Geoff Martin was born in Epsom, Surrey, but spent most of his youth in Ruislip, Middlesex. During the early 1970s, Geoff became interested in medieval warfare, and using much of his time researching the subject, he soon turned his hand to making useable armour and trying it out. Taking his hobby a step further, Geoff started meeting people of a like mind, and having picked their brains, extended his knowledge of the period. Thus armed with this good understanding of the Middle Ages, he has written *Saint Robert and the Devil* with an insight gleaned from four decades of study.

To Roger

Lots of Love

Geoff XX

SAINT ROBERT AND THE DEVIL

Geoff Martin

SAINT ROBERT AND THE DEVIL

Vanguard Press

VANGUARD PAPERBACK

A CIP catalogue record for this title is
available from the British Library.

ISBN   9781784652029

*Vanguard Press is an imprint of
Pegasus Elliot MacKenzie Publishers Ltd.*
www.pegasuspublishers.com

First Published in 2017

**Vanguard Press
Sheraton House Castle Park
Cambridge England**

Printed & Bound in Great Britain

To the lovely Helen Richmond, whose words of encouragement gave me
heart to keep writing.

INTRODUCTION

The following story is based on factual events, and although some of the main characters were in fact alive at the time, sometimes their roles have been changed to suit my story, as have the actual occurrences which may not necessarily be wholly correct, or in chronological order, many of which are purely figments of my imagination to enhance the tale.

Since the year 1296 the war of Scottish independence from England had been raging. Edward I of England had initially made some noticeable gains, including winning the battle of Dunbar and the taking of Berwick, both in the first year, also managing to remove Edward's disobedient, puppet king John Balliol from the Scottish throne, aiding the English successes, and allowing them to create a headquarters at the abandoned key site of Stirling Castle, known as, 'The gateway to the Highlands'. However, the Scottish rebels led by William Wallace won a famous victory at Stirling Bridge in 1297, beating the much larger English army led by Hugh de Cressingham, who was killed and then flayed, forfeiting his skin to be tanned and made into a baldric to carry Wallace's sword.

The main blame for the English defeat was laid squarely at the feet of John de Warenne, sixth Earl of Surrey. Panicking when faced by the rampaging enemy, he deserted his position and prematurely destroyed the bridge in his retreat back to Berwick, abandoning what remained of the isolated English garrison in Stirling Castle to the mercy of the besieging lowland rebels, soon to be starved out and imaginatively murdered in retribution for what they considered were their past crimes against the Scots mutineers. Now once again in the hands of the Scots, the castle gave them hope for an overall victory against Edward I, only for their aspirations to be dashed when their armies were humiliated at the Battle of Falkirk in 1298. Once more abandoning the castle to the English, who, having repaired and strengthened the fortifications, surrendered it again in 1299 when an army led by Robert Bruce laid another blockade to the fortalice, and the cash-strapped Edward refused outright to come to its aid.

In 1303 the castle was the only stronghold in Scottish hands, and King Edward sent an army complete with his chief siege engineer Sir Robert Jeffrys and his son Alain, to oversee fourteen siege engines, including the giant trebuchet, 'Warwolf', which alone was held responsible for the destruction of the gatehouse during the lengthy blockade. The English eventually re-took the bastion, accepting the surrender from Sir William Oliphant, and thus opening up the road to Scotland, which eventually lost the war completely in 1304 when the whole country was conquered, leaving the fragile internal alliance between the Scottish clans to break, resulting in the resumption of bloody conflict amongst themselves.

Arising from the chaotic turmoil of leaderless post-war Scotland, in February 1306, Robert the Bruce emerged from amid the warring factions to take upon himself the mantle of king of Scotland after murdering his main rival for the throne, John Comyn, following an argument at Greyfriars Monastery. Bruce ended up being crowned king on the 25 March 1306 at Scone, filling the vacancy with an iron like fist, and re-opening the war of independence with England. Using some old grievances, Robert the Bruce incited and bribed the Scots to all-out conflict with King Edward, only for him to be defeated by the English and subsequently be forced into hiding in somewhere in the Hebrides, 'where he was alleged to gain inspiration to keep trying from an industrious spider'. Then he went to Ireland, from where he returned again to raise an army strong enough to beat Edward's forces at Loudoun Hill, afterwards entering into a guerrilla war and meeting with many successes against the English; and now, with carte-blanche to do what he willed, went on to destroy the pro-Edward Comyn clan and any other who stood against him, and adopting a scorched-earth policy against them he razed all their properties to the ground.

In early summer 1307 King Edward I of England, at the age of sixty-eight, was already suffering from poor health, developing dysentery on his way north to reinforce and organise the army fighting Robert the Bruce following the defeat at Loudoun. On 5 July the army made its encampment at Burgh by Sands, just south of the Scottish border, and when Edward's servants came to feed him on the morning of 6 July, they lifted him so that he could eat and he dropped dead in their arms, creating a void, it was going to be very difficult if not impossible for his less militarily astute, weak and unreliable son, also called Edward, to fill.

With most of his internal Scottish enemies subdued, the Bruce was able to hold his first Parliament at St Andrews in 1309, and between 1310 and 1314 he accomplished many military victories, defeating the remainder of his internal opposition and thus gaining control of nearly all of Scotland, allowing him to organise attacks on the remaining English strongholds, including

Stirling Castle. As a sign of respect to his second-in-command, Robert trusted his younger brother Edward Bruce with command of the siege of Stirling Castle, and subsequently it was the younger Bruce who reached a forced agreement with its commander, Sir Philip Mowbray, that if relief wasn't received by mid-summer 1314 the English would surrender themselves and the castle without a fight. This challenge to the new English king's authority was all but impossible to ignore by Edward, as he desperately needed something to stamp his authority on a mutinous English aristocracy. The head dissenter was Edward's own disillusioned royal cousin, Thomas Earl of Lancaster, who fell out of favour with the king after an argument over his part in the execution of Edward's unpopular best friend, chief advisor and suspected homosexual lover, Piers Gaveston.

Having lost nearly all control of his barons, Edward decided a decisive victory in Scotland was the only way he could see forward to bolster his popularity and follow in his martial father's footsteps and thus cement his precarious position as a worthy monarch of England. Therefore, he sent a large army north, consisting of probably two thousand heavy cavalry, supported by around fifteen thousand infantry, many of whom were expert longbowmen, to succour the starving garrison. On their arrival they found the path to the castle barred by Robert the Bruce with about eight thousand men, out of which only around five hundred were lightly armed horsemen, the rest being spearmen, with only a mere handful of archers.

My story starts in the early hours of Sunday morning on the 23 June 1314 in the English camp on the edge of Tor Wood, the uplands adjacent to the boggy marshland alongside the meandering River Forth and within sight of Stirling Castle and hearing distance of the Scottish host.

CHAPTER 1

"Fucking bagpipes, I hate fucking bagpipes! Only the fucking Scots could like the sound of strangling a cat to death. Dick get some clarions up that hill and give them some of their own back."

Obediently, Dick scurried off on his errand as commanded by his thirty-year-old master Sir Henry de Bohun, sitting alongside his inexperienced banner man, Sir Lawrence Buckenham, sipping some Rhenish wine, spiced and warmed with a red-hot poker by the now-absent body, squire Richard de Mauville. Happily at ease with his life, Henry de Bohun lounged back on a flimsy folding chair, his massive barrel of a chest and muscular broad shoulders appearing too much for the flimsy item of campaign furniture which creaked and groaned as he stretched his arms wide to give a giant yawn, screwing up his intelligent hazel eyes and splitting his swarthy, scarred, craggy face in two, showing what seemed like too many teeth for his mouth. Henry was the flower of the English knights; his great prowess on the battlefield was legendary, as were his feats of arms and honest disposition, which were famed among the host of Edward II, who knew that when the famed knight's war flag was unfurled, the tangible sense of relief and expectation of imminent success and safety could always be felt among his adoring followers.

In a total contrast to the larger-than-life Henry was Lawrence Buckenham. Although roughly the same age as Henry, Lawrence was a much slighter man, unused to warfare and terrified of getting hurt, and was only present at the camp because, against his wishes, his wealthy family paid for his knighthood. Using the family's considerable fortune, they begged and bribed his way into a senior position in the retinue of Sir Henry, to try and get him out of sight, and away from the many irate fathers of de-flowered underage maidens, whether willing or not, which regularly hammered at the gates of their Wiltshire fortalice, wanting justice for their daughters. Often offering single combat with the smooth-tongued womaniser, whose soft tones and easy way with words nearly always met with success when he applied his lecherous intentions to any unsuspecting female, whether she be high born or low, ugly or pretty; but always in the most danger from his practised patter were the easily impressed, innocent, youngest of young girls, he liked best of all.

Lawrence definitely wasn't a handsome man, nor was he pig-ugly; his greasy jet-black hair capped a sallow, high cheek-boned, waxy-skinned face, with close-set, beady, restless brown eyes which constantly scanned those he spoke to with his thin-lipped, mean mouth. He was cowardly, pigeon-chested, thin and walked with a hint of a stoop, making it a mystery to most what it was the female of the species found so alluring about the reluctant hireling. Although Henry held his arrogant, outwardly brave, second-in-command in contempt, the revenue generated by his inclusion into his household was more than useful to him. Publicly, he afforded Lawrence much more respect than he deserved, openly treating him as almost his equal, but inwardly detesting the low morals of the man who had nothing of use to offer other than mere gold.

Both men were enjoying the tepid wine as they chatted increasingly heatedly about the day ahead, with Henry making his best attempt to sound interested in Lawrence's empty bravado. "I'm looking forward to seeing the look on Bruce's face when we cut his scabby bollocks off and make him eat them," Lawrence said, licking his lips in anticipation of the expected victory the next day.

"Don't get ahead of yourself, Lawrence, we've got to beat them first, and they're going to be a hard nut to crack! Curse that fucking noise. Won't someone put an arrow in those fucking pipers?" Henry, who was much more of a tactician than the rest of the English generals, moaned. Having spent lots of time surveying and assessing the Scottish position, he realised that only a narrow frontal assault was possible, as the Scots had carefully selected the battleground, using the terrain to funnel any English horsemen along a shallow valley, where they had dug pits alongside the road to prevent a broad-fronted cavalry charge from swamping Bruce's small army.

"I don't know why we don't just ride over this pathetic bunch of mangy highland bastards and put the fucking lot to the sword for their fucking cheek?" the inexperienced Lawrence gloated, overfilled with a false sense of confidence which warranted his military superior to put him squarely in his place.

Disgusted by his second-in-command's martial ignorance, Henry swallowed his wine in one gulp, amazed at how incompetence like that just shown by Lawrence was still rife in the ranks of the English. Tutting his aversion, he wiped the last ruddy drops from his purple-stained lips to chastise his underling. "Like we did on that bridge sixteen years ago when fools like you ignored the wise words of Richard Lundie, and fell into a trap a child could see, when they also assumed that the Scots and that bastard William Wallace were just another ignorant rabble of tribesmen who didn't have a fucking clue about tactics."

"I heard it was our own cowardice that beat us then, rather than the Scottish bravery," Lawrence said, spitting out his words in a shower of wine, aggrieved at being likened to a fool. Feeling annoyed at his superior, Lawrence poured himself another large goblet of the scarlet juice, and very deliberately didn't offer Henry any in a poor attempt to make his point.

Aggravated by the snub, Henry turned on his underling. "Then you are fucking wrong! They were the bravest of the brave who died there on that fateful day. They should never have been made to ride onto the bridge to be trapped like rabbits in a warrener's net! No thinking, no planning, all wanting to prove they're better than the man next to them; bad leaders, bad result, it's always the same. Good men led to their deaths by idiots like you, playing at being fucking soldiers without a fucking clue, most of them not even knowing which end of the sword to hold!"

Normally such open insults led to bloodshed between proud noble antagonists, but in this case, knowing how infinitely more practised Henry was at the warrior arts, Lawrence decided to swallow his pride, preferring to stand, glare a beady-eyed stare for a second, spin on his heel and flounce out of the pavilion in a petulant huff, but still avidly clutching his brimming goblet to go and drink alone, rather than to challenge his expert leader.

The embroidered flaps to the de Bohun's tent were still flapping after the hasty departure of the unpopular Buckenham, when the fair-haired, blue-eyed sixteen-year-old, ever-obedient stripling Richard de Mauville burst in, looking red and breathless from dashing around on his allotted mission. "That's done, my lord! I've got eleven of the noisiest musicians in the whole army stuck up on the top of a hill, and they should start up any second!" Then, as if by magic and exactly on cue, a cacophony of noise struck up about a hundred yards from where the camp was positioned. There were trumpets, clarions and nakers all blaring and thumping as one, drowning out the sound of the bagpipes with a tune not dissimilar to the one that reputedly brought down the walls of Jericho over two thousand years before.

Looking sideways at Richard, Henry swigged half the contents of another goblet of wine freshly filled by the diligent squire. Putting it down on a nearby folding table, he freed both his hands and placed his fingers in his ears to protect his hearing from the dreadful din. Shouting his thanks to the youth,

Henry exaggeratedly mouthed his words to make them more easily understood. "Well, at least we can't hear those fucking pipers, I suppose!"

Beaming a wide, adoring smile at his lord, Richard showed him some oily sheep's wool he had liberated from a nearby gorse bush, and, pulling off two clumps, he gave them to Henry, who promptly stuffed them in his ears, laughing and still shouting to be heard above the din. "That's better! You can tell them to stop now, tell them I've had enough, I give in. I yield! I yield!"

Outside, those who could sleep were now awake and the whole camp was starting to stir as the first signs of the coming dawn lightened the sky to the east. The imminent daylight prompted a huge flock of noisy rooks to take off as one, adding their strident caws and screeches to the already intolerable racket which filled the morning air, where the perfumed smell of wood smoke, which hung vaguely about all night, suddenly got stronger as the cooks and smiths blew to re-kindle their fires in preparation for the day. Out over the mist-filled Forth valley the risen dark fumes refused to mix with the pillowy-white vapour and it hung in the still air in great dark, ragged shreds, slowly rising to fade as the rising sun gently warmed away the morning chill.

All of a sudden, as if turned off like a tap, the hideous row halted, leaving a few moments of incredible complete and utter silence before being interrupted by a single smith when he started musically hammering on his anvil to straighten out a bent piece of armour. His melodious ringing strikes were immediately a cue for the many others who also needed to urgently ready the trappings of war for their masters, and within minutes the whole camp was echoing with the noise of preparation for battle. Even when the Scottish pipers resumed their task, their dissonant notes, instead of reverberating around the quiet of the sleeping camp, were now accepted as just another vague sound to add to the rising clamour of the day. Everywhere knights and men-at-arms were arming themselves. Easily putting on their leg-protecting chausses and schynbalds themselves, they then needed the attending swarms of squires and pages to help them wriggle into the stiff quilted gambesons or padded haquetons of canvas or leather stuffed full with goose down or sheep's wool. The next, and probably most important stage was to assist the warriors into either the mid-thigh-length mail hauberks, or the antiquated long mail byrnies with their attached hoods. The nervous assistants' trembling fingers struggled with the thick, greased, bull's hide straps and stiff buckles to safely secure armour, prior to lacing tight the coifs of mail around the face and the cuffs on the sleeves, ready for the old-fashioned flat-topped iron casques, or the new-style pointed, pig-faced visored, steel bascinets with their already-attached aventails of mail and reinforcing plates, which were just coming into fashion with the richer nobles. That done, the last task was to add the knight's final identifying layer by putting on either the outmoded calf-length surcoats, or the fashionable hip-hugging jupons, emblazoned with their identifying coats of arms, or marvellously contrived heraldic devices, such as blue lions with huge red claws, griffins, unicorns, or many other of the mysterious beasts which had never walked the earth, like the mythological cockatrice, a fierce huge-beaked cockerel with the wings and tail of a dragon.

In other places the archers were busy oiling their mighty six-foot longbows or checking the flax strings for any slight flaw which might cause it to snap. Individually, they eyed up each arrow, inspecting the goose-feather fletchings and waxing the points on each before lovingly placing them in the quivers. Satisfied their main weapon was in order, they whiled away the intervening time by sharpening their short swords or the curved knives preferred by the many Welshmen in their thronging ranks. Separated from the main body of soldiers, the lowly peasant spearmen were also busily occupied in affording their bodies with as much protection as possible. The luckier ones equipped themselves with odds and ends of outdated armour stripped from victims of other battles; those without, wrapping their limbs with torn strips of cloth designed to deaden the force of any connecting blows.

On the picket lines, the grooms and ostlers were putting the final touches to the spirited, champing war-horses, removing any last specks of dirt from their gleaming summer coats, plastering down any unruly tufts of tail or mane with water or polishing the bridles and saddles, making sure that their charges were without any blemish which could reflect so badly on the pride of the haughty riders. Finally, they covered their glistening hides with the blazoned caparison of embroidered cloth, which announced to all the name of the otherwise anonymous, armour-covered knight. Eventually, and after over two full hours of frantic preparation, Edward's army was at last ready to do battle with Robert the Bruce and his small mixed army of penniless Scottish knights and the even poorer desperate clansmen.

Up on the higher slopes, the Scots prepared for the fight in a similar way, but in general they were much more lightly armed than their enemy, and there being much less of them, with only five hundred horse as opposed to the English's two thousand, it took them less time to ready themselves. And as it was a Sunday, they had enough time before the battle for a full-length mass to be hurriedly read to them as they kneeled in the morning sunshine, thankful to be absolved of their sins by the sinful, overly pious Bishop of Scone, whose desire not to be there was barely hidden by the condescending blessing he speedily yodelled over the massed ranks. The virtuous words barely having left the bishop's slavering lips, when he turned to leave the danger area with a promise to King Robert that he'd come back, in the unlikely event of a Scottish victory, to say a mass of thanksgiving. That done, with more speed than dignity, he left to return home to his wife and eight children, not, however, before stopping at several taverns and a brothel or two on the way back to his devoted family.

Mass said, with souls purged and sins forgiven, the Scottish army rose from their knees to take their allotted defensive positions and wait for the eager English onslaught. Like clockwork they formed three large polished schiltrons of well-drilled pike men, each under the command of a mounted veteran, one by King Robert the Bruce himself, the second by his younger brother Edward Bruce, and the third by Sir Thomas Randolph, the doughty Earl of Moray. The Scots, however, were not as the English expected, and instead of the raggle-taggle army of untrained, ill-disciplined, poorly led highlanders, they were, in fact, a battle-hardened crew, who learnt the art of war on their many looting forays and guerrilla raids plundering the north of England for much-needed booty, necessary to support the economy of their justly aggrieved, beleaguered and poverty-struck nation.

Some six hundred yards to the east, the armed and ready English, instead of marching straight away on the Scots, were sweating in their heavily padded armour with the risen June sun burning mercilessly on their exposed backs, forced to wait what seemed like an eternity for the customary bolstering speech from their tardy monarch. Without care for the comfort of his men, the over-fastidious king took his time to make sure everything was to his complete satisfaction before delivering his address, and eventually, after an hour of being boiled alive in their shells, the slurring red-nosed Bishop of York arrived standing unsteadily on the back of a cart, to wail a falsetto, undulating and incoherent blessing in Latin to the steaming men in preparation for the impatient host to receive Edward II of the house of Plantagenet. The last strident utterances from the drunken cleric were still echoing across the valley when, in a flamboyant show to impress his men, King Edward cantered imperiously before his army. Screeching to a halt on his magnificent dappled, pale-grey destrier, lavishly caparisoned from head to hoof with the royal arms of the Plantagenets liberally dotted among a scattering of open broom pods, the badge of his house, all heavily embroidered in expensive coloured silks and precious metal thread. Edward himself was armed cap-a-pie in the latest mode of armour, in gleaming gilded mail with etched polished plates of the finest Spanish steel strategically placed to protect his regal neck and limbs. On his head he wore a new-fashioned silvered bascinet, heavily embossed in gold with a replica of the English crown around its brim, open-faced so the whole army could see that it was indeed his royal majesty, apparently ready to shed his blood for the cause alongside his loyal men. Like Charlemagne, freshly descended from heaven, he sat his restless charger, easily controlling the champing beast with a subtle hand gently chiding on the reins and an easy spur to place the massive barrel facing the kneeling throng. The risen sun now bright and high reflected back off the mirror-like, brightly burnished plates into the eyes of the squinting multitude, giving the king an aura-like halo, as if personally sanctioned by God himself.

An eddy of murmured wonder spread through the gawping superstitious ranks, awe-struck by the vision and the carefully choreographed theatre of the king's late arrival, only to be cut dead when the heavenly apparition actually spoke. Standing tall in the stirrups, Edward raised his voice, attempting to deliver his speech so that even those at the very back could hear his slightly stammering, shrill and woman-like reedy tone as it cut through the air. Managing their job well, the strident tones even reached the furthest away. "Peace amongst you, my loyal s-subjects!" the king screeched as the murmuring gathering hushed to a spellbound silence.

Not a sound was to be heard, except the faint distant pipers, their notes now drifting harmlessly away in the opposite direction on a rising breeze, and a coughing man, whose choking was suddenly halted with a thunderous slap on his back. "Today we are assembled to do God's w-work, to rid ourselves of the false king. The false king who d-dares to raid our northern lands, and who claims Scotland to be h-his and not the rightful realm of the English throne. I look to you my loyal s-subjects to aid me in England's quest, to rightfully restore back to her what is hers, and to r-rid these shores of he who calls himself King of Scotland. To cut down Robert the Bruce and put him where he belongs, where all traitors belong, toasting themselves alongside the devil in the f-fires of hell!"

Having heard the encouraging oration, as one, the whole army rose from their knees to shout in acclaim of the would-be warrior king, creating a great cheer which filled the whole valley with its clamorous approval reportedly being heard up to six miles away, but also acting as an alarm to the patient Scots, whose battle plans were ready to be put into place. Unlike the Scots, the English really didn't have a specific strategy. The arrogant self-confidence of the rotund but well-meaning Humphrey de Bohun, the fourth Earl of Hereford, and the slighter more warlike Gilbert de Clare, the eighth Earl of Gloucester, dictated the plan of attack. Ignoring the judicious words of Humphrey's war-wise, but hot-headed nephew Henry de Bohun, their idea was for the vanguard of just over a thousand horse, supported by seven and a half thousand infantry, most of whom were longbowmen, to simply hurtle at top speed towards Robert the Bruce's rear-guard schiltron, to assail the almost impenetrable formation of spearmen head on, and rely on the following weight of numbers to overrun the Scots and break their will to fight. Meanwhile, as a second prong of the attack, Sir Robert Clifford and his force of seven hundred cavalry and only one and a half thousand foot soldiers were given the task of simultaneously assailing the enemy vanguard on the Scottish right flank, commanded by the seasoned Sir Thomas Randolph, first Earl of Moray, to break them and then ride on unchallenged to relieve the besieged garrison of Stirling Castle.

The king's rallying address finished, it became time for action and after the last fine adjustments to horse or armour, the English van assembled. At the head of the eight and a half thousand were both Gilbert of Gloucester with his entourage and Humphrey of Hereford with his retinue, containing his favourite nephew Henry de Bohun and all his attendants, including Henry's youthful squire Richard de Mauville and his overdue banner man Lawrence Buckenham. For vanity's sake Lawrence always dressed himself in the very best available, so mounted on a fine but unmistakable jet black steed, itself unique due to a singularly odd, gleaming sickle-shaped blaze on its broad forehead, and accoutred in the latest fashioned mail and plate with a plumed pig-faced bascinet completing his attire. Thus the weak-spirited Lawrence arrived looking every inch the brave rich warrior he wasn't, as sadly for him all the expensive showy trappings were paid for by his wealthy family in their eagerness to absent him from their sight. In a glaring contrast to his companion, the much poorer youthful Richard, although of noble birth, was orphaned at a very young age and, having no estate to support him, was charitably taken in to their household by Henry and his wife. With little money to pay for his outfit, Richard's mount was in the not-too-distant past a farm horse, and his armour consisted of a hundred-year-old battered flat-topped casque to protect his head, which itself had visited the Holy Land more than once. And to defend his body he wore a much-repaired, ancient hooded mail hauberk over a tatty padded arming jacket, all tightly belted around his waist to make them fit, and, to finish off his attire, a repainted shield daubed with three gold roses on a red field, the arms of his master. All old-fashioned hand-me-downs begged and borrowed from friends and relations in their bid to equip him for war; all, that is, except for his prize possession, a German-made, beautifully balanced, lightweight tapering sword of the highest quality given to him by his mentor, Sir Henry, as a gift on his fifteenth birthday.

It was the mid-Sunday morning by the time the marshals finally felt suitably prepared enough to signal the attack. First contenting themselves the brave king and his personal division of around a thousand chosen body-guards of knights and mounted archers were comfortably installed at a prepared vantage point on a small hillock at the rear, high enough so the valiant Edward could safely witness for himself the savage punishment being meted out to the mutinous Scots army of Robert the Bruce. After what seemed to be an eternity, the heralds at long last gave order to attack, loudly announced for all to hear in the form of a blaring fanfare, commanding the advance. With a giant rustle the many multi-coloured blazoned war banners, flags and pennons were proudly unfurled and held high over the army's heads, to flutter noisily in the rising breeze at their backs. Every single one garishly announced the fame of he to whom the arms belonged, imaginatively emblazoned with colourful heraldic devices, chevrons, bends, saltires, crosses, fantastic beasts, or actual birds, and even a bloody Saracen's head or two, all brightly portrayed in tincture on metal, Gules on Argent, Azure on Or, with representations of the furs, ermine or vair, some with cadency marks to identify succession, a label for the first son or heir, a crescent for the second in line, and so on.

Slowly but surely, the growing rumble of thousands of walking hooves from the high-blowing, sweating and snorting horses, combined with the sound of metal rubbing on metal, creaking leather and the ripping noise of the straining banners, the earls and their vanward rode forward. Most were eager to ride over the impertinent rabble of Scots, who they believed would simply run at the first sight of the mighty English host in all its pomp and glory. Yet some wiser heads like that of Sir Henry de Bohun knew different, and with a feeling of shame at already knowing its fate, he rode alongside his uncle at the head of the phalanx, followed closely by Lawrence and Richard.

Setting out from the encampment in Tor Wood, the main battle formation slowly made its way along the narrow Roman road which crossed the swamp, to meet the cheeky Scots, who stood barring their path to Stirling Castle. The canny Scottish engineers had prepared their field defences well. Along with the many deep trenches, dug at regular intervals on the wide verges at either side of the road, and incidentally used by the whole defending army as communal latrines for the past week, they had scattered wicked caltrops, the four-pronged steel spikes guaranteed to always land with a point facing upwards, on the level ground in between, where they'd hammered in thousands of pointed stakes leaning both forward and backwards, to prevent the cavalry from wandering off the narrow road either in advance or retreat. So in a lengthy parade, five horsemen wide and hundreds of yards long, the

English host went forward. Occasionally, either through utter stupidity, loss of control over the fretting, pent-up steeds, or pressure from behind, a warrior would burst free from the forcedly sedate parade, leaving the safe ground of the lane to meet a grizzly fate at its edge, with horse lamed and rider impaled or drowned in a pit of sewage, each unfortunate incident being met with volleys of cheers by the laughing, pointing Scotsmen.

At last, having crossed the bridge over the winding River Forth, the English had some room to spread out a little and organise themselves, with all cavalry at the front and foot soldiers behind, only to witness the crafty opposition retreating into New Park Woods in an attempt to draw on the English into the heavily wooded area, again preventing a mass charge of lance.

Some two hundred yards ahead on the open ground in front of the woods, Robert the Bruce was tauntingly out in the open, lightly armed from head to foot in fine silvered mail, helmet-less, with nothing but a thin circlet of gold around his coif. The only sign of his kingly rank was the red and gold royal arms of Scotland blazoned on his shield, heraldically described as *'Or, a lion rampant gules, armed and langued azure within a double tressure flory, counter flory for the second'*. And instead of sitting astride a great heavy-boned destrier as a formidable warrior like Robert normally would, he rode a slight-framed, elegant, pale grey palfrey, waving his only weapon, a mighty battle-axe, in a contemptuous display of defiance at the frustrated English host. The highly polished axe's gleaming blade caught the sun's rays, making it flash mockingly into the eyes of the perturbed and fuming Henry de Bohun, who, on seeing that it was the Scottish king that goaded him, brutally prick-spurred his already fractious destrier into action. Feeling the sudden pain in its flanks, the horse opened its red nostrils wide, and, shrieking a loud neigh of pain, leapt four feet in the air, cocked his jaw and rushed headlong up the hill, blindly bolting across the grassy slope, leaving squire Richard flailing in its wake, trying to urge his clumsy horse into something like a canter to follow his hot-headed master in his death-or-glory bid.

Hauling with all his strength on the reins, Henry battled to steer the foaming equine, just about managing to point its head directly at the impudent false monarch. Travelling at a full-bodied gallop, he quickly closed the gap, and at about fifty feet from his target Henry leaned forward in the saddle, levelling his lance with the intention of skewering the stationary saucy royal antagonist on its point. Watching coolly, Robert sat astride his horse, apparently unmoved as the flying man, beast and pointed weapon, forming a deadly missile hell bent on his destruction, hurtled at uncontrollable speed in his direction. Allowing the opponent to get within just more than a spear's length away, Robert nudged his responsive slender horse sideways, dressage style, to evade the deadly tip, allowing it to whistle past his ear, at the same instant smartly bringing down the heavy razor-sharp axe on the weaker back plates of Henry's war helm, splitting it and the head within, killing the valiant knight outright.

Stone dead, but clamped firmly in his deep socket saddle and still grasping the lance in his convulsed grip, Henry appeared alive and unhurt to the spectators, as his trapped corpse galloped on, finally toppling off the horse as it swerved violently in the face of the moving unrecognisable shapes sheltering amid the dark boughs at the edge of New Park Woods, to fly back to the safety of the English lines. Henry's body tumbled in a heap at the feet of the Scottish pickets, causing a mighty pained groan to issue from the ranks of the English, appalled to see their greatest champion so easily felled, only to be drowned out by a colossal cheer from the crowing Scots, heartened by the sight of their king, holding aloft his broken weapon and shouting so all could hear. "Wha hea, Scots! I've brake my good axe!" Robert bellowed, laughing triumphantly, bowing from the saddle to accept their plaudits, as his men emerged from the trees to dance derisively, humorously lifting their kilts and exposing themselves as they begged the English to fall on, knowing that safety from a mass cavalry charge was only feet away within the tangle of trees.

Seeing that the demoralised, panicking English were bent on revenge, the Bruce commanded his schiltron to quickly form up at the top of the slope, to repel several disorderly groups of knights, who'd disobediently broken away from the main phalanx and, ignoring Gilbert de Clare's pleas, charged to avenge the death of the ever-popular Henry de Bohun. Among them was a distraught Richard de Mauville, still struggling to cajole his reluctant horse to a fast trot, let alone a gallop. His main aim, though, was not to enter the fight, but to retrieve the body of his beloved master, with a view to return it home to his family crypt in the church near Hereford, where the bones of his forefathers rested and were remembered in effigies of stone and brass.

No matter how hard the commanders of the vanguard screamed for their charges to return to the ranks, the foolhardy troops, taken in by the heat of the moment, kept going towards the waiting enemy. Those who remained, fearing their staying might be construed as cowardice, in ones and twos also joined the senseless fragmented attack, drawing others, until the whole eight and half thousand mixed horse and foot were thundering in small groups up the hill to fall on the Scottish ranks. Falling on in dribs and drabs, the English assailed the tightly formed impregnable schiltron of war-hardened troops, whose serried ranks of spears bristled in the faces of the attackers, stabbing and skewering horses, riders and footmen alike, killing hundreds as the English futilely threw themselves on the ready points of the Scottish pikes, their fruitless efforts having absolutely no visible effect on the solid formation.

Not actually wanting to put his life in danger, the gutless, lily-livered Lawrence Buckenham was among the very last to leave the safety of the English lines, and then not by his own doing. The herd instinct of his unruly horse had taken over when it saw its fellows leaving, joining them with utter disregard to its rider's wishes; it was soon hurtling alongside its stable-mates, up the hill to add to the waves as they crashed on the impregnable rock which was the Scots. It was useless for the English; even if they had attacked as an organised group, it was doubtful whether they would be able to break the Scottish formation, and instead of dying *en-masse* they perished singly, run through by the lethal spearheads, with only the very fortunate ones returning unharmed to tell their tales of near misses and lucky escapes. Thinned and broken, attack after failed attack, the English still fell on, time after time meeting with no success, eventually being forced to retreat and watch as about fifty recently arrived, expert mounted longbowmen went to their work, mercifully despatched by Sir Ingram de Umfraville to succour the failing assault. Unable to miss, the archers aimed their waxed bodkin-tipped arrows high so that they dropped fizzing from the sky into the compacted stationary target. The lethal shafts taking their toll amongst the barely armoured Scots, filling the air with the noisy thuds, where the arrows embedded themselves in the held high, small round leather shields preferred by the highlanders, or squelching plops, as with murderous effect the missiles found their fleshy human targets. With a feeling of helpless impotence, the despairing King Robert watched as his ranks started to thin, and soon he realised that to stand would be their downfall, as, locked together without room to move and thus incapable of defending themselves from the deadly hail, they died where they stood. So, on Robert's orders, a herald blew a long blast on a clarion, giving the signal for the hard-pressed schiltron to break ranks and advance.

The long gradual slope was in the favour of the Scots, and to the absolute horror of the disorganised English host, two hundred lightly armed Scottish cavalry simultaneously burst from the woods to engage the remains of Edward's broken vanguard. At the same time the berserk spearmen were released from the confines of the orderly schiltron, to come leaping and screaming, sprinting to chase away the importunate English, most of whom panicked and ran when they saw the thousands of clansmen tumbling down the hill like molten lava streaming from a freshly erupted volcano. There was only one course of action for the broken English: retreat; so, in total disorder, the shredded ranks struggled back across the burn, the heavily armed horses sinking up to their hocks in the sucking swampy mud, slowing their flight to a crawl. The unlucky hindermost were picked off one by one, dragged from their mounts and without any offer of mercy, died horribly, torn to pieces at the hands of the rampaging vengeful enemy. A scant few survivors finally reached the narrow road back, only to be hampered as they jostled, clumped tightly together to escape to the safety of the English camp, again losing men to the pursuing Scots and to the traps laid along the verges, reducing their numbers to just over five thousand by the time they reached the safety of the English camp. Among them, and lucky to be alive, were Sir Lawrence Buckenham and the empty-handed, bereft squire Richard de Mauville.

Four hundred yards to the right, Sir Robert Clifford, the first Baron Clifford, and his seven hundred cavalry supported by fifteen hundred infantry and bowmen fared little better in their bid to relieve the besieged garrison of the castle. Their attack on the schiltron protecting the road to Stirling, ably led by Thomas Randolph, the first Earl of Moray, was as fruitless as the vanguard's. Once again the Scots had selected their defensive position well and having placed their force protected on three sides by a natural rocky barricade, the English had little choice other than a frontal assault. Yet the need to clamber up the steep craggy bank to challenge the opposition made the use of horse virtually useless, forcing most to dismount and, unable to make any headway, harmlessly threw up axes, maces or any other makeshift projectile in frustration at the securely placed schiltron.

The English lost many men in the attempt, when the Scottish spread out along a ridge and hurled back not only the Englishmen's own weapons, but boulders, clods of earth and anything else available, down on to the heads of the cowering, ensnared assailants. Clifford's men only met with a modicum of success, when under the leadership of some wily old campaigners, and the bowmen took charge to cover the escape of the trapped English. Using the same tried and tested tactics as the other archers, they stood at a safe distance with the rising wind at their backs and fired high, allowing their shafts to drop vertically down on the targets, ignoring the few Scottish bowmen's feeble reply, when having lost their fight against the stiff breeze, most of the arrows fell short, to clatter harmlessly amongst the rocks, with only the odd one finding an unlucky victim.

The time gained by the archers amply gave what was left of Clifford's division the ability to retreat. Sir Robert himself, staying to the last, along with a body of volunteers, held off the Scots from charging in order to allow his troops to leave with as much dignity as possible. Sir Robert Clifford sadly lost his own life when an almost naked Scotsman dashed from the cover of the bank and hacked through the hamstrings of his horse, causing the poor animal to instantly collapse and tumble down the slope, crushing the rider and attacker in the process, when the massive beast rolled on them both. Leaderless and confused, Clifford's knights and captains, along with his entire demoralised rabble, departed in total disorder to go back to the camp and make their excuses to the furious and tearful Edward, screaming with rage at the embarrassing rout of his prized army, brought to their knees by what he thought were nothing better than a handful of ignorant scruffy clansmen led by a useless false king.

On the evening of 23 June 1314, after the first day of the battle, the king summoned all that remained of his commanders to attend a post mortem on what had been nothing less than an utter disaster. Miraculously, both Earls of Hereford and Gloucester survived the failed assault on the Scottish rear-guard and were there, including John Comyn, Lord of Badenoch, William le Marshal, great grandson of the famous marshal of Ireland and renowned man at arms, Maurice de Berkley, the monarch's friend and advisor, Baron Dennis Dussingdale, the ever-present aide to the king, and also, expressly at the king's wishes and to the amazement of the others, the turncoat Scottish knight Sir Alexander Seaton, whose dubious allegiance had been bought by Edward's gold. Last but by no means least, completing the war council and filling the empty seat of the late lamented Henry de Bohun, Sir Ingram de Umfraville had been invited to attend in recognition of his quick thinking and prompt action, which saved much of the English van, when he sent the hobblers to relieve their plight. Clear for all to see, the strategy of the day's events was catastrophic.

The English were used to the set-piece tactics where the knights, squires and other nobles would enter into individual jousts before the main battle, following which, the cavalry would charge each other on open ground after the archers had fired all their arrows, leaving the foot soldiers to fight hand to hand to reach a conclusion. Not so with the cunning Scots, who had changed the dynamics of war to suit themselves, and sneakily used their lightly armed soldiers with mobile flexibility, changing defence to attack or vice-versa according to the situation, sometimes setting traps, or hiding and jumping out on the unwary, making their next moves impossible to anticipate.

Fearing that once again the Scots might simply ignore the accepted protocols of war, and use the cover of night to attack the English as they slept, Edward's war council sat and hatched a suitable counter-measure to nullify that possibility. Their carefully contrived plan was to leave nothing but a skeleton guard at the camp to protect the baggage train, and during the darkest hours of night, quietly despatch almost the entire English force over the burn to take up a position where the Scots wouldn't expect to find them. The idea was to place the archers in hiding behind the cavalry, from where, unseen by the enemy, they could shoot their arrows over the heads of the horses, and thus surprise the Scots on their advance, then meet their thinned ranks on equal terms in open ground at the front of New Park Woods, giving their still superior numbers the definite advantage. All the nobles involved in concocting the plot both came up with ideas and listened to the others when they spoke of theirs, soon reaching a mutual agreement. Not one of them, however, noticed that the one paying closer attention than anyone else was the scheming treacherous Scot, Sir Alexander Seaton, who listened very carefully, adding almost nothing of note to the plan, and disappeared very quickly as soon as the meeting was concluded.

CHAPTER 2

It was the small hours deep in the night of 24 June, Mid-Summer's Day on the feast of St John the Baptist, and one of the shortest of the whole year, when the English army crossed the burn to lay in wait for the unsuspecting Scots. Each man was warned to silence on forfeit of their lives, so, preparing themselves, they muffled the horses' feet with rags, strapped their scaffolds extra tightly closed and even went to the lengths of of tying down any loose item of armour or any other thing that was in danger of giving a warning rattle which might alarm any vigilant Scottish sentries.

Stealthily they crept over the boggy ground, crossing the ebbed tidal Forth, like ghosts moving silently through the gathering mist with almost no sound at all, except the occasional muttered oaths from some of the clumsier soldiers, or the whinny of an anxious horse, but nothing out of the ordinary to alert the wary Scots. A good way away from where the English were starting to settle down in their new position, and very close to the woods where the vanguard had been broken to red ruin, a lone figure leading a sturdy saddle-less grey carthorse wandered sadly among the dead and dying. Fruitlessly searching by the dim light of a pathetic lantern in the inky blackness of night was Henry de Bohun's distraught squire, Richard de Mauville, looking for his beloved, fallen brave and wise master among the gruesome mangled corpses of the slain. His ears filled with the weak and plaintive cries of the suffering, their moans sometimes being cut short by the invisible looters who flitted to and fro like dark wraiths from hell, dragging their sacks of booty, robbing the poor souls of anything of value, after mercilessly murdering them as they lay injured and helpless in the pools of their own gelling gore. More than a hundred dead souls he had inspected without success, and was in the process of heaving another's cold face to the sky, when a deep mellifluous voice emanated from somewhere in the gloom in a language totally unfamiliar to him. In response, Richard replied politely to the shadows, hoping not to incur the wrath of the invisible speaker, whom he suspected was a Scottish picket asking for identification in Gaelic.

"I only speak English and French, sir, if you wouldn't mind," he answered, surprised when, instead of running at him with a sword and striking him dead, the body-less voice spoke again, this time in very courtly English with only a hint of a Scottish accent.

"I said you won't find anything worth taking here as they were stripped hours ago!" it informed the incredulous stripling.

Indignant to be suspected of such behaviour, Richard retorted irritably, his angry breaking voice warbling nervously between bass and falsetto, "I'm not here to rob these men, sir, I'm here to find the body of my master so that I can take it home to his family."

"Who's your master then, laddie?" the voice asked sympathetically, as its owner strode out of the gloom, revealing a well-built man whose fine quality polished mail twinkled in the feeble light of Richard's fitful flame.

"My master, sir knight, was Sir Henry de Bohun, sir! He was the first to die in single combat with the Bruce himself," Richard declared, pulling his shoulders back with pride to be associated with his hero, only to be shocked by the mysterious stranger's reply.

"Aye, a brave man. I didn't mean to kill him, it was a fluke. I caught him on a weak point on the back of his helm. His damnable armourer should be hanged for his murder," the voice half-apologised, giving away its owner by the content of the explanation.

Struck speechless for a moment, with his entire body tingling from head to foot, Richard fell to his knees in deference, overawed by the super-human presence and giant aura of the man who called himself the King of the Scots.

"Get up, son, you don't have to kneel to me, I'm not your king. Come on, on your feet, let's talk while I walk with you," Robert said, bending down to grab Richard's arm and aid him to his feet, feeling his half-developed biceps in the process. "However did you think you were going to lift a great lump of a man like Henry on a horse on your own, brave laddie?" Robert politely asked the lad, who was just starting to get over the shock of meeting him.

Feeling emboldened by the familiar kind manner of the man he was led to believe was nothing but a monstrous ogre who slaughtered women and priests, grew fat on the flesh of English babies, and had brutally murdered his fellow Scot John Comyn, simply to eliminate him from the race for the vacant Scottish throne, Richard huffily puffed up his chest and, craning his neck to look the foot taller Robert squarely in the eye, answered the famed Scottish king a little tetchily, "My lord, my name is Richard de Mauville, body-squire and I believe friend to Sir Henry, and I would have managed somehow, and if it please you, my lord, I need to continue with my work before the wolves and foxes do theirs!"

Pausing for a second, Robert scratched his kingly head before answering and, putting his mighty arm round Richard's adolescent shoulders, decided to aid the young squire in his difficult quest. "I think I know roughly where your master lies, and I will help you with your search, young faithful Richard de Mauville, as I admire your dedication and steadfast loyalty and I am telling you the truth when I say I would be a very proud king to have a fearless man like yourself in my train."

Still with his arm draped around Richard's young shoulders, King Robert led his boy enemy, chatting and walking together like old comrades who hadn't seen each other for some time as they picked their way carefully through the tangled sea of slain, over to where they found a battered corpse laying not fifty feet from the woods. Although stripped totally naked, and robbed of all which marked him as knight: armour, boots, spurs, even his blood and brain-spattered clothing had gone, all valuable assets to the thieving ghouls who followed armies to profiteer from battle, the body was still unmistakably that of the valiant Henry de Bohun.

Sobbing loudly at the sight, Richard collapsed to his knees and attempted to say a short prayer for the dead over his once-haughty master. Seeing the difficulty the overwrought lad was having in getting his words out, Robert knelt beside him and muttered the Latin words which had stuck so painfully in the tearful boy's throat. The prayer said, Robert cast his eyes to the lightening eastern sky. "Come on, laddie, we need to get you both back to your lines before day breaks. I will get some help to lift him on. John! Walter! Here to me!" Robert uttered, and barely needing to raise his voice above a whisper, summoned John Stuart and Walter Grint, his two burly bodyguards, who all the time had been secretly lurking protectively at close hand in the gloom, and, as if by magic, two huge mail-clad figures came sweeping out of the gloaming to assist the boy with the dead knight. The grizzly task of throwing the broken bloodstained body of Henry across the horse was soon completed with the aid of the two large strong men, who at Robert's insistence had covered it with one of their own cloaks to preserve what dignity Henry's naked, mutilated remains still had, and then secured it safely with a discarded baldric on the horse's back.

"Away with you now, laddie, and remember me in your prayers. I'll probably need them when day breaks," the Scottish king said a little sadly, with more than a hint of foreboding in his voice, as though he doubted the outcome of the coming battle.

"I will, my lord, always, I promise!" Richard replied, as the king bent down to hand him a bulging leather purse in gratitude. At first Richard refused to take it, but at Robert's persistence he accepted the gift with the same good grace with which it was given.

"Take it, I insist! Buy yourself some new armour with it!" Robert smiled; scanning his mischievously twinkling eyes up and down at Richard's outdated, poorly fitting harness, whilst chortling to himself at the sight. "By God, I think you've earned it, putting your life at risk in your dedicated loyalty to your lord. Accept it with my thanks for being my friend when I most needed one." And with those words still in his ears, Richard turned his horse to trudge back to the east, where the merest hint of the imminent dawn was just visible in the lightening sky, and the first chorus from the more insomniac members of the avian community heralded the coming second day of battle.

The slow journey back to the English camp was a sombre one for sad Richard and his precious cargo. The relatively un-blooded pack animal took its time to slowly weave its tentative way through the many mangled corpses of the scattered dead, which either lay in dense swathes where they had stood, fought and died, or in long drawn-out trails of the face-down slain, brutally killed from behind in their hurried disorderly headlong rush to get away from their attackers and back to the safety of the English camp. To Richard's relief the same avaricious robbers who haunted the bloody field that night and stared so greedily as a mere stripling of a boy led a valuable horse and what could be priceless pickings through their ranks, disappeared quickly as the daylight grew. Fearing the swift justice of the provost marshals, they melted away into secret hiding places to inspect their ill-gotten gains in the cold light of day and haggle with each other, bartering one precious looted piece in exchange for another. Richard had managed to reach the far edge of the battlefield quietly and unscathed, when to his surprise, his young sharp eyes noticed about a hundred yards away in the half-light, a knight with his squire, he recognised as the Scottish defector who fought for English pay, Sir Alexander Seaton. Crouched low in the saddle, riding hell-for-leather towards the enemy's camp, they appeared as if they were on a life or death mission, as their busy spurred heels flayed the poor horses' sides bloody in their anxiety to cross the open ground on the Scottish side of the burn.

Taking mental note of this strange incident and drawing the obvious conclusion that there was a nefarious reason for Seaton's changing sides, Richard started repeatedly slapping the reins hard on his stubborn horse's neck to hurry it up. In response to the constant urging, the heavy-footed nag, which in civilian life did no more than walk in front of a plough, started to clatter its clumsy way more urgently down the slope to the river, when suddenly and from nowhere he was silently challenged by a group of English pickets.

Jumping out from their hiding place behind some scrubby furze bushes, two archers and two spearmen blocked his way. Their sudden appearance startled the stumbling horse to an abrupt halt, almost unshipping the precious load when the nag planted its feet in surprise, frightened by the soldiers pointing their drawn bows and spears at Richard's head to bar his way and demand to know his business in a place where he hadn't expected to find them, on the Scottish side of the river. Holding their fingers to their pouted lips, the men warned Richard, on peril of death, to speak quietly, and at spear point he whispered an explanation for the reason for his appearance from the wrong side of the army, resorting to pulling back the cloak covering Sir Henry's body, to show his inquisitors the well-known, pallid, dead face to give credence to his story. Believing the tale, and after some discussion as to what they should do, the pickets eventually decided to allow Richard to leave and resume his journey with the re-secured grizzly cargo, back to the rear and deposit it with the physicians and priests, who loitered safely out of harm's way in the almost empty English encampment.

Paying the holy-men with some of the Bruce's gold to say some prayers over Henry's remains, Richard instructed them to look after him well and carefully wrap and truss his body and place it on a cart, promising them more money if the job was done to his satisfaction, before hurriedly returning to his dreaded duty under his newly allotted master, the wretched, weak-minded Lawrence Buckenham. Richard's new master wasn't hard to find, as knowing that where the senior nobles gathered, the sycophantic Lawrence wouldn't be far away. Sure enough, after a short search through the new position, Richard found him, slumped on a seat, sipping copious amounts of warmed wine against the early morning chill, and listening to a heated debate between a group of eight seated nobles. Amongst them, were the pale-skinned, golden-haired effeminate King Edward, Henry's uncle, the plump bulbous-nosed Humphrey de Bohun, Earl of Hereford, and the impetuous redheaded, ferrety freckle-faced Gilbert de Clare, the Earl of Gloucester.

With all urgency Richard raced up to Lawrence, anxious to tell him about what he had witnessed concerning Seaton. Obviously having drunk much more than the others, Lawrence merely nodded at Richard, and barely bothering to acknowledge the information, gulped down the remainder of his draught. Then seemingly without a care in the world, Lawrence simply handed the empty vessel to Richard, and giving him a limp-wristed languorous wave, sent him away to get another goblet of liquor, while he listened as the bones of contention were raised and discussed with the confused-looking king. Obeying the command somewhat begrudgingly, Richard returned as quickly as his legs would take him, and handing Lawrence the refilled large goblet of mulled wine, took his place standing diligently at his knight's shoulder in case he was needed to do further errands. Feeling frustrated and powerless, Richard fidgeted from one foot to another, watching on impotently and forced to remain politely mute as the valuable time was wasted while the senior nobles squabbled.

In total ignorance of the new game-changing information, each of the good and great put forward their own personal reasons as to why they were the best man to lead the army. Initially, Humphrey de Bohun demanded the leadership of the van, citing his senior Earldom as a reason. Responding, Gilbert de Clare sarcastically questioned Humphrey's fitness to lead a thirsty donkey to water, let alone a demoralised army into battle. The verbal joust ended up with Humphrey throwing a glove in rage at his rival for the position, and having accused him of gross mismanagement the previous day, was adamant he was still the only senior noble fit to do the job. Sardonically, Gilbert picked up the symbolic insult between a finger and thumb, holding it as far away from his turned-up nose as possible, and hurled it back at his opponent's feet as if it were a foul rag, promising to resolve their differences in single combat after the battle. Then, smugly turning to the monarch, Gilbert stated his case as being the most experienced in warfare, which in some ways was true. The information swayed the decision his way, prompting Gilbert to glare triumphantly at Humphrey when the king accepted his plea, and told him that he had the honour of leading the deflated English army into battle.

Gilbert's smug victory smile instantly faded, when Richard, who had been hopping up and down on the spot with silent impatience and fear that his master's unwillingness to inform the gathering would reflect badly on him and endanger the mission, blurted out what he'd been bursting to say. Unable to contain himself any longer, Richard bravely butted in to the rather heated discussion, and without being asked, accurately related the events he had witnessed earlier, describing what he had seen, and the obvious conclusion he had drawn all about his suspicion that Alexander Seaton had treacherously betrayed the new English position to the enemy. Now awakened to the probability that the English stratagem was now known by the Scots, and correctly surmising it was a danger to the whole army, Gilbert decided to recommend an immediate withdrawal until another day. His apparent reluctance to join battle prompted the king to openly accuse him of cowardice in the face of danger, the royal affront resulting in Gilbert stomping off in high dudgeon with his entire retinue, to mount their horses and wait nearby to see how things panned out for the English, leaving the poisoned chalice to Humphrey, as second choice to lead the vanward.

Once again, in the bright warm sunshine of the new day, the king retired safely to the rear, while at the front the cavalry mounted their steeds, this time a little less eagerly, in response to being informed by a recently returned reconnaissance party that the Scots were already on the move. However, ignoring the impending danger, a tidal wave of activity spread through the whole ranks as each individual prepared himself to face the headlong assault by what they hoped were going to be the surprised Scots. Some touched lucky charms, others kissed either the keepsakes and mementoes given to them by loved ones, or the cross on the swords where the hand guard meets the blade, but everyone without exception uttered a favourite prayer to their adopted saints. Some of the more devout promised to light candles and offer gifts to the Church, if God thought them fit and helped them to survive the day.

Behind the lines of cavalry, the ranks of archers were equally as ready, their bows tested and strung, their waxed arrows planted in the freshly soiled ground in front of them. Eagerly they waited, heads cocked and ears straining to hear their captain's bellowed command to, "stretch and release", the well-known signal to fire their arrows, in this case blindly over the heads of those in front, and with any luck on their side, into the unmissable massed ranks of the charging enemy.

The strain of the wait in the hot sun had started to tell on the English force. Riders wrestled with the fidgety, sweating, foam-flecked horses, trying to control the pent-up energy in the fretting beasts. Some reared in anticipation, or bucked on the spot, doing anything other than to stand still, knowing full well what was next in store for the flight-prone animals. Similarly worried, the fretting bowmen started unstringing their bows, fearing that under the constant strain, the strings might stretch and reduce their effectiveness. Many swore, when, as often happens, their fingers got nipped in the release of the taut flax cord. Perspiring with heat and frustration, they all waited for what seemed like an eternity, until with a kind of terrified relief, the unmistakeable distant rumble made by a body of fast-advancing horses could be faintly heard, getting louder and louder as they speeded up for the charge.

Everywhere there was confusion in the English ranks, as once again, instead of doing what was expected of them and meet the English head on, the Scots, cunningly led by Sir Robert Keith, and armed with the latest intelligence of the new English position, charged along the broad grassy banks of the river into the unprotected right-hand flank of the unsuspecting lightly armed archers. Unable to protect themselves in the confusion, the Scottish cavalry hurtled into Edward's infantry at top speed, parting the ranks like a hot knife through butter, scything them down in defenceless swathes, preventing the bowmen from even firing a single arrow. Their numbers became even more hampered when the tightly compacted lines were further compressed as Humphrey de Bohun and his astonished mounted troops hurriedly jostled to turn their horses round to meet the surprise direction of the attack head on, only then for them to be assailed on their exposed backs by the divisions of Scottish spearmen, who, using part of the old dried up moat as cover, all the time lay hidden in total silence no more than thirty yards away from the English horse, waiting for the chance to implement the cleverly devised outflanking manoeuvre.

Still in his petulant huff and surrounded by his equally annoyed entourage, Gilbert de Clare watched powerlessly from his horse some three hundred yards from the action, as the bloody conflict unfolded before his eyes. Seeing the impossible position the outmanoeuvred English army found itself in, Gilbert forgot his sulky argument with Humphrey and the king, and, gathering some forty odd of the bewildered, leaderless escapees from the massacre, galvanised them and his household knights into a small cohesive unit of seventy or so mounted warriors, to counter-charge in a glorious suicidal attempt to save the surrounded shrinking English host from certain obliteration. Adopting a wedge-shaped formation, Gilbert and his men crashed into the nearest schiltron, penetrating the wall of spears, and desperately fighting ferociously and without fear, they felled and trampled scores of spearmen, only to be eventually overwhelmed by sheer weight of numbers. Gilbert himself fell to a lowly bred clansman's broken spear: when thrusting it upwards, he luckily found the soft target where the mail is at its weakest under the arm, the point piercing all the way up, and out through the side of the neck of the unfortunate warrior, killing him outright with a cascade of foaming blood from severed veins and arteries in Gilbert's throat.

Although outwardly a failure, Gilbert's brave try gave a little breathing space for the panicking hemmed-in English. The valiant venture opened a forty foot breach in the Scottish attackers' lines, allowing several hundred of the hemmed-in English to escape before it closed again, trapping Humphrey de Bohun and the remaining men to their fates, when they were pushed ever backwards by the pressing Scots. Eventually, the English retreated into the flooded burn, where unknown to them, the tide had risen and was now at its highest, causing them to flounder hopelessly in the unexpectedly deep water. Horses and men drowned, cramped into a dwindling space and weighed down by their armour. Beleaguered and confused, any resistance soon petered to nothing, as the few who remained alive yielded, offering up their swords to anyone prepared to accept them.

Among the troops freed by Gilbert's brave sally was Sir Lawrence, whose fine helmet of Milanese steel had somehow disappeared from his head, without his sword never having left its scabbard, as in his alcohol-impaired state, the sozzled knight's complete attention had been concentrated on staying on the beautiful, but poorly broken destrier. However, protected by his new squire Richard de Mauville, who, with only a folded blanket instead of a proper saddle and no stirrups, skilfully cajoled the same unresponsive horse he used to retrieve Henry's body and fought bravely in defence of his helplessly drunk master, preserving his useless life twice before leading him to safety. Somehow managing to avoid the gnashing teeth of Lawrence's panicking horse, he grabbed the reins of the foaming mount, dragging both man and beast away from the lost cause, to join the broken ranks making their disorderly flight southwards to head back to the English border and safety beyond.

Seeing the day was lost, the king also decided to make his escape to the nearest remaining English stronghold at Dunbar Castle, from where he planned to take a ship back to England, along with his personal bodyguard, including the distraught and highly embarrassed Sir Giles d'Argentine, who categorically refused to run away. Almost in tears, proud Giles stood in his stirrups to announce his intentions to everyone nearby. "I for one am not accustomed to flee from such a rabble!" he cried, and with those words still reverberating in the ears of the assembly, he screamed his war cry, and turning his massive warhorse around, spurred him to gallop single-handedly at the nearest band of Scots, only to be slain, along with his brave steed, when both were impaled on the serried spears, the momentum of his charge taking the tumbling corpses deep into the schiltron, crushing many Scots on the gory path through their cramped ranks.

With the flight of the noble Edward and the capture of the senior captains, all order was lost among the English, and the retreat soon became a rout. Thus in total confusion, with their tails firmly between their legs, what remained of the king's mighty host ran for their lives. In the scrambled disorderly withdrawal, the English left all behind, deserting everything, including the stranded garrison, which, seeing sense once abandoned, surrendered themselves along with the contested castle, hoping upon hope that Robert the Bruce would be in a merciful mood after his great victory over the tactically naive and hopeless general, Edward II of England.

Knowing that he probably wouldn't be so lucky a second time, the victorious Robert ordered the aptly named and famously merciless Black Douglas to leave his own private army to take personal charge of the relatively fresh Scottish cavalry and bolt off in hot pursuit of the fleeing English king, to hopefully overtake and capture him before he could make good his escape to the safety of Dunbar Castle, where he could possibly re-form his army to resume the conflict another day. Obeying the command, Douglas left behind three of his most bloodthirsty captains in charge of his own five-hundred cold-hearted revenge-filled Scottish clansmen, to chase the shattered English as they all instinctively bolted south and homewards in headlong flight the ninety miles back to the border and England beyond. If caught, which many were, they had to endure a fate worse than death itself, many being nailed to trees whilst still alive, or castrated then disembowelled and dragged along the stony roads by their heels; some being burnt to death after lengthy spells of imaginative torture meted to them by the rancorous Scots, in reprisal for the years of cruel suffering endured under Edward I.

Richard Mauville, who until then had shown no sign of his inherent tactical ability, did the complete opposite to the rest of the survivors; having considered all his options and thinking what Henry would have done in the same circumstances, he decided it would be best to tow his uncaring, oblivious master northwards, on an illogical lengthy circuitous route to avoid the remaining Scots not involved in the pursuit. Nevertheless, before doing that he sneaked back to the ransacked camp to hopefully pick up the cart, along with the body of Henry de Bohun, meeting with utter disappointment, when he found nothing except a few acres of desolate scorched earth, littered with hundreds of rifled broken crates which once held the all-important victuals to feed the men, some smouldering remains of the tents and pavilions, dotted with bodies of men and horses, scattered among sundry debris that was not long ago the vibrant colourful heart of Edward's defeated army. Tearful, tired, ashamed and filthy dirty, Richard, suffering the feeling of abject failure, searched through the site for the disappeared cart and Henry's body. On his way round he used his time wisely by picking up anything he thought might be of use for his long journey home, and placing any worthwhile finds in a pair of conveniently discarded, looted saddlebags he'd found nearby and now were strapped safely over the cob's broad back.

Luckily for Richard, his search turned up trumps, when an unharmed, stray magnificent dark bay destrier wandered rider-less back to the safety of familiar ground, a large dark red splatter of clotted arterial gore on the saddle and horse's withers paying testimony to its rider's death in the battle. Well used to handling Henry's high spirited animals both from the saddle and the ground, Richard easily caught the great beast, and using a handful of freshly plucked grass and a horse-handler's unique two-tone soft whistle, made friends with a reassuring pat on solid cresty neck and a welcome scratch on its massive head, the horse responding with a soft whinny of greeting. The bond was instant, confused man pleased to find beast, and equally confused beast pleased to have found a friend to tend him.

Having already spent too much time in the dangerous position, Richard felt forced into giving up the useless search for Henry's remains, and fearing the Scot's imminent return, tied a length of rope to the old cob's bit and quickly secured the gleaned goods in the bulging saddlebags, ready to mount the new horse he'd already decided to name Solomon after the great and wise Biblical king. Gathering the cob's rope and the reins of his master's steed, complete with the semi-comatose Lawrence still slumped forward over its neck, trapped by the deep front and back of the war saddle, and then urging Solomon forward, he dragged both animals sweating and puffing from the heat of the high summer's day along a rocky track to the northwest, and away from Stirling.

However, the progress was far too slow for Richard's liking, as his plodding old mount was sluggish and clumsy. Nevertheless, making the best time he possibly could, he headed for the coast on a new, much bigger, more elegant horse than the one he had arrived on, this time with the luxury of a good deep, comfortably padded socket-saddle, slipper stirrups and the finest of fine, top quality leather tack. Solomon was as good an example of a destrier as Richard could imagine, selectively bred in the pink from the very best of stock and fit for a prince, now unbelievably his property, and with a feeling of returned pride, he sat comfortably astride the highly schooled mount. His downcast spirits quickly lifted from the abyss of defeat, the sadness and woes of losing his friend and mentor not forgotten but temporarily put behind him, when boyish inquisitiveness took over. Youth was on his side and he started enjoying the experience, experimenting on his ability to control his valuable beast with a gentle nudge here or a subtle squeeze on the reins there. Very soon he rediscovered the joy of riding, after the horrendous bumpy feeling the saddle-less clumsy jerky carthorse gave him, and still leading his fast-sobering reluctant companion, Richard zigzagged along a stony track, ignoring Lawrence's moans and groans which issued with each trip and stumble of his leg-weary, tired horse.

The calamitous day was fast drawing to a close, and smelling the distant sea on the rising westerly breeze, Richard felt happy that he was now far enough away in the wrong direction from Stirling to feel relatively safe from marauding Scots. Noticing the sun was becoming slightly watery and all the time getting lower in the cloudless sky, Richard reckoned it was about half past eight, leaving enough time to find shelter and settle in for the night. Now riding directly towards the sinking sun, he continuously scanned to and fro, looking for a suitable spot to set up camp and sleep reasonably comfortably for the approaching night. Eventually selecting a safe-looking place at the bottom of a grassy slope on a rocky hillside, he found a suitable sheltered spot in a natural ten-foot-deep hollow, under an enormous overhanging slab of yellow and green, lichen-mottled grey granite, supported by a badly split supporting boulder about twelve feet in front of a cosy looking mossy back, making a sort of crude room for them to rest in.

As was his duty, Richard first assisted a very relaxed, swooning, limp Lawrence from his mount, and made him as snug as he could on the soft moss, by placing a folded cloak under his head as a pillow, before stripping the exhausted horses and stowing the tack and bags in a dry place as far at the back of the overhang as possible. Happy all the gear was safe, and Lawrence as comfortable as he could be, Richard led the thirsty beasts to a nearby watering place, which he couldn't help but notice earlier, when he was taken aback by its stunning natural beauty. Dropping the reins, Richard plonked his weary behind on a convenient boulder to take in the splendour of the idyll, thinking that it must have been at a very similar setting where Lancelot and Guinevere fell in love. A place where a mystical fairy pool of crystal clear water had gathered in a broad grassy hollow, fed by a twinkling rivulet, illuminated pink by the sun's fading rays, which sprung as if by magic from an emerald green grassy bank, and tinkled off to the underworld down a crack among some rocks. Suddenly, a noisy crow interrupted the daydream by cawing loudly as it flapped overhead, searching for a late supper, its raucous cries snapping Richard back to reality, and remembering there was still work to be done, he set about hurriedly rubbing down the dried sweat-stained beasts with plaited wisps of dried grass and then hobbled their front legs, permitting them to graze almost freely in the lush fetlock-deep forage without letting them stray too far.

Back at the camp, Lawrence was clearly dissatisfied with the bed Richard had made him and had found himself a different cosy little place out of sight, wedged at the back of the overhang where the baggage and tack had been safely stored. After obviously being dreadfully sick all over himself, he was now sound asleep on a sort of cluttered couch made out of the goods, snoring sonorously in a sound not dissimilar to the accursed bagpipes. The discordant noise tore Richard's mind to the first day before the battle when his teacher and friend, the larger than life Sir Henry de Bohun was alive and well, not having the slightest inkling that in under ten hours the fickle hand of fate would see him stricken dead at the hands of the enemy to England, Robert the Bruce, and his remains would be missing somewhere in the Scottish wilderness.

Sleep didn't come easily to Richard that night; although completely and utterly exhausted, he was unable to take his mind off the feeling of wretched failure he experienced on seeing the demise of the English army. Adding to his inability to find rest, apart from his own terrible hunger and gurgling stomach, was his noisy fellow camper, who along with the noisy snoring, now muttered loudly through all the hours of darkness, accompanied by the constant flashing of far-off lightning and the deep rumbling booms of distant thunder somewhere up in the highlands. Somehow, Richard eventually managed to find his slumber just before dawn, only to be awakened shortly afterwards by the unfamiliar frightened high-pitched whinny of his new horse Solomon.

CHAPTER 3

Alerted that everything was not as it should be, Richard jumped up with a start, the unaccustomed but distinctive sound of his new horse's anxious neigh plucking him from some sweet dreams of his happy early childhood days, that he was otherwise unable to remember. Unlike most youths of his age, getting up in the very early mornings was easy for him, as never in his life had he ever been afforded the luxury of festering in bed until the sun was high in the heavens. And because of his position as squire to the very strict Sir Henry, every day at first light Richard always had many stable duties to perform and horses to exercise before he was allowed to even consider having breakfast. A complete contrast to his notoriously idle new lord, Lawrence Buckenham, who by being banner man to the dead knight, had inherited Henry's martial responsibilities, including his squire Richard de Mauville. And as was usual the late-rising Lawrence was still fast asleep and snoring, not knowing what time it was, let alone being aware of any impending danger.

Thankfully, however, Richard was instantly alert, so grabbing his beloved sword he went to investigate what had caused the alarm. Instead of rushing head on to investigate, as many impetuous young squires would have done, he craftily sneaked round the back of the massive overhang and approaching furtively, staying close to the ground to view from the cover of a small pile of rubble, over to where he'd left the horses peacefully grazing the previous evening.

As Richard was all too aware, there had been some overnight heavy thundery showers over the higher ground to the north and to his surprise the little clear sparkling rivulet had transformed into a frenzied, mud-coloured waterfall, which thundered and gurgled over the grassy bank into the small clear pool which was now approaching the size of a large village pond, hemming in the restricted horses on a bright emerald green mound surrounded with swirling brown water, which instead of disappearing into the ground as it did before, now overflowed and stormed noisily down the hillside in a murky frothing, raging torrent. Nonetheless, the horses seemed completely unperturbed by their latest predicament, and rather than rolling their eyes in fear at the risen water, they were standing erect on the edge of the islet, with long strings of un-chewed green grass hanging from their mouths, their red nostrils wide, ears pricked and heads held high while snorting loudly and looking over towards a strewn mass of boulders, where something they found disturbing had caught their wary eye. Understanding how sensitive horses were to anything they thought might pose a danger, Richard peered, squinting against the low sun twinkling brightly reflected off the water, over to where their attention was riveted. Shading his bleary eyes, by cupping his hands either side of his head to focus, Richard could just about make out two or three silhouetted figures, some one hundred and fifty yards away, and judging by their shifty demeanour, they were apparently up to no good, as they were slyly creeping up on all fours towards the rocky shelter, where he thought his master was still sleeping.

Richard had no time to waste, so with as much speed as he could muster and staying low while running, trying not to be seen by the intruders, he went straight back to the camp, where to his surprise Lawrence was now sitting bolt upright and wide awake, rubbing his questioning eyes in dismay. With little or no memory of the chain of events which placed him in his present situation, Lawrence asked in his usual eloquent manner, while flicking bits of dried puke off his sleeve, what had befallen. "Where in fucking hell are we? What the fuck's happened? Where the fuck is everybody?"

"Shusssh, I'll tell you later! No time now, just listen; there are people sneaking up on us and I don't think they just want to say hello," Richard whispered to the confused fuzzy-eyed Lawrence, who in his befuddled state merely nodded acceptance for his underling to take complete control of the parlous situation. "We're outnumbered; I think there are at least three of them, so we can't fight them in the open. What I think we'll have to do is, if you make believe you're still asleep while I'll hide between those rocks," Richard advised, pointing nine feet away to a narrow dark space, where the age-old crack in the nine-foot-tall supporting granite boulder had been widened over the years by frost, time and pressure, to be just about broad enough for the slim youth to slide into. "You stay where you are with your back to the gear facing me, and don't forget to do your best to look as if you're fast asleep, but keep your dagger at the ready. Don't let them see it, and when one of them is near enough to you, just stab him as hard as you can, in the guts or balls or anywhere, just maim or kill him, and I will take any others from behind. Got it?"

"Got it!" Lawrence replied, nodding a timid yes, as he settled back down, and screwing his eyes tight shut as if rehearsing his imaginary sleep, but in reality the expression was in sheer fear of the imminent fight ahead.

Bewildered and still drowsy, Lawrence nodded again when Richard suggested that he tried to appear a little more relaxed, so with his eyes less firmly shut, he made a better attempt to appear asleep. Barely daring to breathe, and with whitened knuckles where he clutched his dagger in a vice-like grip, Lawrence stayed doggedly hushed while Richard slipped into the tall fissure complete with sword held high above his head, ready to strike.

They didn't have long to wait, and by the time they had settled into their positions, one, two and then three distinguishable armoured shapes, of what Richard thought were probably escapees from one of the armies, crept in, staying close to the sides in an attempt to remain unseen. In total silence the first intruder, brandishing a large curved rusty knife, sidled furtively up to the baggage where the apparently sleeping Lawrence lay completely still and struggling to hold his breath until, with the need to fill his lungs, his short-lived moment of courage ran out. Panicking, he burst to life, blindly lunging upwards with his aptly named bollock dagger at his surprised victim, as the puzzled intruder paused to deliberate the best way to dispatch the unwary, slumbering, mail-clad man efficiently without damaging the valuable armour. The timing of Lawrence's strike was as lucky as it was poor; he should have waited a second or two more for the man to get closer. However, the blade, instead of going deep into the assailant's abdomen, pierced him through his scrotum ending up with its point embedded deeply into his groin, severing the femoral artery, dowsing the prostrate Lawrence with steaming bubbling blood, as the dying assailant collapsed in a crumpled, bleeding heap, helpless to do more. Simultaneously, Richard jumped out of his hiding place, and leaping high in the air to exert all his power into the swing of his beautifully balanced sword, brought it down on the back of the second man's helmeted head, the steel blade striking sparks as it skidded off his pointed bascinet, hitting his less well-protected shoulder with a crunching squelch, cleaving a good third of the way down his torso, slicing through his ribs, lungs and muscle, exposing his faltering heart, striking the man instantly stone dead in a scarlet explosion of life's vital fluid.

As Richard expected, the men were from the military; not Scots, as he initially suspected, but, as it transpired when the remaining villain spoke, English infantrymen, who by the look of them were deserters, their hotchpotch of rusty stolen armour and grimy, shabby, soldier's attire suggesting that they probably had been on the run for some considerable time.

The heroics of Lawrence were short-lived, his fleeting moment of bravery fading quickly into an uncontrollable bout of blubbering terror. Holding his trembling hands clasped together over his exposed fresh frothy gore-covered head, Lawrence hid his eyes behind his forearms when he saw that Richard was now out in the open, facing a third burly, war-hardened, looking brute, dressed in the manner of an archer, with a tatty filthy padded studded brown leather jerkin covering his barrel chest, bull's hide bracers guards on his knotty wrists, criss-crossed laced leggings, and a dented round steel cap over his seamed scarred face, the whole outfit lending him a look of invincibility as he approached the comparatively tiny boy. Brandishing a short cheap archer's sword in his right hand, and opening and closing the other much like a wrestler seeking to gain a hold, the bully spoke menacingly to his youthful opponent. Curling a sneering lip, he addressed Richard in a thick East London accent. "Give it up, little fellow, your fucking useless mate over there ain't going to fucking help you now, is he?" the man said, flicking his mean eyes over to where Lawrence was still sobbing with fear. "Come on, boy, you don't want me to beat you to a fucking pulp and leave you to bleed to death in fucking agony, do you?"

The gift of a sword to Richard wasn't simply because of his birthday; it was largely given as a reward for being an excellent and very diligent pupil in the training yard, where under Henry's personal expert tuition, he proved to be extremely apt at the art of war. To the surprise of the would-be assailant, instead of doing what he expected the mere boy to do and run at the first threat from the surly giant, Richard stood his ground and without showing any outward signs of fear, planted his feet eighteen inches apart with both knees slightly bent, and raising his plain, but extremely well-made glaive above his head, pointed it up, and slightly behind him, ready for either offence or defence, exactly as his expert tutor had taught him to do whilst waiting for any opponent to make his first move. The man, whose experience of fighting was more akin to drunken brawling in taverns with knives and clubs rather than the higher skills of swordplay, started to look somewhat less self-assured when he saw his opponent's professional stance, combining both grace and poise with a steady unblinking look of resolution in his unerring piercing blue eyes. Not really knowing what to do, the man resorted to speaking patronisingly with false bravado, again trying to extricate himself unharmed from what he now perceived as possibly a perilous situation. "Come on, boy, put that big pointed sharp thing down, give me what I've come for," he said, almost pleading, giving a sidelong glance over to where the valuable pile of tack was still being used as a refuge by the cowardly Lawrence. "Cross my heart, I promise I'll let you and that snivelling cunt live if you do," he added hoping upon hope that the suggestion of a compromise might do the trick.

Richard, however, remained unmoved by the appeal, and holding his position, bored his steely glint manfully up into his opponent's eyes. Yet brave as he was, his undeveloped arms were starting to feel the strain, and for no more than a micro-second he allowed the sword to waver in his grip. Seeing this as his chance, the man rushed like a bull at the boy, trying to get inside what he thought was the useful range of the blade, to gut the lad with his shorter, more effectual close-contact weapon. It was Richard's arms that were tiring, not his legs, and with the reflexes of a cat, he sprung backwards, finding relief for his arms by swinging down his weapon in a shimmering arc to catch the aggressor down the side of his small round helmet, slicing off part of his left ear on its path, and cutting through the padded leather on the point of his left shoulder, carving off a thin steak of bloody flesh, and paralysing the arm in the process. With a howl like a wolf, Richard's opponent rushed on trying to overpower the stripling with his sheer bulk; nonetheless, the impetus of the blade hadn't been wasted, and in a glinting figure of eight, the young practised swordsman brought the perfectly honed razor-sharp tip with full force horizontally across just below the ribcage of the man, laying open his abdomen and spilling a small bucketful of his greenish purple entrails on the emerald-green mossy floor.

Seeing he was mortally injured, the beaten man looked startled for a moment, and then, with an expression of utter dismay on his disbelieving face, dropped his weapon, and staring in wonder at the mini-assassin, fell to his knees and, scooping up his spilled insides with his good hand, put them back in the yawning gash where they once belonged.

Richard had never killed a man in cold blood before, and he knew that although badly injured, his opponent's wounds meant that without a surgeon's aid, they would result in a slow painful death, probably from gangrene. After a short-lived pause to consider whether he should allow the defeated bully to suffer or not, Richard sheathed his stained sword, and went across to Lawrence to assure him that at least for the time being he was safe, leaving the crumpled heap of whimpering humanity to suffer the same agony he threatened to inflict on Richard only a few minutes before.

Dreadfully embarrassed by his display of abject cowardice, Lawrence followed Richard around like a faithful puppy while he went about his urgent business, offering lame excuses in explanation for his behaviour, partly citing his hangover and the resulting headache as one reason, and his blurred vision as another, both of which Richard knew were just more lies which fell so readily from Lawrence's scheming, dishonest, craven mouth. Most importantly, the next errand was to rescue the hobbled horses from the pool which had so unexpectedly sprung up overnight. Leaving the victim where he sat, fighting to hold his slippery guts in place, and ignoring his moaned pleas to be mercifully dispatched to save him from more of the searing pain he was already experiencing, Richard rushed to where the animals were stranded. He was astounded when, such a short time before there had been a torrent of murky water feeding the deep gurgling tarn, now there was just a small peat-coloured pond and a brown trickle, flowing away through the middle of the water-swept grassy stone-strewn sward with the horses peacefully munching at the grass on the dry, if somewhat squelchy, land.

Satisfied the horses were safe and well, Richard gazed at the welcoming looking shallow pool, and, not having had a proper wash for days, he stripped off to bathe in the alluring freezing water. Jumping into the pond stark naked, he couldn't help but take a great lungful of air when his breath was stolen by the shock of the chill. Splashing about like a water baby, laughing and gasping, Richard washed away the weeks of camp-life grime and with it the horrors he'd witnessed, leaving it all behind in the water along with a part of his boyhood. Emerging as if baptized, cleansed and happy, he was pleased with himself having fought so bravely, knowing how proud Henry would have been to see his taught skills so effectively put to use, feeling that at last he could honestly say he was indeed becoming a man.

Back at the camp, the still very green-looking Lawrence had composed himself a little, and was in the process of shedding his vomit-soiled hauberk and gambeson, so he could also wash, bending forwards and wriggling to allow the weight of the mail and padding do the work and fall to the ground. Hell bent on his own comfort, Lawrence ignored the fast-fading man, who was still alive and propped up against a rock, bleating and mumbling hideously, begging for his confession to be heard and then put out of his misery. Richard arrived back in the nick of time for Lawrence, just as his master was starting to rinse his arms and bloodstained face in some stagnant green rainwater that collected in a natural basin formed where two rocks met. Timidly nodding an embarrassed welcome at his approaching saviour with almost, but not quite a smile of gratitude, he cupped his hands to liberate some of the polluted water to throw over himself. On seeing the foul soup, Richard urgently stopped Lawrence before he polluted his reeking body even more, informing the half-naked knight about the pool and its supernatural refreshing qualities. Pleased to have an alternative other than the revolting stinking slime to bathe in, Lawrence rushed off in the direction where Richard was pointing, where the magic pond with its amazing rejuvenating properties was shrinking fast.

Alone together, the victor and vanquished eyed each other for a second or two, Richard with an expression of sadness and pity for the dying man, who looked back pathetically, and imploring Richard to do the decent thing, automatically lifted his good hand away from the wound to gesticulate as he spoke in a mumbled groan to the lad who had so easily bested him. "Save me dog, will you, mate? I've chained me dog to a tree, and he will starve to death. Do what you want with me, but please save my little Sammy?" the fading man begged.

The pathetic plea struck a sympathetic chord in Richard, who was more than a little amazed by the doomed man, who although suffering the last stages of an agonising death, his thoughts were focused rather than on his own misery but on the wellbeing of his dog. "Tell me a few things I want to know, and if you answer me honestly, I promise I'll find him and look after him," Richard suggested, proffering a listening ear to his dying adversary.

Hearing Richard's offer, the man looked up from replacing a wayward entrail which escaped when he lifted his hand, and wincing with pain, he feebly spoke. "What do you want to know from me?"

Seeing the man didn't have much left in him, Richard replied instantly, perplexed as to why the men were willing to take such a risk in attacking armed men. "I want to know where you're from, and why did you want to murder us last night?"

Once again grimacing with effort, the man replied, croaking with thirst, "Hear my confession and I'll tell you all!"

With a little nod, Richard signified his acceptance of the terms, and offered a soothing sip of water from a flagon to the grateful recipient, to aid him talk and explain where things had gone so badly wrong for him. "Two or three weeks ago I escaped from Baron Dussingdale's squadron; they'd accused me of murder and theft and having found me guilty on all counts were going to hang me the next morning. My brother and pal didn't get caught with me, though, so they sneaked up the night before and rescued me."

"Go on!" Richard urged the swooning man, as he paused to recover his fading breath before continuing.

"We've been on the run since, stuck hiding in a sort of cave next to a stream. Just follow where the water runs down that little glen and about six hundred yards east of here you'll find our camp," he explained. Rolling his hazy eyes in the direction of his hiding place, the doomed man carried on, screwing up his pallid face with each uttered word. "That's where my Sammy is! Him and me was out hunting when we saw you and the other bloke arrive with the nags; all we wanted was them to get us back to England. When we sneaked in last night we only wanted to nick the tack without waking you up and you know the rest." The effort of the confession was taking its toll on the fast-weakening man, whose voice was growing fainter by the second.

"Was the accusation of murder warranted?" Richard demanded, bending close to hear the man's reply, repeating the question twice, wanting to know if justice was being served in the end, before the man's last few fitful breaths left in his failing body. Mustering enough strength to own up to the crime, with a half nod, the man, who such a short time before was a merciless, larger than life bully, admitted his guilt and died smiling, believing in his ignorance that the admission had cleansed his soul free of the crime, allowing it to take its place in heaven along with the good. After uttering a brief prayer for the departed over the body, Richard went about searching the bodies of all three deceased to see if there was anything of use about their persons, finding nothing of particular interest, except the very obviously thieved, latest style of pig-faced bascinet, which so recently furnished the rather large head of his first victim. Trying it on, Richard adjusted the laces in the lining to make it something approaching a proper fit before cleaning it thoroughly, by energetically burnishing it to a deep shine with one of the dead victim's mail mittens, before discarding his old helmet, to put the new one in its position along with his mail shirt and quilted arming jacket, placed to air in the morning sun to freshen them up, ready to put on before leaving to find the bandits' hiding place, and as promised rescue Sammy the dog.

The pool had also worked its mysterious magic on Lawrence, who returned after his lengthy bath scrubbed and glowing from the magic waters, now free from his hangover and with a bounce in his step. His eyes, however, immediately alighted on the new head-piece which now shone like new and glinted in the corner. "I see you've found me a new helmet; I think I lost my old one in the battle!" Lawrence declared, sounding as if he had actually taken a useful part in the battle and making the incorrect assumption the piece of armour was for him.

"It's mine, not yours," the astounded Richard corrected him, and testing out his newfound manhood, raised his breaking voice a little and stood over the disputed item defensively. "By the laws of chivalry it's mine. I killed him and thus his property now belongs to me... sir!"

Feeling rather stunned by the insolent riposte, Lawrence replied, and reddening with building anger at his impertinent squire, shouted aggressively to remind Richard of his rightful place. "I am your liege lord, and you get your spoils at my say so, so give me that fucking helmet now!"

Once again Richard tried out his new power, answering somewhat sarcastically and a little dismissively at the aggrieved Lawrence. "You can't change the chivalric code to suit yourself, but you can have my old one if it pleases you, my lord!" he sneered, tossing the old out-dated, dented flat-topped casque over to the feet of Lawrence, who, spurning the gift with a foot, kicked it back to Richard. Aggravated at knowing he was wrong and fearing that to argue further might result in a very one-sided fight, Lawrence spun on his heels and went to where his own armour was still in a muddled heap and, sulkily refusing Richard's conciliatory offer of help with the awkward process, offered as an olive branch to appease his petulantly brooding master, started to put it on.

Armed, mounted and ready for the day ahead, bare-headed Lawrence and helmeted Richard rode away from the camp, both starving hungry, towing the lazy pack horse to where the dead criminal had indicated his hiding place lay, soon becoming alerted that they were in the correct place by the whining of a dog and an unexpected very human feeble plea begging for help. Vaulting off tall Solomon, Richard tossed the reins to the still-ruminating Lawrence, and carefully approaching the source of the noise, drew his sword in readiness at what might meet his wary gaze. Stopping dead in his tracks when rounding a corner, he found a completely naked young girl of sixteen or seventeen years old, gagged and bound, laying on her side, covered in thick layers of accrued muck, tethered with a short length of rope to a stunted six-foot pine sapling, next to a chained sleek young grey and brown-mottled hairy lurcher, which sympathetically was licking clean an area on the girl's grubby cheek in concern for the terrified lass. Not being entirely sure what action to take, as he had never before seen a naked female, Richard shouted loudly for Lawrence's urgent help to deal with the matter as he ran towards the poor trembling waif, the hastily adjusted lining of his new bascinet making him appear to frown, as he urgently drew his dagger to extricate the girl from her savagely tight bonds. Naively, Richard failed to understand the reason for the utter terror in her bright green eyes, as he knelt down next to the shivering wreck with his dagger poised at the ready. Confused by the shouting and having misread the way Richard drew his blade, thinking it was to murder her and not to free her, the lass braced herself to receive the expected strike, when to her surprise the blade slipped with ease through the restraints, releasing the girl from her bonds, allowing her to scuttle out of reach of the armed stranger and remove the gag herself.

Lazily and without any hint of urgency whatsoever, Lawrence deigned to wander over to the encampment as if he was simply going for a Sunday morning walk, deliberately dawdling to take more time than really necessary to tether the horses to a convenient stump. Making sure he had wasted enough time for any possible confrontation to be over and done with before appearing, Lawrence paused on his way in to shoot a disapproving scowl at Richard, annoyed at being given orders by his underling, and thus be treated as though he was the squire and not the knight. His grumpy expression soon changed to one of joy when it lit on the young naked female. Lustfully scanning her nudity and having had his eyeful, in a bid to impress her, he turned to Richard, admonishing him for nothing in particular, demonstrating to the girl, that it was he, not Richard, who was actually in charge of the delicate situation.

Ignoring the futile attempt to belittle him, Richard politely instructed Lawrence to fetch a scavenged cloak from the saddlebags, and bring it to preserve the girl's modesty while they tried to find out more about her plight. Realising by means of a stony stare from Richard that he really meant what he said, Lawrence forgot his seniority and begrudgingly trundled off to do what he was told, this time returning quickly, complete with a flask of clean water to slake the girl's thirst. First the girl and then the very thirsty dog drank deeply when offered the water, and then, suitably refreshed, she covered her nakedness with the sage green cloak before speaking timidly to thank the strangers for her rescue. In her overwrought state her faint words were virtually incomprehensible, but clear enough to shock both men, as her accent was one cultured in the shires of England, not one, as they had expected of a Scottish lass who mainly spoke Gaelic. "I must thank you, sirs, for my life, I think," she said, forcing her parched, cracked lips into a weak smile of gratitude.

The girl's voice quickly faltered as she tried to speak, the release of pent-up emotion overtaking her as an uncontrollable quivering of her lips heralded the release of the fought-back tears she desperately wanted to remain behind her eyelids. First just one single salty droplet trickled down her grimy cheek, its meandering course leaving a starkly clean trail among many other tracks from where she had been sobbing a short time previously, soon to be followed by another, then another, before a whole cascade of its fellows came streaming in pursuit of their lost friend. Both Richard and Lawrence watched in awed silence for a good five minutes, while the girl cried uncontrollably, partly in relief at being saved, partly in shame at what she had endured. Now and then she clutched the hem of the cloak to mop her water-filled, swollen eyelids, making them look oddly white amid her muck-striped face. Eventually, her bitter sobbing abated into gentle hiccups, punctuated with deep body-shuddering sighs. When at last the poor lass managed to regain adequate composure, she volunteered to tell her harrowing tale of woe.

Sitting on the ground like a lost stray with the cloak wrapped tightly around her like a winter blanket to protect her from an imaginary chill, she introduced herself as Yolanda Bellew, and commencing her woeful tale, started at the very beginning. She was born in Market Deeping, a small town near Stamford in Lincolnshire, to a reasonably wealthy retired professional soldier turned spice merchant and his wife. The eldest of eight children, three boys and five girls, for the first fourteen years of her life she lived with her family in total happiness, wanting absolutely nothing, even receiving a reasonable education from the local priest, until everything changed when her mother died unexpectedly from a mystery illness. Yolanda believed her father came from a long line of the recently disbanded Knights Templar, and seemingly was unperturbed about the death of his spouse of fifteen years, as he very quickly re-married a much younger woman. It soon became patently obvious that her new stepmother despised her very being, and manipulating her new husband to her will, within a few months Yolanda had been sold and shipped off to a nunnery, in the middle of nowhere, several miles from the outskirts of Ripon in wildest North Yorkshire.

The convent, instead of being a holy house, turned out to be little more than a religious brothel, where the nuns were merely prostitutes who prayed all night and day when they weren't otherwise engaged in servicing the many customers who frequented the house of leisure. The clientele, rather than being lay folk, were mostly priests, bishops and even the odd cardinal or two, on sabbaticals to indulge themselves in sexual fantasies away from the public eye. As a newcomer she was tied, whipped and beaten into compliance, before agreeing to be taught the many advanced sexual techniques, worthy of Salome herself, that were necessary to please the paying guests. As well as enjoying females of all different ages, the guests often craved the favours of young men, small boys and even the odd animal or two, but whatever type of perversion was required, the Abbess, Mother Godeliva, always did her best to cater for the special needs. No matter how far-fetched or bizarre the request was, she always managed to come up with a suitable answer to keep the customers happy and sate their weird and wonderful perversions. However, on hearing that a large English force was heading north to Scotland to fight Robert the Bruce, the mother superior realised that there was a small fortune to be made, and with that in mind she dispatched a mixture of her dual-purpose holy prostitutes, including Yolanda, to set up a tented brothel within half a mile of the army's base and fulfil some of the carnal needs of the hundreds of lonely, woman-less men. It was there where she was kidnapped by two of the three bandits. All three having enjoyed the facilities provided, categorically refused to pay, criticising the quality of the service as an excuse, and they started to leave, doggedly pursued by a persistent and very noisy, naked nun, who hung on to one of their sleeves, shrieking loudly, attracting lots of unwanted attention by demanding immediate payment for her time, only to be heartlessly killed by the most vocal complainant, who slit her railing throat to shut her up. Realising the gravity of their crime, the men attempted a panicky bid for freedom and as the smallest female to hand, Yolanda was dragged as a hostage with them. Leaving at speed to escape the ensuing commotion, they lost one of their number, who unluckily for him, was caught by a couple of Welsh captains as they entered the brothel with high hopes, a purse of silver and full of their manly expectations, only to witness the event and, sadly for their raging libidos, capture one of the perpetrators, subsequently to leave disappointed, having to take their captive back to suffer the swift justice meted out by the hastily convened martial court.

Yolanda's time as captive in the bandits' base was worse than being at the brothel. On her arrival she was immediately stripped of all her clothes, which were subsequently hidden in a secret place to encourage her not to run away, and then forced to suffer three weeks of constant torture, tied up, gagged, kept naked on a six-foot leash in the open, and only fed the bare minimum to keep her alive. Regularly being mocked, brutally beaten, and raped, sometimes several times a day, her only solace during the captivity was the year-old lurcher Sammy, who licked off the worst of the grime and curled up with her, sharing his warmth on the chilly upland nights. The story of her dreadful ordeal ended with the arrival of Richard and Lawrence when they heard her muffled screams and came to her timely rescue.

Both men appeared visibly moved by the sorry saga; even the stone-hearted Lawrence pretended to almost shed a tear on hearing the sad reality, but it was the youthful, naive Richard that was most affected by the story, and listened open-mouthed as the particulars were told, hardly believing people, especially holy ones, were capable of treating a fellow human being in such a manner. In an attempt to make amends for the cruelty and relieve the emotional trauma Yolanda obviously suffered by telling all, Richard suggested that she took a bath in the nearby brook, while he searched for her missing clothes. Agreeing to the idea, Yolanda shuffled off, shrouded in the cloak, to where a stony-bottomed mountain stream gurgled through a patch of green sward, to bathe her sore abused body with hopefully only God and the birds as her witness.

Unable to find the clothes, Richard rode back the short distance to the old camp to retrieve some items of useable garb off the corpses which he thought might be useful for Yolanda to wear. Returning quickly from his errand complete with a bundle of assorted garb, he arrived back only to be greeted by a female's shrill scream of terror, issuing from the area near the stream. Fearing the worst, Richard leapt off the mighty horse, and ran to where he thought the shriek emanated from, but on rounding a large rock an unbelievable sight met his incredulous eyes. It only took Richard seconds to work out what had happened. Lawrence had watched secretly as the lass bathed, her youthful loveliness gradually being revealed, as she busily scrubbed her muck-covered skin with a wad of dried grass, turning it to flawless pink ivory with washing. The sight built up Lawrence's urges to a point of no return, when his lustful nature took over, and losing control, he sexually assaulted her in the middle of a grassy bank next to the stream. Without a care for Yolanda's wellbeing, Lawrence was on top of the struggling, naked girl, preventing her further screams by clamping his hand firmly over her mouth and nose, almost suffocating the helpless lass, as he humped and grunted like the rabid cur he was, mercilessly raping the freshly bathed female, who writhed and thrashed, trying to escape the unwanted attentions of the frenzied predator.

Looking up when she saw Richard, her weepy, sad green eyes mutedly beseeched for help, to save her from yet another forced indignity. The look was enough, so without considering the situation further, Richard raced up to the rising and falling pallid backside of the partly clad Lawrence, and, using the flat of his sword, mustered every last ounce of his strength to slap it as hard as he could with an almighty thwack. The stinging strike instantly stopped the rape mid-stroke and after a giant long-drawn-out animal-like howl of utter agony, Lawrence rolled off Yolanda, his limp cock falling out of the girl, shocked into immediate flaccidity with the unexpected severe pain.

Still panting from his exertions, Lawrence looked evilly up to identify the interloper, lust, pain and bitter disappointment still visible in his bulging eyes, as recognising the culprit as his own squire, screamed abusively in frustrated rage. "You fucking little bastard cunt, I'll have you fucking hanged for that!"

His empty threat was wasted on the deaf ears of Richard, whose sympathy lay entirely with the assaulted girl. "You, my ignoble lord, are nothing better than those dead men that rot not half a mile from here, and it is in my mind to despatch you to a place where the damned souls like you are licked by the flames of purgatory, but in this life, I for one will have nothing more to do with the cowardly criminal I now know you to be," Richard spat with audible disgust in his voice, before turning his back on his rejected master to tend to the hurt of the dumbstruck, uncontrollably trembling poor Yolanda. Sticking his sword safely back in his belt, Richard supported the traumatised, weak-kneed girl with one hand and holding her cloak together with the other, escorted Yolanda back to the place where Sammy was still tied. His turned back offered an easy target to the rampaging Lawrence, who, seeing it as a chance to get even, raced at him silently over the spongy sward with the intention of stabbing his departing ex-squire squarely between the shoulder blades. Luckily for the trusting Richard, Yolanda's unsteady legs failed her exactly at the precise moment when the cowardly strike was timed, causing them both to stumble sideways and hence avoid the onrush. The flashing blade missed its intended target but unfortunately made contact with Richard's unarmoured wrist just below the cuff as he thrust it out sideways from his body to regain his balance. Hardly crediting his luck, Richard watched the dagger whistle harmlessly past him, along with Lawrence, who in missing his blow, tumbled forward with the effort, and ended up sprawling five feet in front of his target, impaling himself through the thigh with his own knife on landing.

Now steadied from his stumble, Richard looked down at the prostrate man, chiding him mockingly as if he was an errant child. "You can't even get that right, can you? Stung by your own stinger," Richard said, shaking his head with contempt as he bent down to pluck the intended murder weapon out of Lawrence's oozing leg. Laughing derisively at the hapless fool, Richard cast the blade far beyond retrieval, out into the brook. Doing his best to keep his injury hidden from Yolanda, they both departed, Richard supporting the distraught sobbing girl with his good hand, back to the camp, leaving the hate-filled Lawrence hobbling alone at the rear, clutching his bleeding leg, slowly getting further and further behind, his bellowed vile curses slowly fading in their youthful ears.

When Yolanda had recovered enough to be spoken to, Richard sensibly advised her to find something to wear; so, obeying him, she urgently set about rummaging through the retrieved pile of clothes, to select some to make herself half-decent. Meanwhile, Richard made his best effort to wrap his throbbing wound before searching the bandits' hideaway for food or anything he deemed useful for the journey homewards. His efforts were well rewarded when he found among some bags of assorted loot, an all-important flint and striker, some meagre army rations of musty dried meat from an unknown beast, and a linen sack half-full of weevil-infested thick oat biscuits. However, thinking something to eat was better than nothing, he pouched the poor fare safely into the saddlebags but put enough to one side for a scanty meal for them both before starting their lengthy journey home.

Although taking the matter very seriously, Richard couldn't help allowing a stifled laugh to leave his lips when he saw the newly dressed, still-traumatised Yolanda emerge from behind the rock she had used as a modesty screen. Wan-faced and attired in an ill-fitting faded brown leather man's jerkin, some coarse woollen red leggings, which being at least eight inches too long, sported a giant turn-up which almost reached her knees, and short serviceable boots that were several sizes too big, looking down at herself, Yolanda flapped her arms like a wet sparrow, demonstrating exactly how badly the garments fitted, almost managing a smile when she saw Richard's amazed expression.

Silently taking her old place alongside tied-up Sam, Yolanda started wondering what on earth was going to be served up next, which happened to be a meal when Richard presented the starved girl with a sort of breakfast. Accepting it, Yolanda started eating, picking at the food trance-like, gazing at an imaginary distant horizon, removing the maggots and other inedible bits, sharing some of the choicer morsels with equally as hungry but much less fussy Sam. Having finished the apology for a repast, all three settled down after washing it down with gulps of water from the freshly filled flask, which almost, but not quite, got rid of the rancid taste, afterwards resting to digest for a while without a single word being said.

Sensing Yolanda's deep unhappiness, Sam rested his furry streamlined head sympathetically on her lap, rolling a loving eye and licking her hand, asking to be stroked, giving the bitterly unhappy lass some crumb of comfort, when suddenly without warning Sam looked up from his personal bliss, pricking his ears and staring into the distance as though he had seen something. Suspecting that Lawrence may have returned, or maybe some belligerent Scots had found them, Richard immediately stood up, holding his precious sword, he always kept no more than an arm's length away, ready to fend off any potential aggressor.

Fully alert and ready to strike, Richard scanned the surroundings to spot the reason for the dog's reaction, at first seeing nothing, until on further inspection, he noticed a distant big brown rabbit, sitting on its haunches, munching some tasty greenery, some sixty to seventy yards away. Remembering that Sam's dead ex-master had mentioned he had been hunting with the dog, Richard whispered the general command of "fetch" to the beast as he unleashed the anticipating trembling hound. Freed from the restraining rope, Sam shot off like an arrow, skirting wide off to the left, closing quickly on the unsuspecting animal, stretching hard the last twenty yards to gain full speed, outflanking the coney to take it on the blind side and picking it up at the full gallop by snatching at it on the way past. The naturally talented lurcher then swerved, to canter back, returning very pleased with himself, and presenting the still-living creature into his best friend's hand. Then with a practised skill Yolanda had learned from her father, she silently took hold of the virtually unharmed and kicking full-grown rabbit by the ears, and dispatched it with a sharp rap to the nape of its neck, afterwards rewarding the dog with a vigorous scratch along his back and between his shoulder blades for his trouble.

Although well-educated by Henry in the subtleties of riding, warfare and the chivalric code, Richard hadn't yet mastered the culinary arts, and with an unsure shaking hand, he prepared himself to undertake gutting and skinning the rabbit. Looking at it in a puzzled fashion, not knowing precisely where to start, Richard incorrectly put the unfortunate animal belly down on a suitably flat slab and braced his dagger to make the initial incision in its back, only to have the blade unceremoniously snatched from his hand and himself pushed to one side by Yolanda. Overtly turning the dead creature the other way up with its legs in the air, she shot a little amazed smile at Richard's ham-fisted effort, and neatly butchered the animal with an expert hand, throwing the offal, as another reward, to Sam, who had been patiently waiting and intently watching every move, energetically wagging his entire body from behind his ears to the tip of his tail in anticipation of the morsel. Casting the danger aside, Richard, who in reality was still starving hungry, helped by a much more relaxed and more trusting Yolanda, gathered several armfuls of dry wood and a few dried pine needles for tinder. Using a well-practised technique with the flint and striker and a high degree of skill, Richard easily started a blaze, and feeding the fire for upwards of half an hour, let the flames die down to a pile of glowing grey ash. Then, using a green stick as a makeshift spit, Yolanda cooked the tempting rabbit over the residual heat, and after another half hour of suffering from the mouth-watering sight of the sizzling lunch, made worse by the excellent meaty smell of the cooking flesh, all three sat together to enjoy an extremely welcome and very tasty meal, before departing on their arduous long trek south.

Riding side by side, they departed the robbers' camp, Richard on his tall bay destrier Solomon, and Yolanda on the uncomfortable slow grey carthorse, with Sam doing his own thing and cantering happily at their heels, leaving behind them a good third of the disgusting food for Lawrence, along with all his gear, his unpredictable steed, including its fuming injured owner, who secretly watched them as they ate, whilst inwardly plotting his dire revenge from a safe distance.

CHAPTER 4

Thirty miles to the south-east of where Richard and Yolanda had deserted the raging Lawrence, Edward the king, his entourage and bodyguard of five hundred chosen lords, knights, bowmen and foot soldiers, were also in the process of making their escape from Bannockburn. Their intention was to travel the sixty or so miles due east to the coast, and the safety offered by the English-held Dunbar Castle, hopefully avoiding the hotly pursuing Scots, led by James 'The Black', Douglas and his own small army, whose sole intention was to overtake the English, bar their way to the port and engage them in battle, capture the king, thus instantly obtaining complete recognition of the Scottish demands, and probably end the war. As it was, with Edward still free, the English had enough strength in depth to go back to England and consolidate their forces to resume the war at a later date.

Initially Edward and his retreating bodyguard made good speed. However, the rear-guard of three hundred heavily laden foot soldiers, composed of fully armed English spearmen and a corps of Welsh archers led by Sir Maurice Berkley, made pitifully slow progress as they grew weary. Over-burdened and still tired after the battle, they struggled along the unfamiliar, poorly made stony road to Dunbar Castle, holding back the rest, who were obliged to stop and wait for them to catch up every now and then.

The king himself rode somewhere in the middle of the phalanx, surrounded for protection by twenty of the best of the best lances the country could offer, including the notable soldier and wise councillor Baron Dennis Dussingdale, who always rode at the king's elbow. Nevertheless, the household knights, mounted on their speedy steeds, were becoming more and more frustrated and somewhat frightened by the snail pace of the retreat. Fearing that James Douglas would soon overtake and out-flank them, they begged the king to break away from the slow-moving foot. It seemed to make good sense, so after a brief discussion among the nobles and taking Dussingdale's advice with Berkley's agreement, the order was given by the king for the cavalry to make their own headway, un-hampered by the retarding infantry, and leave them to make their own way back to England the best they could. In loyal devotion to his men, Sir Maurice bravely refused to flee with the cavalry, and against the king's wishes insisted on staying and ushering his dedicated men all the way back home to England.

Amid a volley of howls, whistles and cat-calls, the king, his nobles, and the two hundred mounted knights urged their horses to the trot, leaving the dismayed infantry gazing after them, disappointed, alone, demoralised and stranded miles from home. Their only hope to survive lay in staying together as a unit, under the more than adequate auspices of the valiant and wily Sir Maurice Berkley, who gave them hope by making a public oath in front of his men, promising to get them all home safely or die with them in the attempt. The declaration caused a clamorous cheer to issue unanimously from all three hundred souls, so loud it was heard by the now-distant king and his followers, who assumed the noise was caused when Black Douglas caught up with the deserted men and joined them in battle. Ignoring the fact that they thought Berkley might be in trouble, the selfish king, hell-bent on making his escape, implored his followers to make more speed, as he assumed the Scots were not far behind. So, at a noisy canter, the two hundred wound their way along the rocky track, their steel-shod horses' hooves clattering, and making showers of sparks off the grey granite as they tried to make the best of what they hoped was some stubborn resistance from the English and Welsh under Berkley. They'd covered all of ten miles at speed before they dared allow their wheezing, blowing horses some respite by slowing them to a trot and then a weary walk. Many men were left behind, some because of lameness to their steeds, either having trodden on stones or stumbled in the flight, and others simply having fallen off in the press; but in the main, the body of horse remained complete.

Caring little about the losses, the king and his retinue continued on as fast as possible, through the evening, only making two stops overnight, to dismount for water, and briefly rest the thirsty and weary horses at convenient pools or ponds. Without respite, the panicking bodyguard rode on, ever eastwards, heartlessly deserting any stragglers to their fate at the hands of the pursuing merciless Black Douglas. They rode through dawn into the morning, until a couple of hours after first light, stumbling and limping, the breathtaking sight of the mighty and ancient, forbidding Dunbar Castle loomed in front of them, its massy battlements silhouetted jet black against the risen sun, the lofty heights surrounded with screaming seagulls, gleaming starkly white against the blue morning sky, circling the perpendicular walls perched on an impregnable precipitous grey-brown rock dominating the natural haven below.

Safely moored in the sea harbour, two English merchant ships were unloading their cargo of supplies for the isolated garrison, their bobbing reflections shimmering on the calm blue swell of the sheltered water, shielded from the vagaries of the North Sea by the natural formation of towering craggy rocks. The piers and jetties were busy with milling men, loading and unloading, readying the ships for the expected coming of the king. John Binham, the warden of the port, only having learnt of the royal visitor a few hours before, had been informed by a messenger whose horse died of exhaustion minutes after his arrival with the news from Stirling of the unexpected visitor and the woeful tale of the calamitous defeat of the English at Bannockburn.

Crestfallen from failure and faint from fatigue, King Edward II, rather than being safely surrounded by his bravest knights as he had been, now rode wearily at the head of his hundred-and-sixty remaining men, slowly leading the bedraggled parade as they ascended the steep slope through the gates of the castle, feeling relieved for the horses', the men's, and his own sake, to dismount his completely spent, faltering, favourite war horse Hector. The king himself almost collapsed with relief, when at last he felt the solid and reassuring English territory under his feet.

Standing to attention, waiting to greet their liege lord and master, was the constable of the castle, Sir Hugh Fernsdale, along with John Binham, the port warden. Both of the men hoped to ingratiate themselves with the monarch and conduct him to a good meal in some hastily prepared quarters. Instead, though, they had to catch the shocked, distraught king when his legs failed, ending up supporting his limp form to the nearest seat, where Edward mustered just enough energy to feebly command the nearest grooms to take care of the valiant Hector, before being escorted inside the castle. All the new arrivals were at least in a similar condition, if not worse than the king. A lot of the horses were even poorer, and in all twenty-three of them had to be put down because of the injuries sustained during the hurried retreat. Their flesh, however, not going to waste, the carcasses were instantly butchered and sent straight to the kitchens, where it was going to be put to good use in feeding the always-hungry garrison with the rare commodity of fresh, wholesome meat.

For eight weeks the king remained in Dunbar, taking his time to recover from the distress of defeat. Edward made a good attempt at relaxing in the sea air and forgetting about his situation, but the indelible images of the forced humility unbalanced his fragile mind further. The desperation mixed with grief, addled his wits, making him even more prone to flying off into his sudden, famously erratic moods, that always were accompanied by uncontrollable bouts of tears, or the screaming fits, which never again left him and beset him for the rest of his days.

Many of his knights and nobles, terrified of incurring his randomly fickle wrath, or frightened at being subjected to unwarranted blame for the defeat, left for England, sailing off in the two cargo ships, which were already there at their disposal, or any other convenient vessel that visited and proposed to leave with unfilled space for passengers. In all, more than a hundred survivors of what was left of the king's bodyguard made their excuses to return home, leaving the king and a reduced entourage of only a scant fifty of his closest attendants in the castle.

With nothing to do in the hemmed-in fortalice, the retinue simply whiled away their time waiting for the advent of the purpose-built royal cog, the *Saint Luke*. Edward categorically refusing to take a less luxurious ship home, preferred to bide his time and wait until the only vessel he deemed magnificent enough to carry his regal self arrived to convey him home to his long-suffering wife Isabella and his young son Edward, back in Southampton, on the south coast of England.

With the arrival of July came the hottest spell of summer weather Scotland had experienced for a hundred years. Surrounded on the two landward sides by the Scots and thus unable to leave the sanctuary of the castle, the complement stifled and perspired as they whiled away their time in the sultry oppressive heat, playing cards or other gentle games, which didn't generate even more soaking sweat with the effort. However, the unbalanced king still sulked about the humiliating crushing defeat, and decided to shut himself out of sight in an airless room, away from the imagined pointed fingers and wagging tongues of those around him. Stubbornly, Edward refused to accept any audiences with his subjects, including the Baron Dussingdale, who needed to urgently discuss the present perilous situation in the stronghold with the disturbed royal, who, instead of being interested in the wellbeing of the garrison, preferred to wistfully sulk in total silence, and gaze out of a closed glazed window over the sea, thinking of what should have been. Only at the dead of every sweltering night could the king's voice be heard, when his haunting nightmares turned into terrifying ranting screams, which echoed around the sleeping castle, annoyingly waking those experiencing happier dreams.

Thwarted in its attempt to rush to the aid of Edward, the royal ship, the *Saint Luke* and its sailors were in a little better state. Hopelessly becalmed, they drifted midway between the shores of East Anglia and Holland in the windless sea. Its scarlet sails hung limp in the heavyweight turgid air, as without even a hint of a breeze, it needed to be towed along by the ship's pathetic rowing boat with eight labouring sweat-soaked tars, heaving at the oars, making little or no headway north against the tidal flow which twice daily funnelled southwards, drifting the stranded vessel as far backwards as the oarsmen had made forward during the slack water, resulting in a stalemate, where until the wind rose neither side could win.

Back in the castle of Dunbar things were getting worse. Adding to the almost intolerable conditions, a virulent summer illness had broken out, infecting the weakened population crammed into the confined area. The king and the forty-seven remaining men exacerbated the squeeze and like a whirlwind the voracious stomach bug swept all before it. Everywhere the stench of vomit and faeces hung heavily in the air; gagging servants ran about with brimming buckets and dripping mops where people failed to hold their bowels or unexpectedly threw up without warning. The very young, the old, or the weak started dying with the illness, and with no place to bury them, their yellow jaundiced bodies were merely thrown over the seaward wall into the ocean, where they floated together in a festering raft of reeking human flesh, attracting the seabirds from miles around, who enjoyed the bounty and grew fat on the bloated carcasses. The highly contagious disease forced Edward and the more senior nobles to lock themselves up in their stuffy quarters, pleased to be sealed behind closed doors and hopefully safe from the mini-plague sweeping the castle.

Meanwhile the useless frightened priests could do nothing, except drone prayers all day and night, and fight off the devil-inspired sickness by sprinkling Holy Water wherever they went. The inept physicians also did their bit by burning unguent herbs, and spending the rest of their time shut up in the apothecaries, concocting strange potions to combat the pestilence, which could strike anyone without warning, no matter who they were. Without the regular shipments of supplies, which before the arrival of the windless weather were ferried almost daily from England by sea to the outpost, the food stores started running dangerously low, so with the agreement of the constable and the Baron Dussingdale, the horses started to be slaughtered to feed the starving, sickly population. The first to fall to the butcher's poleaxe were the unlucky donkeys, mules and sumpter horses, and when they ran out it was the jennets and hacks; last of all it became the turn of the knights' destriers to forfeit their lives for food, some of the more sensitive lords saying lengthy, often tearful goodbyes to their old beloved friends, thanking them for their loyal service, before the butcher's axe fell and their flesh divided into joints for the ovens.

With the coming of August and still no sign of a change of weather, everywhere in the castle there was a sense of doom. With no means of escape, the people were trapped in, the seaward side an impossibility because of the un-scalable sheer cliffs, and on the landward side the unseen Scots, who, understanding full-well the misery being suffered behind the walls, waited to pounce on any absconders from the hell on earth. Inside, the food was poor and getting worse: sweetmeats, nuts, fruit or vegetables were a distant memory, there was no bread, and even the fresh horsemeat took on the sickly sweet rancid smell which permeated everything in the citadel. Mercifully, in the second week of the month, the weather broke, as a blustery front swept in from the west, taking with it the sickness as quickly as it came, leaving behind in its wake, gaunt shadowy people that only a month before were among the plumpest and best-fed in Scotland.

With the wind, the promise of expected relief lifted everyone's spirits, including the king, who emerged unannounced from his confinement a wreck of humanity, hollow-eyed and pale, with filth-matted hair and skin loosely hanging off him in folds, his unchanged, soiled attire reeking from the detritus of his self-imposed imprisonment. The first act in his newfound freedom was to scream for the servants, berating them severely for not being ready at his beck and call, savagely slapping an innocent page to add force to his demands, which included a change of clothes, a much needed bath and some food, other than horsemeat or the broth made from the unfortunate creatures' bones. On hearing the king's impossible-to-fulfil last request, the slapped page ran off, not to cry as expected, but signifying that he had something that might be suitable for the king to eat. The boy returned within minutes with a well handled, if not slightly grubby, large marzipan sweetmeat made in the shape of a graceful white swan, he had been saving for months, because of its beauty. Kindly, the boy handed the sugary sculpture to the king, who without as much as a thank you, snatched it out of his hand and greedily ate it.

Satisfied after the snack, Edward took his bath in a large wooden hooped tub, brim-filled with almost unbearably hot water, and then, assisted by the same rather disappointed page, he changed into the finery more befitting the great and powerful monarch he aspired to be. Bathed, refreshed, although stick-thin and hollow-cheeked from lack of food, the cleaned king looked very much more like his regal old self. All except, that is, for a newly acquired single lock of grey hair which strangely had sprung up during his confinement, contrasting starkly amid its golden fellows at the front of his hairline.

With a returned sense of pride, Edward took his place at the head of his hastily summoned, depleted council of senior nobles, including the Baron Dussingdale, Sir Hugh Fernsdale the constable of Dunbar and John Binham the warden. Unusually, the normally impatient king waited with self-control as he sat at the head of his councillors, only the tapping of a royal foot betraying his true nature while he waited for an update on the present situation; to eventually be told what he wanted to know, when the baron bravely explained everything of relevance, about the toll taken on the inhabitants, firstly by the disease, then the starvation and the present total lack of food, also adding that he didn't know when succour was due.

For once in his life Edward bothered to listen; taking in what was said, he cast his eyes at the ceiling as if looking for divine inspiration, suddenly suggesting that maybe a raiding party could be formed to sally out at high speed, burst through the Scottish cordon, and steal some very necessary supplies from the surrounding farms. More than pleased with his inspirational idea, the king looked round the gathering, expecting some united, smiling, animated vocal support for his brilliant idea; but instead of gazing round at the inspired happy faces he thought would be looking admiringly back at him, each person sported the dejected glum expression of impending doom. Wondering what the reason for the negative response was, he asked one and then another to explain themselves, learning nothing from their down-turned closed mouths, until his newfound patience ran out. Turning back to Dussingdale, he banged the table, demanding to be informed why it was his scheme had met with so little support. As brave as the baron was, he still needed to take a giant gulp of air as though he was bracing himself for a plunge into icy water, and then, after an emboldening slurp of wine, he blurted his answer nervously to the incredulous monarch. "Because of the horses, sire!"

"What about the h-horses, Dennis?" the bemused king inquired, his brow furrowed questioningly.

"They've all been eaten, my lord," Dussingdale replied falteringly, frightened that he had incurred the Royal wrath by his honest answer, being fully aware how prone Edward was to dreadful bouts of violence to those who vexed him.

"All!" the king screamed, his voice piercing and high like a woman's.

"Yes, my lord, all! They were needed to feed the people, there was just nothing else to eat, sire."

"Even my faithful Hector?" Edward demanded, looking sad and shocked, thinking that his noble horse had been slaughtered to feed mere commoners.

"I'm afraid so, my liege. He never recovered from the journey from Stirling, sire, he was suffering," the baron lied, crossing his fingers to ward off any curse, in case the Devil was watching. In reality, Hector was in no worse shape than the others, but he thought the truth would inflame the volatile, unreasonable king even further.

"What! My p-poor, poor noble Hector has been eaten by base peasants! Who the hell dared to give the order to do it?" Edward shrieked, his gathering anger clearly visible in his reddening face.

"You did, my lord!" Dennis lied again, this time, though, designed to save the poor souls who did the deed without knowing to whom the condemned steed belonged. "I'm sorry, sire!" Dussingdale added, still keeping his fingers crossed, not out of superstition, but hopeful that the untruths wouldn't be found out and hoping that, in the depths of the king's depression, Edward wasn't interested or aware of anything, not even the demise of his favourite horse Hector.

"Oh y- yes! I remember, at least I think I remember," he said sadly. It was the king's turn to lie, and with a tear in his royal eye he got up from the table, helpless and impotent to influence the outcome of this particular chapter in the history of Dunbar Castle, to while away the time hoping the expected succour would arrive before having to yield himself and the fort to the Scots and hence lose the war.

The wait for relief wasn't too long, as a day after the dangerous session with the unpredictable king, the westerly wind which accompanied the fresher weather backed to a strong southerly, favouring the supply ship's run up the North Sea. Speeded by the breeze at their backs, a distant splodge, thought to be a ship, was spotted from the lookouts posted on the highest point of the castle, its imminent arrival being announced to all by the energetic ringing of the castle's chapel bell. As if being magically switched on by an invisible hand, the listless starved population, who'd previously wandered about aimless and without energy as they went about their daily routine, suddenly, with the prospect of new hope, started urgently rushing about, tripping and stumbling as fast as their weakened legs would carry them, excited by the thought of actual food, the last remnant of nutrition having been wrung out of the horses' bones a few days before. Those who manned the seaward battlements craned their necks to peer down the channel, some leaning dangerously far out off the walls, pointing, shading their eyes against the sparkling sea, trying to gain a glimpse of the approaching relief. It was true, ten or so miles distant, just distinguishable against the glistening white foam-specked water, a single scarlet and black dot was beating straight up the channel, directly towards harbour. Within minutes everyone gazed to the south, watching, concentrating, as the approaching ship became clearer and more defined. It was unmistakable; it definitely was the *Saint Luke*, the painted red badge of a Winged Ox, the apostle's insignia, clearly visible on its forward billowing sheet, causing the air of anticipation to ratchet up a little more, becoming almost frenzied when a very small sharp-eyed boy sitting on his father's shoulders announced he could see more. Sure enough, a minute or so later, just visible some five miles behind the *Saint Luke* there was another, then another, in all four ships were running with the wind, hurtling across the choppy seas, bringing eleventh-hour supplies to rescue the famished occupants of the impregnable Dunbar Castle.

Heralded by a colossal cheer, the first and fastest of the ships turned its gilded prow towards the narrow steep cliff-sided entrance of the sheltered harbour. Furling up the main sheet, it glided in under its own impulsion, gently through the reeking flotsam made entirely from the last remains of floating humanity, trapped like a strange oily scum of bleached flesh drifting aimlessly on the tide. The ship's precarious path was aided by rows of sailors along its sides, each armed with a long pole to prevent its gaudily painted wooden hull from coming into contact with the dangerous jagged rocks which lurked unseen just beneath the surface and which in the past had caused the demise of more than several less wary vessels. With a frenzied urgency, hundreds of pairs of hands aided the unloading; everyone helped, from an old withered crippled woman, still dressed in her mourning robes for her long-dead husband, to the muscular, bare-chested, out-of-work farrier. Even Baron Dussingdale himself rolled up his sleeves to join in with the toil, where each and every person carried as much as they could to stock the empty larders, and in no time at all the mouth-watering smell of baking bread filled the air, its sweet yeasty scent even overpowering the all-invading siege smell which had assaulted the nostrils of all those trapped for the past several weeks.

For the first time for ages the population ate decent food, a stark contrast to the rancid flesh and thin, flavourless, watery broth their taste buds had become used to, many over-filling themselves and bringing the welcome rations back up as fast as they had eaten them, their shrunken empty stomachs unable to cope with the sudden influx of the solid wholesome fare. With their bellies filled and lives back on track once more, a tangible sense of well-being was soon present in the castle. Where, before, the people had simply plonked themselves down anywhere, to wait with hopeless resignation for the inevitable, and the only music was that of the priests chanting dirges for the dead, all the misery was now forgotten and replaced with happily occupied folk, singing and whistling as they scuttled about their tasks with a renewed sense of purpose and meaning. Even the king was unusually upbeat, taking some time out of his busy schedule prior to leaving on his voyage back home, talking with the constable and warden of Dunbar, reassuring them that he would come back to defeat Robert the Bruce and re-take the lost ground in Scotland. Also, with a hopeful glint in his eye, he informed them that fresh troops and horses were already on their way to defend the stronghold. Even making a solemn oath to them, Edward swore before God that he personally would return within a year and resume the campaign, offering them tempting rewards in anticipation of their keeping the key strategic site in English hands.

Two days after the arrival of the ships, the time came for Edward to depart. Almost everything had returned to normal and back to the clamour of a fully functioning castle, where the new batch of reinforcements had joined the garrison complete with horses, fodder and the raw materials to make work for the farriers and grooms, bringing with them all the latest news from England and giving the women something to gossip about as they went about their tasks. The men resumed practising the martial skills necessary to keep their senses honed ready for conflict, the bowyers, fletchers, armourers and all the other tradesmen now busy, gainfully employed in their workshops, noisily turning the new supplies into useable weapons and the paraphernalia of war.

The evening before the regal departure, as warden to the port John Binham organised for the *Saint Luke* to be turned round so that its painted and gilded bows now pointed seawards ready to leave, and not wishing to cause offence to the petulant monarch's olfactory senses, the grizzly task of skimming most of the stinking human flotsam off the water had been completed by some strong-stomached volunteer sailors. Inside the harbour the morning was fine and still, and now the royal ship patiently waited for its regal guest, swaying gently in the sheltered haven, its deep mirrored reflection sharp against the calm blue-green swell, the perfect image occasionally interrupted by the white diving birds as they picked up their breakfast of odd remaining tasty morsels of sea-bleached meat here and there.

Eventually, after what seemed like an interminable wait, a blaring fanfare of trumpets at last announced the imminent presence of the king. The clamorous notes were still reverberating around the cliffs when, in all his finery, the noble Edward arrived amid the pomp and ceremony befitting his kingly status, to board the *Saint Luke*. His nobles, knights and the dignitaries of Dunbar all lined the stone quay, bowing reverently on sight of him, hoping to catch his eye, as he planted his first royal foot on the flamboyantly bedecked gangplank. That single step was the signal for two sailors, stationed ready at the stern of the ship, to unfurl an oversize royal flag sporting the arms of the Plantagenets, promoting a huge orchestrated cheer to issue from the whole populace, obliged to look on and bid farewell and safe journey to the departing pompous monarch, most of whom were more than delighted to see the back of. All watched as the ship was warped out from the windless sheltered harbour into the open sea; once there, the breeze filled the raised sails and picked up the limp ensign, signifying all things were set fair for the voyage home.

The constable and warden inwardly breathed a huge sigh of relief as the ship's stern finally disappeared from view. Overjoyed to see it and the king gone, they were relieved because of Edward's unpredictable turbulent nature and his tendency to fly off the handle for no apparent cause, and fearing that, as trustees of the castle, they would be made scapegoats and be blamed for the disastrous events which almost led to the loss of Dunbar, both very pleased, if not somewhat amazed, to have survived the visit unscathed, unbelievably with their heads still firmly attached to their obediently loyal, steadfast shoulders.

CHAPTER 5

Five days after the battle, which came to be known by the historians as Bannockburn, the victorious Robert the Bruce sat proudly at the head of his chiefs around a massive table in the great hall of his new royal headquarters, the recaptured Stirling Castle. Rocking backwards on a sturdy carved oak chair, with his feet crossed on the mighty slab of oak, he watched with a huge grin on his sun-tanned face, as on his orders, all signs and hints of the English occupation were being totally erased from the building. The banners, shields, coats of arms and everything considered not of any use to the Scots, associated with the enemy occupation, were ripped down or prised off the walls, to be carted outside and piled high, ready to be burnt in the very centre of the courtyard.

At the pyre's summit a crudely made cloth effigy of Edward II, tied on a broken chair, took pride of place, to be ritually cremated that evening, much to the pleasure of the gloating Scots, who lit the offensive material as soon as twilight fell, and to the incessant sound of screeching bagpipes, they danced and frolicked around the blaze, swigging at flagons of the highly prized strong-amber coloured liquor they were famed for making.

That same evening, inside the castle, Humphrey de Bohun, the uncle of Henry, Maurice de Berkley, John Segrave, the second Baron Segrave, Warden of Scotland, Sir Marmaduke Tweng the Yorkshire knight, Baron Ralph de Monthermer and most of the other captured English aristocrats were being entertained by Robert the Bruce and his senior lords, including the turncoat Sir Alexander Seaton, who in celebration of the famous overwhelming victory, had organised a lavish banquet, and out of respect for famed enemy warriors, had invited them all to attend.

The food was fantastic, offering the very best of Scottish cuisine, including the finest roast venison, grouse, and capercaille, with a fish course of fresh salmon, fat trout, smoked haddock, and wonderful plump stewed eels. Yet strange as it was to the English, the most prized food of all were the boiled sheep's stomachs, stuffed full of a mixture of spiced offal and oatmeal, treated by the locals as edible gods, introduced into the gathering held high on wooden trestles and heralded by a long deafening wail of the accursed pipes. The last strident notes were still ringing in the guests' ears, when Robert himself drew a sword, and with great ceremony took the first slice of the hallowed steaming sausage, promoting a rousing cheer to issue from the eager Scots in anticipation of the much-vaunted delicacy. To the English the dish was mealy and disgusting, but to the Scottish majority it tasted delicious, as amid a chorus of approving lip smacking, they devoured the strange food, many asking for seconds and some of the greedier even demanding a third helping, ending up eating it down to the very last crumb. At the head of the heavily laden table Robert sat between two leaders of the beaten English army. On his right, the unhappy portly red-faced trencherman Sir Humphrey de Bohun scooped the more edible better-known fare into his mouth as fast as he could; and on his left, eating much more selectively, the much-respected older and blatantly honest, languid-seeming slim form of the highly experienced grey-headed constable of Nottingham Castle, John Segrave, who, unlike Henry, seemed happy, accepting his captivity as merely another peril of war.

The Scottish king spoke to them both with great respect, addressing the apparently disinterested John first. "Yesterday evening I lay in bed wondering to myself where it all went so wrong for the English, Sir John."

In deference to good manners, John was delicately picking at a piece of salmon with two fingers of his left hand, pausing to think for a while and consider a tactful reply, eventually answering with a hint of a hybrid Scottish mixed with north country drawl, making the vowels long and drawn out. "I think, my lord king, apart from some faulty tactics, it was the terrain which beat the English, as without your prepared ground, we would have simply ridden over your spearmen without much trouble to ourselves." Following his frank assessment of the English failure, John shot a wry smile at Humphrey, who spat out some half-chewed venison on hearing Segrave's verdict.

Shouting out angrily in defence of the approach, almost breaking a blood vessel in his blood-suffused purple face in the process. "The tactics were sound, it was the disobedience of the cavalry on the first day, and the next day we would have won if it wasn't for Seaton's damnable treachery!" Humphrey shouted, glaring at Seaton, who in response tossed his head dismissively, and casually flicked some imaginary crumbs off his sleeve in Humphrey's direction; but under strict instructions from Robert, avoided the prolonged eye contact which could have so easily led to more bloodshed. The argument was short lived, quickly defused by Robert who wanted the occasion to be one of peaceful celebration rather than beset with petty quarrels, which in the turbulent times could so quickly turn violent.

Speaking this time to Humphrey, who was mumbling and grumbling in between large mouthfuls of each type of food and gulps of the sweetened warm wine so loved by the hierarchy, Robert made a surprise announcement. "I believe I have something of yours, Sir Humphrey, something to take back with you when your ransom is paid."

Looking up from his platter, Humphrey ceased his muttering, and speaking with his mouth full of food, frowned with interest. "What might that be, sir? What it is that is mine which you have in your possession?"

Robert looked back at Humphrey with a forlorn expression. "Sadly, my lord, I have the body of your nephew, and at this precise moment it is being preserved by my physicians ready for the journey home to your family crypt, where a brave man like him belongs."

"How do you know it is him that you have, sir?" Humphrey asked, preferring now to listen rather than to eat.

"Because the night after the first day of battle, I found his brave young squire Richard de Mauville wandering among the dead searching for his body, and together we found him and wrapped his remains in a cloak given to me by my bodyguard Walter Swan. Richard obviously returned him back to your camp because that is where he was found, exactly as we left him, still wrapped in the cloak and dumped with the all the priest's ransacked gear."

Humphrey fostered a great love for his younger kinsman, and inwardly mourned Henry's passing deeply, managing to keep his grief well hidden from everybody except the astute king of the Scots, who knew how much the retrieval of Henry's mortal remains meant to him. With moist eyes and a genuine smile, Humphrey thanked Robert, who accepted his proffered hand. Grasping it firmly, Robert shook it, having just one more thing to add. "Really, it isn't me you should be thanking; it is Master Richard, if he has survived. On your return to your castle in Herefordshire, you will, I trust, honour him for his steadfast devotion," the king advised, hoping that he soon would be released from Humphrey's rather firm clutch.

Still retaining his vice-like grip on Robert's fast-purpling hand, Humphrey looked into the king's sad eyes to earnestly reply, "Sire, you have my solemn word on it. On my oath, I will reward his loyalty when the next I get to see him."

Mercifully for the Scottish monarch, the sincere conversation was cut short, leaving Robert inspecting his bruised hand, when with a heralding blast on a badly played clarion, accompanied by some clashing cymbals and a coordinated cheer from the willing audience, a motley group of mummers spilled leaping and tumbling into the room, rattling tambourines and banging drums, to amuse the banqueters with their hastily prepared production of a play they amusingly titled, 'Saint Robert and the Devil', which was an imaginatively clever, but far from accurate re-enactment of the recent battle. The victor, Robert the Bruce, was played by a tall man on stilts, dressed in silver-foil armour with the royal arms of Scotland painted somewhat crudely on his surcoat and a golden halo wired above his head. His escort consisted of three larger than average-sized men dressed in kilts and white shirts, with their sleeves stuffed to look like huge bulging muscular arms holding mock spears in their hands to represent the Scots army. Opposing them, King Edward was played by a dwarf attired as a female demon with ridiculously large pink-nippled breasts, which probably were a comment about the English king's suspected sexual leanings, and on his head he wore a long gold-coloured wig topped off with a battered, verdigris-coloured crown tipped haphazardly on one side. In contrast to the Scots, his army comprised of eight of the smallest possible deformed midgets dressed as very satanic-looking chickens with tall scarlet combs flopping on their heads and holding sticks of rhubarb in their hands in lieu of weapons, and who cowered and hid at every glance from the Scots.

All was taken badly by the English captives, whose chorus of boos were soon drowned out by laughter from the superior numbers of the Scottish contingent, except for John Segrave, who accepted the satirical portrayal of his royal master with good grace, wondering quite correctly what would have happened if the boot was on the other foot. Once the melodrama was over, the pious Scots, having slain all the English Satanists and then wrapped the devil king in rusty chains, they hurled him unceremoniously back down to hell amid a burst of sulphurous smelling flame, signalling it was the time for a bard to take centre stage. Mysteriously manifesting from the residual smoke, the poet appeared in the form of a hunchbacked, pitifully thin, toothless, elderly and bald man, whose deeply furrowed leathery face spoke of much time spent in the open air. Under his arm he clutched a crude type of lyre, and on his back he wore nothing other than what could only be described as an ancient-styled scarlet Roman toga. His arrival was greeted in silent reverence by the Scottish court, whose noisy revelry stopped the instant he appeared. Creakily bowing to Robert and taking the crude seat that appeared with him, the ancient storyteller carefully positioned himself on the three-legged stool, ready to play and sing for the hushed gathering. The half-poem, half-song was completely unintelligible to the amazed English, who sat for half an hour patiently listening to the nonsensical lengthy tale, all chanted in ancient Northern Isles Gaelic. The deft old man's horny fingers glided across the strings to make melodic points during the performance as he croaked his way through the song. Often rolling his cloudy yellowed eyes skywards as if he was looking to a divine being during the most exciting parts, he ended his chant with a flurry of wildly played notes, and spoken words, then drifting to silence as the saga was finished, prompting thunderous applause from the momentarily awestruck audience.

Fortunately for the Englishmen, Robert translated the tale during the whole performance, which was originally about the Scottish tribesmen in the north defending themselves against all odds from a Viking invasion in the ninth century. However, to bring the yarn up to date, the bard had simply, but cleverly substituted certain words for ones pertinent to Robert's victory over the English, much to the pleasure of those who actually understood the obsolete foreign language. Having massaged their warrior egos enough for one evening, it became time for the real entertainment to start, and at the invitation of Robert, the same six pipers who had amused the cavorting masses outside during the evening, were invited inside to play.

First lining up in single file, on a signal from their leader, they simultaneously thumped the wheezing bags and, straining themselves purple, they puffed their cheeks and blew into the mouthpieces to prepare them to produce their music. Satisfied all were suitably inflated, and on a single note from him, as one it started, filling the high-ceilinged hall with the strident noise, which was torture to the English but heaven to the Scots, who, seemingly enjoying the row, took to the empty floor and placed their swords in cross formations, then in time to the tunes they danced barefooted, skipping bravely either side of the razor edges, holding their hands high and yelping and shrieking in delight as they gyrated, narrowly missing the sharp blades. The copious amounts of the heady alcohol were working well and the dancers were fading fast, one by one taking to their seats puffing and panting; they then refreshed their thirsty throats with even more delicious mind-altering liquid, eventually leaving an empty space where a short time before they flitted and twirled above the dangerous glaives, knowing one false step could mean serious injury to a careless performer.

The hour was late, and the time came for the last of the evening's entertainment to take the floor in the form of a troupe of professional dancing girls: professional in more senses than one, as their heavy make-up and the skimpy outfits testified to. In all, twenty scantily clad, beautiful young females floated in as if on a breeze, their pale yellow gauzy gowns transparent and revealing as they twirled to the beat of a single tabor. Those who were conscious enough gawped as the garments rose and fell during the performance, revealing glimpses of the nude forms of the girls, suggestively thrusting their hips backwards and forwards in simulated copulation movements, and making their naked, rouge-nippled breasts bounce to the rhythm. The erotic performance whipped up the few who were able to respond, to a frenzy of sexual fervour by the time the dance ended, and as a finale to the celebration each girl whipped off what little she was wearing to stand completely bare, waiting to be selected for a service of a more personal nature.

Each of Robert's captive guests was offered a free choice of the females, most gladly accepting the gift, except for Sir Humphrey, who was too far gone to be of any use to the lovely allotted to him. Marmaduke Tweng, who took his marriage vows seriously enough to decline the tempting offer, and sober John Segrave who seemed more interested in the resting pipers rather than the naked female form. One at a time the sober senior nobles left, leading a giggling female to their room for their carnal entertainment, each of them being reminded on the way out, by the clear-eyed lucid Robert, that they were not to over-exert themselves, as directly after Sunday mass had been conducted, they were to go hunting with him.

It was Sunday 30 July 1314, at five in the morning, when the servants were despatched to wake the English guests and resident Scots to attend an early mass of thanksgiving for the victory, to be conducted by the freshly returned Bishop of Scone. The bishop barely bothered to hide his annoyance at being plucked from his warm bed away from his favourite concubine, and forced to travel overnight the whole thirty miles without a stop, back to Stirling to oversee an event only a week before he thought was merely an impossible fantasy dreamed up by the illusionary king. Minus any enthusiasm, the revellers from the previous night filed into the castle chapel to hear the droning prelate enjoy listening to himself, as he hypocritically preached about the value of principles and moral virtue, his undulating, over-sanctimonious voice rising and falling, echoing round the bare vaulted building, falling on the deaf ears of the congregation, otherwise engaged in trying to stifle their poorly concealed yawns. Suffering from a severe hangover, Humphrey nodded off during the sermon, only to be prodded awake by a giggling Marmaduke, who boyishly enjoyed disturbing the bleary-eyed earl. Accidentally overstepping the mark when one of the pokes was harder than intended, he caused the sleeping Humphrey to shout out in surprise, interrupting the bishop's wordy flow, who made his display of chagrin obvious to everyone when he glared menacingly at the guilty pair.

Mass said and Sacrament given, His Grace the Bishop disappeared as quickly as he arrived, leaving without so much as a farewell to the king; Robert merely shrugging as the churchman scurried away to get in the back of his official conveyance, mercilessly commanding the driver to whip the horses to action, in order to make as much haste as possible. Back to the woman who promised to be ready, waiting and eager on his return to their little love nest not a stone's throw away from where he lived with his blissfully unaware wife and nine children at his palace at Scone.

The dust from the speedy departure of the cleric was still settling, and the relieved but weary worshippers had already left the chapel to head towards the castle, and sleepily return to their snug warm beds. Seeing the direction of the departing assembly, Robert good naturedly questioned the nobles, asking where they thought they were going; laughingly he reminded them that the stables were in the opposite direction and the horses were saddled and ready for the Sunday morning stag hunt. In their alcohol-induced hazy state, most of the nobles had forgotten everything about the arranged event, and the unwelcome news was greeted with a long resigned groan as the men changed direction, and trance-like, plodded their way towards the stables to mount the anticipating eager steeds jiffling in the stalls, stamping their hooves and bristling with enthusiastic excitement at the forthcoming gallop.

In total, Robert's Sunday morning hunting party consisted of ten suitably attired bodyguards posing as hunt servants, leading three couples of enthusiastically baying large hounds, seven English and seven Scottish nobles and knights. Most of them suffering from hangovers needed to be helped on the champing horses with varying degrees of ease. Having imbibed less than the others at the banquet, the king mounted his horse effortlessly, as did John Segrave, but when it came time for portly Humphrey to ascend the fifteen hands high, weight-carrying solid grey cob provided for him, he struggled hopelessly trying to get on, even though two of the strongest grooms heaved and grunted with effort to assist him by trying to leg up his limp heavy form on the perplexed yet resolutely steady beast. Eventually, in pure frustration, the weakening assistants resorted to leading the bemused animal to a low wall, bidding Humphrey to clamber on the stonework, and then climb into the saddle from there. In the end, managing the feat with difficulty, his efforts cued an amused ragged cheer to issue from the grinning spectators, while the other riders remained silently wrestling with their overeager mounts that keenly wanted to get going.

Once the king had satisfied himself the assembly were all safely on-board and ready to go, he gave the go-ahead with a wave of his hand at the head servant to blast a long moot of a spiral horn as the signal to move off. Pre-empting the lengthy note, Robert galloped ahead just as the musician lifted the instrument to his lips, his surprise exit being closely followed by the body of horse as they raced out of the castle yard, in pursuit of the speeding king, who was, as usual, riding the swiftest of speedy hunters. The whole band soon became obscured by the clouds of dust thrown up by the horses' flying iron-shod feet, which sprayed the gathered onlookers that now stood sneezing and blinking away the debris as they gazed after the fast-disappearing band heading north towards Pisgah Woods.

At first they galloped hard to expend some of the pent-up energy in the steeds and thus making them more manageable for the half-awake, jaded riders to handle. Robert the Bruce, though, was as brave a rider as he was a warrior and as if all the devils of hell were on his heels he urged his horse on, feeling freed from the burden of kingship, and doing one of the things he loved best. Yelping and shrieking with joy, Robert scrubbed his horse's neck and dug his spurred heels into its flanks to encourage it on, squelching across the marshy flatlands in the Forth Valley at full-speed, hurdling the many small tributaries which ran into the main river, jumping the low wooden fences and walls marking the boundaries between different holdings, leaving the others floundering at the rear; especially so for the heavily laden ten foot servants, burdened with the paraphernalia of the hunt and fighting to control the six massive, straining staghounds, pulling relentlessly on their leashes in their desperate attempt to keep up with the vanishing horses. The same servants who were sworn on forfeit of their lives never to let their royal master out of their sight, now lagged over a mile behind their carefree king. Elated with his lungs full of the exhilarating fresh morning air and having at last rid his pent-up spleen of all the worries associated with his royal status, Robert checked the animal to a medium canter and back to a walk, giving his horse a chance to recover and for the others to catch up, which they did a full ten minutes later, when the fragmented group reunited, puffing and panting, to at last actually go in pursuit of the game.

After enjoying a permitted brief period of recuperating rest, and a quick drink, the foot followers were sent on by Robert to spot any likely targets up in the woods. Thankfully, they released the shoulder-wrenching hounds to explore where no man could follow amongst the tangled brambles and undergrowth in the extensive Pisgah Woods, where a regal stag of fourteen points had been reported to be living with his harem of hinds. In all, a mixed assortment of fourteen English and Scottish knights and nobles, including the fast-recovering, but wheezing, Humphrey de Bohun, sat on their horses, while

Robert passed around some flasks of wine. Together, the old enemies chatted between swigs of the refreshing liquor, watching with common interest as the huntsmen and hounds went to their strenuous work.

Making as much noise as possible, the beaters went from covert to covert, shouting, whistling, crashing and banging through the thickets, as they tried to bolt the stag out into the open, with no result, until from deep in the heart of the copse a sudden chorus of spontaneous baying and a long drawn-out moot on the hunting horn, followed by a series of shorter notes, the signal was given that the quarry was found, and the chase was on.

Then the frenetic action started and amid the echoing cacophony of hallooing, a more excited baying of hounds and a long series of different notes, the magnificent, massive, imperial, liver-chestnut, red stag of Pisgah Woods burst from the edge of the trees and came blinking into the bright sunlight. Over four feet tall at the shoulders, with a golden shaggy mane and its massive six feet-wide antlers clogged with matted undergrowth, the hart arrived out into the open, pursued by two of the more determined offending canines close on his heels. Looking rather annoyed at being disturbed from his domain, he proudly hurtled headlong towards the supping group of lords. Galloping at them with his head held high and nose stuck pompously in the air, he leapt effortlessly out of range of the dogs' jaws, twice spinning round to face his chasers with a mind to confront them, but considering discretion was the better part of valour, he pranced away, changing direction and using all his speed he tried to elude the resolute beasts by sprinting along a lengthy grass slope which led back towards Stirling. Within seconds everyone was in full flight, and in a line across the rolling Scottish countryside both hunters and quarry dashed across the sward. First the stag, then the hounds, next came Robert the Bruce on the fastest horse, with the others strung out in a long line back to Humphrey de Bohun on his slow, steady cob, which laboured far behind, gasping for air. Last but not least of all came the hunt servants and gillies, who, still blowing their horns between giant gulps of air, manfully tried to keep up, sweating hard in their robust thorn-proof clothes in the warming day, running as fast as their legs possibly could, to decrease the lead the others had on them.

For two miles they ran zigzagging over the undulating terrain, until the pace of the tiring hart slowed to a canter, whilst looking right and left for a suitable place to make his last stand, eventually finding a likely spot next to a bare rocky peak at the top of a long energy-sapping slope where he decided to turn and face the relentless hunters. Bracing his hind legs against the shock, he lowered his lordly neck, offering the sharp tines on the deadly antlers to meet the foremost of the hounds as it leapt for the kill, and with a single nonchalant toss of his weary head he discarded the yelping canine as if it was nothing more than an annoying leaf which dared to flutter past his noble muzzle. However, with his effort to thwart the first dog, he opened up a chance for a second, which with the skill of Orion's eternal hound, skirted around the deadly prongs to clamp his powerful jaws on the near foreleg of the doomed animal; digging his paws into the turf, he tugged violently backwards, safe from the scything strokes aimed to disembowel him, soon to be joined in his lone effort by one of its kennelmates who did likewise. Alas for the unfortunate regal stag, whose ebbing strength was failing fast, and with one mighty last defiant bellow he succumbed to the relentless hounds, pitching forward on to his nose; with his front legs pulled from under him, he tumbled on the sward, to be pinned fast by a third dog, and wait for his inevitable death, which came at the hands of the Bruce himself.

As first on the scene Robert athletically vaulted off his blowing, sweat-soaked horse before it had even stopped, to run over to where the quarry lay. In a blink of an eye he was on its back. Gripping his powerful crossed long legs around the tangled mane of the stricken beast, he pulled the exhausted sculptured head ever backwards, to expose the animal's pulsating chestnut hairy throat and with one powerful stroke of his hunting knife, slit through both jugulars and carotids. With a spout of foaming pink froth, and a roll of a disbelieving bloodshot eye, the magnificent animal expired: giving the worthy beast a well-deserved quick and noble death at the hands of a brave and mighty monarch.

In dribs and drabs, the outpaced hunters eventually turned up to join Robert. Lagging behind and last of all the riders, a wheezing, purple Sir Humphrey arrived at a slow walk, only a couple of minutes ahead of the fatigued servants. Ignoring their personal tiredness, they immediately did the necessary evisceration of the dead animal, removing all, throwing the inedible entrails to the deserving dogs and saving the liver and kidneys for themselves, yet they reserved the heart, as the highest-valued piece of offal, for the bravest and most forward of the hunters, which, in a small ceremony, was rightfully presented to the deserving Scottish king.

The journey back to Stirling was relatively short. The chase having taken the party from Pisgah Woods, where the stag was initially put up, a whole four miles east to Tullibody, where the splendid beast finally met its end, leaving only a three-mile trip back west to Stirling, so with the carcass thrown across the rump of Humphrey's unflinching heavyweight cob, a weary bunch of horses, riders, footmen and hounds, trudged their shattered way back to the great hall, proudly sporting their great prize and worthy opponent, the magnificent imperial stag of Pisgah Woods.

It was well past lunchtime when the king arrived back at Stirling Castle. With a sense of admiration and more than a hint of sadness, Robert watched as the dead beast was unloaded and placed in a special, purpose-built, below-ground store for the flesh to mature. After paying the moment's final respect to the brave creature, Robert joined the others from the hunting party in the buttery, where a cold buffet was already prepared and waiting for their arrival. Tired and slightly sore from the breakneck ride, the fifteen nobles sat to enjoy their meal. Once again, greedy Sir Humphrey was first to load his platter, and was about to start on his heaped repast, only to be reminded, as you would a naughty schoolboy, that it was Sunday and Grace was to be said; and so, with their heads bowed and their hands clasped together, the gathering of affable enemies said a small prayer of thanks before the famished group at long last broke their fast.

All the talk at the table was of the hunt. Robert sat quietly in his place at the head of the board, modestly listening, starting to feel uncomfortable and somewhat embarrassed as the plaudits were piled on him. He was pleased to find some respite from his displeasure when one of his liveried servants entered the room to whisper something in his ear, while pointing to a person standing at the opened heavy oak door. In a bid to change the subject, which was becoming monotonous and boring to him, Robert decided to share some of the less than important secret information with the others, turning to Sir Humphrey, who was busily gnawing at the leg of some sort of local wildfowl. "This might interest you, my lord Earl?" Robert enquired, looking directly at Humphrey, who on feeling the gaze boring to him, looked up quizzically from his fare, where he was engrossed in selecting another tasty morsel, whilst still chewing at a piece of recalcitrant gristle, its grease, his saliva and other sundry debris clinging to his half-grown beard.

"What might that be, my lord, is it...?" Humphrey asked, accidentally allowing the bit of meat to drop out of his open mouth, picking it up to inspect it and then putting it back in, before continuing the attempt to masticate it and to finish his question at the same time. "Is it news from home?"

"In a sort of way, I suppose," the king replied, kindling the interest in the other Englishmen, who looked hopefully up from their half-eaten plates of food to listen. "It concerns your nephew's banner man, Sir Lawrence Buckenham. He's been captured, and you'll be pleased to know, he's in reasonable health considering the three nights he spent alone, badly injured and wandering lost in the Trossachs."

"Pleased? You should have left the weasely bastard there to rot!" Humphrey interjected, spitting out the same mutilated lump of food he had been wrestling with. "It's a shame that useless lump of shit was ever born, and how he ever rose to the rank of fucking banner man is still a fucking mystery to me?" he railed, giving the king a straight-faced glare of disapproval.

Blinking in disbelief, Robert looked somewhat stunned by the sudden outburst. "Well, I can assure you that he won't be troubling you for quite a time, as he's now a prisoner of my not-so-pleasant constable of Dunstaffnage Castle, that disgraced old Templar Sir Thomas Dewar, and I doubt very much if he will let him go until every last penny of a very hefty ransom is wrung out of him. And while I'm about it, may I ask why it is you hold Sir Lawrence in such low esteem, sir?" Robert asked, staring hard at Humphrey, waiting for his reply, whilst delicately sipping some wine, when John Segrave surprisingly replied in his stead.

"Because, my lord king, he is a cowardly, lying, drunken child abusing bastard, whose family bought his knighthood to save him from gaol or worse."

Nodding his agreement, Humphrey added his pennyworth in support of his fellow. "The last time I saw him, he was being dragged away from the battle by the young fellow you mentioned to me yesterday, Richard de Mauville."

"Why Richard?" the king questioned, placing his empty goblet on the table, signifying with his forefinger and thumb for a page to only half fill it while he listened.

"Because that poor unlucky little sod was allotted to him as his squire when Henry was killed, and like the brave boy he is, he saved Lawrence's worthless skin when he was too drunk to fight."

Laughing aloud at the condemning opinions, Robert got up to leave with the same armed stranger that loitered in the doorway to the room. "Well, I'll find out for myself soon, as I'm now going to Dunstaffnage Castle on some supposedly urgent business, and trust me, I'd much prefer being here with your pleasant company, rather than to be at that damnable place, stuck on a rock, surrounded by the sea, with nobody but that filthy, lecherous, foul bastard Thomas Dewar as my only fellow diner." With that, the king left with the unknown stranger to go about his duty, fifty miles northwest to possibly the bleakest of all the castles in the whole of Scotland, leaving the captives under the charge of their ex-colleague and self-confessed traitor, Alexander Seaton.

CHAPTER 6

Refreshed and feeling somewhat rejuvenated after the meal and a bath, Richard and Yolanda kept riding westwards, eventually getting close enough to the sea to hear the continuous rumbling noise of the waves as they made landfall on the craggy Scottish shore. This was a new experience to Yolanda, who always, having lived in a coast-less county, looked frightened and perplexed in her ignorance. Reading the uncertainty in her demeanour, Richard dragged Yolanda another half mile, right to the edge of a cliff, to show her the reason for the noise, and together they listened and watched mesmerised as the giant, white-crested turquoise Atlantic waves rolled in one after another and threw themselves at the rugged grey rocky shore, roaring and crashing, breaking into massive plumes of white foaming water before retreating loudly back into the sea.

For ten whole minutes they sat their horses side by side, looking at the spectacle, when without any forewarning, Yolanda put her hand out and trustingly clasped Richard's as it held onto Solomon's reins. Wriggling her fingers into his palm, she squeezed it in silent thanks, her voice still trapped in her throat, taken from her by the ordeal of yet another traumatic savage rape, this time from someone she believed she could trust. In response, Richard automatically squeezed back, to reassure her that he was there to look after her without conditions, no matter what, the comforting touch not going unnoticed by a sad and lonely Yolanda, who'd started to form an emotional attachment with her young saviour.

Already having wasted too much time gazing at the ceaseless ocean, Richard turned his horse's head, left, to go southwards and home, planning to hug the coast in order to aid his navigation and avoid as much civilisation as possible. Not for one moment did he realise how many towns and villages there would be on that route, and how much further it would be, having to ride round the many inlets and coves which were plentiful on the north-eastern seashore. Together they rode, Richard high on his tall horse, trying to experiment with the unfamiliar beast and find out the extent of Solomon's education. Inadvertently, Yolanda hampered his efforts, as she reached uncomfortably up and across from the shorter cob, still clutching at his hand, not wanting to let him go in case he might run away.

Awkwardly, they proceeded on their arduous trek, slowly making progress, held back by the slow clumsy carthorse which found the undulating stony terrain more than difficult; tripping and stumbling, it tried to keep up with its surefooted cousin, frustrating both riders. Richard, because of the slowness of the rate of progress, and Yolanda, because at every lurch of her mount the grip on Richard's reassuring hand was broken, causing her to desperately re-establish it, slowing everything even more, and only covering about six miles before realising it was time to stop for a necessary break. Selecting the perfect site on a grassy cliff top, where a small crystal-clear brook tumbled over the edge and down sixty feet to join the sea below. Richard also decided it was a lovely spot to finish the cold rabbit as a small repast.

After the meal was finished, the pair took the time to digest and rest for a while. Still without a single word being said by Yolanda, they lay back side by side on a small mossy slope to doze in the hot sunshine, giving the horses long enough to fill their empty bellies with the abundant forage, and Sam to lope around, sniffing and peeing up every suitable upright, marking his territory in the unfamiliar new place.

As ever, Yolanda stayed glued to her protector, not wanting the physical contact to be broken. Even when the necessary ablutions had to be performed before resuming the journey, she hovered as near as possible to remain polite during the act, and only specifically on strict orders did she absent herself behind a convenient boulder to do hers. Returning, she found Richard bathing his arm in the stream, wincing with pain as he clumsily dabbed at an angry-looking gash on his wrist. Until that moment, Yolanda was oblivious to Richard's wound, but on seeing it she raced over to tend to her injured rescuer, and with a little squeak of concern she brushed his calloused hand to one side, halting his ham-fisted effort at nursing. Confiscating the moist rag, she went about delicately wiping away all the matted tissue which had oozed from the infected wound, soothing the reddened area with more water, peering closely, tutting and taking sharp intakes of breaths as she inspected it. Satisfied the cut was as clean as she could get it, Yolanda made a poultice of fresh moss, binding it as tightly as she dared without cutting off the blood supply to his hand, easing the throbbing, and with thanks Richard tried his damaged limb, opening and shutting his hand to test the amount of pain and find out if he was fit to continue the journey. Coming to the decision he was able to carry on with the trek, Richard considered whether the utterly exhausted poor broken-down cob was as well, heartbreakingly arriving at the obvious conclusion it would be better for both man and beast to abandon the suffering animal where he was, up to his knees in flourishing green grass with plenty of fresh water to hand.

In order to make it possible for them to continue with only one horse to carry them both, it was imperative to reduce their luggage, so with practicality in mind, Richard discarded all items not absolutely vital for their survival. He reduced the amount to barely one quarter of what it was before, even getting rid of the oat biscuits, giving them to the faithful old nag by way of a farewell, feeding them one by one from his flattened hand, and with a goodbye kiss on its soft grey velvet muzzle and a moist eye, he left the beast to its own devices, sadly walking away without daring to glance back, frightened he might weaken and change his wavering mind.

With at least six hours of daylight remaining, and hundreds of miles to travel, Richard loaded Solomon as quickly as his ailing left arm would allow, finding it a monumental effort to aid Yolanda up behind the saddle, before struggling on the horse's back to resume the journey southward, and with hope, eventually home. The new travelling arrangement worked much better; unencumbered by the lame old cob and Yolanda's reluctance to release Richard from her grasp, they made much better headway. The girl was now happily ensconced behind him, her arms wrapped securely around his waist, squeezing at regular intervals, which Richard naively believed to be for safety reasons, unaware that the girl was starting to harbour more amorous feelings towards the only person on earth she found it possible to trust.

All afternoon they rode thus, Richard's injury worsening with each step; even though the day was hot and he was still attired in the padded armour, he shivered convulsively now and again, feeling cold although he sweated profusely. In a swoon he plodded forward, barely noticing the sun was descending in the heavens and turning pink as the daylight drew to a close, only being made aware of the time when Yolanda started to violently shake him, urgently needing to empty her brimming bladder. Wakened from his semi-comatose state, Richard dreamily eased the tired horse to a halt, shocking Yolanda when he nearly tumbled off Solomon, too weak to dismount properly. Distressed and angry with herself that she had failed to realise Richard was in a terrible state, Yolanda slid from her place, somehow finding the necessary strength to aid his helpless limp form off the steed and drag him to a sheltered spot. Her first concern was the wound; so, removing the poultice quickly, she pulled off the sticking bandage to inspect it while daylight lasted. Finding the gash scarlet and boiling hot as she exposed it, and after giving the wrapping a quick sniff, she knew that speedy treatment was utterly crucial to save her brave young rescuer's life.

Some few hundred yards away, Yolanda could hear the sea, and remembering the tales she heard from the nuns of the salty water's magical healing qualities, she tied the perplexed Sam to a handy bush to guard Richard, and scurried off in the direction of the noise, carrying with her one of the larger flasks to retrieve some of the curative liquid. With comparative ease she found her hazardous way down the natural valley to a sheltered sandy cove, luckily with no steep rocks to climb down to the water's edge. Easily filling the flask at the shallow water's edge, she quickly clambered back to tend to her patient before the pitch-black moonless Scottish night had completely fallen.

With the utmost care, Yolanda lovingly bathed Richard's festering wound: sluicing it thoroughly with seawater, she removed the congealed blood, crusty dried lymph, and pus, allowing the efficacious salt to reach the infection to do its job of sterilising the damage so that it could heal. Afterwards, she wrapped the injury in a brine-soaked clean strip of cloth to prolong the contact with the natural antiseptic; then, having made sure Richard was as comfortable as possible, Yolanda set about the other urgent task of attending to Solomon. Considering Yolanda was a complete novice with equines, she managed admirably with the finer points of dealing with the animals. Doing exactly what she had seen Richard do, she tethered the horse to the same convenient bush Sam was tied to, removed the tack and rubbed Solomon down with a plait of dry grass, and then lengthened the rope so that he could put his head down to graze. Satisfied with her achievement, Yolanda returned to where her young cavalier murmured in the first stage of delirium. Ignoring the danger of overheating herself, she snuggled up tightly to Richard, calming his shuddering body, helping keep him warm to save his energy and help him fight the infection.

All night she lay diligently wide awake at his side, cooing with concern as he mumbled and groaned in his burning fever, half-hourly dampening the dressing to stop it sticking, at the same time mopping his sweating brow with her sleeve, praying for the ague to break. At one stage Yolanda even fetched Sam to join them and act as a living blanket during a particularly violent fit of uncontrollable trembling. By the time morning arrived there was still no sign of improvement in Richard's condition: he was still firmly in the grip of the infection which Yolanda knew was the most dangerous stage. Swooning in and out of lucidity, Richard occasionally mustered the strength to open his bloodshot rolling eyes, his blurred vision always seeing the same worried face of his vigilant nurse. In his confused state he occasionally believed he was dead and she was his own private ministering angel. On other occasions he called her mother, and another time he cried out for dead Henry to help him, before drifting back to sleep either to die peacefully, or for the fever to break and hopefully recover to live a full rewarding life, brought about by the passionate entreaties to God, and prayers to the Saints by his constant new companion, the young, unappreciated, beautiful Yolanda.

For two full days Richard was completely unconscious, beleaguered by lengthy bouts of the burning sweats and writhing, battling his illness right up to sunset on the third evening, when Yolanda's prayers were eventually answered and mercifully the fever broke. Richard slept peacefully and deep that night, exhausted from his battle with the Grim Reaper, having only narrowly missed being harvested, protected from the hungry scythe by the diligent attention and heart-felt supplications of his volunteer carer. As Richard slept, recuperating from his delirium, he dreamed dreams of more pleasant times, when his beloved Henry was still alive. In his half-conscious state, he recalled a time when both master and pupil sat together, listening to the noises of the breaking dawn and the first birds, as they woke to herald the day. Richard soon realised that the birds were indeed real, and were calling to him to stir from his sleep, telling him to open his eyes. Struggling to obey their melodic entreaties, he woke, expecting to find Henry's fatherly, kind face looking at him, instead finding the delighted Yolanda, who squeaked with happiness on seeing him lucid once again, as she spooned minute sips of clear rabbit broth between his cracked and parched lips.

Several minutes elapsed before Richard was able to actually grasp what had happened. Looking about him in his confused state, he could see a well-organised camp set up on a flat clearing three-parts surrounded by a wall of large mottled boulders. At the dead centre, a smokeless wood fire was burning well, with Sam sprawled as close to the flame as he dared, guarding Richard's laundered clothes, which were spread out on some imported bushes to dry near the blaze, on top of which his sooty bascinet with the lining, visor and mail removed, was propped upright with green timber, now acting as a cooking pot instead of his head protection, and emanating clouds of steam, accompanied by a very welcoming smell. At the edge of the sward a partly constructed crude shelter was half-built, near to where his armour was scrubbed and neatly hung between two forked sticks, with a pole threaded through the armholes. Within close proximity to the shack, Solomon was tethered, gleaming and polished to perfection as he stood in the sunshine, munching happily at a large armful of long, freshly plucked, very green grass, alongside an age-old perpetual trickle of peaty water, which dribbled musically from an eroded groove in one of the larger rocks and tinkled off to join a little brown puddle at its base.

Miraculously, as Richard was soon to find out, Yolanda's inability to speak had gone, as, amazingly, she had found her lost voice in the protracted conversations with God and the Saints, when she begged them for Richard's life to be spared; and now, with renewed vigour, she found herself able to explain exactly what had transpired during Richard's fever. Initially, she berated Richard for not mentioning the injury straight away, informing him sternly that in her opinion if it had been cleaned then, the life-threatening illness would probably have been prevented. Continuing her tale, she related that over the two days and three nights of illness she had bathed the wound hourly with curative sea water, believing it was the main factor in beating off the infection. Also, she told him how every morning she had dressed the injury with clean fresh cobwebs, which, according to her old mother superior's superstition, had to be collected at the crack of every dawn, while they were still wet with the morning dew. Richard listened to her distressing tale of selflessness for over an hour; enthralled by the noble saga, he gratefully tried to stammer some thanks for Yolanda's diligence, but she would have nothing of it, adding that in actual fact Richard owed any gratitude to her favourite Saxon Saint Winifred, because it was to her she prayed when the fever was at its worst. Yolanda carried on putting her restored voice to good use as she scurried about making things neat and tidy, all watched by an incredulous Richard, harmlessly oblivious to the fact they were both for the best part naked, Richard with just a hacked-off strip of the old cob's blanket tied around his waist to cover his groin, and Yolanda with a square of the same cloth wrapped around her, tied in the middle with a plaited belt of wood bark to hold it together.

As Richard's mind gradually cleared, and with the aid of Yolanda, his memories came flooding back to him, recollecting everything, when of a sudden it dawned on him they were both almost nude. When he asked why, he received a frank reply from the girl, who, pointing to the laundered attire, told him that in his sweating fever, the rank perspiration polluted them both when she used her body as an extra cover to keep him warm during his fits of shivers, and not wanting to smell like a billy goat she washed them the previous evening so that they could dry overnight ready to put on in the morning. Unworldly Richard thought for a few seconds, before the realisation set in that in all probability Yolanda had been sleeping with him. "May I ask, exactly where did you sleep at nights?" he asked, as she went to the fire to fetch him some morsels of cooked rabbit out of the helmet.

"With you, to keep you warm," came her reply, looking over her shoulder whilst squatting, to retrieve a tit-bit from the steaming makeshift cauldron, and speaking to him as if they had been sharing the same bed for twenty years.

"And last night?" he asked, feeling the blood rushing to his face.

"With you again!" she answered matter-of-factly, returning with a pulled-off piece of choice meat, and offering it for him to eat.

"You dressed like that, and me like this?" Richard queried, starting to sound concerned and reddening with embarrassment, thinking that he might have committed a cardinal sin.

"No, it was hot so I was naked. I only put this on this morning to do my chores. Don't worry, I didn't interfere with you. I just wanted to be near in case you woke and needed me. Now eat up while I get dressed."

Hearing the explanation, Richard duly obeyed and ate a reasonable portion of the stew, but found it difficult to swallow as his throat was still dry from the effects of the fever. Wincing with pain, he gulped the last lump down, and gazed with awe as the scantily clad girl walked away to change. Feeling a little stronger after forcing a decent helping of the rabbit down, but still too weak to leave his temporary bed of dry bracken, Richard's curiosity got the better of him, so secretly propping himself up on one elbow, he stole a little peep, as Yolanda went to dress herself behind the poor cover of three-foot high windswept bush. Casting off the make-do tabard, she stood with her back to the young Peeping-Tom, and totally aware he was watching, turned to give an accidental glimpse of her breasts for her audience's approval, meeting his apologetic eyes with hers, and quickly snatching them away quickly with feigned bashfulness, but letting them dwell long enough to notice that the loincloth had moved somewhat.

From that day on, Richard and Yolanda's relationship took on a different nature. Since her recovery from her dreadful traumas, which started when her virginity was haphazardly plucked away from her by an overweight drunken archbishop, when he grunted his way to ejaculation without a care for her unsullied body, up to her happy release, and the subsequent inflicted brutality of Lawrence, her attitude to Richard, and indeed everything else, had apparently changed. Instead of the frightened silent girl, who clung to him trembling as they rode together, she had become confident and a little cocky in his presence. True he had saved her from certain death, and she had done likewise for him, making them even on that score, but her time in the convent had removed all innocence and modesty from her; quite the opposite of Richard, whose purity remained intact, and during his time under the auspices of Henry de Bohun an overly deep sense of moral decency and fair play had been instilled in his psyche, making him largely unaware of the mysterious ways of women.

Often he suffered with a pricked conscience, when she overtly bathed herself in front of him and lay with him at night, part of him stoically ignoring her youthful beauty, which was becoming more apparent to him with each dawn, the other half wanting to caress her smooth skin and touch the parts he naively still believed were forbidden fruit, except in the holy sanctity of marriage. Torn by his ideals, the growing manly part of him wanted her so badly, and the boyish youthful part almost blamed her for the time spent with other men, believing it as casual wantonness, failing to understand her apparent casual demeanour towards sexuality was merely her only way of coping with the sordid past.

Together, Richard the growing boy, and Yolanda the well developed, wretchedly confused young woman, travelled south to England. Each night they lay together, and even though it was unseasonably hot, she pushed her shapely firm young body into his, snuggling up to him, amazed that she received no reaction, as he tried to ignore the advances, although his loins acted uncontrollably, and nearly always he struggled to catch his sleep attempting to defeat his carnal desires. For a whole week they persevered, trekking around giant inlets and fording the many rivers and streams which hampered them, sometimes going north as the lie of the land dictated, but as often as possible trying to keep the sound of the sea in their ears, eventually leaving the higher ground and coming to the lower grassier rolling hills, which Richard knew to be the lowlands of Scotland. Regularly they had to lie low to avoid other travellers, or the small homesteads which were dotted around everywhere, travelling many extra miles in circumnavigating the larger settlements, keeping themselves fed by living off some of the wild brassicas which like to live in coastal areas, and rabbit provided by the ever-faithful Sam, who was proving to be a little too much of a free spirit, and with a mind of his own, started ignoring their commands, often wandering off on his own private hunting forays and bringing game back alive without being asked. But no matter what, they resolutely headed south towards home, and hopefully the safety it offered.

For the best part their efforts to remain unseen were successful, but on one particular afternoon, they had just gone over fifteen miles out of their way, to round a mighty inlet, when Richard thought they had come to grief. Not being one bit like his usual self, the increasingly wayward Sam returned from one of his hunting expeditions. Scurrying along with his tail between his legs, and instead of the usual rabbit or hare in his mouth, he had a large live, juicy chicken, squawking loudly, attracting the attention of the angry smallholder, who galloped after the miscreant hound, screaming obscenities and firing poorly aimed arrows from a weedy homemade bow in his direction. The farmer stopped dead in his tracks when, on rounding a corner, he stumbled upon what was to him a doughty man at arms on his mighty destrier, his knightly sword gleaming at his side, with his valiant squire riding pillion. Fearing his behaviour might upset the young lords, the peasant instantly tugged his forelock in respect, lowering his weapon so as not to appear a threat to the pair. In actual fact, Richard was as surprised as he was and on seeing the reason for the man's rage, apologised for the dog's behaviour, and politely enquired where about they actually were. Richard was utterly taken aback when in a mumbled, northern accent, thick enough to be cut with a cheese wire, the nervous farmer informed them that they were in the famed Burgh by Sands, Cumbria, very near to the spot where the ailing Edward Longshanks, the Hammer of the Scots, camped in July, 1317, and was found dead by his servants on the morning of the 7th when they came to help him eat.

Following a difficult conversation with the man, whose English was closer to the language spoken when Ethelred was on the throne, rather than the cultured one Richard was used to, he discovered that they had wandered ten miles inland in their journey around the colossal flats, and were at the estuary of the rivers Eden and Esk. For ten minutes they chatted, Richard informing him how badly the war went in Scotland, which was bad news for the farmer, as being located so near to the border, he had suffered years of raids from the Scots, who annually robbed him of any profitable surplus, making his life there untenable, but as everything he had was invested in the small acreage, he had no other option but to grin and bear it, and stay where he was.

Feeling sorry for the harassed farmer, and feeling rather guilty over the chicken, which subsequently had dropped dead of fright after its run-in with Sam, Richard delved into the purse given to him by Robert the Bruce, and handed the sorry fellow a couple of silver florins, which in fact was more than equal to a whole quarter's income to the farmer. With his eyes on stalks, the man they now knew as Rolfe Catchpole, looked at the gleaming florins and, accepting them gladly, handed Richard the deceased fowl in return and invited them both to a meal at his little farmstead over a hill, about two hundred yards away from where they were. With the promise of a cooked meal other than rabbit, Richard and Yolanda followed eagerly, as he led them to his family home.

Rolfe's lowly dwelling was little more than a badly thatched windowless circle of stones, fifteen foot across with a crude hole in the roof to allow the smoke from the eternally lit peat cooking fire to escape. The entire smallholding consisted of nothing more than a roughly fenced paddock of three-quarters of an acre, and with no spare money to buy building materials, the half a dozen sheds and small barns were cobbled together with odds and ends of strange debris deposited by the tide, including the wreckage of an old boat he used as a more than serviceable roof to the hen coop. The area adjacent to the house was littered with salvaged barrels and crates, where a sundry collection of goats, sheep, chickens and other fowl picked about in the remnants of the summer grass. On the furthest side, over in one corner near an almost completely dried-up small pond, a vicious-looking hairy ginger sow, rooted at the edge of the water looking for tasty titbits in the mud, aggressively telling off some of her more persistent piglets, which insisted on painfully swinging on her badly scratched and bitten teats, scattering a motley assortment of ducks and geese fighting to dabble in the pool of greenish grey slimy sludge which was all that remained of their watering hole.

Outside the low door to the property, a plump red-faced woman stood gazing fixedly up the lane, impatiently tapping her foot, with her rounded dimpled arms crossed in an annoyed fashion across her ample chest, her electric blue eyes watching out for her husband to see if he had rescued the stolen bird or not. The motherly looking female's mouth fell wide open when she saw him, the slinking guilty hound, an armoured knight and his young squire holding the dead hen, mounted on a mighty horse, meaningfully approaching the hovel.

At first she thought her spouse had been taken by some Scots raiders, but when she saw the easiness in their manner, she immediately realised that the atmosphere was convivial in the group and started shouting in the same unintelligible sing-song dialect used by Rolfe, commanding him to make haste. Happy he was obeying her bellowed orders; she then turned and aimed her shrieks towards the up-turned boat where half a dozen grubby urchins of varying ages were squealing excitedly, whilst scrabbling about hunting for lost eggs. On hearing their mother's call, the children instantly ceased their task and scuttled as fast as they could to where their mother was. All six had inherited their mother's unmistakable bright blue eyes, which became instantly noticeable as they formed their welcoming party, staring straight ahead and bolt upright to attention. Graduated by size, they stood in their rags from the smallest, a four-year-old snotty-nosed red-headed boy, standing stock still with his mucky hand clutching his mother's skirt, stepping up in even intervals to the tallest, a blonde girl of about twelve or thirteen years old, who, assisted by her shorter, similar-aged brunette sister, were on the blind side of the mother surreptitiously thumping their oldest brother around the ear for tormenting them with a giant warty toad. The series of clouts caused a stifled yelp of pain from the boy, which instantly stuck in his guilty throat at one stern admonishing look from the clearly very strict matriarch.

With all the grace and dignity, as if they were the king and queen of England, Richard and Yolanda were invited into the dingy but serviceable dwelling. Inside, the furnishings were crude and poorly constructed from whatever driftwood was to hand at the time. In the dead centre of the rush-strewn earth floor were eight homemade stools of varying ages, neatly placed around a rickety old trestle table; against the walls were stowed three low straw pallets adjacent to a curtained-off area where Richard supposed the adults slept. At the furthest point away from the door stood a three-foot square, flat hearth-stone, with a glowing peat fire set bang in the middle, its embers kept from spreading by a ring of carefully placed blackened rocks, upon which a large soot-stained three-legged clay cauldron bubbled and glooped, full of what smelled rather like a mutton hotpot. Before they knew it, the two honoured guests were politely conducted to the seats, where they were each ceremoniously presented with a large earthenware bowl of the appetising, if not a little greasy potage and a large round of some coarse, slightly gritty bread to mop up the gravy.

The mealtime conversation was somewhat limited by the language barrier, but as far as Richard and Yolanda could understand, in his whole life Rolfe and his wife Margaret had never owned as much as four shillings at one time before and it was their great pleasure to feed them as a way to show their gratitude. Repeatedly thanking Richard for his largesse, they offered more food than the hungry visitors could actually cope with. Yet, unlike the rest of the family, Rolfe was totally oblivious that the squire was in fact female, being utterly shocked when Margaret started calling the fresh-faced lad in oversize clothing, "sweet lass". In amazement, Rolfe looked at her as if she had gone stark mad, until with much mirth, he was at last informed of the very pretty, curvy stripling boy's actual gender.

Once the meal was finished, feeling overheated in the warm room, and rather over-stuffed with food, Richard started to remove his armour. The usual difficulty made worse by his full stomach, he luckily found two willing assistants in the small boys, who seemed more than delighted to help with the chore. Hoping for a chance of a short rest before continuing the journey, Richard wanted to snooze. However, his hopes of a nap were dashed when, without allowing the guests any time to digest the mighty repast, Rolfe and the four youngest children obeyed a garbled command from his wife, and meekly following her wishes and without complaint, dragged Richard outside to endure a lengthy conducted tour of every nook and cranny of the entire ramshackle estate.

Left all alone with only Margaret and her two oldest daughters called Alice and Joan for company, Yolanda suddenly felt deserted and very vulnerable as she stared forlornly after Richard, who had barely been out of her sight for over a fortnight. Gently, but forcibly, Margaret stood the poorly clad visitor in a space cleared by her eager daughters, wide enough for her to walk around, fussing over the bewildered guest. Then, grabbing at the folds and creases in the excessively large clothes and clucking like a mother hen over her errant chicks, she pulled them taut to make them something more like a reasonable fit. At one time she pulled a length of string so tightly around Yolanda's breasts to measure her girth it made the girl wince and cry out in pain, and then with a knowing sympathetic look, a series of tuts and a long compassionate sigh, Margaret patted Yolanda's stomach, at the same time bidding her to remove the outfit. Immediately it was off all three started attacking the badly fitting garments with needle and thread, to speedily alter them, leaving Yolanda standing wrapped in nothing but a shawl, watching the busy fingers of mother and children as they snipped and sewed with the air of three professional seamstresses.

For two whole hours, the barely clad Yolanda stood gazing vacantly at the door, waiting in a slightly traumatised state for her constant companion and youthful saviour to return. Her hopes were raised twice when the third oldest child, the tormenting eleven-year-old toad-loving boy called Robbie, entered to see if they were ready, dispatched by his father to see if it was time to return, only to be hustled away from the partly naked Yolanda with a flea in his ear from his mother, along with a message for those outside to be patient. Following a final flourish of frenetic stitching, Margaret announced that she was satisfied the garments were ready to be put back on, adding innocently that she had left in some gussets, designed to be easily let out at a later date when the baby started to grow inside her. For the entire time spent on altering the garments, Yolanda had taken no specific note of anything said or done. Like a statue she had stood while the clothes were held up against her and measurements taken, her entire thoughts taken up with fretting over the absence of Richard. The conversations between mother and daughters harmlessly drifted past her, only half-heard but ignored as they went about the task at hand. Even after getting re-dressed, the comments meant nothing to her until about five minutes after the others returned to admire the magic performed by the proud trio, did it dawn on her the enormity of what exactly

Margaret had said. Feeling confused and in a dream-like state, doubting that she had heard correctly, Yolanda needed to verify what actually was said, turning very belatedly to Margaret, asking earnestly, "What baby?"

The woman, looking straight back at Yolanda, furrowed her brow, somewhat confused by the question, answering it with a little laugh and concluding it was a joke. "Your baby, you silly!"

Yolanda's tearful expression said enough, enlightening Margaret that in fact the poor young girl was ignorant to the fact she was pregnant. Throwing her arms around the confused youngster, Margaret offered Yolanda some motherly advice, patting her back sympathetically and whispering in her ear, "There! There! Hinny, don't worry, lass. I'm sure he'll stand by you. It can't be all that bad, now can it?" Margaret carried on trying to console Yolanda, delivering her understanding words of solace to the sobbing teenager, while shooting accusing glances at a bewildered Richard, who in his youthful innocence didn't realise he was being blamed for being the father and just looked on in dumb silence, not really sure what exactly was happening. Poor confused Richard only found out the guilt had been placed on him, when Rolfe informed that it was how he himself became married some thirteen years before. Somewhat stunned by the accusation, Richard loudly protested his innocence, and then with a silent nod of agreement from Yolanda, he related the whole sorry tale, from the time she was sold into prostitution by her father, her rescue, and the events which led them up to the present moment.

All evening they talked using a cleverly invented hybrid language mutually constructed and understood by them all. Even after the children had been sent to their beds, the four sat at the table in the half-light produced by a single smelly sheep's tallow candle, listening and speaking of what had befallen, all the while being eavesdropped upon by the oldest of the brood, pretending to be asleep, but quietly taking in all that was said. Erroneously believing that little ears weren't listening, they continued after dark, gathered round the feeble reeking glimmer, the pathetic glow barely illuminating their horror-filled faces as they whispered some of the more harrowing juicer descriptions of events.

Having talked themselves to a standstill, they all retired to bed, Rolfe and Margaret to behind the curtain, and Richard and Yolanda to a small dilapidated store-shed where a paillasse of plaited straw had been prepared by the boys earlier that afternoon, just in case their wealthy visitors ended up staying for the night. Richard and Yolanda laid comfortably for a change, being used to the rough rocky ground or the damp dewy grass they'd slept on of late, enjoying the relief afforded by a roof over their heads and the rather scratchy, but soft, mattress of straw. That night the restless Yolanda held Richard even tighter than usual, clinging on to him as he slept, terrified to let him go, this time even more frightened he would escape to free himself of the now-multiplied burden of her and her unborn child. The thought of a desolate future etched inside her eyelids, haunting her as she tried to force herself to sleep, correctly fearing that as an unwed mother, she would be spurned and ostracised by society to live out her isolated days as a lonely spinster, unfairly having the innocence of youth torn away from her, thrust by her father's greed and his new wife's jealously, into a brutal world where she was nothing more than an unwilling victim, collateral damage in a situation over which she had no control. Eventually having sleepily resigned herself to her lot, Yolanda then found the sleep she so urgently sought.

The next morning it was later than normal by the time Richard awoke; next to him and still fast asleep, exhausted from the night terrors which had so destructively pervaded her troubled mind, Yolanda stirred as he tried to creep out of the bed. Squeaking with fear as he went to leave, Yolanda hurriedly smartened herself up to join him, and to go into the hovel to thank their hosts, harbouring a secret hope that a small breakfast might be attached to the bargain.

Outside in the enclosure everything was astir: giant Solomon was being groomed by a tiny girl called Matilda, standing on an upturned box to reach his higher parts, while the oldest boy was absorbed in the task of mucking out the shack where the horse had been housed for the night. The other children, complete with the tied-up Sam avidly watching their every move, were racing about flapping their outstretched arms, deliberately scattering the hens off of their nests to collect the morning eggs. Nearby, the sow and her litter were happily munching into some cabbage trimmings, while the same two troublesome larger piglets, which tormented their poor sore mother the day before, were fighting viciously over one particular leaf they both had taken a fancy to. The only person missing was Rolfe, who was off on an early jaunt rounding up some of the itinerant sheep he kept wandering loose on the hills to fatten up on the abundant upland grass.

Near to the door of the roundhouse, Margaret was sitting on a short three-legged stool milking an obstinate nanny goat that kicked out peevishly at every pull of her milk-filled swollen teats. Cleverly, she avoided the flying foot with much-practised skill, looking up from her task without stopping the energetic yanking at the udder, she noticed the pair as they emerged from the sleeping quarters, telling them that a breakfast was ready and waiting on the table. Inside the hovel everything was spic and span, all evidence of the sleeping arrangements had been packed away, and resting on the table, covered with a clean rough cloth, was a meal of hard-boiled eggs, some creamy soft cheese, all presented on a round of gorgeous-smelling freshly baked unleavened flat-bread, sitting next to a crude earthenware beaker full of fresh, warm goat's milk.

The meal finished and the morning ablutions over, it was time for Richard to don his armour and leave, so, politely asking Margaret for his missing hauberk, gambeson and smoke-stained bascinet to be brought to him, he prepared to go, being amazed when, shining as if new, the requested items were proudly brought to him for his approval by young Robbie, who had spent more than two hours before first light feverishly buffing and burnishing the soot-stained steel helmet until he was able to see his face in it. With the same difficulty as it was taken off, Richard put on his harness, wriggling in to it, eagerly helped by the boy to straighten the mail and do up the awkward straps and laces, the lad bowing proudly on completion of the task and then smiling broadly, he stood back to admire his work.

With a sense of common decency, Richard and Yolanda waited for Rolfe to return before bidding the lined-up family their sincere goodbyes, Richard promising, hand over heart, to return if he was ever in the vicinity, taking the time to thank each child in turn, presenting them individually with a shiny silver penny for their efforts. Giving both Matilda and Rolfe a hug, along with another two coins for the hospitality, they departed on the meticulously groomed Solomon, whose tack was in similar good order, oiled and rubbed to a deep luxurious shine. Richard and Yolanda looked back as they rode away, waving goodbyes over their departing shoulders at the saddened family, once again standing in a graduated line, mopping their watery eyes, watching as the young lady and gentleman disappeared out of sight, leaving the little ramshackle paradise with mixed emotions, both happy and sad, knowing that in two short weeks they had seen both the very best and the very worst sides of human behaviour.

CHAPTER 7

With the late summer breeze in their faces, the *Saint Luke* at first made reasonable, but rather slow progress. For two hours it sailed untroubled, running as close to the Scottish coast as it dared, hoping to pick up the wandering eddying gusts, disturbed by the warming landmass and funnelled by the deep valleys to fight against the existing weather direction and fly in the face of the prevailing wind, aiding the bluff-bowed ship to make good bouts of speed, especially when the wooden vessel could ride the surf of the southerly tidal flow, and very soon the visible rugged shoreline was unmistakably that of Northern England.

Aboard the ship, everything was extremely neat, tidy and scrupulously clean, each item having its own place where it was stowed when not in use. The mousey-haired, solidly built captain Horace Swale, aided by his officers, ruled with a rod of iron, administering summary instant beatings for the most minor of shipboard crimes. On-board his law was final, and he strutted the decks, bull pissle whip at the ready in one hand, brass speaking trumpet in the other, shouting orders to the sailors who struggled and strained with the sheets, trying to husband each puff of favourable wind, to fill the sails and blow the ship southwards down the North Sea to Southampton and safety.

Never having been fond of the sea, nor its peculiar customs, during the voyage the king preferred to be shut away far below decks in his private quarters, where the relentless rocking and swaying had the least nauseating effect on his weakened body. Sadly for him, in his grossly emaciated state, the ability to take food during the sea trip was almost nil, and in the rare event his churning stomach felt able to partake of nutrient, within minutes any chewed food would soon represent itself, mixed with the yellow slime produced by his innards in their delicate sea-affected state. The king's absence from the upper deck was good for Horace Swale, whose tar-stained, weather-beaten face split into a gummy grin on hearing the welcome news, as the last thing he wanted was an interfering royal poking into his business, questioning his commands, and giving useless advice where none was needed. Dealing with the lesser nobles was a different matter for Horace, as, like the king, their only real interest in the sea was merely what could be caught and eaten. And with none of them being blessed with any curiosity in sailing techniques, Horace still remained in sole charge, and his word was law, even though within a few feet beneath his feet the all-powerful Edward II, potent monarch of England was retching and gagging at each wallowing roll of the labouring *Saint Luke*.

Ever since February of 1314, the weather patterns had been erratic and very strange, with bouts of oppressive steaming heat, followed by unseasonable cold spells, with giant prolonged electric tempests lasting days, saturating and flattening everything in their path. Perhaps the weather trends were a sign of things to come, as the next year was the first of a great famine, which swept across storm-battered, soaked Europe, and lasted for more than three years, starving the population from Lithuania in the east, as far south as Castile, all the way up to Norway in the north.

The August weather in the North Sea was little better, and after having suffered from the highest temperatures ever experienced by anyone alive at the very start of the month, the wind direction suddenly changed to the gentle southerly, returning the climate to more like the norm. However, to the sixth sense and trained eyes of the sailing master, nature had one more surprise up her sleeve. Horace Swale's irrational sea-faring nature became aroused by what still to this day is often considered an unlucky omen by sailors, when just visible in the distant south, a pale green sky accompanied by a continuous rumble of thunder heralded some portentous evil heading their way. Horace himself clambered to the uppermost viewing platform on the highest mast to see what it was which made his weather-sense tingle. Rubbing his eyes in disbelief he saw the biggest storm cell he'd ever witnessed, beating its malevolent way at high speed northwards up the channel, on a collision course with the *Saint Luke*, giving the ship absolutely no chance of finding a safe haven before it struck. The towering mass of cloud ascended high into the heavens, and spread out thousands of feet up in the thinner atmosphere forming the anvil, where the gullible still believed the old Norse Gods forged their weapons, the sparks being the lightning and the sound of the hammer producing the thunder. The inky black underside of the great cloud gave a perfect background against which the scores of flashing bolts could be seen clearly leaping a full thirty or forty miles across the sky from east to west or vice-versa.

On sight of the approaching tempest, a fleeting second of panic swept through the crew, and for the blink of an eye, the normal calm order disappeared, as they dropped what they were doing to point in awe at the gargantuan pile of approaching evil. Yet with one bellowed order through the speaking trumpet and a couple of reinforcing thwacks of Horace's whip, all discipline was instantly restored and every terrified soul on board resumed their allotted places, to automatically perform their prearranged tasks, some shinning up the rigging to take down the sails, while others stowed everything loose safely away below decks prior to the storm hitting; but no matter how they were occupied every single hand still kept a suspicious eye on what was to come. Being inherently superstitious by nature, each sailor patted their little trinkets or keepsakes, crossing themselves when skies darkened, blotting out the sun, turning the bright summer's day as dark as midnight, as they prepared themselves for the malignance which was about to be poured on their heads.

The first warning of the storm's imminent intent to unleash its evil was when the weather-wise snow-white seagulls, which perpetually wheeled and circled in shifts squawking around the rigging, arguing over the ownership of jettisoned crumbs of food, deserted the endangered vessel, and as one bolted feverishly landward to safety. The reason for their hasty departure was soon reinforced when the wind dropped completely, producing a threatening eerie calm, where the creaking ship, its company and passengers, bobbed about like a stranded cork in a tub, rising and falling on the growing swell. The wallowing motion caused the poor king's condition to worsen, where, deep in the bowels of the ship, and out of everybody's sight, he crawled around his hideaway heaving and gagging uncontrollably, trying to void his already empty stomach, making his diaphragm and ribs hurt dreadfully with each new retch or strain.

All the knights and even the strong-stomached Baron Dussingdale became affected by the smooth rolling movement, their green-tinged skin paying testament to their lubberly nature. Each of the nauseated nobles decided to take a leaf out of Edward's book, and do the sensible thing to go below decks to lay as low as possible until the storm had passed, eventually finding some slight relief from the queasiness, when at last the wind returned in the form of a massive squally gust, which shuddered through the vessel, shaking everything from mast to keel. The extraordinary force almost lifted the sturdy oak craft completely out of the water, only to release it to plunge back with a giant lurch, producing an ear-splitting clap as it hit, before its weight took the bows beneath the surface and dwelled for a moment below the water before rising with foam, spume and debris flooding off its forecastle, along with two of the crew, swept overboard, taken unawares by the suddenness of the meteorological assault. The rushing water swept them, and everything else unsecured, through the scuppers into the ocean, leaving the lost sailors floundering in the rising sea, unable to be helped by their shipmates as they gazed impotently after the doomed men, watching them and their mute appeals as they were engulfed by the eddying brine. Even the impious Horace crossed himself with fear, as the full force of the ensuing swirling gale hit the helpless vessel, prompting the crew to immediately find their allotted stations to ride out the savagery, leaving two of the strongest aboard to fight with the tiller and keep the prow facing into the churning sea. As one, the volunteers heaved and pulled, striving desperately against the odds to prevent the craft from drifting parallel to the troughs between the waves, where their downfall would be assured. Horace thanked the heavens for the sturdy English oak hull, purpose-made to the highest standards to convey the king, and strong enough to withstand the most savage of batterings.

For a full three hours the seamen struggled to keep the vessel safe. Although it was still mid-afternoon, the tiring crew worked in pitch blackness, their bare-chested, tar-stained forms only visible when their busy shapes became illuminated by the many lightning flashes which blinded as the men relentlessly laboured to keep themselves alive. Two lashed in position on the tiller, also could only withstand thirty-minute stints on the energy-sapping job before having to be replaced, similar to the others below decks, manning the pumps in total gloom, where the thigh-deep, filthy, rank-smelling water sloshed about the bilges in waves from stern to prow, adding to the lurching, as the courageous ship fought bravely to stay afloat, tossed about in the mighty sea, at one moment hidden in a deep dark trough between the towering waves, the next moment forty feet up high on the foaming crest.

All the time spent fighting the tempest, Horace was there, appearing sometimes as if he could be at two places at once, bellowing encouragement through his speaking trumpet, urging and cajoling the tiring hands as they flagged in their efforts, reminding them that the worst was not over, as with each yard the storm advanced north, the wind grew stronger and the sea rougher. At one stage, at the height of the first part of the storm when the thunder and lightning was as its greatest intensity, the rarest and most sacred phenomenon manifested itself in the uppermost rigging, when a colossal ball of violet-blue Saint Elmo's fire ignored the howling wind and danced among the spars. Instead of the apparition being blown far away out to sea as you would expect, it stubbornly clung to the crow's nest for upwards of four minutes, the ghostly lilac light bathing the crew's awe-filled upturned faces as they gazed at the sign from God and Saint Nicholas, the patron saint of seafarers, telling them that all would be well with the *Saint Luke*.

As quickly as it came, the storm temporarily disappeared. The hardy ship plunged out of the darkness from behind the thick vertical wall of grey driving rain, into a patch of brilliant blue cloudless sky and an area of clear bright sunlit calm water, all aboard blinking and squinting in the unexpected daylight, pleased to have survived nature's first onslaught. Peculiarly, though, there was no sense of joy or relief as you would probably expect there might be among the men, everybody knowing full-well what was in store, when the fiercer trailing edge vented its maliciously spiteful spleen on whoever ventured in its path. The twenty minutes of calm weather at the tempest's eye wasn't wasted by the crew, who had to work just as hard during the lull as they had during the initial bout of madness. Like machinery they toiled, repairing and clearing away the broken woodwork and damaged cordage, casting all unnecessary debris overboard, clearing the decks in readiness for the next violent assault.

The valiant effort of the exhausted crew wasn't in vain, and just in the nick of time the ship was as prepared as it could be, the overwrought sailors completely spent from their travails, taking the last few seconds of sanity to watch helplessly as the second thousand-foot-high, black, flash-speckled wall of dire weather inexorably approached towards them, once again engulfing the dwarfed vessel to have its wicked way with those on board. The furious gale again beat the enraged sea into massive waves, relentlessly crashing them over the weakened hull, taking in their wake much of what was left of the rigging, along with nearly all the remaining superstructure. It swept it and everything else that had been stowed on the decks overboard, never again to meet of up with its discarded fellows, left miles and miles from where they were.

The men could do no more; no mortal hand could help them in their plight, and with another half hour of the battering, the ship would assuredly founder. Having resigned themselves to the fate which awaited them, there was only one more thing they could do to aid them, and that was to pray; so they did, every single soul doffing their brine-soaked hats, clutching them next to their hearts to solemnly recite the Lord's Prayer. Immediately after the final muttered "Amen" was said, one of the waggish, older shipmates, trying to lift the downcast spirits of the crew, struck up a familiar but rather inappropriate Saxon song. His rich baritone voice beat the roaring wind into second place with a slightly bawdy rendition of "Summer is a-coming in", soon joined by the others in warbling the well-known falsetto chorus, "sing cuckoo, sing cuckoo, sing cuckoo noooooo!" Even Horace shouted down his speaking trumpet to add his overworked croaking voice to the refrain, as the crew challenged what might befall. Laughing at the black humour, every man bravely stared death squarely in the eyes, singing their way to certain destruction and bracing themselves to face the inevitable, when miraculously, like turning off a tap, the storm spat the ship out, down the slope of water, sucked up by the extremely low pressure, into an area of relative calm, not dissimilar to the one which heralded the mighty storm before its arrival.

Finding it hard to believe, the reprieved crew's singing soon turned to a mighty cheer before they set about embracing each other, astounded at their defiance of Davy Jones and his damnable locker. The celebrations were cut short when Horace once again yelled down his speaking trumpet, this time demanding order be restored, as there was much work to be done to yet save the stricken craft. Then, somewhat sarcastically, Horace pointed out to the happy smiling men that if they bothered to gaze around, there was nothing to be seen except the fast-departing vast black cloud, which in the evening sunshine sported a magnificent double rainbow glowing starkly against its murkiness, where it undoubtedly was getting more of its dire revenge on humanity by subjecting some other innocents to its savage ferocity. Obeying Horace, the company turned on their heels to look all around at the horizon, being totally amazed that there was no coastline to be seen, and the only sure thing was where west was, as the sinking sun indicated on its inexorable journey to below the sea.

There were many things to do on board; true, the robust hull was still just about seaworthy, but the superstructure had all but disappeared, the main mast having snapped off, was gone, leaving nothing except a ten-foot splintered stump where it once stood, although, as luck would have it, much of the broken rigging was still in tow, as during the frenetic attempts to save the *Saint Luke*, the poor soul sent to cut it away in case it dragged the vessel under was swept overboard in the attempt, and forgotten in the melee. The scuppers were clogged with seaweed and other tangled debris, including the smashed tiller handle, minus the two unlucky men lashed to it, taken by a colossal wave and swept away far out to sea, unnoticed and un-missed in the panic. Most of the taffrail had also disappeared; only a few twisted brass posts were left to mark where it had been, stripped from the decking along with nearly all the cordage, which trailed behind like enormous tentacles still attached to the main spar. To the layman, the situation appeared utterly hopeless, but to the professional seaman's eye of Horace Swale, all was not lost, as to him there was still enough to salvage and cobble together a serviceable jury-rig to guide the blasted wreck back to a safe haven.

The evening weather was lovely, the sky was cloudless and the late sun felt warm in the faces of the crew as the ship's bows were cajoled to head westwards, and with any luck a friendly shore, which although invisible to the naked eye, couldn't be far off as several of the gulls had returned, their raucous cries seemingly mocking the battered vessel as they whirled above to spot any remnants of tasty flotsam for supper before returning to land and a convenient cliff to rest their wings for the imminent night.

To prevent the possible overnight loss of the all-important remains of the rigging, in the experienced eyes of Horace it was imperative to gather all the floating wreckage and secure it onboard before darkness fell; so once again, after a series of shouted commands, what remained of the crew sprang to action. In all, twelve souls had been lost to the tempest, a quarter of the whole company, leaving the rest struggling to cope with the strenuous task. Realising the storm had passed, the curious passengers emerged in dribs and drabs from their cramped quarters below decks to survey the damage. First was Baron Dussingdale, who gazed around the blasted vessel with amazed horror, noticing the difficulty the depleted number of sailors were having dragging on the ropes to salvage the trailing rigging, instantly he rolled up his sleeves and joined in like a seasoned tar, hauling on the cables with the chanting men, adding his considerable weight and voice to the effort, setting an example to the haughty knights, as they merely watched the one-sided struggle, shaming them into doing their bit and for the very first time in their whole lives to labour alongside base commoners, which until that day was totally alien to them. A strange mixture of Baron, knights, seamen and cabin boys acted as one, brought together by Horace, who grunted, applauded and cheered as their combined strength gradually overcame the weighty soaked and sodden rigging as it inched towards the vessel. Eventually it got close enough to be manhandled over the bulwarks and onto the deck, and on one word from Horace all hands instantly descended on the tangle, their busy hands bringing order out of the chaos. They carefully unknotted the confused intertwined pile of cords, and then neatly coiling the ropes, spliced them together where necessary, sorting the timber into graduated lengths and profiles, lashing down anything which they thought might be of any use the next day when the running repairs were due to be carried out, to again make the vessel seaworthy enough to convey the hiding monarch to safety.

That night the desperately needed, all-important rest didn't come easily to the exhausted sailors, as without any form of steering, no one, not even Horace, knew for definite what in the pitch black of night might happen. Much to the relief of all, however, Saint Nicholas was on their side and mercifully the sea was calm during the hours of darkness, free from any of the sudden storms which had nearly caused the ship's downfall, as another, even as little as one quarter of the intensity, would in all certainty be the death knell for the ship, condemning the king, knights and crew to a cold watery grave at the bottom of the sea.

On the arrival of daybreak, the first and most important jobs needed to be started, which were to repair the rudder and rigging. With the famed professionalism of the English seafarers and without any word of command, the tired master craftsmen and their weary mates started on their myriad of tasks. Happily they proceeded with the business of affecting the essential repairs, eating a crude breakfast as they went and all singing as seamen do, their hammers and chisels working in time with the tune, bringing the corpse of the ship back to life. In no time, and as if by magic, from nowhere a shortened mast complete with a cross spar sprang up. Shortly afterwards, a serviceable rudder handle, complete with a steersman, miraculously sprouted from where the old one had once been and by the time mid-afternoon arrived, the *Saint Luke* was almost as serviceable as when she first sailed from Dunbar on the reasonably short journey to take the sulking, vanquished Edward home.

For the best part the vital repairs were finished, and the now-jobless hands, having nothing else to occupy them, were now making themselves busy in the everyday chores of seamanship. With a favourable north-easterly wind at their backs, the half-sized sail was raised, the winged-ox which adorned it now no more than just an ordinary one, having lost its wings in the alterations. Quickly inflating it strained the spars, cracking and flapping with urgency and in no time was propelling the lurching ship on its heading south-west, in the hope of catching sight of the familiar English coast. For half an hour the ship glided ever south-by-west, the less-weightier vessel itself seeming to gain confidence as its speed increased, skipping over the waves, turning the blue sea into creamy white foam as it splashed off its bluff bow. Twenty-five feet above the freshly scrubbed, sand-strewn pale ginger deck, standing daringly tiptoe with one foot on the cross spar, the other held out straight as a counter-balance with only one hand gripping the top of the mast for security, Horace Swale squinted against the glare of the water, shielding his eyes and straining his neck making himself as tall as possible trying to get a glimpse of the coastline through the fair weather sea haze. At last espying a distant shore, Horace looked again to make doubly sure, before pointing and announcing the sighting to all with the familiar bellowed cry of, "Land ho!"

Those two pivotal words grabbed everyone's interest, including Edward's, who clambered out of his noisome hiding place, to stand unsteadily on the deck, blinking in the shock of sudden daylight in his badly soiled doublet and hose. The stained royal arms were practically invisible, obscured by the encrusted vomit and detritus of illness, his noticeably dreadful sorry state causing an audible gasp of shock from all aboard except Dussingdale, the only person previously allowed in his royal company, and then not as an act of friendship, but purely to keep him regularly informed with bulletins as to the state of the ship and how well the journey was proceeding. Satisfied with his updated information, the king returned to his sanctuary below decks, back to the accustomed gloom and the continuous bout of endless queasiness.

The sight of land galvanised the fatigued complement, and with a heightened sense of exigency the ship beat towards the land. Horace personally handled the management of the sailing, cleverly guiding the craft with wild gesticulations from his lofty vantage point, waving his outstretched arm to the patches of ruffled water, signifying exactly where the wind was keenest. Under his guidance, the battered hulk made good headway, eventually getting close enough to the coast to realise that the vessel had been blown dreadfully off course. Horace's heart sank to his boots, when he recognised that the not-so-familiar shoreline in front was not that of somewhere in Yorkshire as he had hoped, but the beaches just off Fraserburgh in Scotland, a hundred miles north of the starting point of Dunbar.

As the realisation set in that they were in enemy water, Horace's signalling grew even wilder, shouting down for the flagging men to turn the ship's prow due south, and make all haste to England. Yet for the always-impatient Horace, everything was a little too slow for his liking; so, using the skill gained from forty years at sea, he adeptly slid down a ratline. Snatching the tiller handle from the hands of the bemused coxswain, he took on the role of steering the ship himself as he barked orders to the scurrying men, getting them to jettison all non-essentials and lighten the craft even further to make more speed, fearing they might be recognised from those on the shore and pursued by a faster undamaged vessel, which in their present state would most certainly mean their capture and imprisonment or worse.

Everything not of immediate use was thrown overboard, leaving nothing except a few dry provisions and some water for the voyage to whatever friendly port that would have them. Cutlery, pots, plates and even some of the ballast in the bilges was got rid of, now considered by Horace to be too much counterweight, considering the loss of much of the rigging. With the wind now backing to north-of-west, the much trimmer *Saint Luke* now skipped over the waves; freed and slimmed it tacked south with almost as much speed as before, but always keeping just in sight of the land. Horace himself husbanding every single puff of wind into the inadequate sail, willing and urging the vessel forwards, always kept one eye on the land, for two reasons: firstly, in case there were any possible belligerents in the area, and secondly, keeping watch and looking for familiar points of land which would mean they were in friendly waters.

For over six hours Horace tirelessly maintained his station, exhausted from hauling on the rudder bar, stubbornly not allowing any other than himself to perform the vital job, but always ever watchful and alert, until peering into the distance he thought he could just about make out the ten-mile-wide inlet he recognised as the Firth of Forth on his right-hand side. Barely being able to believe it, he rubbed his tired red eyes, thinking they were playing some kind of trick on him. Still unsure, he turned to one of the younger boy sailors, asking him to use his renowned eagle-eyed vision to confirm that it was true. Holding his flattened hands either side of his head to shield them from any extra, unwanted incoming light, the lad instantly agreed after just a very fleeting glance that it was indeed the massive estuary. Dancing a little jig of joy, Horace bellowed the news down his megaphone to let the whole crew know, the news meeting with a huge cheer from the relieved men. Even the reserved baron and knights joined in pointing to the land, all seeing salvation was at hand, knowing that initially having suffered from some horrendously dreadfully bad luck, fortunately followed by some good, along with expert seamanship and a joint cohesive effort, their lives, against all odds, were once again safe. There was no need for the Baron Dussingdale to rush to the king and tell him the good news; the noisy cheering had woken him from the sickly sleep which had come hard for him to reach. And with a face of thunder he emerged from the hatchway to his private quarters, and glared evilly at the celebrating assembly who were more than happy to share the good tidings with the grumpy-befouled monarch. Moodily, Edward listened for a second, nodded his head in half-hearted acknowledgment of the information, and then, turning round to go back down, he glanced over his bony shoulder at the hopeful company, all beaming giant smiles, obviously expecting to hear a little crumb of praise for their valiant efforts, only to be disappointed by a grunted, almost inaudible command from the miserable, surly king, who ordered them to shut up and be quiet so that he could get back to sleep, bidding them to wake him on reaching port.

Stunned to instant silence by the dismissive attitude of Edward, Horace looked questioningly at the Baron, who merely grimaced to signify his utter disgust at what he had heard. The silent comment received tacit agreement from the captain, demonstrated succinctly when Horace gathered a huge ball of phlegm from his throat and spat it carelessly over the side, paying little heed to the wind, which promptly returned the insult straight back at his feet. Needing to return to the more important matter of safely sailing the damaged ship, with a visible air of sadness Horace and the deflated crew shuffled back to their positions, their keenness and elation all gone, turned to instant disappointment in their moment of triumph, hacked down by the awful attitude of the foul-tempered Edward, who'd returned down below decks where he was once again trying to regain his rudely interrupted sleep.

For the next two hours the depressed and very tired crew laboured ceaselessly, gradually creeping closer and closer to the coast, until they were completely sure that they were in friendly seas and the inhabitants would be loyal to the undeserving King Edward II. Perpetually scanning the land, Horace gazed directly into the setting sun, searching for the recognisable landmarks where he knew there would be a safe haven. At last, an hour before nightfall, he spotted the mouth of the River Coquet, dominated by the magnificent newly built Warkworth Castle and the natural harbour of Amble, and so wasting no time, the adept crew made straight for the shelter, reaching it with only minutes to spare before, as happened every night, the defensive boom chains were hoisted into position, closing the port so that it would be impossible for any enemies to sneak up the River Coquet at the dead of night in boats and, using the cover of darkness, attack the castle while the occupants were asleep.

Mindful that Edward still had to keep up appearances, the ever-faithful Baron Dussingdale aided the king as he bathed his befouled body, helping him get rid of the sour clinging stench of vomit, washing and combing his golden hair, trimming off some of the more matted bits, making the newly acquired grey streak shine out even more obviously amongst its fellows. The baron dressed the king himself, covering his shrunken frame with a full-length scarlet cloak, finally placing his crown somewhat haphazardly on his regal head, presenting a vision not quite, but rather like the one expected of such a great and powerful potentate.

Twilight was descending into darkness and the first stars were twinkling in the deep amber sky, by the time the *Saint Luke* was safely moored and secured enough for the king to disembark. Still with the air of a monarch, it was a much-changed Edward that walked unsteadily down the gangplank, even though he had to be supported by his faithful baron, with knights hovering in attendance in case of a royal slip. Forcibly lined up on the quay to wish their sovereign well, Horace Swale stood at the head of his crew as each sailor was handed an overtly given small gold coin from one of the attendant knights, by way of a belated royal thanks to the men, prompting an orchestrated half-hearted unmeant cheer from the sailors. Horace himself received a bulging leather purse for his trouble, before the king silently departed without a word from himself, to walk the short distance to Warkworth Castle where the constable, Sir John de Clavering, was waiting, panting rather breathlessly and trying to recover from dashing about, organising his staff, only having received less than half an hour's notice to prepare for the dubious surprise of a very tired and extremely unhappy royal visitor.

Accompanied by much bowing and scraping, Sir John ushered his unexpected highbrow guests in through the massive main gate of Warkworth Castle, leading them with all due courtesy, straight away to the great hall, where ready and waiting for them on the table was a hastily contrived small banquet, mostly consisting of cold meats, some reasonably fresh bread and fruit; but, to the delight of Edward, a small pile of late-season, soft-boiled dove's eggs were steaming on a tray to act as an appetiser.

At the sight of the welcome delicacy, the otherwise silent king spoke for the first time since his arrival, his faltering words stunning all those who had known him before. "W-wonderful, Sir John, I r-really f-f-fancied something f-fresh."

Nobody, not even those who were trapped in Dunbar with the king or shared the perilous journey south with him, realised that the slight stutter Edward had always suffered from, had grown into a full-blown speech impediment, destined to stay with him for the rest of his life and always to remind him of the disastrous summer of 1314.

Edward and his small retinue remained in Warkworth Castle for a whole month, the king taking ten days of complete bed-rest to recuperate from his privations, whiling away the rest of his time wandering around aimlessly, morose and sulkily doing nothing. On the other hand, Baron Dennis Dussingdale and the others enjoyed the good hunting, hawking and fishing to be had in the vicinity, whilst waiting for Edward's personal bodyguard to arrive from London. The king insisted on making the trip home, this time staying on land, refusing point blank to take a new ship and the much quicker sea route back to Southampton.

During his stay, Edward's appetite fully returned, perhaps trying to make up for lost time, or maybe to recoup his lost flesh, but every day he demanded at least six cooked meals, and by the end of his stay he had gained a little too much weight, all totally at the expense of Sir John, who was more than obliging to the voracious monarch, tending personally to his wishes, heartened by the empty promises of more refurbishments and updates to the often-beleaguered castle.

The leaves were changing colour by the time Edward prepared to leave Warkworth Castle. In all, two hundred armed knights were charged with the task of trekking from London all the way up to Northumberland to escort the mentally broken king all the way back down to the capital, where the court, his French wife Isabella and family would anxiously be waiting for him to return back to their bosom. With an ostentatious display of pomp and ceremony, the entourage assembled in the courtyard ready to depart, the plumper-than-usual king leaving on a wonderful new sixteen-hands-high specially bred, jet-black riding horse, a present from Sir John de Clavering, not out of esteem for his royal master, but more as a not-so-subtle reminder of Edward's promise to reinforce the castle's battered defences in the spring of the next year. The reason for the gift not going unnoticed by the sovereign, as he waved his farewells and led the multi-coloured meandering cavalcade inland, amid the wonderful russets, reds and greens of the English countryside in autumn, heading due south down the middle of the country on a pre-planned route and hopefully home by November.

CHAPTER 8

Three months before Edward II's lucky escape back to England's capital, the whole of Scotland was celebrating, basking in the afterglow of the great victory over the English. Not so, however, at the bleakest of bleak Dunstaffnage Castle, governed over by the revolting Sir Thomas Dewar, one of the last surviving Templars and the least sociable of Robert the Bruce's constables, who was widely rumoured to have a hidden fortune stashed away to pay for his most peculiar voracious appetite for the younger female of the species. He was famed for being utterly heartless to those under his charge, let alone those who stood against him or called him their enemy, to whom his mercilessness was as legendary as his poor housekeeping, more savage perhaps than the Black Douglas himself.

The fortress itself was situated on a solid rock promontory at the south-west of the mouth of Loch Etive. It was originally constructed to be a suitable seat of power for Duncan MacDougall, the dour Lord of Lorn. However, after losing a war with Robert the Bruce in 1309 and following a brief siege, it duly passed on to the Scottish crown and thus, as the most senior laird in that area of Scotland, into the hands of Thomas Dewar. Although having been built less than a hundred years before from the self-same stone as it stood on, its walls had virtually no shelter on three of its four sides and were blasted and stained from the sea and relentless wind, which could make its uninterrupted way all across the Atlantic Ocean from Greenland and the unknown world beyond. It was to there, where King Robert had been summoned by the less than hospitable Thomas Dewar, to mete out the summary justice to some unlucky suspected deserters from the Scottish ranks, who had the misfortune to fall into the hands of probably the worst possible person imaginable.

As it was ultimately the responsibility of Robert to pass the sentences on those found guilty of such a crime, he decided to go himself, rather than was the usual practice, and let the senior noble, in this case the unforgiving overly zealous Thomas Dewar, to deal with the likely culprits. With a heavy heart, Robert left the relative comfort of Stirling Castle, to travel the seventy miles to the horribly bleak and isolated Dunstaffnage Castle, where he was expected to undertake the unsavoury task of condemning seven uneducated peasants to death, merely because they were probably fed up with camp life, and decided to go home to take care of their wives, children and livestock. Robert only took with him a small retinue of Walter Grint, John Stuart and four other men-at-arms as protection on the two backside-numbing days' ride, crossing right through the centre of the Trossachs, clambering up steep hills and down deep gorges, taking the most direct route but maybe not necessarily the quickest to the dreaded destination.

Eventually, the king and his small party arrived on the third day of travelling, to enter the austere foreboding iron-grey, lichen-covered gateway and the poor hospitality to be had within the permanently dank cheerless but famously impregnable fortalice. Weary and sore, King Robert and his men dismounted their steeds in a gloomy, musty-smelling corner of a granite-cobbled mossy courtyard, where, except for a few days in high summer, the sun rarely shone. Their arrival was greeted by a bevy of rushing scruffy grooms and ostlers whose pallid bleached faces paid testament to the long daylight hours spent lurking in the lightless pile. Quickly and silently, like frightened rabbits, the wraith-like servants took hold of the rider-less horses and disappeared with them as speedily as they appeared, to vanish somewhere in the depths of a large dark damp barn, leaving a pitifully thin, elderly old man to nervously usher the seven guests to the main hall. Attempting his version of a courtly bow, the scruffy servant manfully opened the large mildewed oak door into the hall, its brown rusty hinges screaming a strident welcome to the visitors, whose eyes were very slowly growing accustomed to the gloomy light-less conditions at the castle.

Inside the chamber, even though it was just past noon on a summer's day, a great fire snapped and crackled in the hearth, belching the occasional puff of acrid blue smoke into the already odd-smelling hall. Its glow, however, gave an element of welcome to the otherwise forbidding room, which had nothing of interest to break up the featureless, bare stone walls, that tapered up to an invisible vaulted smoke-stained roof lurking somewhere high above the floor, upon which, at least half a year's worth of damp and festering rushes were strewn. Hidden amongst the foot-thick litter, five sundry mangy old curs munched on partly gnawed old bones, jumping up from their meals in a flurry of barking aggression at the sight of the newcomers, but instantly halting in their tracks when the voice of a man sitting hidden behind one of two high-back chairs facing the fire simply whispered "Stay" to the slavering beasts instantly followed by "Beds." The grumbled command resulted in their sulky return to where they had been lying and back to extract the last remnant of nutrition from their late lunch.

"Who is it, Duncan?" the grumpy voice asked, taking on a surly demanding tone, its owner apparently too idle to look to see for himself.

"I-It's K-King Robert, my lord," the ancient guide answered timidly, as if he feared a wrong word would upset the cantankerous host.

Wooden and rather puppet-like, as if he had been tugged by invisible strings, the owner of the voice immediately jumped out of his seat and turned half in mid-air to face Robert and bow a very low obeisance to his liege lord. "Forgive me, sire, I wasn't expecting you until tomorrow, otherwise I would have had this tidied up," the cantankerous man declared with a wet-sounding sniff, whilst swinging his arm wide as if bringing the king's attention to the horrendous unmissable stinking mess.

"Don't worry yourself, Thomas, I didn't expect to be here until tomorrow. Never mind I'll wipe my feet on the way out!" Robert replied, trying to put his inadequate host at his ease with his humour, forcing a half-smile from Sir Thomas Dewar, the smelly little constable, who was probably only in his late forties although he looked substantially older. Thomas wore his long greasy iron-grey hair scraped back tightly into a ponytail to pull the wrinkles out of his craggy face, where his deep-set, pale-green merciless eyes sat narrowly over a permanently running large hooked nose above his mean thin-lipped moist mouth, which barely moved as he spoke, keeping his brown decayed teeth all but hidden out of sight. And judging by his overall ragged unkempt appearance and the nostril-stinging body odour, the master of the stronghold rarely changed his clothes or visited the bath, if ever.

Barely being able to disguise the tone of repugnance in his voice, Robert introduced his six companions. All of whom had previously heard gossip concerning the infamous hospitality of Thomas Dewar, but they still gazed around them, unbelieving and open-mouthed, as they gawped at the foul-stinking surroundings, utterly amazed at how hugely understated the descriptions were.

The formalities done with and not wishing for his stay to last one more second than absolutely necessary, the king wanted to get down to business as soon as possible, hoping to leave well before nightfall and possibly sleep rough in the wet, rather than having to suffer the awful conditions in the noisome sleeping quarters of permanently damp Dunstaffnage Castle, so filthy he was led to believe, that even the more choosy rats and mice opted to live elsewhere. Wanting to get on with proceedings quickly at the specific request of Robert, with a nod of agreement and a clap of his hands from Thomas, Duncan scuttled off to fetch a trestle table and then two short benches, dragging them and the two high-backed chairs in front of the fire, facing into the hall, making a sort of courtroom for the trial of the seven accused. First Robert took his seat on one of the softer large chairs in the centre, closely followed by Thomas, with three knights sitting either side of them on the hard benches, and then in a tense silence, all eight waited for the sorry bunch of prisoners to be marched in front of them. Obeying a whispered command from Thomas, Duncan raced away on his given errand, closing the screaming oak door behind him on the way out, leaving the assembly with nothing to do but stare vacantly at the bland uninteresting walls around them.

By way of making polite conversation, Robert turned to his dishevelled host, interrupting his idle picking at an oozing boil on his neck. "I hear you have an English prisoner as well as the deserters, one Sir Lawrence Buckenham, I believe?"

Hearing the king's comment, Thomas giggled greedily then rubbing his soiled hands covetously together, he sniffed back a long string of escaping snot as he spoke. "Indeed I have, my lord; he's safely locked up in the cells along with the traitors. Fucking Englishmen, I fucking hate them," he snickered, mopping his filthy nose with his equally filthy, well-used, mucus-encrusted sleeve.

On hearing the surprise revelation, Robert turned to Thomas, his face confused and questioning, and barely being able to believe his ears, he lowered his voice to almost a whisper, "I beg your pardon, correct me if I'm wrong, but did I hear that in your infinite wisdom you've locked up an English knight in your foul dungeon, along with seven Scottish traitors who know that they're going to die?"

Reading the gathering wrath in Robert's expression, Thomas tried to buy some extra time to think by resuming the nervous picking at the back of his neck, and then wiping away the same stubborn bit of snot off his nose with the back of his hand, he answered hesitantly. "Sort of, but not exactly with them, more next to them."

"What do you mean, not exactly with them?" Robert demanded, his obvious rage showing on his face.

Wriggling awkwardly in his chair, Thomas replied tremulously, "I mean that he's separated from them by a sort of cage. He's all right if he stays in the corner; they can't get him if he stays out of reach."

Robert was about to ask another question about the well-being of the guest, when the creaking hinge came to Thomas's rescue as the bound and helpless seven accused were marched in and prodded into place in front of the table by two burly spearmen. The men lined in front of the king and his fellow judges were, by their appearance, no more than a quartet of conscripted peasant farmers, two other men and a pre-pubescent lad. The signs of their captivity were all over them, the filth from the dungeon floor hung off them in clods of muck, with the odd bit of mouldy straw bedding stuck to it. Speaking to the men in turn, Robert asked each their age and then, to see if they were guilty or not, he looked steadily into their eyes to search for any signs of untruths. The first and oldest man questioned said his age was sixty and he was innocent, as did the next, who looked roughly the same age, but didn't exactly know how old he was. Four of the five remaining accused's ages ranged from roughly twenty something to about late thirtyish and all pleaded their innocence; but the seventh, who was no more than twelve years old, stood shaking in his boots and speechless, far too frightened to reply. When asked as to why, when and where they were taken, it became apparent that four of the seven were about their legitimate business when the overzealous captain of one of Thomas's disreputable raiding parties captured them, and without bothering to inquire exactly who they were, he accused them of being deserters from the army and took them into custody. Reading the prisoners' faces like a book, the king believed their stories, except for two very guilty-looking of the thirty year olds, whose shifty mannerisms and sideways glances told another story.

With a mind to redress the unfairness of their incarceration, Robert looked at each innocent prisoner in turn, sighing sympathetically while shooting a menacing sideways glare at Thomas. Bidding them take a step forward as he spoke to them, Robert addressed the guiltless five as one; standing up, he walked over to the men to deliver his short speech. At first he spoke relatively normally, but wavering slightly, struggling to keep his rising anger under control. "I am Robert the Bruce, and I see you here accused of a capital crime against me, your anointed king. Your noble lord Thomas Dewar here," Robert said, indicating towards Thomas and frowning with the gathering fury visible in his face and tapping an impatient foot, he raised his voice a little, before continuing where he left off, "feels that, because of the seriousness of your offence, it needs me to personally deal with you as I see fit, and so I will." Making another poor attempt to suppress his wrath, Robert gestured to where Thomas was sitting, his head cradled in his grubby hands, dreading the backlash from the obviously extremely angry king, who rightly felt that the whole incident was nonsensical rubbish which could and should have been dealt with easily with just a few well-aimed sensible questions. Wondering how to adequately punish Dewar for his arrant stupidity, Robert mused on the possibilities, ruling out most of his ideas, when with a sudden flash of inspiration, the highly aggravated king commanded Thomas to have some of his well-known hidden stockpile of money brought so he could administer proper justice.

Reluctantly, Thomas accepted the order without any argument, and, trusting nobody else to go on the errand to his secret cache, he went himself, traipsing off with a face of gloom, returning after ten minutes with a small, extremely filthy stinking and half-rotted brass-bound coffer full of assorted coins.

Robert waited for Thomas to return before announcing his final judgement. The first two older men he dismissed, finding them innocent on all counts, commanding the miserly Thomas to give them each the equivalent of two shillings, payable out of his own pocket by way of a token of recompense for their unfair treatment. He missed out the next two, still standing a step behind the others, who looked at each other with a nervous guilty expression, knowing the jig was up. Making them wait, Robert addressed the fifth, and then the sixth, administrating the same judgement as the first two, and then, taking a pace forward Robert crouched down on his haunches and beckoned to the boy, telling him to approach, reassuringly winking at him and speaking to him in fatherly tones. "Whatever are we going to do with you, wee laddie? Your mother and father must be going out of their wits not knowing where you are."

Gaining in confidence at having seen the acquittal of four of the men, the boy attempted to answer, his filthy tear-streaked freckled face making his sapphire blue eyes even bluer amongst the grime, his bright red lips trembling uncontrollably with terror as he made his best effort to reply in the hybrid Scottish-English border language familiar to them all. "My parents are dead! The soldiers killed my mother and father when they captured me, sir."

"What soldiers might that be?" Robert asked, trying not to look angry and leaning precariously forwards on the balls of his feet, interested in what the stripling had to say.

Glancing around him, apparently too frightened to reply, the youth decided the best course of action was to stare at his boots rather than to possibly further incur the famously dire wrath of Lord Thomas Dewar, whose ill-disciplined men it was that murdered the boy's parents.

Understanding the reason for the terror in his face, Robert changed tack. "Come here and tell me your name, then we can talk as friends, can't we?" Robert suggested, giving the petrified lad an encouraging smile.

Emboldened by Robert's new approach, the boy took a step right up to the king and stared directly at his royal lips, which were mouthing tacit words, trying to encourage the lad to answer. "My name is Robbie, sir!" the lad mumbled almost incoherently.

"That's better, isn't it? Now we can talk, big bad King Robert to little shy Robbie, can't we?" Blushing a little, the embarrassed small boy nodded a shy yes in response. "Remind me, who were the soldiers who killed your father, young Robbie?" Robert repeated, giving the boy a gentle friendly tweak on his grubby cheek.

In response, the lad looked around him, scanning the room, and then at Thomas, and with tears welling up in his terrified eyes, he blurted out the answer, pointing directly at Thomas. "It was his men, sir! We was looking after our animals when they attacked us. I tried to stop them and they hit me. My daddy was only trying to protect me and they chopped his head off!" That was enough for the boy; overwrought by re-living the sight of his father's death, he crumpled into floods of uncontrollable tears.

Barely able to believe the pointlessness of the unnecessary murders, Robert the Bruce looked appalled and somewhat incredulous at his fellow judges, before suddenly standing up to address all present. His face drained of colour in his rage, he spat out his speech to all, but aimed his remarks directly at Thomas. "Is it not enough that we are in bloody conflict with the fucking English king and his bastard barons who want our lands for themselves, but do we also have to make war on hard-working farmers? To steal what we have to, is one thing, but to cut them down for trying to protect what is theirs by right is another. Are we that hardhearted that small boys and their innocent fathers have to fear us?" Finishing his tirade, Robert looked at the two un-sentenced of the accused, to vent part of his anger on them. "And you two! I know your guilt, I can see it in your worthless faces and you know your fate, but I can assure you those who murdered this poor wee lad's only kin will join you on the gallows, to watch you suffer your deaths, knowing it's going to be them next. This is my sentence!" Robert, however, wasn't finished and, pushing a chair out of his way to give him room, he turned his whole body to face Dewar, who at the time was starting to look a little relieved and relaxed, believing the session was over. Thomas all but jumped out of his skin when the king turned on him. "And you! You who are no better than the murdering fucking English! You, who by birthright are supposed to teach the correct path to the feudal subjects beneath you, allow your men to commit atrocities in my name! Believe me, somehow I shall make you suffer for this outrage."

Still surprised by the verbal attack, Thomas started to mumble an explanation in his defence, only to be cut short by the furious monarch as he continued. "Be silent, and listen to your king! Trust me, if you weren't of noble birth, you would accompany these deserters and your murdering minions alongside them on the scaffold. As it is, I shall hit you where it will hurt you most! In your pocket. I will take this poor wee boy back with me to Stirling, where he shall live with a childless family I already have in mind, and be taught to be a gentleman, all at your personal expense, and when it comes to the time to fit him out, once again the money will be paid by you or your heirs!" Robert roared, straightening up Thomas's already grim visage as he tried to object, only for Robert to once again stop him dead by holding up his open hand. "Furthermore, you shall release Lawrence Buckenham without ransom. Make sure he is unharmed, clean, well fed, and fit to travel; I don't want to send him back to England with tales of Scottish brutality, making them think we're as bad as they are. So do what you must to make him happy and then have two of your best men escort him to me at Stirling Castle. From there I shall release him, as I have something for him and your men to deliver somewhere in England. Now apologise to these four, and give them each a handful of that money by way of a fine, not because of your arrant stupidity, but because I am ashamed that you have done all this in my name. So let's get on with this, as I want to be out of this stinking shithole before mid-afternoon."

The kingly justice administered to his satisfaction, Robert turned to get out of the foetid chamber, almost tripping over a clump of matted flooring in his anxiety to exit himself from the vile company. Stomping out of the room, Robert did his best to ignore the wordy protestations of Thomas Dewar, who barred his path, gambolling around the king's feet, believing he had been treated unfairly by the monarch. Knowing them to be fruitless, Thomas gave up his pleas, moodily throwing himself down in one of the chairs in a petulant sulk, as he watched the six knights disappear with the boy and the four other innocents, and with a simple wave of his hand he dismissed the two spearmen with the condemned. Bidding the men as they left, to arrest the culprits who meted out the swift miscarriage of justice to Robbie's unlucky family, he left Thomas completely alone, and a lot poorer, in the now even more cheerless room, with nothing for company other than the vengeful thoughts swirling around his disturbed brain.

A short while after everybody had left, Duncan returned, standing a good five minutes in silence behind his distraught master, collapsed in the chair, holding his face in his hands and moaning, slowly rocking backwards and forwards in grief at being hurt in his pocket. Trying to be tactful and not make the bad situation worse, Duncan cleared his throat and, using his politest possible voice, spoke to his lord, hoping to bring him out of his sulk and remind him there was a duty to perform. "Is there anything you wish for, my lord?"

The harmless question resulted in Thomas raising his head up out of his hands, to glare viciously at the loyal servant, his venomous answer showering Duncan with spittle as he vented his anger on the innocent old retainer. "Nothing you can fucking do, unless you can bring me that fucking usurper's heart to me in a fucking pie. Now fuck off back to your kennel, you snivelling little cunt, and go and lick your fucking bitch's arse instead of mine."

Quite used to being spoken to in such a way, Duncan ignored the outburst to reply calmly, with more than a hint of sarcasm in his impertinent voice. "Before I go to lick some lesser arses, sir, I must remind your lordship that the king and his royal arse awaits you outside in the courtyard to witness the executions, and he bids you make haste as the hour grows late."

Not wanting to aggravate Robert further, Thomas raised himself up out of his seat, wagging his head from side to side and putting on a childish voice, replied to the cheekily delivered, royal command, "Run along like a good little boy then, and tell that cunt of a fucking king that as fast as my feeble fucking old legs will fucking let me, I'm fucking coming. Now go! Fuck off and tell him!

Ignoring the unwarranted outburst, Duncan shuffled off at speed to the courtyard to relay a diplomatic interpretation to Robert, leaving Thomas cursing and swearing under his breath as he followed his messenger outside into the daylight to watch the king's justice at work.

The captain at Dunstaffnage Castle had been swift to organise the executions. Only an hour after being condemned, a total of five sad-looking accused were prodded into line at the top of the wooden parapet some thirty feet up in the air to stand, hands tied, behind the dangling coarse rope nooses to wait for their punishment. The two guilty deserters were first in line, and having made their peace with God, looked calm and totally resigned to their fate. The remaining three appeared frightened and confused, having expected nothing other than their evening meal, when they were arrested and sentenced without given the right to speak in their own defence.

On the orders of Robert, the whole garrison, including the women and children, had been commanded to attend and watch the fate of those who incurred the king's displeasure. With their faces turned skywards to view the final act, the crowd watched as the first two slowly had the ropes put round their necks by the executioner, who was in fact the burly armour-clad garrison captain himself, him being unable to find anyone else willing to undertake the grizzly task. Announcing the reason for their deaths, and with a nod from

Thomas, the two were brutally hurled off the edge, falling eight feet before the cord tightened, yanking them back up with a sickening crunch, instantly killing them, although they jerked, kicked, twitched and voided themselves, as if still alive.

Next it was the turn of the three murderers, who stood quaking in their shoes, still unsure of the reason for their predicament, only being made aware of what they were condemned for when, at Robert's insistence, Thomas Dewar personally read the charges, having to be reminded twice by the king to speak up so all could hear the pronouncement. On hearing the indictment, a great groan rose from the gathering, one woman's voice heard shrieking above the rest imploring the king to spare her Hamish, when from behind The Bruce a small tremulous voice spoke. "Sir, the one in the middle wasn't one of them."

Robert looked at the lad somewhat bemused. "Are you sure, laddie?"

"Yes, sir, the other two were the ones, but he wasn't there," the boy informed Robert with a reassuring nod of his tousled head.

The last of the three accused men was just in the process of having the noose being put in place around his neck when the king shouted, calling a halt to the procedure. Addressing the central of the trio, Robert cupped his hands to be heard above the murmur. "Oi! You in the middle!" he called, staring directly at the fellow. The petrified man looked right and left before realising Robert was talking to him; nodding timidly, he acknowledged he was listening. "This wee laddie tells me you weren't there when his father was murdered, is this true?" Nevertheless, the condemned man couldn't speak properly as the rope was pulled too tightly around his throat to talk, only managing to squeak his response, making the reply gibberish. "Loosen it, man!" the king commanded, pointing out to the captain which one of the accused he wished to question. Understanding what was required of him, he instantly abandoned what he was doing to slacken the taut cord from around the man's throat, his action leaving unfinished the correct positioning of the noose he was applying on the third culprit, but allowing the poor trembling wretch in the middle to reply coherently.

Half-choking on some spittle he collected to ease his sore throat, the hopeful man rasped out his spluttered answer, "No, sire, I was supposed to go, but just as we were leaving my horse threw a shoe, and I was with the farrier when they left."

"Then it's your lucky day! Let him go!" Robert commanded, turning to Thomas, tutting and shaking his head in amazement. "Do you get everything wrong? Sometimes I just can't help but wonder why I ever put you in charge of this place, Thomas!"

With his ugly face screwed up with utter rage and embarrassment at his own failings, Thomas gave a terse order for the executions to go ahead, and with two shoves from the reluctant captain, the men plunged off the edge. One died instantly when his neck snapped, but the other, because of the king's intercession in saving the third, had the noose incorrectly applied and simply strangled to death. Gyrating, spinning and pissing himself on the end of the rope, he slowly turned blue, his blackened bitten tongue lolling out of his bloodied mouth, gurgling and grunting for all of six minutes before finally succumbing to the inevitable.

Without wasting any more time on worthless chatter, Robert and his small retinue departed as quickly as possible from the unhappy grim fortalice, taking with them young Robbie, riding almost on the neck of Walter Grint's destrier. Behind them they left a sad disillusioned garrison, whose only fault was the mismanagement by the miserly, mean-spirited Thomas Dewar. Unwilling to take any blame for the king's displeasure on himself, Thomas administered the punishments for his own shortcomings liberally among his employees. Accusing everyone of disloyalty, he sacked everyone, from the captain to the cook; even the ever-faithful Duncan fell foul of Thomas's swingeing retribution, losing his job, his master's bitter words all but breaking the old servant's heart by a string of poorly aimed, unnecessary and spurious accusations.

The loss of all the senior staff left the castle even less well governed. With only newly promoted green and inexperienced personnel to oversee the running of the stronghold, apathy and chaos ruled, and every last man wanted things to return to the way they were, including Thomas, who rued dreadfully the day he called on the king to do what he could have done so easily himself.

CHAPTER 9

With a renewed bounce in Solomon's rested step, Richard and Yolanda made their way south. Their intention was to go first to Yolanda's home at Market Deeping in Lincolnshire and there hopefully re-unite her with her estranged family, then onwards to Herefordshire and Henry de Bohun's home, to tell his kinfolk about his glorious death at the hands of Robert the Bruce himself.

Feeling slightly downhearted, Richard and Yolanda left Burgh by Sands in Cumbria already missing their new friends Rolfe, Margaret, their eldest daughter Alice, Joan, Robbie and the rest of their happy brood of children, all of whom had been so kind and generous to them. With a tinge of sadness Richard and Yolanda reflected on the hardships ahead for the peasant family, but content at knowing they were much richer after the visit than they ever had been in their whole lives before. Riding away over the brow of a hill on the mighty Solomon, the more comfortably dressed Yolanda and a smartly attired Richard in his rejuvenated polished and oiled armour, craned their necks to catch the last glimpse of the family, a tell-tale plink at the horse's every fourth step, a sure sign that Solomon desperately needed re-shoeing, and so with a great deal of urgency they sought a town with one of the many smithies which littered the countryside, eventually finding one attached to an inn at a small hamlet called Bassenthwaite, near Keswick in Cumbria.

The village was small but a hive of activity, with many people toing and froing, going about their late-afternoon business. The inn proudly sported a rough sign announcing to all who could read that it was called the Cross and Lamb, reinforced for those who couldn't with a crude depiction of something similar to a bow-legged white goat with a cross between its ears, but the most common well-known indication that board and lodgings were to be had within, telling all, whether they were literate or not, was a bunch of sweet laurel leaves hung from the eaves outside the entrance. The arrival of a soldier and his squire riding one horse, dragging a reluctant hairy brindle lurcher whimpering at the end of a long cord to protect the plentiful loose fowl in the hamlet from his jaws, at this particular time wasn't a thing of interest. And because of the English defeat at Bannockburn, it didn't cause a single head to turn as they plodded a little lamely along the dusty main thoroughfare. Who would notice a man-at-arms and his young servant riding pillion, clutching so very tightly round his master's waist? And who could possibly see the satisfaction in the quiet attendant's beautiful green eyes as he felt each intake of the knight's breath?

Thus they rode to the yard of the tavern, dismounting and leading Solomon to the adjacent smithy, parting with a whole two pennies to the soot-stained, honest-looking, burly leather-aproned smith, in payment for a dry stable overnight, some good hay and a few oats for the horse, with the promise of a brand new set of shoes to be in place by first light. Happy that Solomon would be well cared for the night, Richard, Yolanda and Sam entered the tar-blackened smoke-stained portal of the inn. Opening their eyes wide in the dingy half-light to see, they found a very low-ceilinged room with a dreadfully uneven sloping floor. On the furthest wall, and taking up its whole length, a lopsided dresser was stacked to a ridiculous height with a very precarious pile of crockery which looked as if at any moment it might tumble into the room onto the furniture of rough-hewn tables and benches, all of which seemed to be rather short-legged.

The strange interior caused a giggle of amusement from the pair, neither of whom could be described as tall, but had started to wonder if they had inadvertently wandered into a kingdom of dwarves. Their funny-bones were tickled again when a simple three-plank door from a side kitchen burst open, followed by billows of acrid-smelling wood smoke and a coughing, spluttering six-foot-tall willowy man who emerged from the cloud, his reddened eyes watering prodigiously, as he stumbled into the main room of the tavern, cursing and swearing about an annoying downdraught. On seeing he had some early arrivals, he slammed the door shut, trying to hide the confusion within, and walking very peculiarly with his knees slightly bent and his neck thrust forwards at a right angle, ducking every few steps to prevent his bald head from colliding with the beams, he approached the amazed guests.

The strange sight caused even more strangulated mirth from the amused couple as he requested them to take a seat, while wiping two imaginary clean spots on a heavily stained table with a filthy rag. Indicating it was where they should put themselves, the man then disappeared back into the kitchen, opening the same door he came in by, allowing another giant puff of fumes to belch into the already smoke-filled room.

Leaving Richard and Yolanda sitting uncomfortably with their knees pressed hard against the rough underside of the heavy solid oak table, the ever-faithful hound lying close by on the floor, cramped in between their bent legs, they stared at each other in dumb amazement over the table, trying to suppress their obvious amusement. For the first time since Richard had met her, Yolanda seemed happy and light-hearted, as she struggled to contain her rising mirth. Bending forwards, trying to stifle more laughter, Yolanda wanted desperately to say something to Richard; having to put her hand over her mouth to control herself, she gathered her wits together to start again. Leaning across the table, Yolanda just about managed to whisper the reason for the stunted furniture. "It's the floor!" she said, mopping at her moist eyes while trying desperately to control herself.

Feeling rather confused, Richard peered under the table and around the room, seeing nothing amiss; he looked blankly at Yolanda. "What about the floor? It looks all right to me, I can't see anything wrong."

"The furniture hasn't actually got short legs, it's when they clear the fire out," Yolanda explained, chuckling as she pointedly stared over to a large stone hearth where, although it was very warm, a large log was smouldering. Once again bracing herself, she made another attempt not to burst into a fit of the giggles, her tear-filled green eyes twinkling in the gloom, as she clarified the statement. "Instead of taking the ashes outside to get rid of them, they just spread them out; they're about six inches thick!

Peering under the table, Richard gazed round the room to study the floor and noticing that she was in fact correct, added innocently, "I thought we had to climb up a bit of a hill to get in here!"

That was it, the dam burst, Yolanda couldn't contain herself any longer, and she erupted into uncontrollable laughter, dragging the bemused Richard with her, the mixture of smoke and mirth making the tears run freely. The reason for the merriment was totally missed by the host when he returned, backing his way through the now smoke-less kitchen door with a jack of foaming ale in each hand. Bobbing over to the recovering guests, he handed them each a brew for them to enjoy.

As the late afternoon turned into evening the room started to fill up, not with smoke, like before, but with people, all wanting to be served at once. To help him with the rush, the tall landlord had been joined by a short dumpy woman, who Richard assumed was his spouse, and now two people were flitting in and out of the kitchen carrying beakers of liquor, minus any hint of the choking fumes which polluted the room earlier. Richard and Yolanda relished the experience of sitting together as a couple, laughing and joking, watching as the burgeoning motley band of revellers imbibed the strong beer. Getting louder and louder, the visitors took turns in bursting into choruses of unknown ribald songs, telling stories, or some of the more educated reciting poetry, each one meeting with general applause at the finish. During an interlude, after one of the regular performers had finished ruining a perfectly good ballad, one of the louder voices pointed out that the young squires hadn't contributed to the evening entertainment, prompting the whole gathering to join a chant imploring one of them to do a turn. Eventually, the loud appeals forced Richard to apologise for not participating in the amusement, citing his lack of talent as his reason. However, the rowdy clientele refused to accept the lame excuse by booing and hissing at Richard's rebuff, the continuous heckling obliging him to acquiesce to their noisy demands.

Never having stood up in public before, Richard was at a loss of what to do. Standing silently for some time, he tried to think of a suitable act, but after another short period of impatient hand-clapping and jeering, not wanting to disappoint the company and having no talent in the arts, Richard announced to all that because of his lack of ability he merely proposed to tell them the story of the Battle of Bannockburn, turning the jeers to cheers, petering to utter silence as he started.

At first he set the scene, accurately describing the hour before the battle on the first morning, going into minute detail, painting a vivid picture to the hushed gathering, enthralling everyone attending. Even the landlord and his wife, stopped what they were doing, frightened they would miss a word as the story got into the most exciting parts, when Richard told of Henry de Bohun's valiant charge up the hill, and how he was tragically slain by Robert the Bruce himself. The lurid description met with a general gasp of grief from even the hardest hearts amongst the company, and some of the more sensitive openly sobbed when Richard explained every detail of how the English broke and retreated, losing hundreds as they crossed the blood-reddened, corpse-filled burn back to the camp, arriving there with only a scant three-quarters of the army alive to tell the tale. Finally, Richard resumed his seat with applause ringing in his ears, dying away after more than two minutes to a stony silence as everybody stopped to think about what had been said and the lives lost, each person dwelling on the dreadful nature of modern warfare.

Richard was in the middle of taking a well-earned gulp of his beer when the thick Northumberland voice of the landlady inquired almost timidly, "What about the next day, young sir? Have you nothing to tell of the next day?"

Her appeal was instantly joined by the united voices of everybody else who also wanted to hear what transpired on the second day. "Yes what about the next day? Tell us about the next day!" they clamoured as one. The raucous pleas prompted another, but rather less aggressive chorus of chanting from the imbibers, all wanting to be told the story of the second day of the now notorious Battle of Bannockburn. The hosts even promised as much food and ale as Richard and Yolanda could take if he complied with the demand.

The appeals were too many for Richard to refuse, so, begging for five minutes to recover from the telling of the first part of the lengthy saga, Richard stayed in his seat to think what he was going to say, while the owners of the inn replenished everyone's drinking vessels ready to hear the second part of the harrowing tale. Having taken his time to recuperate and imbibe several sips of the strong courage-giving heady liquor, he resumed. Starting the second half by telling about the sleepless night he spent fretting over his lost master, he went on to tell about the meeting with Robert the Bruce, the retrieval of Henry's body and the final battle resulting in the utter rout of the English. All the assembled company listened very carefully to the sad narrative, but none more so than Yolanda, who was moved to tears more than once by the disturbing story.

Daylight had started to turn to dusk by the time Richard had finished the account. The food which had been ready in the kitchen for upwards of an hour had to be served before going too far to be pleasant, and so with a flurry of hustle and bustle, the earthenware platters were hurriedly scooped off the rickety, overloaded dresser and placed in front of each person, quickly followed by a more than adequate portion of steaming stew and a large lump of coarse bread to mop the remnants off the plate with. All the time during the meal Yolanda gawped at her young companion's face in awe, speculating on the horrors his juvenile eyes were too young to have witnessed and wondering what other terrible sights they must have seen.

By the time the ale and the food were finished, it was getting very late and much of the company had started to wander off to their homes, having overstayed their welcome in listening to Richard's hour-long story. As it was for travel-weary Richard and Yolanda, agreeing it was well past time for bed, they made their uncertain way through the gathering gloom to an outside loft above the stables, already prepared by the landlord for them to stay the night in. Feeling slightly unsteady on their feet, they woozily climbed the ladder, carrying Sam with them to retire for the night, all three cuddling down on a tatty mattress to enjoy a deserved night's rest in readiness for an early start. Alas for the hopes of a good sleep, for within minutes of lying down, some voracious hungry fleas, brought by the previous occupant, started mercilessly biting their soft young flesh with a mind to get their own late supper. All night Richard tossed and turned, itching and scratching, trying to rid himself of the unwelcome visitors; unlike Sam, who slept as soundly as ever, oblivious to a few extra of the annoying dining insects. The whole night Yolanda held

Richard extra close, ignoring her personal discomfort, and she stroked his shoulder, trying to lull her brave young war-hero to sleep, eventually succeeding during the wee small hours, when holding him in a loving embrace he drifted into his slumber.

The sleep was short but sweet, as at the crack of dawn Richard's rest was brutally interrupted when five hungry swallow chicks shouted from their mud nest, built in the shared shelter of the barn, clamouring for their breakfast to be brought with as much haste as was possible by the diligent parents, who swooped in and out, each visit heralded with noisy anticipation of the succulent beaks full of the plentiful gnats and midges which plagued the lakeside area.

Still twitching and itching, the trio descended to a well-prepared breakfast of smoked fish, scrambled eggs with some steaming hot freshly made bread and a small portion of beer, eating and drinking all that was put in front of them before settling the tab. Afterwards, more out of a sense of duty rather than a complaint, Yolanda informatively told the landlady of the problem with the lodgings. On hearing about the infestation, the apologetic woman promptly summoned her husband to berate him for allowing a particularly scabby-looking Welshman to stay there a few nights before. Reaching up, she clipped the lofty man around his ear by way of demonstrating her object of blame for their overnight discomfort; and for the first time seeing Yolanda in the light of day, realising that he was actually a her, she gave Richard a long knowing wink before returning to her morning chores.

On entering the smithy to collect Solomon, Richard found the blacksmith affectionately stroking the horse's noble head to stop his anxious fidgeting in his stall. True to the farrier's word, Solomon was well shod, groomed, fed and digested, stomping his new shoes on the cobbles raring to go, wanting to be out where he loved best, with the springy turf under his feet and the horizon in front to aim for. Richard happily gave the man a small tip for the extra trouble he had obviously been to in caring for the mighty horse, whose deep mahogany coat was curried to perfection, his mane laid, and every hint of a knot carefully brushed out of his tail. Feeling thoroughly grubby, as if they had been dragged through a hedge backwards and then eaten alive, Richard and Yolanda left, riding the immaculate gleaming Solomon from the village of Bassenthwaite to resume the journey due south, still infested with the single-minded, vile biting parasites.

After their intimate evening sharing food, ale and stories, in the somewhat comical and less than scrupulously clean Cross and Lamb, Richard and Yolanda set out with a new sense of togetherness. They had only travelled just two miles out of the village and were in the absolute middle of nowhere, when they climbed up a long, sapping, steep hill; reaching the crest, they found in front of them a stunningly breathtaking vista. A sunlit, tree-dotted, verdant slope swept down to a very inviting-looking-extremely long and wide sky blue lake, where the mirrored images of puffy white clouds scurried across the placid lagoon. The perfect reflection only occasionally being broken by rings of ripples as the resident colossal brown trout hit the surface to take some of the hordes of flying insects. On seeing the marvellous sight, Yolanda couldn't help herself but squeal at the vision. Excitingly beseeching Richard and giving him an extra hard squeeze, she started pleading with him to go down and have a closer look at the alluring, refreshing lake. Thinking it would be nice to be near some clean, calm water after the night of torment, Richard acquiesced to her pleas, nudging Solomon to a trot down the incline right up to the stony shallows at the edge of the giant tarn.

Like a shot, Yolanda was off the horse's wide back and, casting her oversize boots to one side, ran barefoot, throwing off her jerkin as she went, into the cool clear water, and in no time was splashing and kicking at the little wavelets with her bare feet. Laughing and screaming with utter pleasure, Yolanda wanted to share the delight with her two friends, so, calling for Richard to join her and clapping encouragement to the reluctant hound, she ran up to him and insistently pleading, dragged at his arm, begging him not to be shy and dismount and come with her into the wonderfully beautiful mountain lake.

The manly part of Richard wanted to stay on Solomon, ignore the incessant itching under his clothes and proceed with the trip. Yet there was still more boy left in him than he realised, the sight of the partly-clad, dripping wet female playing at the water's edge and the lure of the chance of having a little childish fun was more than his torn mind could bare, so with just one more encouraging tug on his hand, he slid out of the saddle to obey her constant pleas and join her in the water. Doffing his heavy armour and removing his old worn-out boots, Richard jumped into the pool bare-chested in only his hose and under-garment to splash alongside Yolanda, calling for a hesitant Sam to come in too. Quickly getting into the spirit of things, Richard was soon wading waist deep, enjoying himself, throwing cupped handfuls of water over Yolanda, soaking her right through, and she was doing likewise to him.

The youngsters' watery frolics were all watched by a perplexed horse, which opted to stay on dry land to munch at the margin of juicy-looking grass and a fearful dog, who eventually succumbed to their encouragement and joined them, having overcome his fear and been lured in by a thrown stick.

All three ended up playing and splashing like the boy, girl and puppy they really were. Although not outwardly showing it, Yolanda was as flea-bitten and uncomfortable as Richard. The morning sun was warm and her clothes needed washing, so, showing no sign of modesty, she clambered out of the water, and politely turning her back to a gawping Richard, stripped off the remaining soaking garb and piled it on the bank. Then, completely undressed, Yolanda returned to her game, bidding Richard to do likewise and remove the rest of his attire so they could play unhampered. Taken in by a moment of madness, Richard only had to think twice before obeying, emboldened by her nude pleas; his shyness and strict morals forgotten, he removed his leg wear and under-garments and, as naked as the day they were born, the teenagers washed away the troubles and tribulations of their young lives, leaving them, along with their last act of childhood, behind with the trout in Bassenthwaite Lake.

Tired out from their energetic games, Richard and Yolanda collapsed laughing and soaking wet on a soft grassy bank, lying flat on their backs as they listened to the rhythmic sounds of Solomon as he tore and chomped at mouthfuls of lush grass, and the panting of Sam, who was doing exactly the same as they were, trying to recover from the watery exertions. For some considerable time they lay, staring at the azure sky, mesmerised by the scudding white clouds as they contorted into familiar shapes in their race from horizon to horizon, and the screaming swifts as they played their own private game of chasing each other in unruly squadrons, ripping through the air after clouds of flying insects.

"This must be the most beautiful place in the world," Yolanda murmured, as she studied a high-flying bird of prey as it lazily wheeled in search of some unsuspecting prey. "This is exactly where I want my mortal remains to spend the rest of eternity!" she added, whilst watching the bird gradually fade into an unidentifiable dot high in the heavens. "Promise me, if anything ever happens to me you'll bring me here," she asked the dozing Richard and, receiving no reply, repeated herself. "Promise you'll bring me here when I die," Yolanda begged again, and, breaking the magic spell, reached out her hand to squeeze Richard's and breathlessly tell him some things she'd been meaning to say for some time. First, she thanked him for rescuing her and bringing her back from the brink of despair, telling him how much she enjoyed his company, almost mustering enough courage to tell him she loved him, when, propping himself on one elbow, Richard attempted to reply.

The words he wanted to say got stuck in his throat when for the very first time he realised his only companion in life was a beautiful young girl, much

127

more to him than just a friend, seeing things about her he had never noticed before. Her shiny damp dark hair and the mischievous bright green eyes which glinted beneath perfectly arched eyebrows over her slender nose and red full-lipped moist mouth, how her pert nippled breasts were stretched tight as she leaned back with her arms thrown wide to absorb the sun's rays. Looking down, he saw Yolanda's slightly extended, tubby, pregnant waistline, and then to the little patch of dark hair which looked so temptingly inviting to the unsullied eyes of poor young Richard, whose erotic imaginings stirred his loins to uncontrollable stiffness. Turning on his side bashfully, he tried to hide his erection from Yolanda, who, on seeing his discomfort, simply smiled and rolled over, to straddle the poor, confused lad, and placing her hand on the cause of the embarrassment. Then staring fixedly into Richard's perplexed eyes she started to massage, slowly and gently at first, increasing the rhythm, plunging the innocent lad into an ecstatic new world of all-consuming joy.

Afterwards, with his adolescent mind in a whirl, Richard felt the compelling necessity to lay back and close his exhausted eyes to snooze in the satisfied afterglow of his first sexual experience. Yolanda watched for a little while as Richard dozed, studying his sleeping face and watching him breathe, wondering what he dreamed about, and praying it was her she leaned forward to plant a huge, surprise, waking kiss on his unwary lips and then, feeling the opportunity presenting itself, she whispered in his ear the thing she had not dared to tell him before, saying and meaning her words, "I love you, Richard, I really do! I don't want to go home; I want to be with you."

Richard didn't know what to say, but in the depths of his young soul the dawning of realisation had set in, at last knowing the truth that in reality he had fallen in love with her when he first saw her, but in his naivety he simply didn't recognise the fact, obliviously ignoring her longing looks and the loving squeezes, but now suddenly aware of the powerful chemistry which existed between them.

With all the clothes washed, painstakingly picked over to de-louse them and half-dried, Richard dressed hastily, leaving off the stifling armour, to watch, with his newfound appreciation of the female form, as his youthful lover struggled back into her damp attire. Yolanda started by battling with the faded damp red leggings, which, having shrunk in the wet, were now too tight. Richard laughed loudly at her impotent efforts to force her shapely legs into them, lying on her back and waving her feet amusingly in the air, tugging and pulling at the clinging garments, succeeding with one final yank and a satisfied, "Yes!"

Happy the leg wear had survived the tussle relatively unharmed, she stood half-naked from the waist up, looking rather like a peculiar pink-legged fowl, as she donned the rest of the outfit much to the hilarity of her grateful admirer. Thinking back, Richard was amazed at his own blindness, wondering how he could have missed the crystal-clear fact that a simple twist of fate had brought the beautiful, intelligent and witty girl to him, uttering an inward prayer of thanks to God for his infinite mercy in sending him the gift, which was the lovely Yolanda.

The day ahead promised to be very hot and long, so with a mind to Solomon's ease and Yolanda's condition, Richard led the horse, allowing her the sole use of the saddle, with the precious armour neatly rolled up and strapped behind her with the bascinet in front on the high pommel. Thus they travelled, chatting, looking at each other, talking openly about the unfortunate predicament she found herself in, Richard swearing to stand by her, with Yolanda promising eternal fidelity in return. All day they journeyed, only making one stop on the trek to eat some stale bread and cheese Richard had bought off the landlady of the inn. After the brief break, they carried on in the same fashion, right up to nightfall, the increasingly sore-footed Richard leading Yolanda on Solomon, making camp at dusk in a sheltered spot some twenty-five miles nearer to home from where they started in the morning.

That night the sleeping arrangements were roughly the same, only instead of always having his back turned to Yolanda, Richard faced her, giving her a long goodnight kiss on the lips, occasionally touching her as she touched him, feeling her smooth skin under her clothes, but never allowing his sexual desire to come to the fore. Explaining to Yolanda his reason for abstinence, assuring her he loved her, but with the ideals of chivalry firmly instilled in him by his old dead mentor, he wanted to be married before properly consummating the relationship.

For the next several days they travelled in the same fashion, Richard always walking, leading Yolanda riding astride the willing Solomon, and Sam, the tousled grey provider of food with his improving sense of obedience, cantering at their heels. Onward they went, always talking and planning their future together. Each day Yolanda showed a little more sign of the baby growing inside her, and each day the hobbling Richard walked a little slower in his failing boots. Eventually, after ten long days' torturous trekking, they at last reached the market town of Melton Mowbray, very close to Yolanda's home in Market Deeping, the place where Yolanda had lived happily with her parents and siblings, until the sad break-up of the family, as described in her own words: "When my father was bewitched by a raven-haired Harpy, who was only interested in his money rather than him."

The afternoon they arrived in Melton Mowbray was a Friday and market day. Everywhere the air was filled with the loud clamouring hustle and bustle of arguing buyers and resolute vendors haggling to sell their wares. Holding hands and barely able to hear themselves think, Richard and Yolanda walked, leading Solomon through the noisy stands, with the much less errant Sam trotting obediently behind as they wandered among the booths inspecting the goods. Wanting to present a decent image to Yolanda's family, Richard paused at a shoe and boot stall to purchase some new shoes for Yolanda, who could barely walk in the dilapidated oversized ones she already had, and buy some sturdy well-made boots for himself to replace the old worn-out ones, parting with a whole shilling to seal the deal. Having seen to the footwear, Richard stopped once again to spend some more of his dwindling supply of money at a second-hand clothes seller to buy Yolanda a more appropriate new outfit to meet with her kin. Finding one which suited her needs, she tried it on behind a ragged, poorly concealing curtain, finding it actually fitted her, but knowing money was tight she offered her old re-vamped one in part exchange; bartering with it and knowing the way of merchants, she received a decent discount, effectively reducing the asked price by a whole tenth.

The day was fast drawing to its close, so Richard decided to find some lodgings for the night, this time enjoying the luxury of having several half-decent inns and taverns to pick from in the busy market town. He provisionally selected the third visited, it possessing the best stabling and the most honest-looking host, but not sealing the deal until inspecting the room to make sure it was reasonably clean and free from vermin, before approving it as fit to spend the night. Partaking of an early supper, both Richard and Yolanda agreed to take to their bed early that night in order to get a good night's sleep in preparation for the short trip to find Yolanda's missing family the next day.

Richard and Yolanda woke early in the morning, brutally roused from their slumber by a sudden squally storm, producing a barrage of enormous hailstones which hammered on the wooden sides of their sleeping quarters, quickly followed by a single blinding flash of lightning and an immediate clap of thunder which shook the entire building to its base. The primeval savagery of the sudden meteorological onslaught immediately snatched them and the rest of the household from their deep sleep, to a shocked and very wide-wakefulness in the blink of an eye. The summer tempest passed in a matter of minutes, but as the eastern sky was already growing pink, Richard and Yolanda decided there was absolutely no gain in trying to get back to sleep.

Eager to get going, the pair went down some rickety stairs to join the landlord with five other early risers, also disturbed by the squall, who had similarly opted to make an early start. Being told to take a table to dine at, they were soon presented with a delicious slice of spiced local pork pie, some pickled cabbage and a beaker of home-brewed ale to break their fast. Eating it quickly and paying their tab, they asked the landlord to have the horse readied for the departure while they quickly went about their ablutions, Richard donning all his meticulously shone armour to look his best at the prospect of meeting and trying to impress Yolanda's estranged relations, before going outside to fetch Solomon.

As arranged with the host, the horse was tacked-up, ready and waiting exactly at the appointed time. However, instead of the tolerably eager Solomon Richard was used to, the horse was dripping in sweat and fractiously bucking and kicking out in fear, not yet having recovered from the terrifyingly noisy storm. Considering the danger involved in riding a stirred-up, highly bred horse, Richard decided he alone would mount and take some of the steam out of the animal before allowing Yolanda on board. Coolly, Richard took the jig-jogging Solomon around the square ten or so times, the free sideshow attracting a small crowd of early worms, who watched agog as the fractious creature squelched through the sodden muddy streets, Richard gently chiding the disobedient beast with soft admonishing tones, ignoring the occasional bucking and leaping. Looking like a veritable Paladin, he gently calmed Solomon to his normal self before showing off slightly to demonstrate the horse's regained obedience with a circuit of Spanish Walk before halting where Yolanda, the landlord and a group of others stood clapping in admiration at the consummate horsemanship of the young squire.

Satisfied that any danger was past, Yolanda took her usual place behind the saddle where, as normal, she clasped Richard around his waist ready to ride off. Unable to resist just another little show of his equestrian skills, Richard urged Solomon into the restricting bit and demonstrated a few paces of passage before he departed, half-passing left and right, causing another round of applause from the audience before he disappeared out of sight on his way to Market Deeping.

The weather was perfect for travelling, the storm had cleared the air, which was pleasantly warm with just enough breeze to ruffle the high-summer leaves, and even at a gentle walk, a fully recovered Solomon covered the twenty miles in less than four hours, across undulating terrain from Melton Mowbray to the village where Yolanda was brought up. The nearer they got to Market Deeping, the more familiar the surroundings became to Yolanda, who squeezed Richard a little tighter at each turn of the road, transmitting her frightened trembles all the way through the mail armour and padding to the rider. At one stage Richard even resorted to asking her to release the vice like grip so that he could breathe properly, Yolanda slackening it only slightly to retain as much contact with her beloved as possible.

On they rode, making their way through a dense copse called Langtoft Woods, when suddenly the trees thinned and the little town popped up in front of them, its sight causing another mighty shudder to shake the whole of Yolanda's body. Leaning her head a little closer to speak to Richard, she whispered to him to let him know her innermost feelings, "I'm terrified of seeing my father. What am I going to say to him?" Yolanda needed to repeat the question twice, speaking louder each time, trying to be heard through the padded bascinet, ending up shouting the sentiment directly into the hearing holes of the helmet, making Richard jump as he turned Solomon's head to go down the main street.

Obeying a mighty signalling thump on his shoulder from his passenger, Richard pulled up to halt outside what was once clearly a very impressive merchant's house, which was now in a state of awful disrepair and desperately needed some extremely urgent attention. With Yolanda's delicate condition in mind, Richard helped her down from the lofty Solomon, easing her landing as she put her feet once again on the strangely forbidding ground. Giving a snotty-nosed urchin of about ten years old a shiny penny to hold the horse, Richard offered Yolanda a supporting arm as they hesitantly walked towards the ramshackle dwelling. The unusual occurrence of a fully-armed knight, his lady, a mighty destrier and their dog arriving at the dilapidated old house attracted some nosier of the few neighbours to come and gawp. One of them, a lad just a few years younger than Richard, recognised Yolanda and shouted excitedly to gain her attention. "It's me, Simon Byrde. You remember me, don't you?"

Knotting her brow, Yolanda tried to recall who the oddly familiar, scruffy teenage boy with tousled red curly hair, friendly greyish-blue eyes and a heavily freckled face could be. Delving through the muddled confusion of the past three years and thinking hard who he was, she suddenly came up with the answer, pointing an outstretched finger at the sky with inspiration. "Yes, I remember, you used to help my father sometimes, when he was busy. You liked the smell of nutmeg a lot if I remember correctly, didn't you?"

"Yes that was me; have you come to see your poor father?"

"Why do you call him my poor father? Is he unwell?" Yolanda asked, thinking her father had a disease or something similar.

"Not ill exactly, more like not there. Come with me, I'll show you," he excitedly yelled, then like an arrow shot from a bow the garrulous adolescent raced through the rickety door into the building. Beckoning Richard and Yolanda to follow, he plunged into one of the inner rooms which Yolanda recognised as being the old spice store. Opening the door, they were hit with a heavenly blast of the combined smell of pepper, nutmeg, sweet cinnamon and all the other various spices which had once been stored there, but most of all, and much stronger than the rest, was the unmistakable fragrant aroma of cloves. The boxes and sacks of the actual spices were long gone, but their essence stayed as strongly as if they were still there. In the main, the dark and grimy, oak-panelled walls and dusty ochre-coloured sandstone-floored room appeared empty. Except that is, where an errant ray of light shone from a hole in the ceiling where the thatch was damaged and cutting through the murk it illuminated a few broken old crates stacked under a closed and shuttered broken mullioned window. However, as Richard and Yolanda's eyes grew accustomed to the gloom, they could just about see that propped in the corner facing into the room and sitting in a once-expensive but now tatty chair, was a late middle-aged man, completely still and unmoving, staring fixedly straight and for all intents and purposes apparently unaware of the intruders.

With a huge grin splitting his speckled face, the lad looked triumphantly at Yolanda while pointing to the sitting man through the gloom. "Your father. I think he doesn't see or hear anything. Look!" he exclaimed, and to demonstrate, waved his hand in front of the scraggy shell of the man's face, receiving no visible response. "As I told you, nothing there!" Simon pointed out, taking Yolanda's hand to lead her nearer to the living corpse, hoping she'd recognise the withered form of the once-chubby red-faced man she used to call father.

Leaning very close, she felt the skeletal face to verify if it was him or not, as if expecting a reply from the stricken man. "Is it you, Daddy?" she asked, peering closer to get a better look with her acclimatising vision. Still unsure, Yolanda had another feel of the bony visage to make certain. "It is you, it's you, Daddy! Whatever happened?" Yolanda questioned, sympathetically stroking her father's unresponsive hand, having already forgiven the man who had been bewitched into treating her so dreadfully.

Receiving no visible response from her father, Yolanda turned to Simon to ask him if he could clarify what was going on. "How long has he been like this?" she begged, fighting to control her emotions.

"He's been like this since his wife left him over two years ago. We think he likes to be in here," Simon explained, lowering his voice to a whisper and holding a hand in front of his mouth to direct the sound at Yolanda. "My mother thinks she poisoned him," he added with a knowing nod.

"She's gone? Where are my brothers and sisters if she's gone?" Yolanda enquired, looking round as if one of her siblings was going to pop up from somewhere at any moment.

"They're all at work; they have to, there's no money otherwise. She stole it all when she went! My mother feeds him and keeps her eye on him during the day; she thinks he watches her, but I don't."

"I need to speak with your mother, I think," Yolanda added, precisely at the same moment as her father, who had remained completely silent for the whole two years, suddenly grunted twice, the unexpected noise even making Simon jump.

"I've never heard him do that before. I'd better tell my mother." With that, he hurtled off like a scalded cat to fetch Yolanda's father's chief carer. Meanwhile feeling aghast that the blighted man was virtually imprisoned in the gloomy airless room, in something resembling an apology of a tantrum, Richard started battling to open the nailed-closed shutters. His strenuous effort becoming rewarded when, in an attempt to prise one open with his dagger, the corroded, seized hinge unexpectedly produced a shrill scream as it reluctantly acquiesced to the leverage and burst open, releasing it and its partner with a wafting, choking eddy from the years of accumulated, residual clogged dust of the mixed spices, allowing both fresh air and bright sunshine to stream into the dark, stuffy room.

The influx of light, making it easy for Yolanda to see that her father, instead of being merely a shrunken, lifeless hulk, was actually able to communicate and was fully aware of what was going on around him. Sadly for Yolanda, who was becoming increasingly more distraught by the second, her father was completely and utterly motionless in all departments, apart from his eyes, which clearly needed a great effort to move but seemed to be trying to say the things his immobile body couldn't. Yet, knowing him best of all the brothers and sisters, she instantly recognised he had something very important that he desperately needed to tell her. Feeling desperately sorry for her entombed father, Yolanda peered very closely at him to find out exactly what he was tacitly trying to articulate and after spending some considerable time concentrating on his almost invisible endeavours, she started making some sense of the silent message. Speaking to him all the time, Yolanda both asked questions and gave their answers out loud for Richard to hear. "First of all, I think he's trying to say he's sorry for making me go, but he keeps looking at the panels over near the window. What's over there? What are you trying to say, Daddy? There, he's doing it again, look!"

Richard leant forward to see and, noticing the merest hint of a very slight movement in the old man's fixed iris, he agreed with Yolanda. "There's definitely something over there he wants you to look at. Ask him again?"

"What is it, what are you trying to say, Daddy?" she asked, as Richard crossed the room to where the spent and tired man's clouding eyes appeared to be transfixed on an area somewhere just below the open window.

Choosing a position near to what he thought might be the probable spot, Richard started sidestepping six inches at a time, while Yolanda studied her father, searching for any sign that he was in the correct place. The faintest of grunts emanating from somewhere deep in the fast wearying man's stomach gave Yolanda the cue to shout an urgent, "Stop there!" to Richard, who instantaneously halted mid-shuffle with one foot still in the air adjacent to some broken boxes thrown in front of one of the panels. "Is that it? Is that where you want us look, Daddy?" she implored, staring intently into her father's eyes and noticing a slight tell-tale flicker which suggested it was.

Having made sure Richard was positioned in exactly the correct spot as indicated by her fast-fading weary father, Yolanda relayed the message to him. "That's where he wants you to look. I'm sure he wants you to look behind those crates," she informed Richard, whilst planting a huge daughterly kiss on her father's sad old wrinkled forehead, before he yielded to his energy-sapping efforts and went to sleep.

Without delay, Richard obediently kicked aside the boxes and started scrabbling at a loose panel of partly rotten, green-tinged and badly mildewed wood; easily splitting it with his dagger, he revealed an eighteen inch square, heavily carved dark wooden coffer covered in a thick aromatic rind of coagulated spicy dust. Lifting the weighty chest from its gloomy cubbyhole, Richard took it over to where Yolanda's exhausted father was now completely unconscious but still open-eyed, with his sad glazed sleeping orbs staring vacantly in front.

Suddenly, Yolanda looked inspired by the sight of the box. "I remember! That was his secret place. I caught him putting stuff in there when I was about eight. He told me it was for his old age and he made me swear never to tell anyone about it, not even my mother. Quickly, open it!" she commanded, and, as there was no sign of a key, Richard gathered his strength to raise the coffer above his helmeted head and hurled it with all his might onto the stone floor. Hitting the hard surface, it burst asunder, spraying its contents all over the floor like a shower of crushed winter ice, in an assorted mixture of silver and gold coins rattling and glittering on to the flagstones. Richard and Yolanda looked at each other in shocked silence as the last coin rolled in ever-decreasing circles, eventually spiralling to rest with a gentle musical tinkle.

The resulting stunned silence was broken when Richard declared that he'd never seen so much wealth in one place at the same time, exaggerating the amount, and getting closer to the truth than he realised by remarking, "It's like King John's lost treasure; there's enough to last you the rest of your life."

Sporting a little wry smile, Yolanda summed things up succinctly by adding one of her thoughts, whilst furrowing her brow as she struggled with her eyes on stalks to read the strange angular foreign writing on a gold bezant. "It's a sure thing that witch didn't know about it; otherwise it would have gone with the rest when she did!"

CHAPTER 10

Within the cold, wet bowels of Dunstaffnage Castle, deep in the dim lit dungeon and locked away in an eight-foot-square iron cage for his own safety, frightened, frozen and wounded, but lucky to be alive, Lawrence Buckenham whiled away his captivity. With only a single shaft of light shining through the small grating on the door to illuminate the noisome cell, he had nothing to do but plan his dire revenge on Richard de Mauville and the filthy whore whose name he'd already forgotten, but now had convinced himself they were both guilty of cowardly stabbing him and leaving him to die in agony in the wilds of Scotland.

Up until a little earlier, Lawrence had shared the foetid cell with a bunch of wild-looking Scottish captives and was only separated from them by the bars of his cage, but as their hated English enemy, they perpetually subjected him to a tirade of verbal abuse, to say nothing of the regular showers with their bodily waste, all of them suddenly disappearing, leaving him totally alone with only his thoughts for company.

Lawrence was in the process of inanely studying a six-inch-long, giant amber slug as it made its slimy way across a small lit patch on the algae-covered wall, marvelling at how it became almost see-through in the bright spot as it deposited its twinkling silver trail amid the green. His odd pastime becoming noisily interrupted when, without any warning and with an echoing strident screech, the iron-studded rust-stained door was thrown open, allowing a welcome gust of refreshing fresh air and a wider beam of light into the gloomy prison. The sudden influx of brightness made the gloom-accustomed prisoner blink as he peered to see who the unexpected interloper was, instantly recognising the shape as the silhouetted outline of his gaoler. Giving no explanation, the guard grabbed Lawrence's arm and, saying nothing, he dragged him out of the cage and up some slippery damp spiral stairs to a room he reckoned was about fifty feet above the dungeon. Opening the door and using slightly less brutality than usual, the guard shoved Lawrence in, locking the door securely behind him, adding even more confusion and doubt into his already befuddled mind.

The room itself was virtually a prison in its own right, only ten foot across with cold plain walls of un-plastered roughly dressed stone. The main physical difference between it and the cell was the fact that it was relatively dry and quite bright, as there was a small barred glassless window facing out to the sparkling blue sea; but the most noticeable difference, in contrast to the thick polluted air of the cell, was a pleasantly refreshing chilly salt breeze which blew straight off the ocean and in through the window. The furnishings in the chamber at the very least could only be described as spartan, consisting of a low lumpy straw bed with some mangy-looking half-bald animal skins as blankets, a three-legged milking stool for a seat and on a wobbly table with a badly repaired leg, a plate of cheerless cold meats was placed. Yet, after having been virtually starved in the cramped filthy conditions of the cage, to Lawrence it was heaven on earth.

For ten minutes Lawrence inspected his new quarters, walking around, stretching his cramped limbs, chewing on the tough meat. Having made his best attempt to masticate and swallow the inedible gristle, he silently mused on his captivity while gazing out at the Atlantic rollers, watching them break on the shore and listening to the screaming seagulls as they argued over some kitchen scraps, enjoying the prickly air and the refreshing clean smell of the salty spume as the waves crashed with towering pillars of white foam on the craggy rocks at the base of the lofty Dunstaffnage Castle.

Lost in the little world of his own, Lawrence was pondering on what was beyond the sea, when his moment of quiet meditation was very suddenly interrupted by the sound of some noisy grunting and clattering, accompanied by several more sets of heavy footsteps and a lot of swearing in Gaelic, which could be heard coming up the stairs in his direction. Fearing his last moment had come, Lawrence felt relieved when, with the scrape of a key in the lock, the door was flung open to reveal a pair of heaving and straining scruffy servants manhandling a large cut-off wooden barrel into the room. Close behind them, a pursuing host of annoyed-looking soldiers reluctantly carried pails of steaming water and some clean drying cloths for Lawrence; then, glaring evilly at the enemy knight they poured the hot water into the makeshift bath. Having made everything ready for Lawrence to clean his befouled body, the servants and soldiers departed with not even so much as a grunt as they locked the door behind them. Their absence left the badly confused captive alone to peel off his soaked and heavily fouled garb, retching more than once when he saw what the disgusting nature of the filth was. He was in the middle of removing his brown-stained undergarments when, with the sound of another key in the lock, the door was opened again.

of the less-developed but older blonde girl. Beckoning for her to approach, he reached out and grabbed the lass by the wrists to drag her struggling on to the bed. Holding her down spread-eagled by her arms, Lawrence kicked her skinny legs apart, grunting and heaving as he tried to gain entry, causing the otherwise silent child to squeak and squeal with stifled pain as he made his clumsy efforts to penetrate her, prematurely ejaculating with the built-up excitement, mercifully saving the poor lass from prolonged rape, when he rolled off in his less-than-fit state, once again thwarted in his sexual ambitions.

Remembering he was due to attend supper with his captor, Lawrence decided to dress; sorting through the motley collection of clothes he selected a suitable outfit, moodily kicking the rest of the blameless garments into a haphazard heap under the window. Badly frustrated by his sexual failure and too weak to make another attempt, Lawrence broodily resumed the vacant staring out to sea; with yet another problem corrupting his evil mind, he ignored the terrified girls' attempt to comfort each other by huddling under the skins for warmth. Completely absorbed in his own private world of lust and revenge, Lawrence didn't even hear the rattle of keys when, still grumbling about his ailing back, the same servant arrived to inform Lawrence that supper would be ready in half an hour. Stopping on the way out, the bad-tempered minion shot a lecherous leer with a supporting snigger towards the quaking lasses hiding in the rugs, telling Lawrence he would bring them some food, adding with a depraved guffaw that he thought they would need it to keep their strength up. Turning to finally leave, he disappeared, rubbing the seat of the pain in his back, his shoulders twitching up and down, giggling at the girls' unfortunate plight.

Twenty minutes after departing, the grouchy butler returned, this time opening the door to throw in a wooden bowl of kitchen scraps for the girls and moaning bitterly about the hundreds of stairs he had to keep going up and down to go back and forth to the room. Temporarily forgetting about his ailment, he held out an indicating arm and gave a mock bow of reverence to Lawrence, signifying it was time for supper, instantly clutching the small of his back and, with another groan of pain, slammed the door shut, and turning the key, sealed the girls in the chamber to wait for Lawrence's return. Happy they were unable to escape, he bade the reluctant guest to urgently follow him through the labyrinth of tunnels to where his hungry master and recently royally rebuked host, Thomas Dewar, sat still smarting from his run-in with the king and was impatiently waiting for his visitor to arrive at the table.

The route through the disgusting warren of passages below the keep of Dunstaffnage Castle was an adventure in itself. With nothing but the feeble light from a single flickering flambeau to guide their way, the unwilling escort and his amazed follower descended into the pitch-black tunnel. Doing his best to stay in touch with the scurrying guide, Lawrence hurtled at what seemed like a break-neck speed through the narrow maze, ducking the slimy festoons of clinging foul green and black algae, trying not to slip on the wet flagstones, or brush against the dripping stone walls. Seemingly even more disturbed than Lawrence, the grumpy usher moaned about everything as he squelched along, parting the revolting stagnant weed curtains for his guest as he went, his pattering soaked feet paddling through pools of stagnant water, frightened to arrive late with his charge and aggravate his unforgiving master further.

Puffing and panting from their subterranean exertions, they eventually reached a small flight of stairs which led into the comparatively well-lit hall, to be greeted by the faithful old Duncan, once again re-employed in his role of Thomas's personal servant, reinstated apparently because there was nobody else either stupid or brave enough to take on the poisoned chalice. Clearing his throat to speak in his best voice, Duncan yodelled his pompous address loudly to attract his master's attention and make himself heard above the sound of the newly made-up fire's crackling up the chimney. Sitting alone at the head of a newly polished trestle table, dogs at his feet amid a sea of fresh green rushes in the hastily cleaned and cleared hall, Thomas looked round to assess the newcomer and see if his commands had been obeyed. Kicking his foot rhythmically against the table's leg with impatience, Thomas listened as the windy, rather overly formal introductions were made.

"If it please my noble Lord Sir Thomas Dewar, High Constable to King Robert the Bruce's mighty and most favoured Castle of Dunstaffnage, Sir Lawrence Buckenham is here to be received at his table to discuss the terms for his release."

Showing his dislike of unnecessary formalities, Thomas shouted above the minion's voice, halting the speech halfway through. "Enough! Sit him down, here where I can see him," Thomas insisted, waving a grubby hand roughly in the direction of some rather tatty old chairs.

Instantly obeying the order, not wanting to incur the wrath of his master twice in one day, Duncan pulled out a seat adjacent to a tallow candle for Lawrence to sit at. For some considerable while, captor and captive sat just looking at each other, not knowing what to say, until Thomas broke the ice with an outrageous lie. "I hope you're feeling better now? I think I owe you an apology?"

"What's that for?" Lawrence asked, not being sure where the brief conversation was heading.

"For your captivity. I was told that you were just an ordinary English man-at-arms; they didn't tell me that you were a noble gentleman until this afternoon, and that's why I sent you your little presents," Thomas informed the incredulous Lawrence, while rubbing his grubby hands together and almost drooling at his sadistic mental picture of the two naked girls having their virginity brutally ripped from them. "Pretty little things, nice eyes, shame about the tits! Inspected them myself, didn't fuck them, mind! Couldn't resist a little feel though. Both well fucked, are they?" Thomas questioned, grinning a spicy look over to Lawrence, while nodding positively, with a mind on his guest's pleasure.

Not wanting to admit his inadequate attempt to have sex with the girls, Lawrence merely licked his lips and indicated his thanks by raising his eyebrows, adding almost as an afterthought, "Yes, thank you, my lord, they were delicious!" he crowed, the lie however reinforced his resolve to make sure the deed was done properly when he returned to the room that night.

During the meal, Thomas quickly warmed to his dinner guest, finding in him a kindred spirit, even more so when the captive's tongue became loosened by large amounts of strong sweet mead. Very soon Thomas recognised they had a lot in common, as Lawrence was blessed with the same mean sadistic nature and a taste for the younger female that he also had. The single-minded discussion was only heading one way when Thomas asked Lawrence to tell him about some of his other sexual exploits. More than willingly, the vile Englishman proudly obliged, at first relating some of his old tried and tested stories of sexual abuse and subsequent escape from vengeful fathers, the host relishing every miniscule juicy detail, hanging on every word of the heavily embroidered tales which described the de-flowering of virgins, most of them far too young to know they were being seduced by his velvet tongue. Getting into the swing of the sordid conversation, Thomas started to excitedly beg to be told more defined details about all the gory particulars, of how they screamed when penetrated for the first time, or if they bled when forced into and other finer points concerning Lawrence's other conquests with underage females.

At long last, Lawrence felt happy, pleased to have found someone who actually cared to hear the depraved stories as he basked in his element, re-living the events of the generally exaggerated yarns about his manly prowess with the helpless girls. After an hour of listening to Lawrence stirring himself with the descriptions, Thomas surprised him, when suddenly and without warning, he seemingly lost interest in the tales, and out of the blue Thomas bade him goodnight, as without prior warning he'd decided to take his leave and retire to bed. His absence leaving the bemused guest in the capable hands of Duncan, to be escorted back to the chamber to vent his arousal on the two innocents, soundly asleep under the rugs, unaware that climbing up the stairs up to the room with ominous bestial intent was Lawrence, bent on proving to himself his manly desires had returned.

The deeply sleeping girls barely stirred when Lawrence entered the room. With only a shaft of moonlight from the tiny window to illuminate their untainted slumbering shapes, they looked blissfully happy, smiling sweetly in their idyllic dreamland, where loving parents, brothers, sisters and favourite pets were there to comfort them; only to be rudely awakened by the rampant male, who with absolutely no care whatsoever, ripped the covering off their huddled bodies, bathing them in the eerie glow and startling them to sudden wakefulness before stripping the hopefully easier to penetrate, younger dark-haired adolescent, and reveal her china-like pure naked form cowering in the strange fluorescent light. With wide and sleepy eyes, the innocent child looked up at her assailant, rubbing them to focus as the degenerate pounced on her. Using all his strength he pushed her sister aside to pin the shocked victim on the bed, then, carelessly brutalising her thin little legs apart, he thrust his already erect penis savagely into the girl. Indifferent to which orifice he found, he started pumping at the screeching child, soon coming with a colossal groan. Rolling off the shattered girl, Lawrence spurned her from the bed with his foot so that he could rest alone and in peace, leaving a great gory dark purple patch amid the silver-blue where she'd had her virginity so cruelly ripped from her. Satisfied with his brave conquest, Lawrence plunged into something resembling an alcohol-induced coma, to sleep as soundly as a dormouse, ignoring the piteous moaning of his young victim as she sobbed in the arms of her older sister. Who, rocking back and forth, shared her pain and grief whilst trying to staunch the flow of blood from her bruised and battered nether regions, eventually both going to sleep where the pleasant dreams were replaced by horrific nightmares of bloody violence and the deserved inhuman death of the predatory Lawrence.

At the very first sign of the eastern sky lightening to dawn, every single gull, raven or the many other varieties of cliff-dwelling birds on the craggy rocks in the vicinity of Dunstaffnage, decided to herald the coming day as one. And within five minutes of the initial squawk, all had joined in a cacophony of shrieked screams, becoming worse as all the adults took off to find food, causing all the chicks to start shouting with their undeveloped voices for their absent parents' return in a range of varying notes worthy of the accursed bagpipes themselves. Lawrence, a little worse for wear having drunk too much the night before, blocked his ears, trying to muffle the rumpus's incursion into his throbbing head, but no matter how he tried, the noise was still there and for one brief moment he wished he was back in the peaceful solitude beneath ground in the quiet dungeon, soon changing his mind when he remembered the cramped dank conditions of the cell.

Cuddled together, snuggling under the heap of surplus clothes for warmth beneath the window, the two quaking girls pretended to be fast asleep, making their best attempt to remain invisible and shield themselves from the keen westerly wind which was whistling though the bars. Hearing their tormentor stir, they gripped each other a little tighter, each wondering what next would be his pleasure.

Still very sore and weepy after the rape, the younger sister couldn't help but whimper with fear at the prospect of being subjected to a repeat performance, but aware that any noise would probably remind Lawrence of their presence, her caring sibling soothed her to silence by stroking her dark hair. Nevertheless, the noisy birds had got their way, and no matter how deeply Lawrence buried himself beneath the covers in an attempt to block out the raucous clamour, it still invaded his head, eventually forcing him to acquiesce to the uproar and rise early from his bed.

Fully awake and bored, he had two options, which was either to gaze aimlessly out to sea and count the waves as they rolled in, or amuse himself with one or both of the girls. Deciding on the second alternative, Lawrence set about repeatedly kicking the heap to disturb the apparently sleeping pair. With a sense of self-protection from the increasingly more savage kicks, the older less-developed lass obeyed, pulling her smaller sister to her feet to stand in front of Lawrence, who up to then barely had any recall of the events of the previous night, until he noticed the patch of dried blood on the girl's gown, bringing the whole series of events back fresh in his perverted mind. Seeing the bigger-breasted, dark-haired lass was in no fit state to amuse him, he opted for the flat-chested one. Ripping off the gauzy garment to reveal her childlike nakedness, he threw her on the bed with a mind to accomplish what he had failed to achieve the previous afternoon.

To save herself from the cruelty she had witnessed her sibling suffer, without prompting, the girl screwed up her eyes in anticipation of the pain, opened her legs as wide as she could to fully expose herself, and, gritting her teeth, she prepared for Lawrence to enter her if he could. In his partially hung-over state it took more than a little encouragement to achieve an erection, so rubbing himself feverishly, Lawrence managed something like a semi-hard, and satisfied it was about the best he could accomplish, the monster attempted to shove it in, failing dismally, and after three fruitless attempts he slapped the terrified girl hard, blaming her for his inadequacies.

Commanding her to lay still, Lawrence was about to try again when the familiar sound of keys rattling in the lock disturbed him. With a huge degree of relief, knowing completing the job at hand was totally out of the question, Lawrence looked up gratefully to see who had just interrupted him. It not being much of a surprise when he saw the same grumpy servant he had met the previous evening standing above him, who, clearing his throat, sarcastically addressed the heaving lump of flesh.

Barely bothering to hide the rising amusement in his tetchy voice, the man spoke mockingly to the frustrated Lawrence. "I see you're having lots of fun, my lord," he noted, sniggering quietly, then, scanning the room, he allowed his gaze to dwell on the tearful bloodstained lass huddled under the window and then onto the other on the bed, before speaking again in the same testy tone to emphasise his impatience. "Enjoyed yourself, sir? I'd hate to be the one to spoil your morning exercise, but my master is at this moment waiting for you at breakfast in the main hall, so if you wouldn't mind, I would be obliged if you would put it away, pull up your hose and follow me before he grows impatient."

Realising the seemingly polite request was in fact a command, Lawrence rearranged his tousled attire to make himself decent to follow the butler. Turning on his way out, he shot a menacing look at the still-unsullied blonde girl and, pledging her he would come back to resume where he had left off, departed from the room, leaving the terrified girls clutching each other in utter dread of the child abuser's promised return.

His guide was obviously better tempered later in the day than he was first thing, and bombarding Lawrence with a string of complaints about everything from the annoying moonlight the previous night to the accursed kitchen stove which refused to light, he led the mystified guest through the same maze of tunnels to where Thomas was waiting, ready to eat, with the ever-ready Duncan standing silently at his side, ready to fulfil his master's every wish.

The lord of the castle seemed pleased to see Lawrence as he looked up from taking a sip from his regular morning tumbler of mulled wine. Screwing up his face and shuddering at the unpleasant taste, Thomas greeted him with a snigger and, wiping a long icicle of running morning mucus from his nose with his sleeve's crusted cuff, he observed the customary morning niceties. "Did you have a good night's sleep?" Thomas chuckled answering the question himself while sniffing at his runny nose. "Of course you fucking did, with those little beauties to keep you warm, who wouldn't?" and then pausing to inspect his snot-covered sleeve, he continued before Lawrence could answer, "I hope you fucked them long and properly, 'cause you won't be seeing them again."

"Why's that, my lord? You're not putting me back in your dungeon, are you?" Lawrence asked tremulously, as a new wave of dread swept over him, frightened his brutal rape of the little girl had merited a new spell of incarceration in the squalid prison cell.

His fears were soon allayed by Thomas, who seeing his new friend's discomfort, answered to put his mind at rest, "No, not to the dungeon. It's because I like you that I've decided to release you, but first you're going to Stirling to collect a package for King Robert, and then you're going home to deliver it."

"What about my ransom?" Lawrence queried, confused as to why he was going to be freed without the customary large payment from his family.

"Fuck the ransom! It's as I told you, I'm letting you go because I like you, but you must deliver the package. Do you promise?"

"Yes, of course I'll deliver it," he replied, incredulous at the recent string of good fortune and hoping it was going to continue.

Fed up with the present conversation, Thomas decided to change tack to one more to his liking. Giggling in his drink, he looked up at Lawrence to glory in the previous night's abuse. "My man Stuart tells me you fucked one of the girls bloody; just a virgin or maybe a bit too tight! Good was she?"

"I'm sorry about that. I think I might have ruined her, the other one's all right though," Lawrence regretfully informed his host and was about apologise further, when his confession was cut short by Thomas butting in. "I don't care if you fucked them to death! They were only English bitches anyway, captured last week on a raid. I was saving them for my own little bit of fun when I get better," Thomas replied but suddenly stopped, thinking he had already said too much.

"Better?" Lawrence inquired. "You're ill?"

"Just a little man problem," Thomas lied uncomfortably as Duncan deliberately gave the game away by surreptitiously nodding at his master's crotch and simultaneously cleared his throat knowingly. The implied inference incurring a tirade of verbal abuse to issue from an embarrassed Thomas, who glared menacingly at Duncan. "You can fuck off, you know-it-all cunt! Fuck off and fetch some decent sweet fucking wine, not that cheap vinegar you're trying to fucking poison me with!" he railed, then to emphasise his point, Thomas carelessly hurled the full flagon of offensive liquor across the table to Duncan, who simply caught the thrown missile without spilling a drop; then, unmoved by the insults, the old retainer trudged off to fetch a very different beverage. "Can't have any fucking secrets with him about; the nosey old cunt knows all my private business." Feeling a bit more than annoyed at knowing that his personal problem was now public knowledge, Thomas resumed eating his breakfast in silence, unwilling to say any more, lost in his own sulky self-pity, having been so recently reminded about his inability to rouse his useless dysfunctional manhood to anything remotely resembling stiffness.

After only a very brief period of absence, Duncan came scurrying back with a full pitcher of wine; going over to the fire, he quenched a previously heated red-hot poker in it to warm the drink. Satisfied it had reached the desired temperature, he offered some for his master to try.

Sipping it, Thomas nodded his head with approval. "That's better. Here, try this, Lawrence."

Obeying straight away, Duncan cantered around the table with a bit of a spring in his step, struggling to hide a secret little smirk as he filled Lawrence's goblet, who smacked his lips in agreement. Satisfied the lords were now happy with the brew, Duncan then retired to his place, looking over his master's shoulder, inwardly laughing to himself, wondering how on earth half a pint of Thomas's own stale urine could so dramatically improve exactly the same wine he had left with.

Breakfast done and digested, the goodbyes said and done with, it was time for Lawrence to join the two allotted guards already mounted in the courtyard waiting for him to arrive, trying to calm their impatient steeds fractiously stamping their hooves and fidgeting in their anxiety to get going. Somewhat tardily, as having vainly spent too much time on his own appearance, Lawrence rode proudly into the yard on the same badly broken, oddly marked and still bad-tempered horse he owned before, which during his time in the dungeon had been given as a reward to one of the men-at-arms at the castle. Delighted with the valuable gift, the soldier spent all his spare time re-training the wayward beast, improving it beyond belief, only to have it confiscated and returned to its English owner, a much better-schooled horse than the one he got. Looking every inch a lord, and wearing a welcome gift from Thomas of a fashionable red-plumed, visored bascinet completing his armour, Lawrence eventually took place in the yard with his escorts, who as instructed by Robert were two of the best fighting men in Dunstaffnage Castle. Dressed cap-a-pie in shining steel, with bright colourfully painted shields and gaily pennoned lances held high, they looked like Galahad and Percival in the bright morning sun. Positioning themselves either side of their charge, all three rode out of the main gate, observed with interest by all, but more so by the two little blue-eyed wan faces crammed cheek by jowl, peering through the little window on the tower, relieved to see their hated countryman disappear, hopefully for good.

The trip to Stirling on fresh and rested horses took less time than expected, only having to make one overnight stop at a comfortable inn in the village of Inverarnan, just north of Loch Lomond on the foothills of the Trossachs. Having slept well, all three got up early to make the arduous last twenty miles across the rugged countryside to Stirling Castle. Outside, the weather had changed, and instead of the hot oppressive summer sun, which everyone had got used to of late, a fresh westerly had blown in a short spell of miserable misty drizzle over the high ground, too light to shelter from, but persistent enough to eventually soak through the sturdiest of garments.

With the horses' tails clamped firmly between their hind legs to protect their backsides from the prevailing wind, the sodden group of three made their damp way southwest across the formidable hilly terrain of the Trossachs. For four hours they rode in the low grey clouds capping the high terrain of the mountainous area. The scudding mizzle chapped their wet behinds, making them stick uncomfortably to the soaked saddle, and even through the sturdy boots their calves were pinched red and sore on the tacky stirrup leathers. Finally reaching the top of a hill, they could just about see the unmistakeable grey outline of Stirling Castle, stuck high on a crag, barely visible through the distant ragging mist. Buoyed with the hope of a dry-out, and a warm meal, they urged the weary horses to a trot to hasten their arrival at the welcoming sight, hurrying down to the lower ground and mercifully out of the drizzle into fairer weather, taking less than half an hour of brisk riding to reach their imposing destination. In a sense of irony, just as the trio were at last plodding their exhausted mounts the last few steps up to the main gateway, the bright sun burst through the shredding clouds, returning the climate to what was now the norm, and in no time at all the ground was steaming along with the three riders, filling the nostrils with that unique smell of wet horse and warm damp earth.

Gratefully, within seconds of their expected arrival, three ready and waiting well-trained stable boys grabbed the reins of the bedraggled steeds, first aiding the riders to alight; they then took the animals into a barn for a well-deserved meal in the warm. Similarly, the three-armed visitors were ushered into the castle to recuperate before the scheduled meeting with King Robert of Scotland.

Bathed, dried and re-dressed in their own miraculously aired and laundered clothes, the three were summoned to the main hall to join the king for lunch, taking their places at the massive board to wait for Robert, along with the main five English captives: Sir Humphrey de Bohun, Baron John Segrave, Sir Marmaduke Tweng, Baron Ralph de Monthermer and arriving a little after the rest, Maurice de Berkley.

Seeing Lawrence at the table, Sir Humphrey stared at him with a fixed glare; silently hoping for a riposte from the coward, he didn't bother to hide his distaste for the worthless individual. As did John Segrave, who voiced his disapproval somewhat more eloquently and politely than Sir Humphrey was capable of by goading Lawrence in a matter-of-fact way. "I see, thanks to young Richard de Mauville, you made it out of the battle intact. You must consider yourself very unlucky as through your drunken haze you probably missed all the glorious action."

The perfectly aimed insult caused all the gathering to look at the victim of the slant, to see his reaction if any, leaving their reviled compatriot with no option but to stand up and face his tormentor. In a show of mock bravery, Lawrence daringly clasped the hilt of his sword, knowing the guards on either side of him were duty bound to protect him, prompting John to reply in his languorous, inimitable half-humorous way. "Oh, please do it! How I wish you would do that! Please be my guest and draw your glaive! I'm sure it would be such a relief for your poor family's pockets to hear that at last you've been dispatched to the underworld where you belong."

Humphrey was about to put his two-penneth worth in when Robert and Alexander Seaton entered the room, causing the company to immediately stand up out of respect for the Scottish king. With a mischievous glance around the table and noticing the stony stares amongst the English captives, Robert smiled a naughty smile, and slowly and deliberately taking his seat, he invited the guests to sit back down and join him in a meal, adding his assessment of the situation to insert a little spiciness to the chatter. "If I'm not very much mistaken, I seem to sense a little discord in your ranks. Is it perhaps the attendance of our new guest that has caused you to look so chagrined, Sir Humphrey, or maybe it is you who is most upset by Sir Lawrence's presence here, my lord baron? May I ask what it is you find so distasteful about your fellow countryman, sirs?"

Feeling braver now the king was there to prevent any physical clash between the adversaries, Lawrence decided to speak on his own behalf. "It is jealousy, sire; ever since I joined Sir Henry de Bohun as his banner man they've been envious, of my money, of my horse, my armour, my looks, my way with women and everything about me!"

Up to that point the two guards were overawed by the exulted company and had stayed rather quiet while the debate raged; only reacting when Lawrence mentioned his looks did they glance at each other shrugging, baffled at Lawrence's high opinion of himself. As were the others, especially John Segrave, who listened very carefully to Lawrence's lame excuses and decided to add a little aside, much to the amusement of the English. "Well, I for one certainly am not jealous of your valour in battle!"

The pointed remark prompted Humphrey to join in with the rebuttal, "And your famed abusive ways with the fairer sex, now there's definitely something not to be jealous of."

Robert had heard enough; content he had stirred plenty more discord into the mix of verbally brawling knights, he demanded silence for two reasons, to prevent the argument from becoming violent, and to tell the gathering his plans. "Well, *Gentlemen!*" Robert shouted, holding up his hand in a quietening gesture and putting the emphasis on the word gentlemen. "Your fellow English knight, Sir Lawrence here, and these two liegemen of Sir Thomas Dewar," he said, turning to wave his hand in the direction of the two guards and Lawrence, who, believing he had won the skirmish, looked rather smugly at his fellow countryman, "are going to be my messengers. My Lord Dewar has kindly allowed Sir Lawrence out on his own parole and under my protection; he, along with these others, will take a package along with your letters and my demands for your ransoms to England for me. So, sirs, after we have eaten, I would be obliged if you would return to your rooms and prepare a document for your families. Now, no more arguments please, let's eat!" And with a clap of his kingly hands, the food was brought and placed in front of each person, and in a tense silence they ate together before going off to write their letters home.

Sweating profusely in the heat of the strong afternoon sun, the captives assembled, each holding their written missives, standing lined up in the courtyard to see off the messengers. Taking it in turns, they handed the important little sealed bundles to the armour-clad Lawrence, who arrogantly accepted them with a little self-important malicious grin. Handing his over, Humphrey gave a secret little whisper out the side of his mouth into Lawrence's ear as he passed the package. "When I'm out of here I'm going to make it my personal business to take Richard de Mauville to see King Edward to tell him exactly what transpired on that fateful day, and let him judge your worth, God help you!"

Unfazed by the threat, Lawrence gave a sly wink to his tormentor as he snatched the letter from Humphrey's still closed hand and, leaving a shred of torn paper in Humphrey's clenched fist, he answered back almost silently. "If you think your precious little Richard will still be fucking alive by then, don't forget, unlike you, I'm free now and, believe me, I also have plans and he's a major part of them!" Having said that, Lawrence walked away to where Robert had just turned up to witness the departure.

With a self-important cocky bounce in his step, Lawrence approached Robert, proud to be selected as the king's private courier. Shooting a victorious smile at the Englishmen, he addressed the monarch like an old friend. "Robert, I'm ready to leave, so you can give me your package now, if you please?"

"Oh yes, I nearly forgot," the king fibbed as he waved his hand to where two dark brown, giant flat-footed hairy cart horses tolerantly waited, steaming between the shafts, ready to move off in front of a two-wheeled wagon with a long narrow crate tied securely on the buck.

Seeing the king's signal, the driver flapped his reins, urging the slow beasts into laboured action, halting near Robert, who looked cheekily at the haughty Lawrence, fighting to hide the rising mirth from breaking free. "Here's my parcel, and out of all the English captives I considered you were the most apt person to deliver it for me," Robert smirked, still struggling to keep his laughter under control.

Peering quizzically at the large long box, Lawrence furrowed his sweaty brow to state the obvious. "It looks just like a coffin, sire!" he said, looking quizzically at Robert and thinking he was going to say the cargo was something of high value.

"It is! As I said, I thought you were the best man for the job, and in a role which seems to suit you best, you shall deliver the body of the noble knight Sir Henry de Bohun to his family in Herefordshire." And with that the laughter Robert was attempting to stifle broke free, and, tittering like a miscreant child, he spun round to face the English spectators, who to a man had joined in with the hilarity, leaving the overly-proud Lawrence red-faced with embarrassment and not appreciating the joke one little bit.

Not dissimilar to a small cortege, the two guards were followed by a downcast Lawrence, the pair of gently nodding nags drawing the cart, complete with driver, baggage and most importantly of all, the coffin, which in reverence to the dead knight now had a newly painted shield lashed to the lid. Departing from the mighty castle, the short procession wound its sad way off the concourse and out into another merciless hot Scottish day. Sir

Humphrey, holding a kerchief to where an off course wayward fly had accidentally flown into his watery eyes, couldn't help but forlornly wave, thinking of Lawrence's thinly veiled threat, as the earthly remains of his dead favourite relative disappeared south to England and home to the tomb where his noble bones belonged.

For the next five nights Humphrey found it hard to gain his sleep. No matter how he tossed and turned trying to get snug, the vicious departing words of the malice-filled Lawrence haunted him. In his semi-conscious state between sleep and wakefulness, the implied violence the ignoble knight intended to inflict on the loyal Richard kept going round and round in his mind, gaining impetus in his insomnia, putting wild pictures of the lad's dreadfully mangled corpse in his head, conjuring horrible images of the poor young man's life being brutally taken from him.

On the sixth morning after the departure, Humphrey was unusually late for his breakfast. Instead, as was normal, of him being first at the table, knife in hand, waiting to be fed, the meal had started well before he arrived, Humphrey's delayed attendance causing some consternation among the diners, especially Robert, who'd grown rather fond of the knight. As if in a trance, he came shuffling into the room, the hollow dark rings beneath his eyes paying testament to another sleepless night, raising a stir of concern among his fellow breakfasters. More so when Humphrey clumsily took his seat and went about pouring himself a goblet of wine to freshen his mouth before eating; completely missing the vessel in his bleary-eyed state, he tipped the purple juice directly onto the table, stunning the assembly to mystified silence, worried the ageing knight might be suffering from some kind of grief-related seizure.

In total silence the diners carefully watched Humphrey's every move, as without a single word he mechanically ate some food, stirring Robert to speak and ask what all the others were thinking, couching his words carefully so as not to alarm the sickly looking knight. "How are you feeling this beautiful morning, Sir Humphrey?" he asked buoyantly.

The king's sympathetically enquiring voice broke Humphrey's trance, suddenly bringing him back to reality. Shaking his head and blinking as if he was trying to recover from a hefty blow, he answered, "Pardon me, my lord, I was daydreaming. What did you say?"

"I asked how you are feeling this fine morning, Sir Humphrey," Robert explained, exaggerating his lip movements as though he was talking to a deaf man.

"I'm just a little tired, that's all. I keep thinking about something Lawrence Buckenham said as he left," Humphrey replied, as his lucidity gradually returned.

"What is it, may I ask, that's been said to you, which is so serious it's keeping you awake at night?" Robert inquired, interested in what the despicable Lawrence had said to disturb Humphrey's sleep.

"In essence, Buckenham said to me that he's determined to catch up with Richard and kill him before he tells the truth to King Edward about Lawrence's dismal failure to take any part in the battle," the sickly looking knight explained, shrugging his shoulders in resignation at young Richard's pending fate.

"Are you sure he wants to kill Richard? Why would he? After all, he's only a lad! And while we're about it, Edward's hardly likely to string Lawrence up for being a useless drunkard! Is he?" Robert queried, looking somewhat perplexed, as he stared into Humphrey's bleary eyes, waiting for him to give extra validation to his fears.

"I think there must be something more as it seems strange to me that Lawrence was alone when he was captured, and we know on his own admission Richard is still alive, so something must have happened between them, as I know in my heart of hearts he wouldn't just desert his liege master without having an extremely good motive," Humphrey explained, giving his head a quick scratch to aid the thinking process.

Having listened very carefully to the reasoning, all those that had actually met Richard agreed that he was a person with the very highest of principles and it was highly unlikely that he would have abandoned Lawrence without a very good cause. Backing up the reasoning, Humphrey quoted some words of his deceased, chivalrous nephew. 'As Henry told me some time ago, Richard has a natural sense of fairness and real moral fibre.' Hearing the evidence, the whole party, including Alexander Seaton, concurred that Richard certainly wasn't the sort of person to fail in his given duty, and knowing the scurrilous nature of Lawrence, they drew to the mutual conclusion, that he must have had a better than good reason to leave his wounded master stuck in the middle of nowhere.

Robert sat finishing his breakfast as the debate unfolded, looking from man to man as they made their points, all unanimously in support of Humphrey's theory. Having gained first-hand experience of Richard's steadfast devotion himself, Robert agreed wholeheartedly with the general assessment of the squire. Pondering on what he could do to foil the plans of the despised Lawrence, Robert considered the options for some time, and reaching a conclusion he banged the table to call the jabbering diners to order to announce his plan. "Gentlemen! Gentlemen, please!" he called out to gain the diners' attention.

Taking heed of the polite interjection, the guests instantly stopped their exchange of ideas to listen to their host and his take on the situation, surprising the company with his scheme. "Gentlemen, I know you to be good honest men! I have listened to you and I sympathise with your concerns. Therefore it is in my mind to release you, my Lord Earl, Sir Humphrey, on your own cognisance of your ransom, and you, my dear old friends Sir Ralph and Sir Marmaduke, without any financial demands as a reward for the friendship and generosity you both once showed when I was your captive. However, on your sworn knightly honour, you must follow this rogue knight, and do all you can to thwart his dishonourable scheme. So go now and rest yourself well, Sir Humphrey, Sir Ralph and Sir Marmaduke, for this time tomorrow I shall be bidding you all farewell and God speed."

For the rest of that day and the following night, Humphrey slept soundly, safe in the knowledge that although Lawrence had six days' head start, he and his two fellows would be on fast, athletic chargers, while the quarry would be a slow-moving target encumbered by the sluggish heavy cart and the clumsy horses, sure to be overtaken before Lawrence could do any of his promised harm to the lad who'd saved his life more than once.

CHAPTER 11

It was early September when suddenly the prolonged spell of hot, sunny, summer weather dramatically changed to something more akin to late November. Everywhere an unseasonably early, freezing north wind stripped the leaves from the trees, and with it came a great gloom which descended across the whole of known civilisation. From Norway in the north to Sicily in the south and from Portugal in the west to Byzantine in the east, the murkiness persisted, depressing the whole population of Europe and beyond. To the beleaguered population it seemed as if God himself was punishing the wicked world by hiding the sun and moon from it. It was the same in Market Deeping, where Richard was planning to use Yolanda's newfound wealth wisely, by repairing and updating the dilapidated house and stabling in preparation for what promised to be a very long, cold and cheerless winter.

All the tradesmen from miles around rubbed their greedy hands in glee when they came to survey the damage and found it was a mere boy they were dealing with; however, they hadn't allowed for the wily merchant's daughter who stood forever at his elbow, ready to assassinate their avaricious plans. After assessing the work with a host of sharp intakes of breaths and a whole series of tuts, the unscrupulous workers proposed the very lowest of low prices they could possibly accept to apply their constructional expertise, and then only make the smallest of small profits. Naively, Richard, more used to dealing with the wily subterfuge of horse traders rather than builders, would have gladly accepted the quotes without quibbling. Nonetheless, with Yolanda constantly standing at his side ready to save the day, their vision of making huge gains was soon foiled. Always prepared to haggle, she resolutely beat down the price to something more like a fair one. The workmen openly berated the day they accepted the work for such a low profit margin, but all the time knowing the return was still heavily weighted in their favour.

There was the roof to re-thatch, doors and windows to be repaired or replaced, the rickety stairs needed reinforcing, and all but one side of the barn needed to be totally rebuilt, going right through the house, even as far as having the chimney properly swept. But most importantly of all, a specially designed secret small upstairs room was to be converted specifically for

155

Yolanda's stricken father, where he could quietly stay out of the way and amuse himself by escaping from his eventless world in the dingy old spice store, to watch, strapped safely in a chair through a specially lowered window, the comings and goings in the street below and rue his dreadful deed when he was bewitched into poisoning his poor wife to free him to take another younger one. And then become her victim when, tiring of her older husband, he too was poisoned by the sorceress, damned to live out his days, mind intact but helplessly locked away in his own frozen unresponsive body.

Yolanda's three sisters and four brothers were more than happy to give up their menial jobs, slaving hours on end for the odd parcel of food and a penny or two on a local farm, as their labour now was needed to assist in the rejuvenation of their home. All five spent weeks cheerfully clearing up after the labourers and tradesmen, or busying themselves happily splashing whitewash on the walls, ceilings and even over the now-piebald dog Sam, who was forever under their feet wanting to play.

By the middle of October the restoration work was finished and the house returned back to its former glory, making it look more like the home befitting a wealthy merchant and his family. During the time spent renovating the premises, the beautiful Yolanda's waistline had burgeoned, as had her breasts, stretching her clothes drum-tight across her torso, showing off her pregnancy to all who had eyes. Yolanda's condition attracted muttering and knowing nods from the envious men, jealous of he who did the dirty deed, and unwarranted salacious gossip from among the less-occupied womenfolk in the village, all of whom automatically blamed Richard for her predicament. All, that is, except for Simon Byrde's widowed mother Matilda, who along with her son had learned the truth while assisting with the repairs. Working together they chatted freely, hearing all about the whole sorry sordid tale of beatings, forced prostitution, murder, death and rape, moving the friendly neighbour to tears more than once on hearing the details.

Having known Yolanda's mother a long time before her untimely death and considering herself to be a close friend of the family, Matilda decided on taking a maternal role, volunteering to put herself on standby when the hour of the birth grew nearer, which, having had plenty of experience in the midwifery sphere, she guessed was some time in January or early February.

One day, when the two women were alone, scrubbing and dusting the old house, Matilda seemed to be unusually quiet, prompting Yolanda to ask if Matilda was all right, worried she must have done something wrong to upset her friend.

"I'm fine!" came the abrupt answer.

"No you're not!" Yolanda replied a bit tetchily, surprised by her mother figure's terse manner. "Tell me what's wrong with you."

Realising that her unusual silence was out of character, Matilda told of some deep-festering concerns she had about Richard. "I just can't help thinking he's going to bring grief to this house, when I close my eyes; I know he's going to bring us unhappiness. I just wonder if it's just your money he's after."

"Don't be silly, Matty. On our trip from Scotland Richard spent a small fortune on me and never asked for anything in return. I shouldn't tell you this, but he's never even made love to me, even though I did my level best to get him to. I think it's this bloody weather that's depressing you; it most certainly is getting to me!"

"Perhaps you're right," Matilda replied, still unable to hide her concerned far-away look.

The chat seemed to do the trick: after that day it appeared that Matilda's irrational fears had been allayed and it started to seem as if she had changed her mind about Richard and gave the impression that she had started to be getting to know him quite well. However, although she pretended not to, on the odd occasion Yolanda still caught Matilda giving him funny, suspicious, doubting looks, yet when she saw him together with Yolanda it was plain to her experienced eyes that he really did love her as she did him.

As was customary in the Bellew household, Yolanda organised an evening party to celebrate the completion of the works, inviting all the participants in the project, including the invaluable Simon and his normally sober mother Matilda. Not used to the tongue-loosening beakers of Richard's new favourite drink, the locally made strong cider, Matilda tipsily pointed out in passing that the couple were made for each other and should get married. At first Richard looked stunned at the idea, but, stopping to consider the prospect for a couple of seconds, he turned to Yolanda, who as usual was clutching his arm, and falling on to one knee as he had heard in the stories of King Arthur and his knights, asked Yolanda to marry him in front of the whole assembly. Planting a loving kiss on Richard's trembling lips, Yolanda instantly accepted the proposal whispering, "Of course I will!" softly in his ear, the words causing a spontaneous round of loud clapping and cheering to erupt from the gathering of family, friends, and tradesmen. The drink-fuelled clamour shook the house to its foundations, even reaching the ears of Yolanda's vegetative father, who heard the uproar, but as were his just desserts, was unable to react, trapped in a shell, alone with his thoughts in his own private hell.

Using the temptation of a gift of money to the church as an inducement, Richard circumnavigated the usual channels of arranging a wedding. The local priest needed little convincing when he saw the state of the bride, eventually agreeing to perform the service without the normal protocols such as reading the banns; but more for his own gratification, as Richard suspected he categorically insisted on hearing the couple's confessions before the service could be considered.

As required, Richard and Yolanda attended the small church on the outskirts of the village to cleanse their souls and confess their sins in the presence of God. As normal, the groom took his turn first, privately telling the priest of his transgressions, taking a short time and only receiving a small penance for the odd dirty thought and an occasional few other minor wanderings from the straight and narrow. However, when it was Yolanda's turn to admit her sins, she roguishly went into every tiny detail of her life as a sex slave, taking over half an hour to describe the debauchery and her sinful existence since her last confession some four years before. Eventually, Yolanda emerged from the booth to give Richard a saucy wink as he waited in the body of the church for his soon-to-be wife, her exit from the stall being quickly followed by the scarlet straight-faced cleric, walking awkwardly bent forwards as he scurried into his changing room with more than a hint of an erection beneath his drab priestly gown.

On the day of the wedding, Richard arrived looking magnificent in his meticulously polished armour with his bascinet subtly adorned, to add a touch of grace to his otherwise warlike attire, with a plaited torse of pale lilac and cream silk ribbons around the crown. His striking appearance, though, paled into insignificance next to his stunningly beautiful bride, who wore some magically produced, pink honeysuckle and the last of the wild summer daisies interwoven in her long dark hair, complementing the new primrose-yellow satin gown trimmed in the same shade of lilac silk, bought two days before from a merchant in Stamford.

Together they painted a wonderful picture for the gathering of gawping, holier-than-thou village gossips, fuelling their already full arsenal to talk about the lovely young couple as if it were the first time ever a pregnant girl and her young groom took their wedding vows. Four days after their confessions, the partially recovered priest conducted the brief marriage ceremony of Richard and Yolanda. There were few guests in the old damp church as the couple had no true friends, other than Matilda, her son Simon and Yolanda's siblings. All through the service the deeply disturbed cleric stuttered and stumbled over the words, from time to time shooting funny looks at Yolanda, wondering how such a beautiful creature could be so bestially corrupted in the manner so graphically described to him not a week before.

United as man and wife, Richard walked hand in hand with the stunning, if rather plump around the middle Yolanda, leading her under the eternally grey miserable skies the short cold distance back to the old merchant's house, where now, with thanks to Matilda and Simon's hard work, a warming fire was already burning in the hearth and a small but sumptuous feast was laid on a sturdy oak table to greet the couple.

As a gesture of goodwill to the less than amiable neighbours, the doors to the house were thrown open, welcoming all to the celebration. Yet it was more out of a sense of inquisitiveness rather than one of friendship that the locals arrived, each one feeling pangs of jealousy, as they pried at the interior of the newly renovated dwelling, where all the dilapidated old fixtures and fittings had been replaced with smart new ones of the best quality. The free rein to inspect nearly everything inside and out still wasn't enough to sate the neighbours' curiosity, and they still scratched their heads in frustration as the main burning question still remained unanswered: wherever on earth did the newfound wealth come from?

The evening celebrations were quiet and short-lived and as soon as there was no more food to be eaten, the curious guests started departing in ones and twos. Staying behind to clear up the mess, Matilda, Simon and the family removed the debris whilst Sam volunteered to clean the floor; meanwhile, the newlyweds sat by the fire, holding each other's hands, a little frightened at the huge commitment they'd undertaken and musing on what their future together might hold.

Satisfied everything was in reasonable order, Matilda and all her tired helpers also left, to spend a pre-arranged night at her cottage, leaving Richard and Yolanda alone together for the first time as man and wife. Upstairs, the main sleeping room had been secretly decorated by Yolanda's three sisters. Out of their own pocket money they had bought pink ribbons and fake red flower petals to adorn the bed, causing the slightly overawed Yolanda to weep a little at the sight, before helping her husband out of his mail, quilted gambeson and the rest of his clothes. With love in her beautiful green eyes, Yolanda pushed the stark naked Richard backwards on to the bed to land face up, so, bathed in the fading light of the day, he could watch her disrobe. With as much grace as her swollen belly would allow, Yolanda removed her clothes, all the time staring lovingly into her new husband and saviour's eyes, her nervous fingers trembling as she struggled with the stubborn laced opening up the front of the bodice, to slide the garment over her bump, pulling her stomach in to allow the new gown to tumble onto the floor, revealing not the girl, but the loving wife she had become.

For a few luscious moments Yolanda stood like an antique statue, the fading flowers still woven into her tumbling dark tresses, giving Richard time to take in her beauty, before she walked over to join him on the decorated bed to carefully consummate the marriage. And so, after all the waiting, the adoring newlyweds finally made love, there in the old house, alone except for the desperately sad soul in the nearby room who gazed desolately out into the darkness, pretending he was deaf and wishing he was dead as he should have been.

Ever since they first met, Yolanda knew Richard had important duties to perform. She had always been fully aware that at the first opportunity he intended to travel to Herefordshire to see Henry de Bohun's family and first-handedly tell them the manner of his death, only being sorry that his efforts to retrieve Henry's body and take it to the de Bohun home met with failure.

Sadly, Yolanda watched as Richard started on his final preparations for the journey; nonetheless, he wasn't going to travel alone, as in concern for his safety, Yolanda had negotiated for a young and eager Simon Byrde to act as travelling companion and accompany him. She discussed the boy's future long and hard with Matilda, who with much humming and hawing reluctantly agreed that for the boy's own good, she had to cut the apron strings and allow the lad to follow his ambitions, which were to do what he always wanted to, and be a bowman as his father was before he died from an injury acquired in a skirmish on the Welsh borders some seven years previously.

Simon needed virtually nothing other than a horse to outfit him for his adventure into the wide world. He was already quite adept with his father's old four-foot hunting bow, left to him along with a steel cap, a quiver full of useable arrows, and a short sword, the preferred side-weapon of the archer. Sensibly, though, he didn't even bother to consider the powerful six-foot-long war bow, which graced the wall of their house, knowing it was too much for his thirteen-year-old arms to draw. More as a thank you to his mother and with her permission, Yolanda raided her funds and gave Simon enough money to buy the necessary horse and tack, which he planned on taking to a dealer in Melton Mowbray, wisely asking Richard to accompany him, knowing how much he knew about the finer points of equines and their foibles, learnt during his time as squire to Sir Henry.

It was a slightly jealous Yolanda that watched alongside Matilda as Richard mounted Solomon with Simon in her old place as pillion and trotted off out of sight through a grey, seemingly impenetrable wall of misty drizzle, on the mission to find a suitable mount for the lad. Both women felt saddened to be separated from their nearest and dearest, each seeing it as a rehearsal for the next time when they knew it would be a lot longer than just a single day.

It didn't take too long to reach the dealer's yard on a farm somewhere approximately about a mile on the Market Deeping side of Melton. For the whole journey Simon gabbled excitedly, glad to be unleashed on the wide, outside world for the first time; never before having left the town of his birth, he'd spent every day since his father died cooped up under the auspices of his over-protective mother. Ignoring the cold soaking rain, Simon perpetually urged Richard to go faster, clinging on tightly when Richard occasionally gave in to his pleas when the terrain was suitable, delighting the boy by nudging Solomon to the occasional canter. On they rode, always knowing they were heading in the right direction, but in the poor visibility unsure of the exact location.

Stopping Solomon, they asked directions from a sheltering mendicant friar, who evidently took his solemn vow of silence very seriously as he persistently rattled his begging bowl in Richard's direction, silently demanding a penny before giving up the desired information with a grunt and a wag of a horny, gnarled finger roughly southward. Following the vague directions for half a mile or so, Richard and Simon finally arrived at a smallholding, it clearly being the correct place, as, outside in a muddy stockade, a new intake of assorted colts and fillies were being broken. Simon loved it, watching agog as the high-spirited young horses bucked and leapt through the mire, attempting, often successfully, to get rid of their obdurate riders. Without the wisdom of Richard, Simon would have purchased all of them, especially one giant black monster whose evil rolling eye, flattened ears and red flaring nostrils gave more away about him than could be hidden by the smooth-talking seller. The dishonest dealer made much of the specimen, saying lots about his good points, ignoring the bad, truthfully adding, to give credence to his dubious description, that he thought the horse was a bit green, and might need a little more time. The trader also conveniently forgot to mention the two injured handlers who were inside the dry shack nursing their bruised bodies and egos, gained during their latest attempt to school the unpredictable beast.

How easily it would have been for the unprincipled salesman to cozen the inexperienced boy out of his purse of coins. However, much to the chagrin of the dealership's owner, Richard was there, spoiling his sales pitch with annoying questions, looking at the teeth, inspecting and criticising every broken nag the man led up for Simon's perusal. Using his experienced eye, Richard rejected each one as being either too old, too young or unsuitable for a novice, until out of the corner of his eye he caught sight of a good honest-looking strawberry roan cob of about fifteen and a half hands high.

"What about that one?" Richard asked, tilting his head sideways and squinting to assess the beast with his expert eye. "I like that one! How much is he?" he queried, drilling his blue eyes unrelentingly through to the dealer's convincing orbs all the way to the back of his scheming skull.

Sniffing a profitable sale, the salesman answered dishonestly, trying to build up the asking price while calling for a groom to fetch the animal. "He's a lot of money, sir. There's a good market for good strong horses like him. I've already got a buyer for him, but if…"

"Well, if he's out of our price range you'd better put him back," Richard said uninterestedly, having seen the game played before by Henry's head groom, and was somewhat in his comfort zone when it came to horse trading. Showing a side of him not seen by many, he cut the salesman's rhetoric short and turned his back on the horse of his fancy. Reversing the psychology, Richard pretended to leave, passing a matter-of-fact comment to whet the dealer's appetite. "Don't worry, I've got plenty more to see. I might come back in the spring when feed is cheaper."

The suggestion alarmed the trader, who in thinking he was about to lose a valued customer, gambolled after his departing prospective buyer, knowing Richard was in fact correct, that in the winter the feed was indeed more expensive, leading to the annual dip in the price of horses, whether they were good, bad or indifferent.

Poor Simon was hopelessly confused; he didn't know whether he was coming or going, never before having entered into the fickle, shady world of horse trading, and it wasn't until Richard had an opportunity to whisper to him, did he grasp what exactly was going on. "Just follow my lead and nod knowingly now and again, but don't say anything unless I speak to you first. Got it?"

Good to his word, Simon nodded a silent yes to Richard as they walked away from the paddock, apparently disinterested in what they'd seen. Fearing he was going to lose a cash-bearing customer, the dealer soon called them back, telling them that he had reconsidered his position and wanted a price of ten shillings for the horse, looking amazed when Richard, closely followed by Simon, both nodded their heads negatively. "I could get him re-shod included in the price," the vendor added, almost begging his youthful clients to purchase the horse.

"The saddle and bridle perhaps could be included in that price?" Richard asked, using his best flinty resolved expression to again bore unerringly into the seller's eyes.

"Too much, you ask for too much; maybe for sixpence more it could be done," the salesman suggested, almost on his knees pleading and almost beaten at his own game.

"No! That's my final offer, take it or leave it." Richard said, crossing his arms resolutely, making it clear he wasn't going to budge, the finality of the gesture breaking down any resistance completely.

"Yes! Yes! YES! It's a deal, take it before you demand a year's feed and stabling as part of the bargain! There, it's done; your hand on it, young man."

Agreeing that they'd reached a mutually acceptable arrangement, Richard offered his hand to the distraught man, who spat on his palm and clasped the outstretched hand to seal the deal, accepting on this occasion the baby-faced assassin was better at his chosen occupation than he was.

It wasn't just the cob which needed new shoes; Solomon also desperately needed the services of a farrier and with the arduous trek from east to west in mind, Richard took the opportunity to have his horse attended to at the same time, happily paying a little over the odds to ease his pricked conscience at beating down the salesman so mercilessly.

All finished and fit to travel, the two young friends mounted up ready to head off, almost having to fight the dealer off when for the first time he scrutinised the magnificent Solomon. As Richard left, the trader skipped after him, incrementally raising offers for the horse, until Richard categorically refused the man's final bid of ten times the price he had paid for the cob.

Not wanting to seem a total novice in front of the professional horsemen, Simon did his best to appear at ease riding the stout roan he had already decided to name Uther, after the king in Arthurian legend, and together the two young men disappeared from sight, leaving behind them one very sorry dealer peering into the scudding grey mizzle, rueing the day he had welcomed the shrewd young fellows into his yard.

Simon was as new to equestrianism as he was everything else in the outside world away from his protecting mother, so as they rode Richard used the chance to give him a practical lesson, telling him to "sit deeper in the saddle", or to "relax your hands and use a little more leg", but all the time teaching the raw recruit, knowing that in only a short while they were both going to undertake the lengthy ride to carry the sorry news all the way across the country to Hereford and tell Henry's family the sad story from his own mouth.

By the time Richard arrived back at Market Deeping, his apt pupil had gained quite a reasonable grasp of basic riding. Trotting proudly up the street, they brought the two horses to a square halt outside the house, where Yolanda and Matilda had been waiting, anxiously peering up the road, looking for the return of Richard and Simon with their purchase. On sight of the pair they excitedly ran outside in the wet to greet their gallants, who, even though a stiff breeze had turned the mist into horizontal soaking sleet, still sat bravely erect in the saddle.

With garbled excitement, Yolanda's brothers and sisters took command of the sodden, frozen beasts, taking both animals into the dry, fussing around the patient cob, patting his neck and rump, feeding him handfuls of some fresh grass they'd gathered in preparation for his arrival. The children needed to be reminded about their old favourite Solomon, who looked a little peeved at the attention showered on his new stable-mate but who was soon receiving his, accepting it with a long soft whinny of appreciation.

Content the horses were set fair for the night, everybody went inside the house to warm up in front of the eternally lit fire and then eat. Yolanda listened with pride as Simon garrulously related every detail of the story of the purchase, and how resolutely Richard had dealt with the tricky trader, all about his protracted riding lesson and what he had learnt, and telling them why he had decided to name the animal Uther after King Arthur's father. Yolanda surprised all with her range of knowledge, when, on hearing the new cob's given name, pointed out an oddity, which was that Richard's name meant powerful ruler, and Solomon was famed for being a visionary and listening king, whereas Simon's name literally meant a visionary listener and Uther was a legendary powerful ruler, amazing the poorly read Richard, who asked in his ignorance, "Wherever did you learn that from?"

Looking at him askance, Yolanda replied a touch sarcastically to inform Richard of her educational standard. "I can read, you know, and don't forget I did spend three years in a convent," she informed him, pouting a little petulantly.

"However could I ever forget that, after the stories you've told me about it!" Richard added, looking at her bump to reinforce his point, and crossing his arms in a bit of a grumpy, jealous sulk, thought about all the men who had enjoyed his new bride prior to him.

Knowing that she had accidentally upset him by her glib tongue, fully aware of the hurt she had caused and considering how understanding he had been, Yolanda instantly regretted her clumsiness, leaning close to catch his gaze. "I didn't mean it like you think I did. I love you and only you, please don't be angry with me, I'm really sorry." Saying that, she slid her arm over his shoulder to comfort and reassure him. To which Richard initially responded by petulantly pushing it off, only to have it insistently put back with a whisper and a gentle blow in his ear. "Please, forgive me, please?"

It was no good; Richard wasn't the broody sort, so he grabbed Yolanda's hand and giving it a squeeze, apologised for his grouchy behaviour. "I'm sorry too, for being so touchy."

Happy the whole incident was finished and done with, Matilda decided it was her time to chip in with motherly wisdom of her own. "You do realise you've just had your first row. Now get to bed and make up properly. Anyway it's time for me to go home soon, as we've got a very early start in the morning. Now off you go, while I clear this lot up."

Normality restored and clasping repentant hands, Richard and Yolanda retired upstairs to each other's arms to forgive each other as only a loving young couple could. Everybody else going to their respective beds, except Matilda who pottered around the house, finding already-neat things to tidy up, and imaginary spots to clean, reluctant to even try and sleep, inside fretting dreadfully over her only child. She worried about the almost-forgotten feelings she had when she first met Richard, the perils and dangers Simon was likely to face in his new position as assistant to a squire, on their hundred-mile journey across the wilds, all the way to the same Welsh borders where her beloved husband and Simon's father had lost his life all those years before.

The next day it was another unseasonably cold, damp, dreary morning where the feeble sun's inability to penetrate the sullen low clouds made it exceptionally dark. The gloomy weather depressed everyone except Simon, who was up and about before the cock had even contemplated crowing. Rushing around like a scalded cat, Simon prepared everything, for what in his eyes was an adventure of a lifetime, paying minute detail to both horses and gear, getting everything ready but himself, by the time Richard arrived to breakfast.

In her sleepless state, Matilda had taken the opportunity to bake some bread overnight and was roasting some bacon rashers in the hot oven to accompany it. The combined welcoming smells of the warm loaves and the sizzling fat attracted the whole household out of their beds to where the bleary-eyed matriarch was bravely preparing the table for a farewell meal. The last to appear at the board was Yolanda, also suffering after a poor night's sleep for two reasons: partly worry about a prolonged separation from Richard, but mainly because the inconsiderate unborn baby decided it was only comfortable in a position lying awkwardly on her bladder, necessitating many visits to the ever-ready wooden pail which she had taken to keeping near her at nights.

The delectable breakfast was eaten in virtual silence, Matilda and Yolanda too tired and upset to say much, the children deciding it would be prudent to respectfully remaining silent out of respect for the downcast elders, and Simon, who ignoring his dreadfully sore backside and legs from the previous days' time in the saddle, bolted down his food without a word, and having eaten the last scrap, disappeared the short distance home to dress for the journey, arriving back in a flash to stand rigidly at attention in his soldierly attire, waiting for his mother's approval. Without the luxury of expensive mail, Simon wore a simple thick brown, greased bull's-hide jerkin as his only body protection, and a steel cap rammed on his head, a nimbus of ginger curls escaping from all around the rim, looking like little red flames licking up the side of a pot. On his legs he had some new knee-length riding boots, bought for him as a gift from Richard, and around his middle, his father's old belt, altered to fit his slim waist, with fresh holes bored through the substantial leather to accommodate the buckle's new position on the strap, which held the short burnished sword tucked at his hip. Across his shoulder rested a quiver of snow-white feathered arrows complete with the unstrung bow jutting above his head, making him look every bit like the archer he aspired to be. Matilda couldn't help but clap her hands together and cheer at the sight of her son so gallantly dressed. The sight of her excited son allayed her doubts and lifted her downcast spirits out of the doldrums, knowing for the first time it really was time for Simon to spread his wings and leave the nest. Signalling for the others to join the applause, they made the young lad's freckled face split into a beaming grin as they shouted their approval, Simon thanking them with an emotional waver in his voice, inwardly hoping his father's spirit was hovering somewhere nearby to oversee him taking his first steps into maturity.

Half an hour later, after saying his final goodbyes to Yolanda in private, Richard emerged still only half-armed, as her nervous wavering hands were unable to fasten the stiff straps and leather laces on the hauberk and bascinet. The state of undress was noticed by Simon, who pounced on Richard to complete the unfinished work; making himself busy, he put the final touches to his master's armour, all, that is, except for the old worn sword belt, which much to Richard's annoyance had strangely gone missing overnight. However, his rancour was short-lived when Yolanda presented him with her parting gift: a scabbard crafted in the latest fashion, which, with the complicity of Simon, had been created in secret by a local leather worker, who made it to exactly fit Richard's trusty sword. As a final touch to his attire, Yolanda personally wound the seven-foot-long, beautifully crafted belt twice round his middle, buckling it in the latest mode so the wonderful gilt-bound sheath rested low on his left hip, and with a final kiss and an unshed tear, Yolanda tied one of the lilac wedding ribbons to his arm, bidding him mount and go as she could take no more.

With hidden sorrow in their frightened, tear-moistened eyes, Yolanda, Matilda and the family stoically watched as Richard and Simon mounted up to leave. The children fought to hold back the lurcher Sam from joining the two young warriors, a long piteous howl from the restrained dog adding extra pathos to the occasion as they turned the horses to finally depart.

In the worsening weather, the pair had barely reached the end of the street before their indistinct silhouettes blended into the morning murk, Matilda craning her neck to get the very last glance of Simon, who'd already forgotten all about his mother's anguish and boyishly practised his newfound riding skills. Snaking the cob along, Simon pretended to be avoiding some enemies which were upon him, imagining what it would be like to be in the heat of battle, striking right and left, defeating the non-existent foes which threatened him and his young master. All the time though, Simon kept one listening ear on Richard's instructions: "feel the horse's rhythm and relax your hands", or, "push with your left knee", or something of that ilk. None of Richard's advice was wasted on his keen pupil, who in his newfound freedom, wanted to learn everything possible, to help fulfil his main ambition and become a professional bowman like his father was before him.

The initial leg of the journey was simple to navigate, as southwest in the familiar territory was simple to find, but the further they got from home, the more difficult it became to establish exactly which was south, north or anything, except up. The leaden skies totally blotted out the sun from dawn to dusk, and without even the stars at night to guide them it was almost impossible to find the direct route, having to halt at towns and villages to ask directions, most of which were given to the travellers good naturedly, but occasionally they had to pay or purchase some wares at the inns on the route to gain the desired information.

On one such occasion in the late afternoon, when the visibility was particularly awful, Richard and Simon became hopelessly lost in the middle of nowhere. Fearing they were just going round in giant circles, they sensibly decided to ask the way at the next sign of civilisation. Eventually, after wandering around in the murk for upwards of an hour, they came across a likely looking small shantytown of crudely built hovels, stuck in the middle of a deserted wilderness, roughly ten miles south of Tutbury in Staffordshire.

With the best of intentions to merely ask for directions, Richard and Simon rode over to an indistinct murky shape of what they assumed was a female, busily throwing a bucketful of putrefying stinking slops into a sty crammed full of badly malnourished spotted pigs. Richard innocently asked which way was which, when, without the slightest warning, a bunch of at least another half-a-dozen scabby-looking inhabitants accompanied by some equally mangy, fierce-looking curs emerged from their poorly constructed dwellings and started menacingly walking around the pair, waving an assortment of knives, cudgels and staves, swearing abusively and spitting at the unwelcome visitors. The loudest, a filthy, gaunt, wiry man Richard assumed was their ringleader, took a step too far when he poked Solomon with the sharp end of his iron-shod staff, drawing blood and making the mighty horse jump with pain, the unwarranted assault causing Richard to draw his sword defensively, with Simon taking his lead and quickly following suit.

The raised glinting blades initially achieved the desired result in making the aggressors take a step backwards out of range of the edges, but still within compass of the chief's long pointed stave. Having roughly assessed the monetary value of horses, armour and weapons, the rogue needed no provocation from the others to use his often-successful technique of jabbing the horse in the rump, hoping to cause the beast to rear, unseat the rider and thus make him an easy target to overwhelm, kill and rob. However, Richard's spontaneous reaction surprised the man, when the rusted head of his weapon was easily lopped off its ancient staff by his lightning blade before it could make contact with Solomon's hide, and then in a glittering arc, was deftly brought back round to be poised and ready to strike again. The foolish robber, more competent at stealing off defenceless wanderers, rather than dealing with practised soldiers, even if they were very young, thought he'd seen his chance. Clumsily making an attempt to sally inside the effective usefulness of the sword, he dived in to grab and pull Richard off the horse, only to have the pommel of the glaive smashed down on his greasy-haired skull, splitting the skin and bone, making the stunned man reel backwards again into range of the blade, which Richard instinctively swung down, cutting into the side of the man's scrawny neck, half-severing the criminal's head with a fountain of spinning blood which reddened Solomon's sides and Richard's new shiny boots.

On seeing their leader fall, the other bandits, aided by the goaded, snarling curs, rushed en-masse at the two horsemen, trying to swarm over the pair, to avenge their deceased friend. Their ill-considered sortie met with little better success; one was quickly sliced into by the razor point of Richard's whirling sword, and a second unluckily tripping over one of the yapping hounds, fell on the yelping animal, only for man and hound to be trampled to death, trapped under the hooves of the gyrating horses, both man and beast ending up looking like mangled scarlet rags, half-buried in the mire.

On the other side of Richard, Simon was doing his part, striking at everybody coming close enough to whack with his short blade, making contact with a reeking, stumpy, bald-headed fellow who attempted to batter him out of Uther's saddle with a log. The carefully honed edge of Simon's new sword connected just in front of the man's ear lobe, lacerating all the way through the cursing mouth, and going out of the other cheek, taking on its path most of the yellow teeth, accompanied by the best part of his railing tongue in a cloudy puff of pink bloody spittle.

With four of their number either dead or rendered useless by injury, and poorly equipped as they were, the robbers soon realised it was futile to continue with the foolhardy attack on two mounted well-armed soldiers. Thus they very quickly to the conclusion that their best option to stay alive was to retreat, along with the surviving scurvy dogs. So in a show of utter disarray, they bolted to the safety of the buildings, dragging the wounded with them, leaving at least two corpses and two dead hounds lying mutilated beyond recognition, blended to invisibility, trodden in the freshly churned patch of mud and blood.

Gasping for lost breath, Richard and Simon watched their flight, relieved, yet amazed how simply the unnecessary deaths could have been avoided, where the plain question posed could so easily have been answered and probably rewarded, without so much as a bad word.

The brief skirmish over and done with, Richard thought it sensible to make a considered withdrawal before the beaten gang had time to re-form and mount another attack, which in his consideration could lead to one or both of them, or the horses, getting injured or worse. Making as much speed as he could muster in the deep sucking pool of mud, Richard grabbed his novice companion's reins and shouting for Simon to "hold on tight!" he spun Simon's cob around, and, dragging them both, he cantered out of the enclosure. Slowing on the way through to bend out of the saddle and with one slashing stroke at the rope holding the gate on the sty closed, he freed the starved pigs, adding more confusion to the already-bewildered settlement. Towing Simon on the slower horse, Richard galloped away from the scene, putting at least a mile between them and any would-be pursuers, before reining the horses to a halt and having a breather, ready to continue.

The previously un-blooded Simon and Uther trembled uncontrollably as they drew up. Attempting to hide his waxing emotion, Simon fired an endless confused string of pointless questions between large gulps of air at Richard, the verbal torrent suddenly breaking into a bout of meaningless jabbering, as the reaction to his first taste of real confrontation set in, soon to be followed by a cascade of passionate tears in remorse for the dead, and then relief to be still alive.

Having himself suffered from a similar response after being involved in his very first bloody armed conflict, Richard waited patiently, and still holding Uther's reins just in case, he peered through the misty veil, saying nothing, but still alert to any possible danger, allowing a quiet period for Simon to cry himself out. Understanding that sympathy was not the best medicine, Richard did nothing as the distraught boy collapsed forwards in the saddle, burying his face in Uther's gore-clotted mane, until the shuddering sobs petering to soft sighs as the misery slowly dissipated, taking some considerable time before Simon felt fit to face his friend once again.

Looking up from his tear-soaked hiding place, the pink surrounds of his rubbed eyes making them appear even bluer in his grief, he gazed appealingly for Richard to say something to make him feel better. Fully understanding how the trauma had affected the adolescent, Richard spoke kindly to the lad, telling him the truth with exactly the same carefully considered words Henry had used on him when he was in the same predicament. "Feel unashamed; you have done your duty, and remember only those without a heart don't feel the grief, so dry your eyes, and feel proud that you have borne yourself so bravely and well." He added with a smile to the recovering lad, who was making a dreadful mess by mopping his wet-streaked face with a tuft of Uther's bloodstained mane, "Come on and pull yourself together. We've got to find some lodgings for the night before it gets too dark. I for one don't want to be outside in this God-awful weather, and I don't know about you, but my throat is parched."

With a sense of real urgency, but not having a clue which direction was which, they pointed the noses of the steeds on no specific course and rode heading to nowhere in particular. Fortunately for them, they quickly stumbled across a well-used road. Opting to follow it, on the flip of a coin they luckily turned left, and within less than half an hour found an isolated roadside tavern suddenly loomed up in the murk. Outside was a sign sporting a smart painting of a stag's head, hung under the obligatory bunch of greenery, stating that refreshment and lodgings could be had within. Without hesitation, Richard made the decision that it was where they were going to rest their heads that night and although there were no obvious signs what the time really was, Richard suspected that total darkness wasn't that far ahead. So, sliding off the relieved Solomon, he handed the tired horse's reins to Simon and disappeared through the inn's door.

The inside of the tavern was very well-lit and hospitable, a large fire crackled and spat in a large carved pale-stone and heavily smoke-stained fireplace, which apparently once belonged to a noble's house, as each side of the opening a chained hart in all its splendour was marvellously carved deeply into the stone, along with a poorly scratched-out Latin motto on a long winding ribbon which draped over the animals' necks, and around a centre shield where the heraldic badge of the disgraced de Blay dynasty had been crudely obliterated. At regular intervals around the room several bright cressets were burning well, their sweet resinous odour filling the air, the flickering light showing many beasts of the chase, real and imaginary, galloping round the walls followed by queues of hunters and hounds, all painted with some expertise on the startlingly clean lime-washed plaster.

In an instant a jolly-looking, apron-wearing, round smiling man was there to greet him and ask his needs, and after a brief discussion followed by a few quick words from the host through an open door, two small lads shot out to tend to the horses. Freed from having to guard the steeds, Simon entered the inn to join Richard, who, oblivious to his appearance, stood warming his numb behind with his hands crossed behind his back to the fire, looking into the well-furnished room, watching the very few fellow guests with an expectant grin on his thirsty lips.

First things first, the friendly landlord introduced himself as Owain, and, looking slightly askance at Simon's weary blood-streaked face and Richard's stained boots, twigged they might appreciate a clean-up; however, too polite to ask what had happened, he kindly offered them the use of his own private washing facilities to make themselves presentable. So, having showed the guests where to go, he darted off to his taproom for two leather jacks brimming with his homebrewed good frothy ale and placed them on a table near the fire, ready for the travellers to sit at and get the chill out of their frozen bones on their return. Interested in how they became in such a state, he took a seat for himself and, hoping they'd let slip what happened, interestedly asked where they were from and where they were going to, mentioning how pleasant it was to see some new faces in his hostelry, adding how slow trade had been of late, sombrely giving it as the reason for having time to chat. Realising his motives were without artifice, Richard chatted freely to their host, drinking and telling of his mission, berating the gloomy weather, saying how it was making navigating impossible; in passing and by way of a brief explanation of his and Simon's state, Richard mentioned how they blundered into the thieves' settlement in the fog.

The innkeeper's ears pricked up at the news, asking with a little more than a twang of lost Welshness in his Midland accent, "I don't want to appear nosey, but if you wouldn't mind telling me, whereabouts did that happen, gentlemen?"

Hoping that the unsavoury crew weren't friends or relations of Owain, Richard replied hesitantly, telling him some of the details, remaining vague, not wanting to give too much away, maybe upset the man and possibly lose the lodgings for the night. "About fifteen or twenty minutes' ride from here, up on the moors. I don't know if it was north or south, we were hopelessly lost, and incidentally very lucky and glad to find our way here."

"Was there a short, ugly, bald rascal and his tall beaky-nosed cousin there? Did you see them?" the curious landlord asked, clearly having some knowledge of the unsavoury crew.

However, the way Owain spoke about the thieves reassured Richard enough to candidly tell the whole tale, asking one more question just to make sure he wasn't going to get himself and Simon into hot water. "You describe them very accurately. Were the friends of yours?"

"Friends, pah! They're no friends to any honest man; they've robbed and killed without fear, terrorising everyone. Even the law could do nothing, no witnesses see, just rumours. Some believe they fed their victims to the pigs, and I for one don't doubt it, stuck out there pretending to be good honest farmers." Owain very obviously harboured a deep hatred for the little community of miscreants, clearly wanting to hear more about the travellers' brush with the objects of his disgust, hoping to hear of their demise and not being disappointed when the story was told.

Richard continued after a long pull at the ale from his refilled tarred leather tankard; wiping a blob of foam off his nose, he carried on. "Well, there are at least four less of them now than there were this morning! We only asked for directions and they mobbed us, trying to pull us off our horses. I smashed the skull of the one with a big nose and sliced open one of his men at the same time, my horse Solomon trampled a third, and Simon probably killed the short, fat, bald one, split his face in half, at the very worst he'll never eat solid food ever again, or speak, come to think of it!" he explained, taking another draught of the ale.

Clapping his hands with glee, the landlord called loudly for his wife. "Gwyneth, come here quickly!" he called out, aiming his words toward a slightly ajar door before shouting the good news to his guests. Then turning to speak to Richard and Simon, he beamed a smile of gratitude. "Thank heavens, gentlemen, our trade will quadruple now they've been put in their place. It's because of their notoriety this place is so empty. Most sensible wayfarers have avoided the road out of fear, preferring to travel an extra ten miles rather than to risk their lives with that thieving band of bastards on the loose, and now because of your deeds we're free of the curse!" Just as Owain finished with his assessment of the situation, his very-pregnant wife ran into the room brandishing a large kitchen knife, wondering what all the commotion was about. Soon relaxing when seeing there was no imminent danger, she flopped down in a chair, placing her hands on her huge bump to get comfortable ready to listen. Her pregnant state reminded Richard of Yolanda, who thought of her as he once again related the tale for the eagerly listening woman. The story of the robbers' defeat apparently pleased her just as much as her husband, knowing the welcome news would in all probability now make her life much more tenable than it was at that particular juncture of time.

With a vigorous air of unbridled joy, the landlord hastily arranged a small party for the seven guests, sending the two lads to their beds and commanding his wife to remain seated, he went about making the group as welcome as possible, producing plenty of food and drink for the assembly. Blatantly very pleased to hear about the downfall of the thugs, Owain asked repeatedly to hear the story again, listening carefully and joyful of every detail of the demise of the unsavoury band which had so significantly blighted his trade, happy to have something to celebrate for a change. He was ecstatic that the days of commiserating with lucky escapees and hearing many tales of woe and near-misses, which had plagued his ears for years from any brave-enough soul to dare the perilous route across the wilds to the isolated tavern on the one-time busy road, halfway between the villages of Hinstock and Eccleshall, were at long last over

As Richard and Simon were planning an early start the next morning, they declined the offer of copious amounts of the free-flowing alcohol, knowing the effect it might have on them the next day, nevertheless he accepted the food from the grateful hosts which consisted of several slices of succulent boiled pork served on a large slice of bread. Richard always thought he had a very good appetite, but watched amazed as his fully recovered, ravenous fellow traveller Simon went three times to where the food was being served to heap his bread with more than any normal stomach could cope with.

Filled to capacity with food and drink and feeling tired from the day's exertions, Richard and Simon asked if they could be shown to where they were going to sleep, the landlord volunteering to escort them himself, slurring his repeated thanks as he wove his unsteady way to the chamber. Mimicking him while they walked, Simon repeated everything he said, tittering a little bit tipsily, emphasising each mumbled word, until they arrived at a neat, small, clean room with two somewhat roughly made but comfy-looking beds placed bang in its middle. At the sight of the sleeping quarters, Simon forgot all about his duties as assistant to a man-at-arms and threw himself down on the nearest bed to hand, instantly going to sleep, leaving Richard to undo his own hauberk and gambeson so that he could rest peacefully for the night, pleased to be unrestricted by the cumbersome garb which was made purely with safety in mind rather than the ease of the wearer.

To Richard it seemed as soon as he had closed his eyes it was already time to get up. Outside, a throttled-sounding cockerel had started crowing, going through his repertoire of good morning cries as if his squawking beak was no more than an inch from Richard's ear. Awake with no possibility of going back to sleep and with a mind on the long day's riding ahead, Richard decided to disturb his travelling companion from his resonantly snoring, comatose state. Lying curled up, thumb in mouth, Simon was sweetly oblivious to everything, including Richard, whose efforts to rouse him became more and more vigorous, eventually succeeding with a hefty prod in Simon's ribs. Sitting up with a jolt, he looked startled for a fleeting second, patted his swollen stomach, went a little green and urgently raced outside to the midden to immediately rid himself of the excesses of the previous night's festivities.

Returning somewhat lighter, Simon was more than ready for the large breakfast waiting on the same table that they sat at the previous night. Simon's appetite hadn't waned and, following his good night's sleep, the signs of the previous day's tribulations had all but disappeared completely as he sat devouring his food, babbling away about the incident to clarify it all in his mind. Almost grasping everything that occurred, except for one thing, gulping down a mouthful of food, he stared apparently a little perplexed into Richard's eyes. "The only thing I don't understand is why did you let out the pigs? I just don't understand why."

"That's simple!" Richard replied, laughing at his mystified assistant, looking up from a cup of small beer he was about to drink. "To give them something else to think about while we made our escape, all those pigs would have flattened the place. Can you imagine trying to catch a single starving hungry piglet alone a whole herd, when there's freshly slaughtered meat no more than a few yards away?"

The explanation was enough for Simon, who now could only see the funny side of the incident and both lads sat finishing their meal, giggling like naughty boys, thinking of the plight of the would-be murderers, picturing them trying to drag the starved animals off the fresh food so generously supplied by their own good sharp swords.

At first, the appreciative landlord refused payment for the board and lodgings from Richard, although, at the first hint of insistence, he very soon accepted the much-needed offered money. Gratefully pocketing the cash, Owain once again offered his genuine thanks to the departing guests, wishing them the best of luck as they mounted Solomon and Uther, to hopefully set off on their last leg to Hereford. Although it was still only autumn, the conditions were still similar to a winter's day, yet much improved to those of late, as a faint September sun was nearly visible through the horizon-to-horizon thin sheet of ominously khaki-coloured clouds which had just started to produce a fine cold, almost sleety drizzle, sure to chill even the hardiest to the bone.

CHAPTER 12

In general, August started in a similar way to July, although the baking heat was now accentuated by an extremely high humidity level; everything was wet, even though it wasn't actually raining. Even the trees and grass seemed to sweat and everywhere there appeared to be a strange and very eerie yellowness in the light which became especially noticeable when looking out to sea, where a peculiarly odd, slightly sulphurous smell drifted in with the mizzly haze, and the more you looked to the horizon the more the jaundiced air became apparent. So it was when Lawrence, his two guards, cart with its two plodding horses, the letters from the captured knights and, most importantly, Henry de Bohun's pickled body in a coffin, started their journey south to meander its way through England and finally to Hereford to deliver the mortal remains of the once-valiant knight.

As fathers of adolescent girls, the conscript escort didn't even try and hide their distaste for Lawrence. The gossiping tongues of the garrison's wives had done their work and now the rather exaggerated activities during his last night at the castle were now common knowledge among the infuriated populace. To the eyes of the Scottish escorts, not only was Lawrence a monstrous, sexually degenerate vile English foe who deserved to rot in a dungeon, but he was also solely responsible for getting them dragged away from their wives' children and what little comfort was to be had in the barracks of Dunstaffnage Castle, to go riding hundreds of miles through enemy territory, acting as guards to a man they knew was nothing better than a depraved abuser of young children. In an unstated gesture of their distaste for the mission, the Scottish men-at-arms insisted on having all their conversations in Gaelic to exclude Lawrence from them, as did the driver of the cart; not, however, for his own reasons, but he had been instructed to by the two insistent soldiers, so purely from fear of the seemingly fierce pair, he too joined in the verbal boycott of the lonely-shunned Englishman.

Unaware it was a deliberate ploy to aggravate him, Lawrence repeatedly tried to engage in conversations with his fellow travellers, sometimes using sign language or speaking very slowly, thinking they simply didn't understand him, but always meeting with the same resulting stony silence or unintelligible answers, which annoyed the confused Englishman to the point of utter exasperation. And only after the first day of being ignored, Lawrence resigned himself to the friendless situation and had taken to talking to himself or with his conveniently deaf horse, whose steadfast attitude to his master hadn't altered and, as usual, he disregarded Lawrence's gabbling as much as he ignored his riding commands.

As another display of loathing the Scotsmen felt for Lawrence, they made him eat and sleep on his own. They confiscated his sword, dagger, saddle and bridle at nights in case he decided to either attack them while they slept or make an escape bid under the cover of darkness to save him from the tedious task of traipsing around with the aloof and surly watchers, whose display of detestation for him became more and more barefaced the further they got away from their home.

Hampered by possibly the clumsiest, slowest nags in the whole country and suffering dreadfully in the humid, overpowering wet-heat, the miserable quartet always headed south. After eight days of laborious ambling, the party eventually arrived at the Yorkshire city of Doncaster, to deliver Marmaduke Tweng's letter to his wife and family. Overjoyed to receive news of her missing husband, Lady Joan Tweng, a blonde, pale-skinned, thirtyish, slender beauty, wanted to lay on some entertainment for the welcome messengers.

With a twinkle of lust in his cunning eyes, Lawrence was more than willing to accept the kind offer and hopefully winkle his way into her affections to unselfishly fulfil some of her womanly needs, to say nothing of his own rampaging desire to bed the lovely. His aspirations came quickly to grief when his grumpy guards forced him to refuse the offered hospitality, as they wanted to leave quickly and carry on with as much haste as possible, anxious to complete their hateful task in the sweltering, grim, damp southlands and return to bonny Scotland at the first possible chance, where they prayed the weather would be somewhat kinder and much less oppressive.

For his part, Lawrence also wanted to get his obligations over and done with, but not quite with as much urgency as his Scottish escorts did. Alone with nothing but his thoughts, Lawrence trudged on, inwardly regretting the one missed opportunity to rest, possibly talk to someone who actually understood him and perhaps fulfil his carnal needs, but buoyed by the prospect that in all probability some other chances would present themselves when making each of the necessary stops. Oblivious to any impending danger, he contemplated some of the other comforts bound to be offered by the grateful but lonely female recipients of his messages, not knowing the three sworn enemies he thought were safely confined back at Stirling were now closing fast and hot on his scent.

With a casual indifference and more pressing things on his mind, Lawrence accompanied his Scottish guards from Yorkshire towards the Midlands. All four were totally unaware that Humphrey de Bohun, Marmaduke Tweng, and Ralph de Monthermer were single-mindedly chasing them, sworn to do their best to thwart Lawrence from carrying out his threat to harm or probably murder Richard. None of them fully understood why such a vendetta existed between the two ex-comrades, knowing nothing of their past history and grudge Lawrence had against Richard, believing it was purely and simply in order to prevent any evidence from being given and resulting in another slur being attached to the increasingly more contemptible Buckenham name.

Having made an educated guess as to which logical course their quarry would take, the posse kept an easy pace, mainly to preserve the horses, but sure in the knowledge that the slowness of Lawrence's accompanying wagon would make his party an easy target to overtake before his mission was complete. Together, the trio surmised that with Lawrence's head-start, he would be long gone from Marmaduke's home by the time they arrived at the fortified manor the knight shared with his wife Joan, his five children, along with several loyal old retainers. Humphrey and his companions were correct in their assumptions as to the route Lawrence and his escorts would take, and were only four days behind Lawrence when they arrived at Marmaduke's not so humble abode.

In an unbridled display of emotional delight, Lady Joan Tweng welcomed her adored war-weary husband home. Excitedly, she shared her thrill with the whole household, all of them feeling the same at seeing Marmaduke for the first time for nearly a whole year. Their joy sadly was short-lived, as, after the initial welcome home hugs, kisses and tearful hellos were over, Marmaduke took the first available opportunity to scotch Joan's belief that he was home to stay. Glumly, the woe-begotten knight informed her of the solemn promise he made to the Scottish king in order to secure his ransom-free release. Truthfully, he reassured her that more than anything else he wanted to stay at home with her, sadly adding that it would be a blot on his honour if he failed to resume the journey as quickly as possible and he planned to leave within the hour.

Shocked at the grim prospect of losing her newly arrived husband so quickly, Joan fell on her knees and repeatedly begged him to stay, even if it was only for a little while; but, steadfast to his promise, Marmaduke refused, repeating to his sobbing, loving wife that his duty beckoned and, for his honour's sake, he had to depart within the hour. When Humphrey and Ralph saw the abject misery in the loving couple's faces, they hastily concocted a story to reassure Marmaduke that to stay was a necessity, using the need to rest the weary footsore horses as a viable excuse and reminding him that with faster-recuperated mounts there was plenty of time to stay until the next morning, and still overtake Lawrence before he got to Hereford. Insistently, his kind friends repeated that it was plain commonsense to stay, take pleasure in the comfort of his own home and the welcome benefits there were likely to be attached to the overnight stop and still keep his honour intact. Taking heed of the reasoning from his equals, Marmaduke reluctantly agreed, but only under one strict condition that they left at very first light.

That evening, Joan and the whole household cobbled together a fantastic meal, raiding the larders of many of the willing locals, who freely gave whatever they could spare, all wanting to share in her happiness at the popular lord's survival. The combined efforts provided something approaching a feast, with spit-roasted beef, chicken, mutton, a baked pie, with plenty of wine and sweetmeats to finish off the repast. Filled to the brim with the welcome food and drink, the tipsy visitors unsteadily followed the very grateful Lady Joan upstairs and, bidding her an appreciative goodnight, retired to some guest quarters she'd had prepared for them to spend the night. Their absence allowed the somewhat over-replete host to happily climb the stairs to his own bedroom, where, with a satisfied smile on his lips, he collapsed into his appealing well-known bed to glory in the familiar surroundings of his home. Yet all his home comforts were soon forgotten when the completely naked lovely Joan slipped in next to him and, wrapping her warm soft body into his, she then said both hello and goodbye properly as only a loving woman could do.

The next proposed port of call for Lawrence and his obligated entourage was to call at Nottingham Castle, the seat of the absent constable Baron John Segrave, to deliver Robert the Bruce's demands for John's ransom to whoever was in charge. And after another two days of a painfully slow ramble across the undulating countryside of South Yorkshire into Nottinghamshire, the four travel-weary messengers at last arrived at the ancient and massive stone-built fortalice stuck looming high above the city on a mighty craggy peak. Situated on its own, the sheer rock jutted up some one hundred and thirty feet in the air and with consideration for the height of the walls and towers, the impressive pile almost reached two hundred feet in the air from the base, its dizzy heights almost getting lost in the grey scudding clouds at its top.

All five poor horses struggled painfully up the steep stone ramp to the gatehouse, unable to find a grip on its weather-beaten surface, which had been eroded smooth by three hundred years of horse and foot traffic. Worst of all were the two carthorses, which received a merciless whipping from their angry driver as they slipped and slid on the moist cobbles, their strenuous efforts producing showers of sparks off their badly worn shoes, which desperately needed replacing at the first possible opportunity. Annoyingly for Lawrence and his Scottish escorts, the diligent guards forced them to stop and show their credentials at the closed iron-bound gates, making them wait a considerable time before being admitted to the garrisoned stronghold.

Once inside, they were to deliver Sir John Segrave's letter to his wife Louisa, who in the absence of her lenient, now imprisoned older husband, had ably replaced him and ruled over the inhabitants with a rod of iron. In truth, Sir John was reasonably happy with his present situation in captivity, housed comfortably, being fed and liquored with nothing but the best Scotland could offer, and more to the point, over three hundred glorious miles from his controlling, overbearing foreign spouse, who hen-pecked him mercilessly when he was at home.

Inside the important castle everything was neat and orderly; unlike most working fortresses, the yard was swept and clean without the normal clutter, even the stables where the horses had been taken to for attention were immaculate, the ostlers going as far as plaiting the straw bedding in the doorways of the stables, to stop it being trodden into the yard.

Lawrence couldn't help but compare the neatness of Nottingham Castle to the utter squalor of Dunstaffnage as he was bustled through the orderly passages by an elderly, short and clearly very important clerk, who shuffled along clutching a rolled up bundle of indentures and documents under one arm. Their hanging multi-coloured seals clattered together noisily as he moved, their tinkling music being accompanied by that of a colossal bunch of keys at his waist which jingled and jangled with every trundled step as he hustled Lawrence the short way to meet with the chatelaine who was attending to the boring paperwork locked in her own private strong-room. The old man's inflexible arthritic fingers struggled with the stiff lock to admit Lawrence, eventually managing to open the door with an ink-stained gnarled hand, and ushering the guest into the chamber where Lady Louisa Segrave was sitting stern-faced, perusing a large leather-bound ledger. Locking the door on his way out, the clerk left Lawrence on his own to conduct the business at hand. While outside and well away from the living quarters, the escorts Louisa considered could be dangerous enemy spies were forced to wait, safely confined in the stark gatehouse, to grumble about the lack of English hospitality.

In silence, Lawrence sat in the exulted presence of Louisa, waiting to be spoken to by the notoriously abrupt, feisty wife to the famous Sir John Segrave, the revered veteran knight and close friend of Thomas, the martial Earl of Lancaster, whose names, deeds and public falling out with King Edward were known throughout the land. Sir John, along with Lancaster, was among the senior nobles who pronounced the sentence of death for treason on the king's best friend and lover, Piers Gaveston, and were present at his execution on the Earl of Lancaster's land at Blacklow Hill in Warwickshire.

Instead of the late middle-aged, fire-breathing, wrinkled, female bruiser surrounded with the paraphernalia of her warlike husband's trophies Lawrence expected to meet, Lady Louisa was in fact a pleasant-looking, elegant, dark-haired, reasonably attractive woman, probably in her late thirties. Looking like the lady she was, Louisa, imperiously dressed in a fine embroidered silk cloak at an unpolished scratched and worn counting-table, sat alone at her work amid an extremely neat, orderly pile of account books and chests brimful of cash. It being the end of the eighth month, Louisa was very busily absorbed in her work, noting down the details of the quarterly rents and other monies paid in advance by her husband's tenants.

Snapping the ledger closed with a crack, Louisa looked up from the papers to greet Lawrence with a frigid stare, her manners letting her down when, without even a hello or let alone any of the other normal pleasantries being observed, she merely held out her hand and instantly demanded to be given the letter from her husband. "Give it to me!" Louisa demanded, as she beckoned Lawrence to approach her, asking to see the correspondence. Those three words gave away her Spanish origins, as she pronounced the 'g' softly with a noise as if she was clearing her throat.

Louisa's relentless stabbing black-eyed stare drilled all the way to the back of Lawrence's skull as he fumbled inside his hauberk to retrieve the all-important parcel. Finding it, he instantly gave it to her, already recognising the Lady Louisa was a woman who always got what she wanted.

"Stand there while I read it!" was her only comment, as she snatched the little packet from his outstretched hand. Breaking the red-ribboned wax seal without ceremony, she opened the folded document to read it. Pointing with her forefinger at each word, she repeated them to herself, mouthing each one as she did. Having read and digested the information, Louisa tossed her head peevishly and screeched a meaningless string of Spanish words when she understood the demands. Staring at Lawrence, she reverted to English. "You want me to reply to this?" she screamed, screwing up the document and throwing it back across the table at the very surprised messenger. "They ask too much for him! How can I raise so much money, at such short notice?" Louisa explained, glancing sideways at the overflowing coffers, and simply pretending they weren't there, straightaway looked appealingly back at Lawrence, the hardness in her eyes softening as she used her womanly wiles on him as if it was he who was making the demands. "Why should I pay all that for an old man whose only interest is war, he who is little more than a stranger to me?" Pausing to brush a stray tear away from her cheek, Louisa continued with more than a little bitterness in her unhappy voice. "Here I am, a warm-blooded normal woman, wanting to live life instead of being stuck in this godforsaken freezing place without so much as a man to warm me at nights. And where's my beloved husband if I need him? My beloved husband who I haven't seen for two long years or more? Locked up hundreds of miles away, that's where! Leaving me here as just an unpaid slave to see to his stupid affairs, that's all."

Lawrence's ears pricked up when he heard the lonely woman's speech, thinking he might have stumbled upon a chance to ply his silver tongue and perhaps manoeuvre the plainly very frustrated Louisa into a suitable frame of mind to oblige him in a casual sexual encounter. Choosing his words very carefully, he began to use his God-given skill with the opposite sex to manipulate her. Gazing forlornly into the distance for accentuated pathos, he set about applying his art. "I fully understand exactly how you feel, as I perhaps, in a slightly different way, also suffer from the dreadful empty loneliness of war," he muttered supportively, surreptitiously glancing at his target to see if his words were having any effect.

Attracted by Lawrence's opening gambit, Louisa looked at him and, pouting her red lips, wanted to hear more. Unwittingly pulled into a conversation by his pretended sympathy, opening her otherwise impenetrable shell to his charms, she asked, "How's that then, sir?", nodding yes to herself and prompting him to tell why he also suffered as she did.

"Because of my nobility and my extensive experience in diplomacy, I suppose?" Lawrence lied, appearing as though he was actually embarrassed by expounding his own manufactured importance. "King Edward begged for me to go to Scotland with him, as he wanted someone he could trust and knew wouldn't lie to him. So I had no option but to leave my pregnant new wife in Wiltshire to go to war, and now she's dead and lying in the cold ground with my son and I'm all alone in this merciless world."

Lawrence's considerable acting skills had been honed to perfection during his many dalliances and, reading a hint of compassion in Louisa's less-stern face, he started to sob, spinning away in mock bashfulness at the crocodile tears he could turn on at will. Sensing victory wasn't that far away, Lawrence thought some flattery might do the trick. Turning back to face Louisa, he stared unblinkingly into her face and started saying words any lonely woman would be glad to hear. "She was beautiful like you, you remind me of her a lot, your beautiful dark eyes and your olive skin, you're so much like her, so much like my lost only love," Lawrence snivelled, giving a long shuddering sigh in a feigned show of sadness to emphasise his point. "Tell me, how did she die?" Louisa asked, her hardness all gone, swept away by the quiet sob story, purely designed to pluck at her strained heartstrings and lull her into a malleable enough condition to acquiesce to his carnal desire.

"In childbirth. Nothing could be done! If I was only there to see her and hold her hand as she closed her eyes for the very last time, I would die a more than happy man," Lawrence weepily declared while gazing pathetically at the sympathy-filled Louisa. Then, in another show of bogus grief, the consummate thespian fell to his knees and forced even more well-rehearsed tears from behind his eyelids, knowing his pathetic tale had played successfully on Louisa's maternal instinct by mentioning the grief of losing an unborn child.

In a sudden wave of empathy for the broken Lawrence, Louisa put a comforting arm around the blubbering wreck of a man to help him back up. Staring into his brimming eyes, she could feel hers start to fill in sympathy as she bent forward to get a good grip to help him rise. "I'm so very sorry for you, you poor, poor thing," Louisa said, meaning it, as she strained, trying to heave him to his feet to soothe the inconsolably sad man.

However, with some less than subtle encouragement from Lawrence, Louisa accidentally toppled on top of him in his clumsy attempt to rise. In the subsequent endeavour to free himself from the resulting tangle, Lawrence mistakenly dragged the fine, green satin cloak off her shoulders, uncovering a lemon yellow silk, clinging indoor gown, flimsy enough to reveal her slender well-formed figure. And then, in another cunningly planned mishap, Lawrence regretfully cupped her still-firm breasts in both hands in his attempt to control her tumble. Feeling her passion-erect nipples in his palms, he offered a panted mock apology for the error as they rolled on the floor with their lips almost touching.

The experience of once again feeling the warm breath of another human on her cheeks snapped the bonds of frustrated confinement, the abandoned woman unleashing her true vivacious self; forgetting about her matrimonial oath, she plunged a kiss on his ready lips. Lawrence quickly responded by pressing his mouth hard on hers, and within seconds they were sharing hot kiss after hot kiss.

Hoping to seal the deal between the burning caresses, Lawrence whispered sweet nothings softly in the lonely woman's ear. "You're beautiful! If you were my wife there's nothing on this earth that could drag me from your lovely side," the cleverly aimed flattery igniting the rising continental passion in the yearning Louisa, whose neglected ageing body often dreamed of some passing amours before it got too late for her.

Complying with Lawrence's practised encouragement, the expertly seduced Lady Louisa submitted herself to him. Tearing open the laces on her gossamer top, she freed her well-rounded, brown-nippled breasts and pushed them into Lawrence's face for him to suck; then, laying back spread-eagled on the discarded cloak, she lifted the gauzy hem of her gown to expose her ready, but rarely used womanhood, anxious to accept the lying, unprincipled womaniser inside her.

Lawrence's plan had worked, and within seconds they were making love on the office floor, feverishly thrashing together on the crumpled cloak and scattering the stack of well-ordered ledgers in their frenzy. Building herself up as he pumped his eager body into hers, Lawrence brought the vulnerable and deserted woman to a quick climax. With the ferocity of a mini Spanish whirlwind, Louisa vocalised her pleasure as he finished the job and with a long drawn-out stifled groan of ecstasy, Lawrence rolled off his prey, to lay next to her while they regained their lost breath.

During the entire time of Lawrence's victorious audience with Lady Louisa, the dutiful clerk had remained some twelve feet from the door. Sitting at a side table, he attended to some paperwork of his own while he waited to be recalled and escort the visitor back to his fellow travellers. At first everything seemed normal in the sealed room; only did he become slightly alerted when the books clattered on the floor. Assuming it was nothing other than a small accident, he continued with his work, scribbling comments in the margin of an unsigned document, but when the howls and moans issued from the locked chamber his instincts told him that things weren't as they should be. Thinking some kind of fracas or robbery was in progress, he started hammering on the door, calling for the guards, who in any case were well out of earshot, playing dice some twenty feet below.

Shocked to sudden alertness by the loud banging, the exhausted couple jumped up from their post-coital repose and, without having sufficient time to recover properly, both Lawrence and his latest conquest did their best to put themselves and the room back in order. Panting in their frenzied efforts, they gathered and re-stacked the scattered books, replaced the removed clothing and attempted to tidy up and return the room to exactly how it appeared before. The whole duration of the clear-up time, a panicking Louisa shouted through the closed portal, trying to allay the fears of the concerned servant, using the seized latch as an excuse for her failure to respond instantly. Eventually returning everything to an almost-fit state, she called for the anxious man to enter, the bewildered servant finding her wrapped in her wrinkled cloak, calmly reading the un-crumpled letter, with Lawrence sitting opposite her as if nothing had happened. Only the out-of-sequence ledgers, their heaving chests, ruddy cheeks and ruffled hair told the truth, none of which was missed by Sir John Segrave's loyal trusted employee, Geoffrey Swyfield, who had been a close friend and advisor to the knight for upwards of thirty years.

During Lawrence's time spent closeted with the lady of the castle, ample time passed for his guards to organise the re-shoeing of the horses, which had been done at full English cost, much to the annoyance of the grumbling Scots, who would have paid less than half the price north of the border. Insult was added to injury when even the food they were given to eat was sold to them for a token price, unlike Lawrence, whose fare was provided for free, him being a fellow English knight of Sir John's.

With all the business finished to everyone's satisfaction, the party left, the horses easily coping with the steep downward slope with their excellent new calcin and wedged shoes. Lawrence grinned to himself as they departed, feeling smugly happy and giving himself a well-deserved pat on the back for his successful liaison with the Lady Louisa. On the other hand, the despondent Scots moaned and whinged about the costly twelve-hour visit, mumbling words that Lawrence had got to understand as special Gaelic curses specifically aimed at their hated English foes.

Two days after the visit to Nottingham, the weather finally broke, and the sultry oppressive heat was replaced by a more seasonable prolonged colder wet spell, and for the next two weeks the small band of couriers meandered across the miserably damp shires doing their duty. The unenthusiastic group stopped now and again on the trek, to call at equally soggy fortalices and manors, delivering the demanding letters to grateful recipients, putting wives and mothers out of their prolonged misery when they heard that their beloved sons or husbands were still alive and well, safely imprisoned in Stirling Castle awaiting the payment of a ransom to secure their release. The visits took them from Nottingham, then first to Norwich, Colchester and lastly Oxford, before heading on the last leg of the journey to Hereford, where they were to deliver the most important package of all, the badly embalmed and fast decomposing corpse of Sir Henry de Bohun to his estates on the Welsh borders.

In their fight against the inclement conditions, the disenchanted cortege slowed with each waterlogged day, blissfully ignorant that now only two days behind them and quickly catching up were the three English knights, Sir Humphrey, Sir Ralph and Marmaduke Tweng, hell bent on hunting down Lawrence to prevent him from doing his intended mischief on the innocent Richard de Mauville, who himself was delightfully unaware that his life was in dire peril.

Following the welcome break at the manor house, Lady Joan Tweng's hastily arranged hospitality and a comfortable night's rest, all three Englishmen decided to appease Marmaduke's guilt for enjoying the stop rather more than the other two by offering to make more speed and make up for lost time on the next stage of the trek to Nottingham Castle, where they hoped to possibly overtake and detain Lawrence. Nevertheless, in their haste on the rejuvenated fresh horses, about thirteen miles into the forty-mile journey, Humphrey's mount stumbled down a hidden rabbit hole while cantering over an inviting stretch of heath land and, pitching on its nose, the unlucky horse tragically broke a leg, hurling the weighty rider into the air, somersaulting about ten feet into some convenient fall-breaking brambles and heather, saving Humphrey from major damage. Without needing further inspection, it was immediately apparent that the poor cob's front cannon bone had snapped, making the disabled animal completely beyond rescue and needing to be put as swiftly out of its misery as soon as possible.

Stunned, in no fit state to do the job himself and suffering from a huge sense of loss, Humphrey watched as the sympathetic animal-loving Ralph was left to do the necessary, humanely despatching the ill-fortuned animal with a slash of his expertly sharpened dagger across its pulsating throat. Whimpering a heartrending soft whinny, the lifeblood seeped out of the mighty beast, and, closing its dying eyes, it gently went to sleep amid a bed of soft ling.

With the demise of the cob, all hopes of catching Lawrence in the near future were dashed. All three men ended up ambling through the wilderness of West Lincolnshire at Humphrey's slow walking pace. Being a large man, the injured Humphrey was far too heavy for either of the other mounts, totally putting the possibility of taking turns to ride, or sharing with either Marmaduke or Ralph, out of the question. Only able to maintain a very slow speed, the bruised and strained Humphrey limped painfully along, having to stop and rest every few miles, forced into making an extra unscheduled overnight stop and taking another whole day before seeing the welcome sight of their destination appear through the mizzle, where the chatelaine's banner atop the castle's lofty keep seemed to brush the distant low scudding skies above the ancient walled city of Nottingham.

Humphrey felt a wonderful sense of achievement at actually reaching the goal in his state as he hobbled up the same ramp to the gateway which Lawrence had descended to leave the castle just over two days before, reaching the top with Sir Ralph, and most importantly Sir Marmaduke Tweng, who as a close neighbour and regular guest during the happier times of peace, was well known to the gatekeeper and needed no credentials to be let in. With open arms they were accepted into the stronghold, Louisa personally supervising their welcome, trying to absolve herself from the overpowering guilty feeling she harboured after her passing moment of idiocy.

In the cold light of day, Louisa realised that, in fact, Lawrence had lied to manipulate her and then, preying on her vulnerability, simply used her as an object for his own gratification. With deep regrets, she made herself extra busy, attempting to put the unfortunate incident to the back of her mind, not lucky enough to have anyone trustworthy to confide in and tell about her stupid moment of weakness.

The band of travellers had no option but to try and enjoy a longer than anticipated forced stay of hospitality. The ageing Humphrey needed more time than expected to recuperate from his heavy fall, the joint-straining injuries exacerbated by the ensuing agonising trek taking more time than first thought to improve. With frustration they whiled away the lost time trying to make the best of the inconvenient holiday, all the while knowing their quarry was getting too far ahead to be overhauled before reaching the final destination of Humphrey and Henry's estates and home castle, part of the string built specifically to protect England from the rampaging Welsh.

Following five days of strict convalescence, Humphrey felt recovered enough to resume the journey, all three deciding, rather than to blindly attempt to follow the lost trail of Lawrence and his escorts, they would simply head southwest, directly to Hereford and there to bide until his arrival. With Humphrey mounted on a borrowed and suitably strong chestnut titan of a horse called Titan, he, along with Ralph and Marmaduke, departed from the castle refreshed and ready to chase down the deceitful Lawrence. Rejuvenated from the rest and feeling stronger after the good food, with a heightened sense of purpose, the three knights rode through the murk and unyielding mizzly gloom, armed with the secret knowledge, honestly imparted by Geoffrey Swyfield with his master's best interest at heart, that in his few hours' stay in Nottingham, Lawrence had committed a dastardly act against a brother knight while he was away doing his devoir in the king's cause, and seduced the lonely Lady Louisa Segrave, in direct contravention of the chivalric code. With that in mind, they rode, now even more hopeful to be the ones to finally bring overdue justice to the lying, scheming woman abuser and coward that was the ignoble Lawrence Buckenham.

CHAPTER 13

The advantage of youth was on their side when Richard and his grateful assistant Simon started out on the last sixty miles to Hereford, on their dreary way across the desolate wet countryside. The flooded brooks and rivers made the progress slow and laborious as Solomon and Uther slipped and slid their tentative way forward. Untroubled by the treacherous going, the adolescent pair made the travelling more tolerable by pretending they were fighting off Saracens or bandits.

Sometimes, when the exuberance of defeating non-existent foes had worn a little thin, Richard would fill the long hours by telling his younger friend all about the war in Scotland and the valiant deeds of his much-lamented master Henry de Bohun. Richard's eager audience hung on his every word and occasionally held his breath frightened he might miss a precious word concerning the value of chivalry and the full sense of honour, indelibly instilled into Richard by the famous knight. Yet no matter what they did to occupy their lengthy time in the saddle, Richard always had an eye on Simon's handling of the long-suffering horse, correcting his seat when he started to slouch, or reminding him to relax when he became tense after a slip or stumble, but forever praising him, making the boy feel as if he was actually achieving something, which in truth he did with every single forward step.

The further they went the stronger their friendship became, taking turns to share their learning. Like understanding masters and attentive apt pupils they rode together, occasionally partaking in the odd puerile joke, but always learning off each other as they went. Up until leaving with Richard, Simon had spent his entire life in the close proximity of his culinary-adept mother and was well versed in the finer points of cookery. He understood all about butchery and the preparation of food and with glee he reciprocated Richard's teaching with some lessons of his own, freely imparting to his companion the sum total of his knowledge, going into great detail about such things as where to cut a joint or how long to mix a dough, and by the time they approached Hereford, Richard felt completely able to tackle cutting up a whole carcase or bake the most delicious bread, pies and pastries which sounded good enough for the king himself to eat.

It was the middle of the fourth morning of travel when the soaked pair of armed lads finally headed their horses through the narrow roads of the bustling outlying districts of Hereford city, where all the dwellings and work places were built strangely clumped as near to the massive castle as possible. Simon's eyes were on stalks: never having been to a city before, he was confused as to why, when there was so much land around, all the population wanted to live squeezed together in such a small area.

Turning to Richard as he had just finished practising a newly learnt manoeuvre on ever-patient Uther, Simon asked if Richard could solve a riddle concerning the ways of cities. "Why is it these people build their homes stacked on top of each other when there is so much available land to be had nearby?"

Giving a little laugh at the unworldly wise lad's naivety, Richard answered as they rounded a corner onto the main thoroughfare towards the main gate of the stronghold. "Because of the thieving Welsh tribesmen; they're only a dozen miles away and every time they need something they can't make, they just raid the city to get it, so the people stay as close as they can to the safety of the castle walls, and dive behind them at the first sight of the Welsh."

"How do you know all this?" Simon asked. "You've never been here, have you?"

Shaking his head sadly, Richard gave Simon a woebegone look. "Only for a short while, when I was first sent here as a twelve-year-old boy to become Sir Henry's squire. But although we left to go to war after only six days and I have been following him ever since, I still feel I know this place well as I've spent hours talking to Henry about it when he was feeling homesick, as he normally did," he sadly recalled, turning Solomon down Castle Street, the main road through Hereford, which was lined either side with multi-coloured stalls and booths, where hucksters, tradesmen, dealers and even some artisans plied their wares for sale. Items from as little as a pearl button to as much as a cart with its horses could be bought by the many browsing pedestrians who clogged the street, hoping to strike a bargain with an unwary seller.

As usual, Simon was lost in his own little martial world, pretending he was in the middle of a ferocious melee as they forced their way through the crowd, luckily reaching the drawbridge over the moat without trampling anyone important. The hollow booming-clatter of Solomon and Uther's iron-shod footsteps on the wooden-boarded bridge, alerted the pair of snoozing guards as Richard and Simon crossed to the other side. Peering through their sleepy, half-closed eyes at the unfamiliar visitors, the sentries stopped the unknown armed strangers before they were allowed to enter. Drawing their swords, they demanded to be told the names, styles and what business the outsiders had at the castle. Hearing their reply, the bemused men looked at each other in a rather surprised fashion when Richard informed them that he was Richard de Mauville, the squire to the late lamented Sir Henry de Bohun, who needed to see the lord's wife, the Lady Beatrice, to tell her firsthand about the manner of her husband's glorious but untimely death.

With a surprising degree of urgency, the clearly less senior of the sentinels obeyed a whispered order in his ear from his older colleague and trotted off as if his life depended on it. Having departed on his errand, he left Richard and Simon being guarded by the superior, who, as if to prevent him running off, clung on to Solomon's reins like a limpet on a rock. Attempting to stifle a giant shuddering yawn, the man gazed questioningly at Richard as if he was either weighing him up or trying to recollect his face from somewhere in the past.

Suddenly, with a flash of distant recollection showing in his tired eyes, he exclaimed loudly, "I know who you are; you're that little brat who arrived here six or eight years ago. Wasn't your father the John de Mauville who was killed in Scotland and then your mother sent you here because she couldn't afford to keep you, or something like that?" he queried, filling in some of the lost details of Richard's sketchy past.

Not actually knowing much about his early years, Richard merely shrugged his shoulders indicating such, but the revelation as to why he was enrolled into Sir Henry's train explained a lot and filled in some of the ever-present tormenting blanks that always loitered in the back of the lad's mind.

During the ten minutes being detained under the gateway, at the forcible request of the sentry, both Richard and Simon had dismounted and, being allowed to hold their own mounts, they stood admiring the architecture of the giant stone castle. Talking in wonderment, they mused on how impossible it would be to lay siege to it and thinking it would be there until the end of the world, both lads pictured battles both past and future, where the Welsh attackers were easily repelled and humiliated in bloody defeat.

Their youthful daydreams suddenly were interrupted by the sound of rushing armoured feet echoing under the archway. In politeness, the young men stepped aside to allow the hurrying guards to pass them in the narrow passage and go on their mission to wherever they were summoned. However, both of them went into complete shock when it became apparent the objective of the armed company was surprisingly the arrest of themselves. On the command of their captain, who Richard now recognised as the man Henry left in charge when he went to war all those years before, both lads were swiftly surrounded and disarmed. Startled by the speed of their inexplicable seizure, the distressed companions just looked at each other in dumb amazement, as neither of them had a remote clue as to why. Without putting up any resistance, the astonished Richard's and a mystified Simon's hands were tied before being manhandled through the courtyard and marched away to the cells in forced silence. Forbidden to even ask why they were being treated so badly, poor confused Simon struggled to fight back his frightened tears as they crossed the yard next to Richard, who was prevented from saying anything by a particularly zealous sadistic soldier who'd taken a liking to repeatedly poking him in the small of his back with the point of his own confiscated, cherished sword every time he attempted to protest his innocence.

The route to the dungeon took the bamboozled pair through the stables, where the first hint as to why they were under arrest presented itself to eagle-eyed Richard when he noticed a singularly odd feature on a very easily identifiable jet-black destrier standing impatiently in a stall. Becoming even more certain of its identity when the ill-tempered beast rolled its evil eyes and stamped an angry hoof as it saw the unwanted incursion into its comfort, only to confirm Richard's suspicions when the irritable horse flattened its ears and collapsed its nostrils to lunge and take a bite out of an arm as the party passed its box. It was then Richard knew that it was definitely the same horse he last saw in the wilds of Scotland along with its less than honourable master, the despicable cowardly rapist that masqueraded as a noble knight, one Sir Lawrence Buckenham.

For a complete twenty-four hours, Richard and Simon languished fettered and manacled in the dark, dank, airless cell no bigger than the back of a small cart with nothing other than some damp mouldy straw for bedding and a leaky pail for a latrine. Confused and flustered at their sudden predicament, the pair talked all through the night. Instead of the normal youthful light-hearted joking prattle they often shared, the discussion was much darker and profound, Simon babbling to Richard about what he thought was going to happen, going through some of the more ridiculous possibilities, repeating some farfetched fantasies out loud to mask his fear. His imaginative ideas ranged from being sent on a crusade to the Holy Land, to being publicly hanged, drawn and quartered in a similar fashion to the notorious Scottish rebel William Wallace.

Mainly to shut him up, Richard decided it was time to explain the reason they found themselves in such a mess and narrate the whole story about his falling out with Lawrence Buckenham, who he more than suspected had orchestrated their present situation. In the total darkness of the cell, Richard related the whole sequence of events which befell him in the aftermath of the

Battle of Bannockburn, from his fruitless search for Henry's body, his meeting Robert the Bruce, the story of the attempted rape, and the furious retribution Lawrence promised when Richard abandoned him injured by his own clumsiness and alone somewhere to the northwest of Stirling in bleakest Scotland.

They were still talking by the time the prison guard brought them what was described as breakfast, when each of them were hurled a bowl of indescribable, putrid-smelling kitchen waste, which was not dissimilar to the food they saw being fed to the pigs only a few days before. Sensibly, Richard compelled Simon to eat the poor substitute for nourishment, reminding him that it could be some considerable time before the next opportunity to feed his growing body presented itself. Used to his mother's better-than-good cooking, to face, let alone to actually eat the unimaginable swill was especially hard work for Simon, but with his companion manfully setting a good example, he managed every last drop, not, though, without retching a few times in his abhorrence at the tasteless rancid slops.

The delicious breakfast finished, the two exhausted youngsters had little to do other than to take the chance to catch up with a few hours' rest and digest. Finding it difficult to actually sleep, considering the present quandary they found themselves in, they eventually managed to close their weary eyes and dream pleasant youthful dreams of better times. Their short period of much-needed slumber became rudely interrupted when a squad of eight guards arrived at their cell and noisily rattled the rusted bolt to open the screeching door.

Without observance to any formalities, the brutal escorts manhandled the fearful lads up some slippery stairs to a reasonably furnished room, where their hastily arranged trial had apparently been partly conducted in their absence. It was with no surprise, by the time Richard's sleep-befuddled senses had cleared enough for his vision to return properly, he saw Lawrence as his main accuser, standing arrogantly at the front of the jam-packed court dressed in a fine black velvet cloak, which billowed melodramatically as he flitted around the courtroom. Stopping dead in his tracks, Lawrence smugly pointed to Richard alone as they were shoved in front of a panel of five seated elders.

"That's him! He's the foul traitor!" Buckenham shouted, triumphantly poking a crooked jewelled finger in Richard's direction. "Not that one, I've never seen him before, he's got nothing to do with this, throw him out!" Lawrence announced, waving his hand dismissively at Simon, who was summarily dragged away, leaving Richard standing on his own and suddenly looking very small to face Lawrence, as he turned his whole malicious attention back to the object of his festering hatred. "That's him, that's Richard de Mauville, my treacherous cowardly squire, who stabbed me in my sleep and left me to rot on a Scottish hillside!" Lawrence screeched, turning to the row of carefully listening judges to dramatically make a stabbing motion with his empty right hand and parrying the imaginary blow with his left; afterward holding them both up in a theatrical appealing fashion to make his point, he added a few embellishing sound effects to seduce the absorbed company, including the guards, spectators and two familiar noble women who both looked at Richard with tangible detestation in their glaring eyes.

Seeing that the demonstration had added some value to his attestation, Lawrence continued, placing his hands on his heart and shaking his lying head sadly. "If it wasn't for my lightning reactions, he would have killed me, there in the foreign land of the Scottish heathens, and so my story would have remained untold, allowing him to be free and do more heinous crimes. Yet as God would have it, fortune has brought this felon to be judged by your noble selves, this felon and false squire to your liege lord and mine, the noble knight, Sir Henry de Bohun." Again using his undeniably excellent acting skills, Lawrence looked pathetically at the two women, before continuing with his fabric of lies. "A loyal husband to a beautiful wife, and a proud nephew to a noble aunt!" Then, spinning round like a giant bat, he turned his attention back to the panel of judges to finish his indictment. Shaking his head in feigned disbelief, Lawrence carried on with his fantasy, but almost taking a step too far with his latest untruth. "A squire sworn always to protect his lord, no matter what the danger, a squire who cowardly deserted Sir Henry on the battlefield, leaving him to meet his glorious death charging the Scots on his own, while Richard de Mauville ran the other way. Yes, ran the other way! I saw it! I saw it all with my very own eyes!" Lawrence declared, summoning a look of mock horror to add credibility to the string of falsehoods.

His deceitful testimony failing to impress everyone present, especially the senior elder sitting in the middle of the other four, who, leaning forward off his seat, looked quizzically at the witness and then, tapping his forehead as if he was remembering something salient, stroked his clean-shaven chin and waved a sinewy hand as a signal for Lawrence to continue. "I weep for these bereft ladies, as I weep for you!" he declared, holding his open arms to the crowd in a mock gesture of embrace and, using some borrowed words from the king's rousing pre-battle speech, he carried on with the damning oration. "But saddest of all sadnesses, I weep for the spirit of this damned squire, who God in his infinite wisdom is sure to condemn to everlasting torture where all traitors like him belong, toasting alongside the devil in the burning fires of hell."

Apparently finished with his incriminating evidence, Lawrence hurled himself down in his vacant seat, hunching forward as if overwrought by the dreadful memories, which to all who watched, were a little too much for his sad and tormented soul to bear.

Richard listened to the false allegations without a single word in his own defence, knowing that to interrupt would be considered another crime while a nobleman was stating his case. However, all was not lost, when, much to his dismay a pertinently awkward question was fired at Lawrence by the head of the bench that Richard assumed had already found him guilty.

"May I ask what you were doing when you witnessed the cowardly acts of this young man here? Were you not the banner man to Sir Henry, and shouldn't your place have been with him when he charged the Scots? Please correct me if I am I wrong, as I don't know very much about the ways of warfare?" he asked, peering questionably at the eloquent witness.

Hearing the difficult-to-answer query, it was a slightly surprised Lawrence that looked up from his pretend grief as, thinking his case was already cut and dried, he hadn't anticipated such an inquiry. Somewhat flustered, Lawrence asked the judge to repeat the question, pretending that he didn't hear it properly, but in reality needing the time to think. Listening for a second time and after a brief pause, he responded somewhat indignantly with a seemingly plausible yet concise answer. "My duty, sir!" he said proudly, whilst mopping a pretend tear from his appealing eye.

Again the inquisitor looked sternly at Lawrence. "And what duty was that which kept you safely out of harm's way?" he asked labouring the point much to the witness's apparent displeasure.

Visibly taken aback by the question, Lawrence hesitantly came up with another ambiguity to buy a little more time while he thought up how to wriggle out of the awkward situation. "As I was instructed by Sir Henry, sir!" he answered, trying his best to look vexed at the suggestion that he might be doing otherwise.

"All I want to know, if it's not too much trouble, is to be told simply, what it was which was so important that it detained you from joining Sir Henry when he charged the Scots? Now answer, if you wouldn't mind!"

Looking surprised at the dogged nature of the probing from the head magistrate and rather taken back by it, Lawrence paused before giving his hastily invented final terse reply. "As I was told to do. *Sir*! I was marshalling our men-at-arms ready for the assault on Robert the Bruce's schiltron, *sir*!"

"There, that wasn't so difficult, was it?" the inquisitor noted, sounding relieved at getting the required response; then, leaning back, he crossed his pale fingers in a woven pattern across his dark gown, apparently satisfied with the difficultly extracted explanation. Pausing to digest Lawrence's evidence the magistrate looked over at Richard waiting to see what he had to say about the matter, having to prompt him to speak in his own defence. "Well then, what have you got to say for yourself, young man?" he asked, once again leaning back comfortably to listen to what he expected was going to be a tissue of outrageous lies.

Already resigned to his fate, Richard appeared startled for a moment at his opportunity to speak, never in his wildest dreams having expected to be given the chance to state his case. Therefore, having considered his options, Richard simply decided to tell the truth, and carefully relate the series of events, deliberately omitting any facts which could be construed as self-promoting, so as not to antagonise the glaring assembly further, which he doubted would believe him anyway. Richard started by telling the court about the first morning before the battle, going right through to the time when Lawrence injured himself following the crime against Yolanda. The entire time Lawrence butted rudely in, shouting interjections such as, "Lies! Lies! Lies!" Or, "not true, not true!" Eventually having to be admonished by the head judge, who finally shut him up with a threat to have him forcibly removed from the courtroom.

Having heard all the testimonies, the five judiciaries drew up their chairs to form a seated huddle and for upwards of a quarter of an hour they debated the case, their soft whispers being accompanied with much head nodding and finger-wagging, as they deliberated on their findings. Meanwhile, out of respect for the solemnity of the proceedings, the hushed assembly talked mutedly among themselves, each drawing their own conclusion as to either the guilt or innocence of Richard, who knew that in the next few minutes a verdict would be pronounced, which in all probability would mean whether he would live or die.

At last the torment of the wait was almost over for Richard, when, with an expectant air of doom, the judges resumed their previous positions and, glowering menacingly at the accused, they waited for total quiet before pronouncing their conclusion. A guard found it necessary to bang the butt of his spear on the wooden boards and shout for silence to gain the spectators' attention and make them obey the command. Abruptly, the hushed conversations faded to a total silence before the senior elder cleared his throat ready to sum up what had been a very short trial. Speaking feebly and unheard by most of the gathering, the head magistrate started to give his reasons as to why he reached his verdict and whatever sentence he felt appropriate for the crimes. Although, at the bidding of one of the other judges, he raised his voice to start again at the beginning, this time speaking louder so all present could hear.

"Having heard all the available evidence, I have no option, as considering that in its simplicity it's the word of a sworn knight of the realm, against that of a mere boy, who in all probability was scared witless when the battle lines formed." Stopping to clear his throat again, the judge continued, "I do believe that, against the law of God and that of our noble king, the second Edward of the Plantagenet house, Richard de Mauville did indeed desert the noble Henry, and act in a way which may be interpreted as cowardice, for which this court in its mercy forgives him, nevertheless..."

At the apparent acquittal, a noisy murmur of amazed grumbling ran around the court, especially from Lawrence, who voiced his protest loudest of all, interrupting proceedings, much to the annoyance of the judge, who glanced at the guard and nodded for him to bang his shaft on the floor once more to bring the courtroom back to order ready for the pronouncement to go ahead.

Satisfied that silence was once again restored, he continued, directing a meaningful scowl at Lawrence, whom he had found to be rather annoying from the very start. "But in our consideration, worst of all, he did make an attempt on the life of his liege lord Sir Lawrence Buckenham, and for that he shall be hanged tomorrow at midday for this transgression and this transgression alone. May God take pity on him? Take him away!"

Poor innocent Richard, the youth who'd manfully stood bolt upright during the entire proceedings and held his head stoically erect as he stared unblinkingly into the eyes of the judge while listening in resolute silence as the string of lies were told about him. Yet on hearing the judgement, he felt his knees buckle slightly, as his forthcoming doom was pronounced so matter of factly. Nonetheless, quickly adjusting his faltering stance, Richard accepted his fate with an almost imperceptible nod to the bench, showing the same air of nobility he had always admired in his lord and mentor, the man he had been found guilty of betraying and the guiding star on his about-to-be shortened life, the noblest of noblemen, Sir Henry de Bohun.

Surrounded and dwarfed by his enormous guards, Richard kept his dignity intact by not uttering a single word of complaint, and without looking to the right or left, he pulled his shoulders back and puffed out his chest, holding his head erect and gazing unerringly in front, he passively marched from the room, deliberately ignoring the triumphant jig and knowing wink from

Lawrence, who found it impossible to hide his joy at the outcome of the disgracefully unfair trial. Only once on his way out did he bother to take his eyes off the giant shoulders in front of him and then it was to glance sympathetically over to where Sir Humphrey's wife and Henry's widow were embraced in their shared misery. Sadly believing everything they'd heard about the devoutly loyal Richard, they watched with watery eyes as the condemned lad was led to the dungeon, where he was to await his appointment with the hangman at twelve noon the next day.

That evening, Richard found it impossible to sleep, even though he was utterly dog-tired from the previous night of insomnia, brought about by his relentless worry over the dire situation and the verbosity of the ever-garrulous Simon, who himself was in little better state than Richard, ashamed that he could be of no assistance to his only friend he knew in his heart to be utterly guiltless of any crime. So, buried somewhere deep beneath the castle's keep, in the dank gloom of an airless stone cell, Richard was left alone with nothing but his imaginings as he wrestled with pictures of his beloved Yolanda. All through the hours of darkness he could imagine her beautiful face when she was brought the news of his execution, inwardly regretting bringing her and their family name into disrepute, even though he knew he was absolutely innocent of any crime.

Bravely Richard resolved himself to face the gallows without showing any outward sign of fear, once again modelling his actions on what he thought Henry would do if faced with the same situation. He knew that any display of trepidation would only enhance the enjoyment of his vile scheming adversary Lawrence, who somewhere above him and without conscience slept as soundly as a new-born baby, having worn himself out in a celebratory romp with two underage prostitutes and drunk more than his fill of his favourite red wine.

Not having a clue as to what the actual time was, Richard's overactive mind started playing mean tricks on him. Twice he thought he heard the footsteps of the guards coming to fetch him for his final walk outside into the fresh air, only to realise it was nothing more than a restless horse, stamping his hooves in the nearby stables. Once even, he could have sworn that he heard the sound of noisy bolt on the door being drawn back and it was with some surprise when eventually the unmistakable sound of synchronised feet moving in unison approached the locked and barred entrance to the cell.

The time had come; this time Richard was correct and his worst fears realised when the heavy oak door was flung open, its familiar creak splitting the quiet solitude, revealing lined up in the narrow dim-lit passageway the same body of burly guards that escorted him there the previous day. Without formality or any care whatsoever for the condemned prisoner, one of the biggest, a sombre-faced giant, who appeared to be the sergeant in command, grabbed the terrified lad by his collar. Using just one massive hand, he hauled Richard to his unsteady feet and dragged him tripping and stumbling in his effort to keep up with the long striding legs of the hurrying squad, outside into the crowded courtyard and what seemed like an extremely bright day to his gloom-accustomed eyes, which in actual fact was just another dull, damp, drizzly, and cold late-October morning.

Blinking his gritty eyes against the glaring light and pulling himself together, Richard wriggled himself free from the grasp of his less than gentle escort. Puffing up his pounding chest, he walked obediently and completely without assistance towards the hurriedly erected, crudely made wooden gallows, built as high as possible on the back of a cart to make it feasible for all the ghoulish sightseers to witness the unusual spectacle of the death of an English traitor.

Most of the gathering had already seen Welsh raiders, the odd deserter or murderer executed, but this was different and the news had spread quickly, attracting people from miles around, filling the concourse to the brim with curious people. Every spectator wanted to see how the accused would face his death, including a wan-faced Simon, who was there for a different reason, as he struggled to get a sight of his condemned friend and catch Richard's eye, to tell him that Lawrence had just left in a blind panic when he saw three riders he evidently recognised approaching the main gate from the east.

Richard's arrival in the yard was initially heralded with a mighty chorus of jeers, cat-calls and whistles, quickly followed by a wave of muttering when it became clear how young and brave he was. Without showing any emotion, Richard climbed up the steps onto the back of the wagon and, standing perfectly still as his arms and legs were trussed, strangely enjoyed the smell of some toasting chestnuts as he fixed his gaze straight ahead onto a scraggy pair of crows that were sitting high on the battlements cawing for their lunch. Half-smiling to himself, he mused on how they were most probably queuing up to feast on his dead eyes when the deed was done. Numb throughout his nervous body, Richard offered his head forward as the hangman put the noose round his adolescent throat. Scanning the crowd to get his last glimpse of the world, he expected his final image to be that of an exultant Lawrence at the front of the throng, grinning and dancing as the executioner did his work, but no matter how thoroughly he looked, it seemed the gloating visage was nowhere to be seen anywhere in the vicinity.

As sometimes happens, luck can work both ways and luckily for unlucky Richard, Lawrence had bribed the hangman handsomely to make his demise as slow and painful as possible, and instead of the instant painless death of a long drop with the correctly placed knot snapping the accused's neck in a split second, the expert executioner deliberately applied his trade less succinctly. Doing exactly what he'd been paid to, the sadist hauled gradually on the halter, hoisting Richard's helpless trussed body no more than six inches off the rough planks, before jiggling the rope to half-strangle and make Richard dance for half a minute for the crowd's amusement, prior to releasing the cable and allowing him to fall in a crumpled heap with a thump on the boards to give his living victim time to regain his stolen breath. Then, in a sadistic attempt to enhance the show, the murderous professional killer took the intervening time to bow and receive a thoroughly deserved round of applause, before grasping the rope once again and with another mocking bow was about to repeat the process and brutally heave his victim a little higher this time. His effort though was suddenly halted when an eddy of activity at the back of the crowd took his attention, stopping him mid-stroke in his playful endeavour to amuse the gathering further, before he could continue and prolong the torment any longer.

Attracted by an uproar of terrified shrieks and shouts, the entire crowd turned away from the main entertainment to see three fully armoured, armed and mounted knights, visors closed, charging headlong into the multitude, scattering men women and children alike in their attempt to halt proceedings before it was too late.

Ploughing through the assembly, the horsemen parted the throng like the Red Sea did for Moses, as they galloped up the cleared path, all the way to the scaffold. Fortunately, their meaningful approach halted the vicious sub-human torturer and prevented him from doing any more damage to the gasping Richard, who by then was sitting back up and was also staring in the same direction as everybody else, towards the anonymous riders as they got nearer and nearer to where he was.

Hurtling up like thunderbolts, they screeched their chargers to a sudden halt in front of the gallows next to a viewing platform, where the five judges, two noblewomen and some other dignitaries stood to oversee the summary justice being done. The senior judge, who incidentally never wanted to pass such a severe punishment in the first place, seemed a little relieved at the interruption that saved him from the vociferous objections of the two ladies which were still ringing in his ears, when they realised that integrity was being served poorly by torturing a brave lad of no more than seventeen years old to death.

The magistrate's wavering voice was barely audible above the uproar as he feebly spoke to the foremost of the three. Peering short-sightedly, he addressed a rotund knight sitting astride a giant chestnut horse with no identifying shield to say who he actually was, remaining anonymous to the nobles. "Who is it, may I ask, that so audaciously prevents the Earl of Hereford's justice from being done?"

"You may ask, Mathias, and I shall tell you," a familiar voice boomed from within the protective armour. "It is I, Sir Humphrey de Bohun, fourth Earl of Hereford, the lord and master of this castle, who so audaciously interrupts his own justice," Humphrey explained, lifting his face-concealing visor to reveal his easily recognisable features to the balcony where everybody, except the females, fell on their knees at the vision of the famous knight. Smiling a relieved smile, Humphrey casually blew a kiss at the elder of the two ladies as she crossed herself with joy at the sight of him, before continuing with the admonishment.

Reddening slightly with each word in his gathering anger, Humphrey addressed the judges. "The justice of the castle I hold in the king's name, where I see there has been a new rule of law instigated in my absence. A law which is so omnipotent, it is prepared to hang this valiant squire, who contrary to what you may or may not have been told, is only guilty of being stupidly steadfast to my poor nephew Sir Henry! So release him NOW! And have him tended to, before I choose one of you to take his place," he threatened, scanning his angry, bulging eyes along the line of the judiciary as if he was going to select one as a stand in, before carrying on with his address, a tell-tale throbbing blue vein at his temple the first sign that his pent-up rage was about to break free. Raising his voice to a controlled bellow, Humphrey demanded answers. "And where is the noble knight, Sir Lawrence Buckenham? Nowhere to be seen, that's where; he who undoubtedly has told you a lengthy sob story of the dangers he faced in getting Sir Henry's mortal remains back here to where they belong in the home of his forefathers." Those last words having been said and still echoing around the walls, Humphrey, in something closely resembling a blind rage, snapped and turned his attention to the morbid gathering of dejected-looking spectators, disappointed and saddened that their much-anticipated day's entertainment had been ruined by the knights' timely intercession. "Whoresons and harlots! Get back to your fucking rat holes where you belong. Away! Away with you!" he yelled, as all three riders set about the mob, kicking out with their armoured feet and belabouring anyone to hand with the flat of their swords.

In a whirlwind of frenetic activity, the enraged knights scattered the crowd, including the vendors, who in their bid to escape the rampaging trio, knocked over their trollies complete with the assortment of merchandise on the floor. In a tornado of action, cakes, sweetmeats, steaming chestnuts and a volcano red of hot coals went flying, just missing the head of a relieved-looking curly red-headed freckled boy who clung doggedly to Sir Humphrey's stirrup leathers, begging to be heard.

Like terrified rabbits running from a hungry fox, the mass dispersed, magically melting away to any convenient nook or cranny, trying to escape the wrath of the frenzied attack, until the whole area was cleared, except for a few of the braver sellers who were trying to salvage what they could of their trampled wares, and the boy who still hung obstinately onto the rampaging earl's leg, pleading for him to listen and hear what he had to say.

As quickly as it came, Humphrey's tempestuous tantrum dissipated and, seeing there was no one else available to vent his anger on, he looked down at the boy, somewhat amazed at his tenacity the lord spoke in softer tones to the wide-eyed, freckled-faced lad. "Stubborn little fellow, aren't you? What do you want to talk to me about?" he asked, expecting to hear nothing of relevance from the stripling's trembling lips.

"About Sir Lawrence Buckenham, sir! My friend Richard told me all about him, and I saw him sneak away just as you were arriving," the lad gasped, trying to get back his lost breath.

"Why didn't you tell me this before? If you do indeed have the ear of young Richard, tell him there are several matters I need to talk to him about concerning that man! Ralph, Marmaduke, quickly, to me!" Humphrey shouted to his fellows who were in the final process of clearing the concourse.

At one word from Humphrey, his two associates came racing up, satisfied the task of driving the dross from the yard was complete and correctly thinking there might be another problem which needed their urgent attention.

"What is it?" they demanded, thinking that some immediate action may be called for.

"It's that slippery little fucker Buckenham, according to this persistent young fellow, who claims to be a friend of Richard's, he's run off at the first whiff of us."

"Can I go and see Richard now please, sir?" Simon asked, once more tugging at Humphrey's riding boots.

"We'll go together. Believe me, I'm in no fit state to go chasing after that bastard. Anyway, I need to see my wife and niece, to tell them all about what's happened, but I'm sure my two fellow knights here will do their best to find him."

Without tarrying any unnecessary time, other than to water their thirsty horses, Humphrey watched as his two friends trotted off in the direction as indicated by Simon, hoping to catch up with the fast-departing Lawrence, leaving Humphrey to painfully dismount and hobble off into the castle, supported by the willing shoulder of Simon, to catch up with his relations and the slowly recovering Richard, whose half-throttled, battered body had been dragged to safety by the same over-zealous guards, wanting to make amends for earlier actions.

Once safely inside the massive stronghold, Humphrey instantly planted himself in the first convenient seat, to be attended by a pair of extremely pretty young female servants, his very anxious-looking wife and newly bereft niece, all four of whom were obviously overjoyed to see their returned husband, uncle and kind master. Circling him like vultures, they inspected and dabbed his half-healed cuts and bruises with soothing salves and potions. Every single move was watched impatiently by Simon, who desperately wanted to be with his injured friend, finding relief when a newly arrived third female attendant whisked him away, leaving Humphrey being fussed over by a very concerned quartet as he told everything he knew of the true tale of cowardice, seduction, treachery, and rape, erroneously attributed to poor sore Richard, who was only a few rooms away and also being nursed. Unfortunately for Richard, instead of a couple of pretty female nurses, his carer was a crusty old black-gowned, wrinkled physician, wearing something like a cut-off wizard's hat jammed over his ears to hide his almost completely bald head. The unsympathetic doctor treated him like an ailing dog, poking and prodding with his horny claw-like grubby fingers, prising open his mouth with two of them to gaze down his dreadfully sore throat and inspect for internal damage.

How pleased Richard was to see Simon arrive; he even managed to force out a muffled grunt of delight when he observed his best friend entering the room. Raising himself off his bed, he grasped and shook his hand thankfully as though they were long-lost brothers who hadn't seen each other for ten years. With a weak wave of his hand, Richard dismissed the rough-handed surgeon so the two could talk in private.

Trying to get all his words out at once, Simon told Richard of all the events, babbling hurriedly as if he needed to say what he had to before he'd forgotten the story. In a continuous string of verbal diarrhoea, Simon told all about the rescue, Humphrey's subsequent storm of anger at the spectators and the elders, even how he upset the vendors' stalls, almost burning him, and then of everything else he could think of except the tragic news of the guilty Lawrence's escape.

Richard could do nothing except listen and mumble occasionally in agreement as the series of hazy events were brought freshly back to his confused mind, which in God's infinite mercy had blotted out most of the traumatic happenings, leaving his only real memory of the episode as the smell of roasting chestnuts, which for the rest of his life would induce a fleeting tremor of terror to course through his body.

After a full ten minutes of ceaseless chatter, Simon had said everything he needed to and, panting to regain his breath, he forgot about Richard's inability to talk back easily. Looking disappointedly at Richard, Simon waited for a comment, which painfully came after swallowing as much spittle as he could muster to lubricate his damaged larynx. With a struggle Richard forced his breath over his bruised vocal chords to croak the briefest of possible questions. "Where's Lawrence?" he asked, wincing with the painful effort.

"Pardon, what did you say?" Simon replied, actually having heard the question but needing time to consider his answer, debating whether a harmless lie to save Richard's feelings would be appropriate, or to tell the truth might be easier.

In rising frustration at receiving no answer, Richard repeated himself, this time with even more difficulty, but managing a little extra volume in his tired, distorted voice. "I said, where is Lawrence?"

Seeing the building aggravation in Richard, Simon opted to tell the truth. "He's disappeared, but never mind as Sir Ralph and Sir Marmaduke have gone after him. The last time I saw him, he was riding as if all the devils in hell were after him, which I expect they are, and I hope they get him!" Simon explained, but, seeing the growing weariness in Richard's haemorrhaged bloodshot eyes as they struggled to stay open, he ceased his nervous babble and decided the best medicine for his friend would be rest. So being as quiet as possible, Simon tiptoed out of the chamber and, closing the door silently behind him, took a position in a seat outside the room, resigned resolutely to stay on guard while Richard slept his crucially vital healing sleep.

CHAPTER 14

For a whole week Richard slept his recuperating sleep, only occasionally waking from his sickly slumber to be instantly attended to by the ever-vigilant Simon, who tended to his needs and fed him the only thing he could swallow, the extremely tasty clear lump-free, nourishing chicken broth, made at the dead of night by his own hand. Other than to make the soup, Simon categorically refused to leave his adopted position on his seat outside the bed chamber, where inside, with the healing properties of Richard's age on his side, each day he looked a little better. The redness in his blood-suffused eyes soon turned yellow, and the great purple bruise on his throat had faded to a greenish brown, but the resulting huskiness in Richard's marred voice remained throughout the rest of his life, giving it a sexy quality, much admired by women of all ages.

With the arrival of November, the weather across the whole of Europe changed for the worse. The perpetual damp, chilly, drizzly-gloom, occasionally punctuated by the odd Biblical-styled deluge, which had hung around since mid-August, now turned to a perpetual icy wind blowing relentlessly from the northeast. Its howling gusts soon turned the incessant rain to hail, sleet or snow, freezing everything in its path, and covering everywhere with a two-foot-thick white layer of powdery ice.

The inclement conditions forced the two pursuers of Lawrence to prematurely return, arriving back at the castle chilled to the bone and empty-handed from their fruitless task of looking for the fugitive. The only news of his whereabouts were several feasible sightings of the wanted man flying north, leading them to believe he had fled back to hide somewhere in the wilds of Scotland.

Inside Hereford Castle the Christmas celebrations were decidedly mute as the sad occupants were still in mourning for the lost Henry, whose festering remains were finally laid to rest beneath a brass effigy on the floor of the castle chapel on St. Nicholas's day, the sixth of December 1314. The saddest of all the bereft mourners was an almost recovered Richard, who lamented him dreadfully and felt as though he had not only lost a friend but a father figure as well.

The great penetrating chill pervaded everywhere in the castle. With temperatures plunging well below freezing point, anything liquid turned almost instantly to a solid. Even the strongest wine froze and, before being drunk, had to be thawed in front of the enormous roaring infernos which blazed vainly in all the fireplaces. Despite being kept permanently stoked night and day, the fires were still unable to cope with the frigid air and even though each of the occupants went about their business wrapped from head to foot in blankets and furs, they still had that purplish-blue tinge on all their extremities and their numbed, cold-stiffened, painful fingers struggled to cope with the simplest of tasks which otherwise would have been so easy.

For the rich in the castle it was bad enough, but for the poor out in the isolation of the Welsh borders things were much worse for the peasant farmers, whose very existence was threatened by the unrelenting cold. The valuable animals they relied upon to provide everything from food, clothing, and even tallow for candles, died where they stood. Some succumbed to hunger or thirst, but most died from suffocation, trapped in the monstrous snowdrifts, the wind-blasted peaks of which were visible as far as the eye could see in a continuous, featureless, blinding blue-white undulating sheet of ice that stretched in all directions from horizon to horizon, blotting out the tracks, roads, hedges and even the smaller trees, making the chance of navigation to the shelter of the warmer towns and villages all but impossible.

Inside the farmhouses, crofts or hovels of the lowly country folk, the situation was awful. With nothing but pathetic peat-fuelled fires for heat, everything solidified; the bread, the meat if they were lucky, and even the very strong syrupy alcoholic mead froze solid, including the melt water, which during the warmer daytime leaked through the thatch, only to re-freeze as soon as twilight fell and by the morning hung in long icicles on the inside, where the shivering families' only remaining option was to stay put, cross their frozen fingers and hope, whilst waiting to see what God in his infinite mercy had in store for their miserable souls.

Everywhere from north to south and east to west, a great sense of gloom descended on the starving population, who had little to do but to huddle together for warmth and pray for the cold spell to break, trusting they would be lucky enough to survive the worst and longest spell of severe winter weather ever to have occurred within living memory.

Up in the colder climes of Scotland things were equally as bad if not a little worse than in England. The so recently fast-flowing streams were now as hard as roads, to say nothing of the once-raging waterfalls which tumbled out of the mountains but were now sculpted into fantastic contorted columns of beige or blue ice. It was so cold that even on the coast the salty turquoise ocean was solid enough for a fully-grown man to walk upon without fear.

It was no better in the desolate squalor of Dunstaffnage Castle, where the newly arrived Lawrence Buckenham had begged refuge from his only ally on earth, the mean-spirited Thomas Dewar. In desperation Lawrence reluctantly accepted the bartered hospitality after striking a very one-sided bargain with greedy Thomas, having to promise on the Bible to take charge of the leaderless garrison and command the essential, larder-filling raiding parties into England without expectation of pay. However, on the other side of the deal, Lawrence would get all his needs, including his old quarters, plenty to eat and, to their mutual benefit, whatever females he wanted, providing he titillated Thomas's perversion with the tales of their rape.

It was with a great sense of irony, Lawrence once again found himself gazing forlornly out of his freezing old room's window over the ice-bound sea. Having many regrets, he mused on how the unpredictable fickle hand of fate had so annoyingly sided with his enemies to thwart his well-laid plans. Without its damnable interfering, what greatness he should have achieved and what might there have been, if only it wasn't for the cursed, meddling, eternal fly in his ambitious ointment, his hated archenemy, the holier-than-thou bastard, Richard de Mauville.

The conditions at Dunstaffnage, although much colder, were much as they were before Lawrence was sent on his forced errand to England. Again he accepted as normal the seemingly endless supply of young girls of all ages, who were magically produced and sent on a regular basis to Lawrence's room, where he was given free rein to do with them whatever pleased him, providing, as promised, the whole distasteful account was related, detail by minute disgusting detail, back to Thomas at the first opportunity. Often in the evenings they would share a thawed bottle of wine or two in front of the continuously stoked blaze in the main hall where Thomas would listen, open-mouthed and dribbling, or giggling with excitement at the erotic, usually exaggerated stories. Loving every moment, he would hang on every word, wishing upon wish that his inactive groin would respond to the stimulus, which unfortunately for him it never did, and for the rest of his sordid life he had to rely on the descriptions of other people's sexual exploits to sate his vile appetite.

No matter how many young beauties Thomas supplied for the ever-obliging Lawrence to de-flower or subject to his farfetched sexual inventiveness, he never felt completely satisfied, as he still harboured sulky memories of the unfinished business of his first carnal encounter at the castle.

During the lengthy re-telling of his experiences, he often asked of the little girl he found impossible to rape, at the time settling for her younger, but more womanly sister, whom he considered was his second choice. The picture of the un-developed blonde lass laying spread-eagled on the bed, her small sweet breasts and childish naked purity, even her piercing blue eyes staring hatefully at him, all were impregnated indelibly into his thoughts. How he wished he had enjoyed the terrified girl, regularly wondering if there would ever be another opportunity to finish the incomplete task.

One evening, after relating the story of a particularly horrendous attack on a defenceless child, Lawrence's curiosity got the better of him. Out of the blue he interrupted the slavering Thomas, who at the time was lost in his own sexual fantasy, to see if there was any possible chance of a future liaison with the unforgotten adolescent beauty. "Do you remember those blue-eyed sisters you sent me when I first came here?" he asked, looking hopefully at Thomas, who looked back at him seemingly a little peeved at being disturbed from his depraved imaginings. "I don't suppose there's any chance of seeing the tall blonde one, is there?" Lawrence queried, gazing optimistically at his repulsive landlord.

"That old cherry, excuse my pun! Nice little tight cunt, no tits, yes, I remember, but there's no chance of that. If you must know, I sold her ages ago to an English brothel-keeper somewhere just south of the border," Thomas answered, mumbling almost inaudibly, shooting a wet-lipped sadistic leer at Lawrence, "and her sister, the dark one, I sold her too!" he said excitedly, sucking at some escaping saliva and then chuckling, "Bit of luck there, as you made a fucking dreadful mess of her's, I doubt if she'll be any good to anyone now though!"

Lawrence looked more than a little disappointed at the reply, knowing he should leave it be, but his curiosity had taken charge, questioning Thomas some more, annoying his host who only wanted to hear about the previous night's events. "I was just wondering where they have gone that's all," Lawrence asked matter-of-factly, while wiping an errant purple dribble of wine off of his unshaven chin and trying to sound as if he didn't care, but pursuing the point rather too long.

The tenacious questioning prompted Thomas to answer angrily and raising his voice he made his aggravation clear. "As I fucking told you, if you'll bother to fucking listen to me this time, I sold them to one of my fucking suppliers somewhere on the border; remember, a fucking brothel-keeper! There, you know now, I've told you! Now can you shut the fuck up about them and tell me all about that swarthy little Irish bitch you fucked senseless last night!"

Nodding as if taking the point, Lawrence carried on telling the salacious tale to the vile, drooling, perverted Thomas, who'd recovered from his fit of pique and resumed listening to Lawrence, who outwardly accepted it was time he forgot about the episode, but still indelibly burnt into the back of his mind was the unmovable image of the naked, sprawled girl and her lucky escape from his merciless clutches.

Across the whole of Northern Europe the February chill intensified; day by day it got progressively colder all the way through March and into April. The deep snow, however, miraculously disappeared gradually without thawing, as sometimes happens when the frozen wind blows directly from the Arctic, blasting the ice crystals into the air to disappear without trace. The strange phenomenon caused the bleak bone-hard frozen countryside to shed its all-covering white cloak, revealing its hidden features and allowing some daytime travel, but, only the bravest dared to go outside to find food, which strangely was in abundance, as the many fallen animals' meat, once thawed, was as fresh as if it had only just been killed. Yet even in the respite, the hardiest of the hardy didn't dare to venture out after dark, for any who did were sure not to survive the penetrating night-time frosts. For three months the whole of the population had been trapped in, or near their dwellings, many of them dying in their wait for warmer weather, their unburied solid bodies merely placed nearby to be interred at a later date, when the ground was soft enough to dig a grave.

The tradesmen and labourers looked on the forced confinement as a penance, preventing them from plying their skills and making a living, but in a peculiar way it was a relief to the farms and homesteads in the northern counties of England, where the regular marauding Scottish raiding parties had become braver and much more daring since the demise of Edward's beaten armies the previous June.

Now, much to the relief of their victims, the Scots were also in a similar strait, not daring to wander far from their homes, giving the English borderers a reprieve from their merciless looting forays. Frustrated, short of food and eager for the weather to break, the professional pillagers did what everybody else did and protected themselves and their possessions as best they could by battening down the hatches in whatever suitable shelter they could find to see out the abnormally brutal winter.

The resulting stalemate irritated King Robert as much as anyone else. Safely holed-up in the warmth of Stirling Castle, the normally positive Robert felt downcast, desperately frustrated at not being able to press home his hard-fought advantage and gain some form of recompense for the costly defence of his realm, highly aggravated with his inability to pursue the essential, royally sanctioned sorties necessary to feed his fragilely united subjects. He was frightened that without the all-important, stolen life-enhancing commodities his home country was unable to produce for itself, the tenuous alliance with his one-time adversaries might snap, returning Scotland to the bad old days when the factions spent their time fighting amongst themselves, leaving the road open for the united English to subjugate their less-prosperous neighbour to their will once again.

Down in the slightly warmer south of England, King Edward II, his wounds licked, body and mind almost restored to something resembling normality, also suffered from a deep depression. Still dreadfully haunted by his catastrophic defeat at the hands of what he considered was nothing better than a Scottish rabble, his awful black brooding moods became exacerbated by the relentless bitter winter, making his bouts of unpredictable screaming temper to get worse with each passing month. Those about him avoided the king's company as often as he would allow, including his long-suffering, young French wife, Isabella, his court and even the ever-faithful Baron Dussingdale, preferred to let the tempestuous monarch stew in his own juice.

Shut away from the outside world, Edward planned his dreadful revenge on the impertinent Robert the Bruce for embarrassing him so thoroughly at the abject military farce which was the famed Battle of Bannockburn. There the cream of the English nobility defied the favourable odds by turning certain victory to humiliating defeat, and were made to look like a band of incompetent apprentices at the hands of what the king still believed was an ill-disciplined gang of Scots peasants.

With the advent of Easter, what was loosely described as springtime arrived and mercifully with it the deep penetrating all-pervading ice gave way to somewhat warmer, gloomy and persistently rainy weather. The temperatures, though, still remained several degrees below the normal for the time of year, putting everything into stasis. Even the trees remained bald, their buds and leaves believing it was still winter, wisely refused to open in the depressing cool damp air, preferring to remain hidden, waiting until improved times. Not unlike the populace, whose inclination to joy in the season of new growth was lost, along with their expectations for a good summer.

The general depression caused the early year festivals of Easter, Mayday or Whitsun, which were such major parts of the rural year, to remain virtually uncelebrated. The famished people preferred not to celebrate the expectation of a seasonal change, and opted to stay indoors to save their energy, hoping for some better more clement days, which, unknown to them at the time, would be more than a long time coming.

All through spring into early summer, the occurrences of regular night frosts were still a problem to those who bothered to till the clogging sodden land. With no heat to dry out the soaked soil, each ploughed furrow filled quickly with icy water making it impossible to use. Even if the toiling labourers achieved such a feat, it was still doubtful whether the planted seeds would germinate, let alone grow into the viable crops so badly needed to replenish the empty larders and stocks of grain so badly depleted by the long severe winter.

And so it was that the three years of the Great Famine started. The climate remained out of kilter with the normal rhythms of the seasons, with freezing arctic winters and cool damp sunless summers, where the crops failed, and livestock drowned in the flooded fields. Starvation ruled, and meat was at a premium: dogs, cats, horses and even vermin were considered good food, and even cannibalism had been mentioned in reports from the strife-torn northern borders of England, where the sickliest children were rumoured to be slaughtered and eaten to keep the fitter of the poverty-struck inhabitants alive. The price of even the lowest quality of foodstuffs shot through the roof, where two onions cost a whole day's wages and the price of lowest quality, uncleaned wheat was at least ten times the price it was before the cataclysm. The prohibitive cost of the most basic of commodities excluded many, especially the poor, from purchasing them, and it was they that bore the brunt of the evil times which took in its destructive wake most of their animals and at least ten percent of the peasant population.

The astrologers blamed the three years' ascendency of Saturn in the night sky as the cause for the catastrophe, promising that with the succession of Jupiter the rains would cease and normality return. Their ideas were not dissimilar to many such learned and sometimes beyond bizarre theories put forward by the educated as to the cause. Yet no matter how the wise men and academics argued, the fact still remained that in a general consensus of opinion, the population believed the dearth was sent by God as a direct act of punishment for the profligate behaviour, commonplace in the church and the ruling classes at the time. This was a time where the wastrel priests, bishops and noblemen lived in the lap of luxury, eating copious amounts of the very best, whilst watching the peasants struggle to feed the same large families they themselves had encouraged the lowly to breed in order to care for the land.

The more outspoken of the dissenters cited the excesses of the spendthrift king as the cause, who in their eyes cared little for his people and wasted what little money the beggared nation could afford on luxurious shows of pomp and ceremony, which were mistakenly designed by him to cheer up the depressed population. In fact, the ostentatious displays had the opposite effect, causing his popularity to plummet and hence forcing him to publicly announce some apparently swingeing, but hopelessly inadequate measures, such as rationing and limiting the number of courses the nobility were allowed at each meal, or the amount of meat which could be eaten at a single sitting, all designed to placate his irate peasant populace, but generally considered feeble and purely designed to deceive his agitated subjects, who subsequently didn't believe a single word they were told.

Eventually, the beleaguered Edward was made by his council of disaffected barons to make an attempt to regulate food prices as a gesture to the desperate poor, but finding the suppliers unwilling to comply, he had to repeal all the new laws and thus, once again lose face with the entire nation.

For three long years, the suffering population did their best to exist through the adversities set before them, universally left by the complacent rulers of the country to their own devices and to make the best of a bad situation. There was no help from anyone, except, that is, the wealthy Church and its inadequate plump priests, who seemed to be faring better than most of the population, as their aid didn't come from their own deep pockets, but was extorted from the frightened lowly folk in exchange for them to pray endlessly on their behalf, for God to show some mercy.

The costly supplications were apparently being ignored by the Almighty as the crisis still deepened, sweeping away the poor's claim to anything remotely saleable in the famine and in it they lost everything of worth, bartered away in a bid to survive, which many didn't, and it was a very different land in 1318 to what it was back in 1316, the year when Yolanda de Mauville was due to give birth to her baby, which if it was a girl she planned to call Matilda after her best friend and if a boy Richard, the same name as her absent husband she had been anxiously waiting for since November, to return from Hereford, where he had gone on important business, hoping to bring peace and closure to the family of his dead master Henry de Bohun.

The months of lingering in Market Deeping since Richard's and Simon's departure drifted together into one long humdrum period, as the filthy weather took its hold over the Lincolnshire town, where Richard's new wife Yolanda lived, waiting, hoping and praying that her absent young spouse would return before the birth of her first child. As the season got colder, Yolanda invited

Matilda, her friendly maternal neighbour, to forsake her draughty cottage and move into the newly modernised house with her, for several reasons: primarily to be available to oversee the delivery of the child which was expected some time in January or early February; secondly to help with the many chores the large household needed to be done to function properly; and lastly to share the cosiness of Yolanda's better-insulated and well-stocked dwelling during the bitter long winter days.

With more than enough money to live a comfortable life, the two women, Yolanda's siblings and disabled father lived a lot better existence than the rest of the jealous community. Very sensibly during the late summer and autumn months, Yolanda spent extra money and stocked the larder to the gunnels with pickles, preserves, salted smoked meats, fish, and enough grain to bake bread for more than a whole year, giving them plenty to eat, causing the rift between them and the locals to deepen as they saw the well-fed family prospering when they were struggling to make ends meet. Charitably, in an attempt to repair the widening divide between herself and the envious locals, at Yuletide Yolanda made the mistake of offering some help to the more needy of the community, making up some small parcels of festive food and giving them by way of season's greeting to a few of the more friendly families. The gifts alerted some of the less principled in the district of the abundance, prompting them to plan a raid on the store, to relieve Yolanda and her family of the scarce and increasingly more valuable commodities.

During one particularly freezing night two days before the arrival of New Year's Day 1316, the whole household were upstairs fast asleep, tucked up in their beds, wrapped in blankets to protect them from the deep chill. Yolanda, as ever, slept in her room, alone except for her faithful lurcher Sam, who never wandered far from her and was keeping his vigil snoring at her feet and at the same time keeping them warm. Rest didn't come so easily to Yolanda as it did to the others, as the unborn child had taken to lying awkwardly in her womb, giving her annoying pins and needles in both feet. She had just got herself comfy when the wary hound sat up with a start, going from completely unconscious to wide awake in the blink of an eye and, most unusually for him, managing to produce an almost silent woof of alarm in the process. Thinking it was nothing more than one of the many hungry visiting nocturnal creatures, which emigrated in their droves from the refrigerated bare countryside to the warmer towns, Yolanda went to investigate.

Trying not to disturb the others, she tiptoed down the stairs as quietly as possible and, accompanied by the vermin-hating Sam as back-up, went to shoo away the unwelcome beast. Dreamily, Yolanda headed straight to the kitchen, where she suspected a furry intruder was foraging for scraps. In her drowsy half-awake state, Yolanda ambled wearily down the hallway, cogitating on her forthcoming motherhood, when instead of seeing an impertinent rat running for cover, she horrifyingly came face to face with two equally shocked, hooded masked locals, blocking the exit and struggling with as much of the valuable groceries as they could carry.

Following their natural instincts at the surprising sight of the householder, the trespassers panicked and, throwing the stolen goods on the floor, they pushed Yolanda savagely to the ground with a thud to effect an empty-handed but speedy exit. However, as quick as a flash, the protective Sam managed to get a healthy mouthful of one of them by sinking his teeth into a fast-departing calf, the severity of the painful bite causing a long drawn out reverberating howl of agony from its escapee owner, as he dragged his mangled limb free from the clamped-on jaws of the offended beast to make his escape.

Of late, the fretful Matilda had taken to sleeping with one ear permanently open, patiently listening for the footfall of her long-overdue son to return home. Hearing the scream of pain from the burglar, she left her bed to investigate what had happened and within seconds arrived on the scene. In nothing but the faint light of the dying, flickering fire, Matilda all but tripped over Yolanda's prostrate form sprawled on the boards with the faithful Sam frantically licking her unconscious face. Stunned and apparently injured, Yolanda lay near a scrap of cloth and a pool of blood, which appeared not to have come from anywhere immediately identifiable.

Initially, Matilda thought Yolanda had also fallen over Sam, who was forever under her feet, but as soon as she saw the nearby scattered groceries all became clear and without fear for herself she went to attend to her fallen friend, not knowing whether the robbers were still in the house or not. Also roused by the uproar, the other, rather less alert members of the family belatedly joined Matilda to carry the limp body of their beloved sister upstairs, back into the bedroom where not that long ago she had been wrestling to find sleep.

In the past Matilda's services had often been called upon to act as midwife and was thus well experienced in the problems associated with a pregnancy, and seeing the blood she immediately assumed it was of a gynaecological nature. nevertheless, after a panicky inspection of every inch of the rousing girl's body, the deeply concerned woman quickly ruled out any internal injury to her friend, whose only outward sign of the incident was a large round bump forming above her right eye. Having rechecked her patient thoroughly, Matilda eventually came to the correct conclusion that her first diagnosis was incorrect and she decided that the blood must have come from one of the intruders.

When the first hint of daylight arrived, the series of events became much clearer to the confused group, and after they had cleared up most of the mess, they put everything back in its correct place, completed a cursory inventory, bolted and locked the larder securely and arrived at the speedy conclusion that in actual fact nothing of real note was missing.

Overnight, Yolanda had completely recovered from the hefty bang on her head and although she wanted to get up and join in with the clear-up, at Matilda's insistence she remained in bed, as in the words of her fussing nurse, she "needed time for her body to recover". In reality, as Yolanda expected, Matilda was pleased to have something else to worry over and take her mind off her beloved son who, despite the weather, should have come back to her over-protective bosom over a fortnight before.

Yolanda's two oldest brothers had their own ideas about the incident, suspecting the culprits were the husbands of two of the most vociferously jealous neighbours, who'd become frustrated when their attempts to stir up bad feelings against the newly arrived pregnant teenager failed. The acrimonious relationship became even worse than when all the money was spent on the refurbishment of the house, and if it hadn't been for the support of Matilda, the dissenters would probably have succeeded in driving her away. Ignoring the wishes of Yolanda, who simply wanted to pretend the incident hadn't happened so that she could put it behind her, the boys decided to go on a search for the truth. Sneaking out onto the snow-covered road, they followed the clearest of blood trails to a nearby cottage, where, as they expected, one of their prime suspects, a known rogue called Ailwin Lyman lived with his loudmouth of a wife named Winifred and their only son Wylie. Having identified the suspect burglars, the boys excitedly raced back with their news, only to be disappointed when they were told to leave well alone as their sister didn't want to stir up any more bad feeling in the already-hostile small community, as in her opinion there was already more than enough to go round.

Throughout the coldest, snowiest January on record, the status quo returned to something resembling normal in the household and things carried on much as usual, except for Yolanda, who in case of further emergencies had taken to sleeping downstairs with the valiant Sam at her side for protection. Matilda thought it was a good idea, as in Yolanda's enlarged state the precipitous stairs were more of a danger to her than anything presented by the noticeably much quieter neighbours, who other than that, had only one conspicuous difference, which was the obvious limp the husband of one of the loudest of the tittle-tattling females had miraculously developed shortly after Christmas. To explain it away to the others, his lying wife said it was a result of frostbite incurred during a hunting expedition. Everybody knew the feeble excuse was a lie, as the prevailing conditions had prevented the less than hardy town-dwellers from going outside any further than a couple of hundred feet from their front door, let alone venturing far from their dwelling to hunt for game, which itself was invisible, sensibly hunkered down somewhere deep underground or hiding huddled together in the thickest of thick impenetrable coverts.

It was the last day of the month when Yolanda finally went into labour. She had been feeling uncomfortable all that morning, jiggling from one foot to the other while making a batch of bread with Matilda, who'd looked at her oddly more than once during the procedure. Using her not inconsiderable midwifery skills, Matilda suspected that the birth was imminent a few days before, when Yolanda's bump very clearly changed shape, and instead of sticking out the front was pointing more to the floor. Her suspicions became confirmed when, without warning, Yolanda's waters broke just as she was in the middle of kneading a loaf into shape. In her role as unofficial midwife, Matilda had overseen many a birth in the small town, and with an air of polished professionalism she organised everything.

First of all she sent the gawking interested boys away, but was prepared to allow the girls to stay for the experience, providing they promised to be quiet, which they did, and within three hours of eye-popping heaving and straining, a healthy baby boy poked his surprised head into the frozen world to exercise his powerful lungs. The rowdy new-born only managing to shut up when he was plonked on exhausted Yolanda's breast, where he quickly found the nipple and suckled greedily while still attached to his weary mother.

Happy the child was safe and well, Matilda concentrated her efforts on the other end, dealing with the cord and placenta with practised skill, using it as a practical lesson for the wide-eyed horror-struck grimacing girls as each step was carefully explained with a running informative commentary during the whole gruesome process.

For the next three months barely any sleep was to be had by the baggy-eyed complement in the house. Without a break, the demanding new arrival mercilessly bellowed his annoyance at being ejected from the comfort of a warm womb into the chilled outside world, antagonising everybody with his incessant screeching. Even the long-suffering Matilda found her turns in caring for the challenging baby wearisome, but was always happy to take a shift, purely to give Yolanda a welcome break in caring for the child who she named Richard after her beloved husband, even though he wasn't the actual father.

The one good thing to come from the perpetually noisy infant was that its continuous need for attention helped to take both Yolanda's and Matilda's minds off the absence of their nearest and dearest, both long overdue, and even after making allowances for the worse-than-awful winter weather which gripped the whole country since November, by the time the end of March arrived each woman feared the worst. Both Yolanda's and Matilda's overactive minds regularly conjured pictures of them, either frozen to death in the middle of nowhere or dead at the hands of the starving wayside bandits or outlaws that preyed on travellers all over the lawless ice-bound wilderness between Lincolnshire and Hereford.

Their dire fears were at last allayed one dreary afternoon during the first week of April, when the murky shapes of two fur-swathed, travel-weary riders appeared out of the gloomy grey wall of thick impenetrable freezing fog and, steering their shivering, plodding horses up the main street of Market Deeping, they made a bee-line directly for the old merchant's house in the heart of the town.

Inside the dwelling, the evening meal was being prepared, its delectable smell wafting on a wayward puff of wind, all the way along the high street to the strangers, who on smelling it encouraged their tired steeds to go a little faster when its mouth-watering homely aroma hit their ravenous nostrils.

As usual in the evenings, Yolanda was sitting cross-legged on a low nursing chair feeding the hungry, fast-growing baby, while at her feet Sam made himself as long as possible in front of a spluttering blaze, where a suspended cauldron of dried peas was glooping in the salty liquor left over from a boiled joint of bacon. Standing over the fire and peering attentively into the pot to stir the thick soup with a long wooden spoon to stop it from sticking and burning, Matilda, blinking the stinging smoke from her eyes, now and then cocked her head over her shoulder to chat about nothing in particular to Yolanda, who, still with the infant clamped firmly, sucking noisily at her breast, responded inanely about the lack of prospects for the coming spring festivals. Also enjoying the warmth and smell in the room and completing the family contingent were Yolanda's five sisters and three brothers, busily amusing themselves the best they could while they anticipated the forthcoming meal.

Sam was the first to indicate something was different; suddenly sitting up and half-pricking his floppy ears, he stared fixedly at the shut and leather-curtained front door. Managing to produce one of his famously rare guttural woofs, he alerted the gathering that something was amiss, reinforcing his warning when he excitedly leapt up to scratch at the entrance, whining and wagging his body violently from his nose to the tip of his flailing tail. The dog's over-exuberant reaction quickly became justified when the sound of horses' feet, clattering on the rock-hard street outside the house, became audible.

Inside, everybody looked curiously at each other, barely being able to believe their ears and not daring to say what they all were thinking. Their wildest dreams were soon realised when, with a flap of the hide curtain and a resulting giant puff of smoke issuing from the fire, the door burst open, revealing two unidentifiable callers hidden beneath the icebound frosted cloaks they had wrapped themselves from head to toe in against the chill. Roguishly, the visitors remained anonymous for at least five whole seconds before allowing the garments to fall, revealing the welcome sight of the travel-stained, smiling faces of Richard and Simon standing in their mud-stained, rusted armour.

At first Yolanda and Matilda just stared vacantly at the pair, rubbing their eyes in mute disbelief, but as soon as it had sunk in who the two visitors actually were, the long-absent brace were swamped in a frantic flood of overpowering hugs and weepy kisses. Everybody, including the yelping Sam, got involved and for a full ten minutes the entire family vied with each other to say their initial, long-dreamed-of cuddled hellos. As soon as Richard recovered his squeezed-out breath, he looked quizzically at Yolanda's flattened midriff, prompting her to introduce the milk-filled and for once amazingly asleep and mercifully not squawking Richard junior.

Although Simon really wanted to stay and enjoy the prolonged greetings, there were still duties to perform; so, aided by Yolanda's excited brothers, he diligently went about setting the wearied horses fair for the night. Satisfied Solomon and Uther were happily tucked up, both Richard and Simon struggled out of their soiled armour and changed into some clean dry clothes to join the others to swap stories while they ate. The whole reunited family sat up until the small hours telling each other the tales of peace, violence, failed robberies, injuries, birth and lastly lucky escapes, Richard showing the enduring raised weal on his neck as testament to his sad tale of arrest, unfair trial, torture and subsequent last-minute rescue. Well beyond midnight the rapt audience listened agog, amazed at the despicable behaviour of Lawrence, finding it hard to believe their ears when they heard of the lengths he was prepared to go to vent his vengeful spleen on any who dared thwart his dire scheming nature.

It was the depth of night when Richard finally slipped into bed; counting his lucky stars, he lay embraced in the arms of his beautiful young wife, remembering the time he went to hell and back, barely being able to credit that at last he was at home and safe, at least for the time being.

Too tired to make love, he just pretended to be asleep while he joyed in the warmth and comfort of Yolanda's soft-skinned body next to his and her soothing hands as they gently massaged his travel-weary sore back, and even though Yolanda did her best to hold back the sympathetic tears, she still found it all but impossible to prevent the odd one from escaping to splash on his resting flesh, when her comforting fingers stopped now and again to stroke the plum-coloured bruise on his deeply scarred neck. Silently, Richard lay enjoying the attention, secretly dreading the morning when he had to tell Yolanda about a reward he received from Humphrey for the diligence he had shown as a squire to his nephew.

Feeling somewhat confused after the series of terrifying events at Hereford and by way of an apology from Humphrey for letting it happen, Richard had accepted a surprise promotion to banner-man in the retinue of the newly returned knight from the English territories in France. His new master was to be Sir Alain Jeffrys, the famous siege engineer and fortification designer, a long-time friend of Sir Humphrey de Bohun's and contemporary to his old master Sir Henry. Outwardly, Richard was glad to accept the advancement, but inwardly he felt a little sad; sad because he knew that with the post, in the very near future, and without any prior warning, he and Simon were going to be called away to a meeting at Warwick Castle. There he was to join up with Sir Alain and, as his second-in-command, accompany him far away to his newly allotted temporary constableship at Carlisle Castle, where Sir Alain was to oversee some much-needed improvements and repair work, all to be undertaken while the incumbent overlord, John de Halghton, Bishop of Carlisle, was actively involved in his other more important position as religious envoy to the French Pope at Avignon, John XXII, on behalf of King Edward II himself.

CHAPTER 15

Fortunately for Richard and Simon, there was no urgent need for them to attend Sir Alain Jeffrys straight away. Mercifully, Alain had been summoned by Sir Humphrey, wanting to seek his advice on strengthening the defences of Hereford Castle in the face of the resurgent Welsh warlords, who, feeling emboldened by the English defeat at the hands of the Scots, had once again become a threat to the stronghold, and it was almost a year to the day since the Battle of Bannockburn by the time Sir Alain's messenger arrived to summon them to his side.

However, as often happens with even the best laid plans, it had been changed at the very last minute. Rather than go to the recently plague-stricken Warwick Castle as previously arranged, Richard and Simon were to make their way to Tamworth, a small market town to the northeast of Birmingham and about equidistant on the road northwards between Hereford and Market Deeping. They were to be no later than the fourteenth of July and meet at the 'Ragged Staff', a tavern named in deference to the arms of the earls of Warwick, who once were said to have imbibed at the hostelry. Once there, they were to liaise with Alain and his retinue, then together travel up the west coast of England to their new temporary home in Carlisle.

It was once again with mixed feelings that Richard and Simon prepared to ride away from Market Deeping. Their lengthy period of rest and recuperation had not been wasted though, as each of them left much more developed and filling their armour a lot better than when they arrived back from Hereford in April. Together they used the whole three months wisely: Richard taught Simon not only the finer points of horsemanship, but all he had learned from Henry about chivalry and the knightly use of arms, hence, every day from dawn to dusk, Richard and his eager pupil practised with horse, sword, shield, axe and lance. In return, Simon had gone to great lengths to show Richard how to use the longbow, spending hours with him, explaining about the correct type of goose feathers to use, when it was necessary to rub the flax cord with glue, and even how the yew was cut off the tree for maximum efficiency; then afterwards, whatever time remained of daylight they spent firing arrows at a sack of straw with a crude sketch of Lawrence on it as a target.

Along with the improved diet provided by the brilliant cooking skills of Matilda, who performed miracles in the kitchen by turning the most hum-drum of ingredients into tasty meals, and the constant physical lessons, both teenagers were almost fully honed, multi-skilled, muscular, if not quite fully grown men-at-arms by the time they left the family home.

Matilda, Yolanda, her brothers, sisters and even a couple of reasonably friendly neighbours turned out to watch through veiled eyes as their loved ones trotted off on Solomon and Uther, to head north-westwards to their duty. Both were armoured much as they were the last time they left; only this time, instead of Simon just having his four-foot hunting bow jutting above his right shoulder, he also now carried his father's six-foot war bow for himself, the old one he kept for Richard's use.

The inclement weather improved a little for the departure. The persistent foggy drizzle at long last had given way to a sickly sun, which feebly shot a few dismal beams through the lifted, ragged, scudding grey clouds as they finally reached the horizon. Richard and Simon both turned in their saddles to get a last glimpse of home and wave a final long goodbye before disappearing out of sight, into the blighted and scarred, desolate, barren countryside of the once-so-beautiful English shires.

With the return of illuminating sunlight, the effects of the horrendous prolonged winter conditions became blatantly obvious. The evidence of the lack of summer growth was noticeable all around. Silence reigned in the depressing blasted wasteland, no birds having the spare energy to sing their cheery songs in the stunted hedgerows, bushes and the scantily leaved blossomless trees, which bore testament to their struggle to survive the harsh conditions. There were no crops growing, and even the hardy grasses showed no more than a very little new greenery in sodden yellowed turf. Everywhere Richard looked there was evidence of the surfeit of water. The ruined rutted roads made travelling so difficult, with bridges broken or swept away completely; and the once-shallow fords were now too wide or deep to cross. In some places the streams had changed course completely, the surging water scouring out yawning impassable gorges, depositing the colossal masses of spoil downstream, creating dammed lakes where there was once dry land.

Now at last the sun was shining, and with heightened spirits, Richard and Simon rode on their way, ignoring the eye-watering stench of half-rotted carcases of drowned animals, which added a strange sickly, sweet, putrid aroma to the already mildew-laden musty air. Without a care in the world and in the exuberance of youth, they made light of the awkward terrain, clambering up the slippery hills and splashing through the mud-clogged flooded valleys, where the signs and smells of death and decay littered the whole steaming landscape.

For two days they rode, enjoying the lukewarm sunshine; nevertheless, the short burst of finer weather soon gave way to its more determined predecessor, when the same chilly gloom that had made life so intolerable for the initial six months of the year returned. The brief period of newfound warmth cozened a few of the hardier flowers into thinking that at long last spring had arrived, daring to half-poke their colourful heads into the world, only to return them quickly, realising it was just a cynically wicked hoax of Mother Nature that had duped them into waking up and showing their disappointed faces.

It was during the grim cool gloomy evening of 12 July when at last Richard and Simon reached Tamworth. Darkness had come early in the murky half-light, and the welcoming sight of the glowing fire-lit interior of the Ragged Staff didn't come soon enough for the bedraggled pair. First depositing Solomon and Uther with the hostelry's grooms, they made their way into the warm, alluring, stale-beer and wood smoke-smelling room. Inside it was unusually busy, as crowds of travellers who'd followed the lead of the local flora and fauna, were also hoodwinked into believing the climate had changed for the better and had ventured out on many postponed or weather-delayed errands. Yet when the murk returned, they realised the error of their ways and similarly were tempted by the appealing wayside inn.

In all, thirty or so people decided to seek shelter within rather than to complete their allotted missions; hence a motley crew of allsorts had noisily gathered in the roomy roadside tavern. Richard's first impressions of the assembly were that, in general, the contingent were simply casual acquaintances, behaving reasonably decently, enjoying the warmth, drinking together like long-lost friends and swapping stories in a peculiarly English sort of way about the dreadful climate of late. In a babble of voices they let out their pent-up depression in a flurry of boozy chatter in order to forget the dismal prospects ahead. However, no matter how hard they tried, it was still utterly impossible not to notice that nearest to the blaze and completely hogging the fire were five drunken rowdy peasant soldiers, he thought were in all probability escapees from the disorder of the disease-ravaged Warwick Castle. Richard arriving at that conclusion because, not only as they were unaccompanied by any superior and were much too far from the sealed stronghold to be merely going about some honest business, but the vestige of the badly erased red and gold badge of Sir Thomas Beauchamp the eleventh Earl of Warwick still adorned the breast of their brown leather jerkins, offering proof to his theory and the final damning testimony to demonstrate their recent service.

Loutishly, the men shouted at each other as loudly as they possibly could, making sure their foulmouthed rantings were heard above the rest. Playing at dice, they noisily slapped coins on a low rough table, swearing and cursing above the amiable buzz, proving to be more than a nuisance to the rest of the polite company.

Eventually one of them overstepped the mark when a particularly mean-looking, bearded giant of a man accused one of his fellows of cheating and threw the dregs of his goblet over the suspect. Missing hopelessly, he showered two hooded and fur-cloaked anonymous innocents, who were sitting quietly tucked out of the way in a corner, minding their own business and ignoring the bullies whilst pawing over some important-looking paperwork. The flying liquor landed squarely on the documents, staining them with the sticky brown syrupy liquid, much to the annoyance of a medium-built if not slightly thin man. Standing up to clearly see who the offenders were that so rudely interrupted him, he angrily threw back his hood, revealing a little shorter than middling height, gaunt-faced dark-haired swarthy man in his mid-forties with a slightly hooked nose over a greying goatee beard.

At first the aggrieved fellow looked calmly at each of the offenders in turn whilst brushing the dark droplets off his sketch; stopping, he gazed a beady brown-eyed stare at the loudest of the group, waiting for some form of apology.

Receiving none from the grinning thug who showed absolutely no sign of remorse, and making his best attempt not to cause a rumpus whilst using his very best baritone voice, the stranger politely but succinctly stated the obvious. "I think you've lost something. Try not to lose any more. I would hate it if your clumsiness ruined my drawings!"

Hearing the subtle admonishment, the bully, who normally relied on his imposing build and mean visage to cow-tow his intended victims without question, looked a little back-footed and somewhat unnerved by the response from the lone objector. Knowing his friends were there to back him up, the loudmouth shot a slightly nervous sideways glance at them to make sure of their support and, receiving their unanimous nodded approval, he decided on a show of bravado to try and profit from the situation. "Fuck your drawing; in fact, I think you owe me a fucking drink for making me spill it, don't you?" he roared, glowering threateningly at the calm stranger.

At the first sniff of trouble, the other louts, including the designated recipient of the thrown drink, stood up elbow to elbow, presenting a united front with their mouthy comrade. A shorter one with a greasy sand-coloured ponytail jutting out from beneath a grimy cap, put his two penneth in, adding a little fuel to the already tense situation. "Yeah, you look like a fucking rich sort of skinny cunt! I think you owe us all a fucking drink!" he added, looking smugly at his fellows to see if they appreciated his bravery.

Feeling heartened by the little man's beautifully phrased interjection, another large aggressive tormentor joined in the debate. "Yeah, I ain't fucking moving neither 'til you buy us all a fucking drink!"

Standing his ground, apparently unmoved by the threats, the stranger boldly faced up to the unsavoury crew, seemingly uncaring, with nothing but a whimsical smile playing on his whitened, pursed lips. To all the spectators he appeared hopelessly out-matched by the aggressive five, who by now were posturing with their hands on the hilts of their short cheap rusty swords.

Still standing his ground, the solitary man spoke as if he was simply addressing naughty boys. "Well, here's a situation! I'm not moving, nor am I buying any of you ruffians a drink! And I would appreciate it if you would mind your language. So, as I see it, something must give and it's not going to be me, so why don't you boys behave yourselves, get your hands off your tiny little weapons, and just say sorry, that's all."

Realising that things were very likely to flare up at any second and using more than a little common sense, the crowd immediately halted their chatter and scattered like spilled grain on a hard floor, to clear a space for the would-be combatants, who by this time were glaring menacingly as they squared up to each other.

Used to such alcohol-fuelled brawling, the landlord assumed it was just posturing and made a move to step in between the antagonists, but quickly changed his mind when he saw the resolute sober man standing cold-eyed and stone-faced against the five, with his cloak now flung neatly over his shoulder revealing an extremely fine double-linked mail shirt and the gilded enamelled hilt of his clearly very expensive yet still scabbarded sword. Keeping his unerring gaze on the gang, the man made his sword ready at his hip by carelessly flicking the securing strap on the hilt with his white-knuckled right hand, at the same time holding out his left and warning his companion to stay where they were, as he prepared to take on all five in what seemed to be a very one-sided contest.

Richard and Simon watched mesmerised from just inside the closed front door as the situation unfolded like a tableau before their eyes, almost being barged through it by some less-brave souls, who didn't want to get involved in the seemingly irresolvable dangerous situation and bolted into the street to vacate the premises. Their speedy departure caused a puff of wind to waft from the hastily snatch-opened entrance, briefly blowing the hood slightly off the face of the threatened man's associate. Catching a fleeting glimpse of the concerned fire-lit expression, Simon noticed to his surprise that it was a woman standing behind the man. With a hefty nudge in his mailed ribs, Simon pointed out the fact to Richard just as things were heating up between the opposing factions, when the drink thrower drew his stubby weapon and started waving it about, making throat-cutting figures of eight in thin air.

Things were fast approaching crisis point in the Ragged Staff as the five cocksure men, feeling safe in the knowledge that their numerical superiority was sure to win the day, advanced en-masse in a line on the lone figure. Without the merest hint of a flicker, the man remained stubbornly transfixed and unmoving as the gang got nearer, permitting them to get within four feet of him before drawing his own weapon with a metallic rasp, as the highly polished thirty-nine-inch long, tapering ridged blade left the scabbard. In a flash its needle-sharp end was gently pricking the flabby belly of the head thug, its lethal point freezing him dead in his tracks, while his friends still advanced in a semicircle, ominously menacing their isolated opponent's flanks and threatening the woman behind at the rear.

It was enough for Richard; he had seen enough of the one-sided match, so, drawing his own glaive, he strode forward with Simon at his shoulder to protect the endangered pair. Their timely intervention halted the thugs' advance, as both lads adopted the same well-practised thoroughly proven stance with their blades sloped resting over their right shoulders, ready to strike in defence or attack. Seeing it was now three professional-seeming swordsmen that faced them, the would be murderers decided that their cheap swords, which were no better than long poorly made daggers, were no match for the youthful men-at-arms and started to wriggle uncomfortably, fearing they might have bitten off more than they could chew.

Sensing that the outcome of any conflict might not turn out as they initially thought it might, the hooligans looked for an excuse to extricate themselves from what might be a very tricky situation. The opportunity presented itself when, safe in the knowledge that he was now supported by the two strangers, the previously lone swordsman deftly twitched the silvery point of his weapon, neatly removing the crude blade from the confused thug's hand and causing it to land with a thud on the floor at his own feet.

"Pick it up if you dare! As I told you, all I want is an apology and a little less bad language, if you please."

To any of the onlookers who remained, it was rather like a David and Goliath confrontation, the unblinking comparatively small man outfacing the weak-spirited monster, whose resolve had dissipated completely with the loss of his weapon. Seeing his large adversary had lost the will to fight, the smaller man continued the admonishment, his voice even deeper than before. "Then we can forget all about it, and I won't have to say anything about this little misunderstanding to my good friend Sir Thomas Beauchamp, whose insignia I notice is freshly removed from your chests. Now can we leave it, or do I and my two very able-looking young friends here have to make our point rather more physically than I was hoping to?"

Relieved to have an excuse to withdraw without losing too much face, the giant took his chance to leave, mumbling a half-meant sorry through his drink-stained matted beard and being forced to repeat it more clearly at the insistence of the nameless man before being allowed to depart. The permission to leave signalled tacitly with a momentary nod of his stony faced head, followed by an almost invisible relaxation of his still-raised sword. Still frozen at the combined poised menace of Richard, Simon and the deep-voiced stranger, the shamed giant beckoned his followers to come with him as he hesitantly picked up the inadequate weapon and went to leave through the swinging door. The unidentified man retained the steady threatening grasp on his ready sword just in case, and adding a touch of insult to injury by asking, with only the merest tinge of sarcastic wit in his voice, "If you wouldn't mind, please tell Sir Thomas, when he catches up with you, as I suspect he will very soon, his old comrade-in-arms Sir Alain Jeffrys sends his heartfelt regards and apologise to him for not not personally calling on him on our journey, but as soon as the castle is free of the sickness, myself and my dear wife would be pleased to visit. And if you wouldn't mind, also remind him he still owes me five shillings for my services."

With that, the group of five went off in a petulant huff, a rousing round of clapping and cheering from the remainder of the guests echoing in their disgruntled ears as they left, to vanish and get safely far enough away into the dismal pitch blackness for the head lout to summon up enough courage to cowardly bellow his promised retribution. "I'll make you fucking pay for that! If I were you I'd keep my fucking eyes open; you never know who's creeping up to slit your skinny fucking throat!" the shrinking voice threatened and added even more vile threats as it finally disappeared into the filthiest of grim nights.

Crisis averted, Alain slickly sheathed his sword and turned immediately to the two volunteer assistants. Grabbing Richard by the hand, he shook it enthusiastically. "Richard de Mauville, I assume, and you, young man, must be Simon. I thought it was you as soon you entered: Humphrey described you both well! Brilliant timing, lucky for me you're two days early. I must admit I was a bit worried there; you were nearly without me before you had even met me! Now that would be a shame, wouldn't it?"

As Simon expected, Alain's companion turned out to be his wife, who, against her husband's wishes, having spent most of the past three years apart, had insisted on travelling with him. She was a woman of around the same age as Alain, good-natured, attractive and like him was very fond of a decent vintage. Because of a series of events out of their control, they were travelling alone, staying overnight wherever they could and suffering from some of the poorest food and wines the starved country hostelries were able to muster. It was no different in the Ragged Staff as the four sat together sharing the very best the inn could offer. Mary's innate sense of humour became immediately apparent, when, taking an enormous gulp of her drink, she bemoaned the weak-watery pink liquid, which in her words was masquerading as wine. Taking another gulp and pulling a funny face, she told the company she would prefer to happily face the plague at Warwick Castle and enjoy some of Thomas Beauchamp's famed cellar rather than to drink the tomcat's piss she had in her beaker. Her well-timed witticism made both young men laugh, especially Simon, who had instantly taken a great liking to the woman who always had a ready joke on the tip of her tongue.

Hanging on every word, Richard and Simon listened intently as a brief history of their sometimes-tempestuous relationship was humorously related to the pair, Mary making fun of Alain and him responding with some clever quips of his own. Screwing her face up with each sip, Mary told the lads some of the funny stories while nibbling at some tasteless dry bread and rather oddly rank-smelling, blue-veined cheese the relieved landlord put in front of them.

After about an hour of swapping yarns and listening to Richard's saga about how he and Simon ended up where they were at that moment, Alain soon made it very clear that he felt it was more important for them to hear all about the essential work they both were expected to help him with. With a huge series of blatant "I've heard it all before" yawns from Mary, he started to explain about the finer points of siege warfare. To some extent, Simon showed interest in Alain's teachings, but it was Richard who quickly became engrossed in what he had to say, hearing all about fortifications and a brief history of how attack and defence went hand-in-hand, from the ancient motte-and-bailey wooden forts of Roman times to the present-day concentric castles with their multi-stage defensive systems. Avidly, Richard learned the exact meanings of parts of the castle like loops, crenulations, machicolations, ramparts and lastly of all the types of weapons to attack them with, such as stone throwing mangonels and the more powerful trebuchets, battering rams, mines, and last but not least the mighty towers of Beffroi, the lofty wheeled constructions designed to be pushed up to any besieged castle's walls, so that the attackers could shoot down from their higher vantage point onto the heads of the defenders.

When it came to siege engines, Alain was in his element. Finding a willing pupil in Richard, his already deep voice deepening even further with every explanatory point, telling him about his father's work on the famed 'Warwolf', commissioned by Edward I and said to be the greatest trebuchet ever built. It needed at least fifteen wagons, fifteen master carpenters and forty labourers to dissemble, move and re-erect it. Going on, he told Richard how he tirelessly worked on improving the designs of everything from the basic battering ram to the complicated springald, a giant crossbow capable of firing leathal four-inch-thick, five-foot-long darts over a hundred and fifty yards or more.

The interesting evening soon melted into night, and as there was an early start and a long journey ahead in the morning, a weary, or more probably a thoroughly bored Mary pointed out it was time to retire, so with visions of massive machines and giant earthworks embossed in his weary brain, Richard slept the best sleep he'd had for months. On the morning of 13 July the weather was much the same as it had been for the previous several months, except, that is, for those two glorious days of more clement conditions which brought everybody outside, erroneously believing at long last the belated spring had arrived, only to be driven back indoors when Mother Nature had the last laugh and brought back the drizzly cold rain.

Following a quick breakfast which was almost as revolting as the previous night's meal, the little mounted party set off, Alain riding his bay stallion called Lamorak and Mary on a fine chestnut hack she referred to as Ferret because of its colour and was charged with the task of towing a heavily laden, small, nameless, coal-black sumpter pony, to go on their trip northwards to Carlisle, which they planned to complete within the week and hopefully arrive at the destination on or about 21 July.

The first half mile passed without incident, Alain having taken up where he left off the previous night discussing with Richard the merits of a new design he had come up with for a speedier reloading mechanism for notoriously slow to re-arm trebuchets. Riding side by side, some thirty feet in front and showing no interest in the complicated workings of war machines, Simon was boring poor tired, disinterested, Mary to death with his ideas of pie making. He was in the middle of describing exactly how to get the crust just right on an apple pie when his explanation was abruptly interrupted by a sudden cacophony of noisy birds. Fifty or so yards ahead in a partially mist-obscured matted clump of trees, half a dozen large black birds could be seen, swooping about and shouting their raucous alarm calls at whatever had upset them. Squinting ahead, Simon's sharp young eyes were just about able to pierce the settling fog to where, in some bushes and bracken either side of the freshly trampled muddy track through a shallow ravine, he could see two or three barely visible murky human shapes, furtively lurking, trying to hide in the scrub and using the mizzly gloom as extra cover to set what he thought was possibly an ambush to trap and rob the unwary traveller.

Having heard many stories of theft, rape and murder committed by the droves of marauding wayside robbers, who in the lawless times of general privation were mostly normal people who'd lost their source of income and had taken to highway robbery to feed themselves and their families, Simon quickly made the assumption it was such a band, which were covertly lying in wait on the road ahead, ready for any gullible souls to wander past and into their vile clutches.

Sensing danger was afoot, Simon followed his first instinct to tell the others, and his second, which was to liberate the bows from their oiled weatherproof case. Doing it with polished ease, he vaulted off the wrong side of Uther to remain on the blind-side of the possible ambush, landing up to his ankles in the deep mud for his trouble. Quickly stringing the great war bow and then the hunting bow, he handed some arrows and the smaller bow to Richard, who, remaining seated on Solomon, surreptitiously pointed up the road, gesturing some unspoken tactical instructions to Simon who, knowing him well, understood every silent word. Then out of respect for his master, Richard gave a whispered brief outline of the tacit conversation to Alain and Mary for their approval. The rapidly devised plan was for the three mounted riders to carry on as they were, the men up front with Mary leading the riderless Uther and their pack pony in the rear; slowing their pace to a crawl, they intended to meander along the track clumped together to make it difficult for them to be counted by any prospective aggressors. Using the poor visibility to his advantage, Simon was to run round the side and when he was close enough, to fire at the gang's exposed flank if necessary. Everyone agreed that the scheme seemed sound and so, like a startled rabbit, Simon dashed off, bow in hand, galloping into the mist on what could be a life or death mission.

Simon was right; as he approached the thicket from behind on the left, he could make out at least four shadowy figures armed with bows, crouching low to stay out of sight of the travellers, and signalling to each other with low whistles and hoots from either side of the track. Foolishly, without bothering to place pickets to guard their exposed rear, the overly complacent attackers' whole attention was totally concentrated up the road on their intended quarry as it approached the mouth of the cutting to come into range.

Spotting the men were on the point of pushing over some half hacked-down trees to block the lane, Simon fired his bow twice. The first arrow found its mark and pierced the nearest one through the chest, felling the victim instantly; but the second missile, wafted off course by an errant puff of wind, missed the furthest away by inches. Fizzing past the target, the arrow clattered harmlessly away into the dense undergrowth, alerting the man that he and his murderous company were under attack themselves. It didn't take long for complete chaos to break out in the poorly led group when they saw one of their number so easily disabled and probably killed. In moments, three others popped up from their hiding places at the edge of the lane. Fearing for their lives and not knowing where the assault actually came from, the four remaining prospective murderers were dashing around in total disorder, running blindly onto the track directly into the arms of Richard and Alain, who, on seeing the bunch of hapless criminals crammed together in the lane, charged, swords raised, headlong into the clumped group, scattering them like skittles, cutting down two of them on their way through and trampling to death a third very familiar-looking fellow, whose greasy ponytail and once-blazoned jerkin quickly gave away his identity as one of the dice-playing absconders from Thomas Beauchamp's plague-hit castle.

With the re-cased bows safely back over his shoulder, Simon remounted Uther to ride away from the ambush site with the others. Taking a moment to glance back at the carnage to where the fallen lay, he found himself unable to stop thinking about the first time he killed a man and marvelled on how much easier it was to kill a second. No longer was he experiencing the overbearing sensation of remorse and suffering the anguish which had so badly affected him before. Feeling merely as if he had just potted a rabbit for dinner, Simon continued without any sign of emotion, self-satisfied that it was his sharp eyes and alertness which saved the day. Holding his head a little higher than before and feeling a more important member of the group, he continued north in the direction of Carlisle Castle.

The bleak travel conditions away from the towns were much as they had been for the whole summer so far, the only difference being that the further north they rode the rockier the terrain became and the more desolate the countryside appeared. Because of Mary's presence in the group, and at Alain's insistence, despite her making it quite clear she didn't expect special treatment, they avoided camping overnight, opting to stay in some of the many wayside taverns dotted along the route. However, the inns and hostelries they stayed at were little better than camping outside in the wet, and where once good hospitality was to be had, now a traveller would be lucky to receive some stale bread and watered wine. No matter how deep your pockets were, it was always the same cheerless conditions with feeble, damp-fuelled fires, poor food, third-rate drink and cold shivering nights under the soaked, rotten, leaky, rat-infested rotting thatch.

For five long, miserable days they journeyed, and even though each were tightly wrapped against the persistently horizontal rain in their hooded cloaks, the wet still found its way through to the chafed-raw skin on their behinds, which stuck and clung to the soaked, reeking saddles with every painful movement. On they plodded through the water-sculpted landscape, where wide lakes and difficult swampy quagmires now replaced the same prime grazing land where hundreds of sheep and cows so recently fed themselves to rotund plumpness, now devoid of wildlife except for the crows and magpies which croaked their raucous cries, satisfied with their bellies full of the abundant carrion which rotted where it fell.

No matter how the weather gods contrived to dampen the spirits of the company, Simon's upbeat boyish exuberance and incessant chattering since the first meeting at the Ragged Staff couldn't help but uplift everyone, including the unlucky Mary, who bore the brunt of his verbose nature with a resigned smile, feigning polite interest when he spoke about his favourite subject of cooking. On the other hand, Richard was genuinely enthralled by Alain's deep-voiced informative diatribe of the state of the defences at most of the castles he was commissioned to upgrade, bemoaning the often poor workmanship he was faced with and how hard it was to get decent masons and carpenters with enough skill to carry out the exacting work.

With the constant, sometimes profound, conversations entered into between the members of the group, the time taken to reach Carlisle seemed to not be much longer than a couple of long days, and with a feeling of almost surprise the travel-stained crew saw the war-battered squat orange stone walls and the mighty two hundred-year-old keep of their destination in the distance.

During the latter stages of the trip everything seemed very recognisable to Richard, as he had taken almost exactly the same route in the opposite direction, through the northern counties with Yolanda on his way back from Scotland to her hometown of Market Deeping. The familiarity of the surroundings reminded him of the solemn promise he made to Rolfe and his friendly family, who barely scraped a living from a tiny acreage at close-by Burgh Sands. With a smile on his lips he recalled how he had promised them that if he was ever in the area he would visit them at their lowly home that was no more than a stone's throw from their final destination, where they were to relieve the absent governor and Bishop of Carlisle, John de Halghton, while he was away on urgent clerical business for King Edward.

The closer Alain got to the castle the more he looked worried at the state of it. The constant battles between the English and Scottish over its ownership and the resulting constant changing of hands over the past two hundred and fifty years had taken its toll on the walls. The signs of crude, amateurish repairs were all over the place, especially on the much-besieged gatehouse, which had the semblance of an organised heap of rubble with a badly patched and repaired gate stuck in the middle. To date the damage remained unattended due to the cost, but now, with Alain in charge and Edward's money in his pocket, things were going to be different at the strategically essential bastion, which was all that now stood between Scottish dominance on the western borders and the English population, who otherwise would be sure to suffer dire oppression under the victorious Scottish heel.

Surprisingly, considering the state of the castle, the guard showed every sign of complete alertness when the small party arrived, and their diligent, temporary leader called Erasan made Sir Alain give all his titles, styles and credentials before even allowing him access to the outer gatehouse. The captain of the watch personally grilled him for a further twenty minutes before eventually satisfying himself that Alain and his companions were who they said they were and, with a show of great deference and apologetic humility, the thorough sentinel finally allowed the party access beyond the inner gate into the main cobbled courtyard of the dilapidated stronghold.

Once inside and dismounted, the very first thing Alain wanted to do was to inspect the defences, so without any delay he immediately conscripted the captain to take him on a guided tour, accompanied by his new star pupil Richard and Simon, who having no real interest in construction begrudgingly tagged on; but with his mind on what was for supper, he found it hard to show due attention to the boring but essential reparatory building work. Unlike Mary, who frankly stated her immediate desire to wash the weeks' accumulated grime off her saddle-sore body, warm herself up, and then inspect the facilities in the living quarters where she and her husband were very likely to spend the next year or two.

Anxious to employ his skills as a surveyor and using his deepest grumbling voice, Alain asked Ewan the captain to take him and his helpers to the worst areas of the fortifications, so he could see first-hand and close up what actually needed to be done. Fortunately, the state of the walls turned out not to be as bad as they first appeared. Unlike most other damaged old buildings, the majority of the massive oak beams were still there, laying trapped under the heaps of nearly all the dressed stone, buried where they had fallen, amazingly not having been stolen, sold on, or used elsewhere for private use, as with the ancient Roman wall near to hand; free dressed stone was abundant in and around the vicinity.

That evening Ewan and the travel-weary quartet enjoyed a delicious welcoming evening meal of thrice-cooked pork, fried onions, fresh bread, and especially to Mary's very clear delight, some better than good vintage heady French red wine, pilfered by Alain from John de Halghton's extensive private cellar, to titillate her bored taste buds. At long last, after being soaked and chilled to the bone for a whole week, now feeling warm, well-fed and comfortable, all four sat at a table in the great hall, drinking more of the expensive vintage whilst listening to Erwan imparting his enhanced knowledge of the inner workings of the citadel. Although it was early evening in July, a well-stoked fire was needed for warmth, along with a few candles to illuminate their work as they organised a schedule for the repairs. Together they came up with a plan to do the work while keeping the stronghold still functioning to the purpose for which it was built.

All was settled quickly and without any argument. Alain had rightfully nominated himself as chief designer and master builder, while adaptable Richard would use his increasing tactical military know-how and take charge of the depleted garrison, temporarily replacing Erwan, who Alain required to use his local influence and arrange the workforce. Much to the joy of Simon, his given duty was to assist Mary in coordinating the culinary needs for the garrison and the growing number of workers necessary to carry out the extensive building work.

For the entire following dismally damp day, Alain spent all his time surveying the damaged areas. Coming to the considered conclusion that in the main, all that was needed to effect the most pressing repairs were some raw materials, such as sand, which was in abundance only half a mile away in the great estuary; lime, which had to be imported in; a small amount of the dressed stone which was there for the taking; with masons, carpenters, and the labourers to do the work.

The local economy had collapsed during the past year of dreadful weather and as soon as the word was out that employment was to be found at the castle, a contingent of out-of-work tradesmen and helpers were queuing to sign up for the welcome pay. Attracted by the promise of a decent daily meal, two pence for the labourers and up to six pence for the master craftsmen, the complement of workers were assembled and in under a week were ready to start the work necessary to return the massive fortress to its former glory.

Everything was going ahead as planned. Both in front and behind the walls it was a hive of activity, each individual expertly going about their allotted tasks with precision. All was carefully watched over by Alain, who diligently inspected every little stage, checking and measuring wherever he went, often to the annoyance of the skilled workers, who started dreading his appearance where they were working, knowing he was sure to criticise or correct their perfectly executed efforts, but needing the work they chose to ignore his extra deep chiding voice and carried on exactly as they had been after he had left.

After the few obligatory initial hiccups, the military side of the rejuvenation started going to plan equally as well. Before, with only the untrained Erwan to control the unruly, badly under-manned garrison, apathy and disorganisation had prevailed, where each individual had their own differing ideas of how to do things best, but in reality not one of them having a clue. Now though, with youthful Richard at the head of the defenders, things were going to be very different. Treating them as he would an unruly horse, he gently urged and cajoled them with his velvet-gloved iron fist, always ready to praise, but also to punish when necessary and having to set a few examples before gaining the total respect of the men. Craftily, Richard picked on a couple of the ringleaders, who, used to having their own way, cynically made attempts to incite others to disobey his commands and do as much as possible to disrupt his carefully considered plans to improve the unwilling garrison of spoiled soldiers.

The strained relationship between Richard and the men came to a head in the first week of his command when the vociferous leader of the dissenters, a notoriously idle, burly, fat brute of a poacher turned reluctant conscript soldier called Edgar, decided to directly challenge Richard's authority in front of twenty of his contemporaries. Deliberately locking horns with Richard by ignoring a direct command from him when he was told to join in a compulsory communal sword practice arranged in the courtyard, which, rather than participate in, Edgar chose to watch, overtly slumped from a vantage point on a convenient stack of cleaned building blocks. Refusing point-blank to obey Richard's order, Edgar swore at him calling him a "beardless fucking jumped up little brat", saying it loud enough for all the men to hear. Laughing derisively, Edgar got up from his resting place and in a stage whisper, threatened to teach "the boy" a lesson in swordplay. Then, adding insult to injury, he made the mistake of starting to draw his sword as he turned to stand facing Richard, who in response drew his, having it poised and ready before Edgar's was even out of its scabbard. Adopting the same tried and tested posture taught to him by Henry, which had served him so well before, Richard stood toe-to-toe with the man, staring unerringly into his beady brown eyes, looking for the merest hint of a twitch, blink or any other sign which might inform his trained eye that his opponent was about to make his move.

Straight away Edgar knew he'd made a mistake with his contemptuous posturing, soon realising he wanted the tense situation to go no further and to just do as he was told and join in the practice with the others; however, that option was quickly removed from the equation when the men gathered round the combative pair expecting to see Edgar put young Richard firmly in his place. Never for one minute did Edgar suspect that the youthful Richard would indeed stand his ground and thus leave him no other course to save face, but to act in the way expected from the arrogant bully. Like an odd pair of statues they stood: Richard, small, bareheaded and ready to act, with a look of stony resolve in his pallid face, against the large helmeted, red-faced, fat man who glanced left and right nervously, regretting his big mouth but not wanting to climb down and lose his credibility with the men.

With no obvious easy exit, Edgar impulsively swung his blade, wildly missing the side-stepped Richard. The impetus of the strike spun him round to once again face the smaller swordsman and finding his opponent's point harmlessly pressing into the dimple just below his Adam's apple. Pushing it a little harder than necessary, Richard spoke without malice or emotion, as though it was a pre-arranged tutorial rather than an unsavoury incident. Lowering his voice to almost a whisper, he advised the man coolly, "Don't let the sword take control. Remember, hold it firmly but don't grip it too tightly, relax your hand a little, now your wrist, now let's do that again."

The man and his comrades merely looked dumbfounded as Edgar, who was expecting to be instantly put under arrest, meekly obeyed. Readopting his initial stance, Edgar made the move again, this time with a little more polish, but with the same result. His effort received some unexpected praise from Richard, speaking to him as if he was a friend, he carried on with the lesson. "That's much better, Edgar, but do it again and just let the sword do the work, and try not to plant your front foot so heavily with the strike."

After half an hour of individual tuition, Edgar showed signs of improvement, so with a little polite thank you, Richard left him and took up with one of the others, to share his expertise with them, leaving Edgar counting his lucky stars, knowing that with a word in the right direction, he could have been thrown into the dungeon or worse.

Pleased with his handling of a potentially very difficult if not dangerous situation, Richard finished the lesson, knowing he'd won the skirmish on two fronts, having turned an enemy to a friend and proved his worth in front of the men. From that day forward the lack of cooperation from the men ceased completely and with each dawning day Richard became more popular with the garrison. Gaining their confidence, he motivated them by cleverly making his ideas appear as if they had been dreamed up by the men, involving them in the strategic planning of attack and defence, giving them plenty of rein, only occasionally having to haul them in on the odd occasions when they stretched their luck a bit too far for his liking.

Every day for the next two weeks Richard drilled the men, replacing the casual indifference they initially showed; they now paid close regard to his every word, listening intently to the little swordsman who really loved conducting the sessions.

Regardless of how much Richard enjoyed teaching the men, always lurking in the back of his mind was the urge to visit Rolfe, who lived so temptingly close by at Burgh Sands with Margaret and their helpful brood of children that had been so kind to him and Yolanda when they so desperately needed it. The chance presented itself when some of the contingent of soldiers were called upon to accompany some horse-drawn carts on a mission to collect the all-important building sand from the estuary. Filled with a feeling of anticipated delight and an extra spring in his step, Richard mounted Solomon to leave the claustrophobic confines of the castle as a more than willing volunteer for the essential escort duties.

At the head of six carts, ten labourers and ten infantrymen, Richard rode the happy and somewhat fresh curvetting Solomon, who himself needed some expert controlling, also wanting to stretch his cramped limbs, pleased to be off the uncomfortable cobbles of the courtyard to at last feel the soft yielding turf beneath his feet once again. The journey wasn't far and within half an hour the workmen started shovelling the pale yellow sand onto the bucks of the carts. The task required about two hours to be completed and be ready to return to Carlisle, giving Richard a window of half that time to make a speedy call on his friends to pay them the long-overdue surprise visit at the ramshackle farmyard.

The closer Richard got to the smallholding the more his stomach started to grind and churn with an inexplicable and overwhelming sense of impending tragedy. In his heart he knew something was dreadfully wrong as he approached the little homestead. Where before, from so much as half a mile away, a permanent blue haze of sweet-smelling peat smoke could be seen hanging in the air, now there was none. Even the outlying paddocks had mysteriously taken on an uncared-for tufty look, but most noticeable of all was the complete absence of the constant buzzing uproar of squealing playing children or the noisy uproar of squabbling farmyard animals. Richard's worst fears became realised when, with a large knot in his midriff, he rounded a small wood, hopefully expecting to see the dwelling as it was when he last saw it, his spirits plummeting at the sorry sight which met his eyes.

Sitting in the middle of some scrubby unkempt pasture, there was nothing left of the razed buildings except for a sooty pile of rubble with the remnants of some burnt timbers sticking up like blackened ribs from a burnt carcase, surrounded by flattened, fit-for-no-purpose, broken fences and wrecked useless outbuildings. The only recognisable signs left of the absent residents were the sad remnants of the dilapidated upturned pointed hull which only a year prior had been their uniquely unusual chicken shed.

With his heart in his boots and the ready tears blurring his vision, Richard dismounted Solomon to painfully pick his way through the pitiful wreckage, hopefully kicking at any piece of the debris he thought might offer a clue to the whereabouts of Rolfe and his family, who so recently scraped the scantiest of livings there. The whole place was now completely devoid of any sign of life, except, that is, for a startled rat which froze momentarily in its tracks when it saw him and, seeing him as no threat, blatantly carried on with its errand as before. Regardless of how hard he searched, all signs of them and what little they had of worth was gone and as he suspected, with it the lives of the happy eight who had been such a godsend in his greatest time of need.

Eventually resigning himself to the fact there was absolutely nothing to be done, Richard merely knelt and closed his watery eyes to offer a small prayer for their souls, trying to picture them as he prayed, in the happier time when he first met them, all smiling, lined up to greet him outside their humble little dwelling. Even though he tried his hardest to remember them like that, there was absolutely no way he could remove the ineradicable conjured image of their murdered mangled faces from behind his eyelids, or overcome the feeling that in some peculiar way he had betrayed his friends by not being there for them in their time of need, as they were for him.

In a state of shock, Richard planted a little kiss on the turf before remounting Solomon to return the short distance back to his duties. Nudging the horse to a canter, he left the woeful site a much harder man than when he arrived, and with it the very last vestige of his boyhood, there in that saddest of sad places.

CHAPTER 16

For more than two long, cold and wearying years, Richard, along with his closest friend and ally Simon, stayed at the isolated Carlisle Castle learning the trade of construction under the auspices of Alain Jeffrys. Similar to everything Richard found interesting, he took to the new skills like a duck to water and proved to be a more than apt, intelligent pupil, spending hours and hours over drawings and designs with Alain, knowing that to finish the repairs to the stronghold was imperative, as the threat of all-out conflict with the Scots was merely round the next corner.

For the best part the war had been put on hold while the great famine still had its stranglehold on Northern Europe, the freezing, longer-than-normal winters and the dismal wet summers retarding the growth of the crops, killing the livestock and starving the population into hiding. Even the garrison were on strict rations. Not knowing when the next shipment of the rare dry goods would arrive, they hoped upon hope that, true to his promise, Edward II would fulfil his undertaking to guarantee the desperately needed support for the isolated border fortress, necessary to prevent it from being starved into submission and fall into Scottish hands, similarly to its badly weakened counterpart on the opposite side of the country at Berwick had done in the April.

The work was well on schedule and apart from the odd difficult-to-solve problem, in the main Alain was very pleased with the progress. Yet a greater worry to him was the fact that the king's allotted monies for the improvements were running dangerously low.

It wasn't the price of the imported materials or the cost of labour which had dug so deeply into the coffers, but the price of commodities required to feed the ever-hungry workforce, and if it hadn't been for the readily available fish and other seafood which could be cheaply acquired at the coast near to Carlisle, the pot would have run out months before. With this foremost in his mind, Alain made the decision that, with Richard acting as captain and Simon as his second-in-command, they would take ten chosen men on an imperative, possibly life-saving mission, all the way southwards to Edward's royal hideaway at Arundel. Once there, he was to ask for an interview with the king and diplomatically remind him of his financial obligations and also politely ask for some of the promised reinforcements to be sent post-haste to Carlisle.

The time was noon on 2 August 1318 by the time the small chosen contingent of mounted men assembled with their panniers and saddlebags bulging with the necessaries for the long trek, ready to leave through the refurbished gateway of Carlisle Castle. On the way out, Richard paused to cast an approving eye over the new work as he turned to wave goodbye to Alain, Mary and the new friends he'd made, as the twelve departed to go on the lengthy journey all the way straight down the spine of England as far as they could go, to the warmer climes of West Sussex and seek an audience with the monarch, safely ensconced in his adopted Royal residence at Arundel Castle.

The proposed route was as direct and simple as possible, except, that is, for a slight detour that Richard planned to make at the halfway stage, to make a surprise short visit to Yolanda, Matilda and the family on the way through.

Kindly, the dreadful weather had loosened its grip a little as he started out and although the inclement conditions across the country were less intense than of late, they still remained unfavourable to those who needed to travel. What a few years before would have been an easy, reasonably straightforward trip, was now made hazardous in the dangerous times. As well as the unpredictably difficult remodelled terrain, the added danger of multitudes of the jobless gangs who'd turned to robbery as a way of making a living, threatened any wayfarers, making the inclusion of the armed guards a necessity in the troubled lawless period, when the despised king lurked in safety, as far away as he could from the burgeoning number of dissenters who seriously doubted his capability to reign.

Everywhere from east to west, in places as far apart as Lancashire, Glamorgan, East Anglia and Bristol, open revolt had broken out against the devil king and his excesses. His popularity with the poor hungry subjects plummeted to an all-time low when the news got out into the public domain about the great riches he generously showered on his new favourites, Hugh Audley, Roger d'Amory and Hugh Despenser the younger, when, in a lavish display of opulence, Edward divided the huge estates of the deceased Gilbert de Clare equally between them.

The deprived, poverty-struck people spoke openly about the accursedly weak, ignoble king. One such person, writing a popular poem called, 'The evil times of Edward II', cited the criminally wasteful Edward as the cause of the famine, being brought down on his subjects as a punishment from God in his anger at their sovereign's lack of regal behaviour. The dissenters' voices reached the ears of the arrogant monarch, whose merciless hand descended in dreadful retribution on them with mass torture, burnings and executions. The leading offenders suffered the awful fate of being hanged, drawn and quartered, before the major parts of their bodies were put on public display to deter any such future treasonous rumblings.

During the two long and depressingly wet years that Richard and Simon had worked alongside Alain, the persistently cold wet weather never refused to loosen its relentless grip. The savage storms utterly ravaged the countryside, making large parts of it totally unrecognisable to those who knew it before, including Richard and Simon, who marvelled at the enormous effect of Mother Nature, who in her anger had so drastically changed the landscape. With furrowed brows and open mouths they stared about them, awe-struck at how her mighty hand had turned great swathes of the once-tilled, well-structured, neat parcels of fertile, arable land into expanses of blighted wilderness, where none but the brave or stupid dared to stray in the wastelands. Forsaken by God, and only inhabited by marauding gangs of wolfsheads, outlaws and run-away master-less men, whose brutal, self-proclaimed leaders ruled with rods of iron over their underlings. Ignoring the bounds of common decency, life was cheap, easily forfeited to those who held ultimate power over their subordinate followers in the profligate encampments, where drunken bestial behaviour was considered normal and wild open-air orgies were a commonplace entertainment for the sub-human inhabitants.

However, for a band of twelve armed and mounted, professionally trained, highly organised, well-led troops, there was no danger and they traversed the land with utter impunity. Fearing nothing, they knew that no one would dare challenge them on the two hundred mile plus first leg of the journey to Market Deeping. The urgency of their assignment dictated the pace, forcing them to eat and sleep on the move, living out of their saddlebags off the meagre rations of dried meat and biscuits. Making as few stops as possible on the route, most of those purely to rest and feed the weary horses. The troupe arrived at their destination almost exactly a week to the hour after they started out.

With fluttering hearts and butterflies in their jittery stomachs, Richard and Simon crossed the final several miles of the once so very familiar and friendly land, which now appeared eerily quiet and strangely bleak in their eyes, as they apprehensively turned up the main street to halt their horses outside the front of the welcoming sight of their home. Inside the house everything was as they remembered it. Yolanda and Matilda were in their usual places at the kitchen table chatting away to each other, preparing some food for the family. Having furtively crept through the house to make the revelation of their homecoming complete, the two smiling travel-besmirched wanderers burst into the room, completing the surprise entrance with too much efficiency when Matilda jumped out of her skin at their sudden appearance. Knocking over her dough trough, she spilled a quarter of the valuable contents on the tiled floor and almost fainted after the first shock when she realised that the two strange men were, in fact, the much-grown and more developed, bearded Richard and down-faced Simon, alive and well, returned to the bosom of the family. Yolanda also couldn't believe her eyes when she saw them, and flinging her arms around her errant husband, she kissed and hugged the man, who, in her loneliest darkest hours at the dead of night, she suspected might be imprisoned somewhere in Scotland or even maybe killed without him ever knowing that sleeping in a room next to the three-year-old young Richard was his own eighteen-month-old son Henry, named out of respect for Richard's deceased mentor, and the result of the several nights of saying his passionate farewells prior to the day of his departure to Carlisle.

By mid-afternoon everyone had settled in the best they could, and with the offer of a few scarce pence, the now much more friendly neighbours rallied round to accommodate the horses and men, finding suitable quarters for all. Nevertheless, in her role as lady of the house, Yolanda insisted that it was down to her to feed the hungry complement of soldiers, being more than happy when her eldest brother called William and Sam the lurcher returned from a hunting trip, complete with half a dozen not too thin rabbits and a couple of decent hares, unluckily for them brought out of hiding by the spell of improved temperatures.

With the sleeping arrangements organised to their satisfaction, Yolanda and Matilda returned to their usual places at the kitchen table. After raiding what little was left in the storeroom and borrowing a few ingredients from the neighbours, they happily set about preparing what they planned would be quite a feast for the company Whilst chatting excitedly, buoyed by the return of their loved ones. During the ensuing conversation, in passing Yolanda casually mentioned how much she was looking forward to being alone with Richard; in response, Matilda generously offered to look after the babies for the night, the opportunity instantly being snapped up by the extremely grateful Yolanda, overjoyed to at last have the chance of some uninterrupted quality time with her long-time-absent husband.

That evening the party ate well; in all twenty people crammed into the main room of the house. In a buzz of chatter, everyone talked at once about the state of the nation, the improved weather, as well as many other subjects which were important enough to be included. Yet the most prevalent subject was the popularity of the king, his notoriety as a cowardly wastrel and how he had been noticeably absent during the current crisis. All agreed that if he didn't change his ways very soon, civil war was becoming more and more inevitable with the passing of each day. During the whole evening Richard kept his devoted stare permanently fixed on the lovely young Yolanda. With his mind elsewhere, Richard poked at his food, not really bothering what people were saying. The man inside was raring to be left alone with her, imagining her naked body in his arms, her soft yielding flesh, her hot passionate kisses on his mouth and the so long anticipated sexual bliss he could barely wait to experience.

Every time Yolanda spoke, Richard's pent-up passion rose. With loving gaze he noticed her every movement, from the way her green eyes twinkled cheekily as they flitted from guest to guest, or how she giggled happily whilst delicately sipping at her wine. Like iron being drawn to a magnet, he watched the way she intentionally licked her moist lips sexily between words and seductively flicked a wayward lock of her dark hair from her eyes as she flirtatiously acted the temptress, audaciously smiling at his discomfort by giving him the odd sidelong wink, suggesting he showed some patience while she was doing the decent thing by entertaining her guests without showing any undue haste to depart to bed. All the time, though, Yolanda knew as he did, exactly the place they'd rather be, eventually acquiescing to his desires by trying to covertly hurry along the mostly cheery, but often profound conversation without appearing too desperate to absent herself from their company and submit to his long-anticipated husbandly embrace.

With everyone full of good food and drink, the problems with the country put to rights and the king firmly put in his place, at long last the time came to retire for the night. Without paying too much lip service to the departing guests, Richard garbled an unseemly speedy goodnight and with the excited ardour of a newlywed, scurried out of the main room to go tripping and stumbling up the wooden stairs, dragging a willing Yolanda to the bedchamber, to make meaningful, ardent and somewhat noisy love to the beauty, who for the past two years had come between him and his sleep many, many times.

Their passionate session reached the ears of the wide-awake, motionless, dumb-mute in the secret attic, praying with the sound of every pleasured groan how he wished God would strike him down stone dead and thus free him from the living hell rightfully sent to him as a punishment for the evil deeds brought about by his mindless infatuation with an ambitious younger female.

That night, Richard's rest was shallow and dreamless, even though his body ached for the deep sleep it deserved after such a tiring long ride, followed by the lengthy and intense bout of enthusiastic lovemaking. However hard he tried, his troubled mind still couldn't escape the fact that in the morning he had to tell Yolanda the sad truth about Rolfe and Margaret, the news he had so carefully avoided the previous day, not wanting to dampen the occasion of the homecoming. Mercifully, after tossing and turning for hours, he was eventually lulled to sleep by the lovely's warm and yielding curled-up body pressed so close to him, who, although fast asleep, instinctively fondled his hair lovingly and breathed in gentle sighs with each blissful soft stroke of her adoring hand.

For the first time for three years, Richard woke up noticing the music of singing, chattering song birds in his ears, the sound he cherished above all others as they announced the dawning of a new day. Feeling heartened by the musical chorus and the rare sight of the rising red sun's rays streaming through the lattice, he lay for what seemed like ages, his outstretched arm touching Yolanda as she slept next to him, snoring quietly while he watched the room slowly getting lighter with the dawn. Staring aimlessly at the ceiling, he noticed a damp patch which needed attention, making a mental note to get it fixed, before his meaningless thoughts wandered into musing on what the birds had to say to each other, thinking it was probably something to do with either the king or the weather. Yet wherever his drowsy thoughts took him, in the back of his mind he dreaded Yolanda waking up, having resolved himself to tell her the unedited blatant truth of the pathetic sight that met his eyes on his visit to Burgh by Sands.

As soon as Richard thought Yolanda was conscious enough to absorb the woeful news, he dutifully told her everything. Holding her sobbing, naked body as tightly as he dared, he shed a few anguished tears himself, in sympathy for the people whose lives had so disproportionately touched them after such a very brief crossing of their paths. Nevertheless, with the usual determined resolution Richard had got used to and loved in Yolanda, following the short burst of crying for her lost friends, she shook off the bout of grief as spontaneously as it came. Standing up quickly, Yolanda thrust her naked, pert-breasted chest out and, stoically brushing away the wet off her face, she re-dressed in her casually scattered apparel, to go about preparing a breakfast for the hungry contingent of troops, who needed to be on the road before mid-morning, to head south to where King Edward was keeping his head down in his favourite south coast retreat in West Sussex.

Once again, inwardly distraught Yolanda and Matilda watched and waved, trying to keep a brave face on proceedings as their precious men-folk left. Their quivering bottom lips struggled not to crumple and betray their misery, their valiant efforts not aided by Sam, who also watched Richard and Simon forlornly as they went, letting out his usual long, melancholy howl as his master left at the head of the small column of men and turned the corner out of sight, leaving both women to return to the most heart-rending task of being wife, mother, or lover to a soldier on active duty, never knowing if, when or what the next visit might bring.

For a refreshing, but very unusual change, the sun was shining as the twelve rode on their way in twos. Their sombre warlike countenance brightened, courtesy of Yolanda, by the addition of some long, bright-coloured ribbons she'd kept from her wedding day and tied to their lances. That, and the bright warm sunlight as it twinkled off the headpieces and burnished mail, made the happy band even happier as they trotted off on their cheery way. Taking a route through the wastelands of rural Lincolnshire, they headed southwards, past Peterborough to Bedford, and then all the way through London, keeping virtually due south, straight on over the West Sussex Downs to the mighty South Coast stronghold of Arundel Castle, dominating the landscape for miles around and situated on a massive tree-swathed clump of rock high above the town, on the banks of the River Arun.

Richard's plan was to take an easy five days to complete the journey, resting where they found themselves at each sunset, living off their dried rations, and saving their cash for a stop at a famously popular inn near Horsham on the Sussex Weald called 'The Spotted Pig'. There they intended to stay long enough to clean themselves and all their gear in readiness to present themselves as a suitably immaculate team of messengers, fit to meet and impress the famously tempestuously picky Edward II and to present him with their letter from Sir Alain Jeffrys, which begged for the necessary extra money to complete the updating of the strategically essential Carlisle Castle, stuck all the way back up in the other end of the country.

The night's stay at The Spotted Pig was as comfortable as could be expected in the present times of hardship. There was little to be had, but the landlord and lady did their level best to accommodate the grateful travellers, appreciating the sudden upsurge in trade caused by the mass influx of the twelve hungry soldiers. Deciding it was time for a little bit of fun, Richard gave the men some leeway to let their hair down and fritter away some of their unspent allocation of travelling allowance after their lengthy journey. In order to retain control of the ten men, Richard was resolutely determined to stay sober, once before in his life having witnessed a group of drink-fuelled soldiers run amok among the populace. Fearing the repetition of such an incident and determined to present a respectable face to the easily upset king the next day, he made sure that the owners of the inn watered the strong ale, to nullify its mind-altering effects, thus saving the men from any loss of control and the resulting hangover.

Richard's cunning plan had worked a treat, and at first cockcrow on 15 August, Simon dutifully awakened the crew with ease, summoning the clear-eyed men to breakfast before joining them in the task of cleaning everything to perfection, including horses, tack, armour, and lastly themselves. Having completed the job to Richard's satisfaction by mid-morning, when following his leader's instructions, Simon delved into Uther's saddlebags and issued each of them with a brand-new, black linen surcoat emblazoned with Sir Alain's coat of arms, 'a rampant lion sable, on an ermine field', he'd kept safely hidden in their depths.

By eleven o'clock the company were suitably preened, polished and mounted on their immaculately groomed horses, ready to travel the last few miles to meet with the famously unpredictable, tempestuous and unpopular Edward II of England. Glistening and gleaming in the midday sun, the party wended their way west across the High Weald, where the confused flora had got itself completely out of kilter with the normal seasons. The short sudden spell of warmer weather had brought everything into flower at once, the summer daisies sharing their space with the winter snowdrops and brightly coloured summer butterflies fluttering around the clumps of egg-yolk-hued yellow broom flowers sitting amid the sea of smoky purple heather. In a strange unfamiliar world, the troop crossed the sandy heath land, going around the copses of dense woodland to join up with Stane Street, the ancient Roman road which went across the South Downs, all the way down to the Castle of Arundel.

It took about one and a half glorious hours of riding before the very impressive castle came into sight. Designed specifically to dominate the surrounding landscape, it was situated on an emerald green, tree-covered, sloped hill, the castle itself glinting almost sugar white in the afternoon sun, surrounded by the town nestling at its feet on the lower slopes, going all the way down to the banks of the slow-flowing green waters at the wide mouth of the River Arun.

Stunned by the magnificent scenery, the awe-struck column stopped for a moment at the sight, taking the pause to each pluck a sprig of broom, which Richard remembered was the badge of the Plantagenets, to tuck it in their hauberks in deference to the king, and then quickening their pace, they arrived at the pale stone gatehouse on the outer curtain wall. There they were made to wait for a full ten minutes outside the locked entrance, before a small door in the gate opened, allowing a welcome committee of six royal-liveried, heavily armed guards headed by a grey-haired, short and rather tubby, over-officious, stern-faced captain, whose gold-tasselled laces stretched tight over the belly on his luxurious, dark red, velvet tabard boldly picked out in gold and silver thread with the arms of the king on the front.

Gasping out his words, the breathless, somewhat portly official insisted that the party dismounted before he allowed Richard to tell him every detail about the armed party. On learning that there was a letter for the king, the little man demanded to be handed it. However, Richard refused point-blank to give it him, having been specifically told by Alain, that it was to be given directly into the king's own hand and no one else's, fearing that otherwise it would be swallowed up by the internal bureaucracy and remain unread if not.

Following a lot of grumbled humming and hawing, the liveried, somewhat over-zealous interrogator reluctantly came to the conclusion that Richard's errand was genuine and it would be appropriate to allow him and only one other admittance to the inner sanctum of the king's court.

Knowing that his best friend had never seen the royal Edward, Richard instantly decided the duty would fall on Simon to accompany him. With that settled, Richard and Simon hurried off with the fast-disappearing, wheezing, fat escort, leaving the horses in the capable hands of the others to be conducted to the stables and after that to the buttery, to partake of some average lunchtime fare of a meatless potage, some small beer and reasonably fresh, if not slightly gritty rye bread.

With much more effort than speed, the pair were conducted through the opulent interior to a bright whitewashed and gaudily painted side-room off the main hall, where the noble Edward was in negotiations with some of his barons. Flanked by two heavily armed guards wearing the same livery as the usher, the king himself was attired in a gold-coloured jupon under a heavy purple damask high-collared cloak, with a thin golden crown placed precisely in the centre of his shoulder-length grey-streaked, yellow hair. Sitting at a rose marble table, he was in mid-discussion about the running of the country with six sober-looking soldierly souls. Edward was finishing what was to him a normal lunch, but to Richard and Simon was a veritable feast of roast meats, baked pies, the finest wines and the king's favourite sweet, swan-shaped white marchpane shapes, all beautifully presented in a glittering display of crisp white napery, gold platters and goblets with superb ivory-handled silver cutlery.

Richard instantly recognised two of the nobles, the rotund, grumpy-looking but famously honest royal advisor Baron Dussingdale he'd met at Bannockburn, and sitting uncomfortably close to Edward was the podgy, mean-looking, clean-shaven Hugh Despenser the younger, a notorious schemer and close friend of the king's, a stark contrast to a very effeminate looking young man he'd never seen before; dressed in a very short green silk jupon and very revealing canary-yellow hose with pointed red shoes adorning his feet, he sat cross-legged like a woman, propped on the edge of the table opposite the king. Speaking to Edward in a very familiar way, the fop called him Eddy, while gracefully sipping some wine and picking at a tiny piece of roasted chicken, letting the morsel provocatively rest on his reddened lips, much to the apparent disgust of Dussingdale, who wanted to discuss the heady affairs of state rather than to see one of Edward's pets openly flirting with the monarch. The disgruntled baron unashamedly reminded the king there were more important things to do, other than gaze into his impudent lover's eyes, his plain-speaking attitude annoying Edward, who was about to fly off the handle into one of his famous rages when the two messengers were loudly and very formally introduced by the red-faced gasping steward.

With a tangible sense of relief, the seated seven looked up, pleased that the new arrivals had diffused a potentially volatile situation. Edward's gaze lingering rather too long when he saw that it was two disarmed young soldiers standing to attention before him; scanning them with a lecherous twinkle in his royal eye, he tried to think of something aptly funny to say at their appearance to ease the tense atmosphere. Noting their emblazoned surcoats, the king instantly realised who the envoys were from and turned to his companions to raise a laugh.

Speaking in his best put-on falsetto voice, he turned to address the gathering, "I see my Lord Jeffrys has sent me some tender young boys for my amusement!" His attempted witticism created no more than a polite titter from the company, except for his gaudily dressed jealous friend, who tossed his head peevishly at the joke, irritating Edward, who, ignoring his covetous associate, continued happily teasing Richard and Simon at the expense of his resentful companion. "And I see these pretty boys are wearing my badge tucked in their tunics. It's nice to see some respect from at least two of my subjects," Edward declared, glaring studiously at the baron, who taking his point, sniffed contemptuously and then, spluttering a pretend cough, nodded a begrudged "yes". "And what is it that I can do for my Lord Jeffrys' young harbingers who honour me by their presence?" the king asked, looking directly at Richard, who cleared his damaged throat in readiness to answer.

Pulling his shoulders back, Richard stared straight into Edward's eyes and, trying not to show any outward sign of the nerves which were jangling throughout his trembling body, repeated a well-rehearsed speech. "Sire, my name is Richard de Mauville; I am squire to Sir Alain Jeffrys, formerly squire to the late Sir Henry de Bohun of your acquaintance."

Before Richard could continue further, the king interrupted him. "Tell me then, Richard de Mauville, why is it you speak so gruffly to your king. Have you a cold, perhaps a sore throat, or maybe you're angry with me?" he asked, looking sternly at the clearly very nervous young man-at-arms.

Taken somewhat aback at the question, Richard considered his reply carefully before answering, deciding to tell the curious king the blatant truth. "Because in your name, sire, I was hanged on the word of the proven liar Lawrence Buckenham, who falsely accused me of treason and cowardice."

Stroking his chin as if trying to recall a memory, the king butted in. "Yes, I've heard the tale; I believe Buckenham has buggered off to Scotland, terrified that Humphrey will catch up with him and cut his balls off and, knowing Humphrey as I do, probably eat them before the rogue's eyes!"

Edward's jest about Humphrey de Bohun's famously large appetite created the round of genuine laughter which his previous attempt at comedy had failed to do; so, satisfied his humour had tickled his courtiers' funny-bones for long enough, Edward held up his dainty jewel-bedecked hand to halt the mirth before continuing. "Well then, half-hung Richard, now I know who you are, tell me what is it you want from your king?"

"I want to deliver this letter from Sir Alain, addressed to you, my liege," Richard announced, breaking with protocol and taking a stride forward to put the correspondence directly into the king's hand, his action instantly meeting with the rasp of two drawn weapons from the silent guards.

"Leave him! Let half-hung Richard approach," Edward screamed, holding out his regal hand to stop the guards, who immediately sheathed their weapons again with a rasp, allowing Richard to put the tied and sealed epistle into the king's outstretched other hand. Tearing it open, he read out loud the lengthy list of requirements Sir Alain thought were necessary for the defence of the northern border. Edward took his time to read the letter, handing it on to the Baron Dussingdale for his perusal and then to Despenser, eventually passing it on to the rest of his council, while he personally digested the information, taking it back to Richard to clarify a few salient points. After having done that, he joined his advisors in a huddle to secretly discuss their findings, deliberately leaving out the fop, who obviously felt annoyed by being so blatantly excluded and without a word stamped his scarlet-shod foot petulantly on the floor and stomped out of the chamber with his nose stuck pompously in the air.

Happy that he and his chief advisors had understood Alain's desires to the full, Edward launched himself regally to his feet with a noisy rustle of his cloak to address Richard. "Well, half-hung Richard de Mauville, I will send a message to your oppressed master. I have listened to his pleas and I will be sending him most of what he desires, and on the advisement of my Lord Dussingdale here," Edward declared, waving an emerald ringed finger in the direction of the baron, "I am also sending him some of my private guards to reinforce his hard-pressed garrison in the hope he can prevent these marauding Scots from making further inroads into our land. So, attend me here, tomorrow morning at ten, and a letter will be prepared and ready for you to take back to my noble Lord Jeffrys."

The royal assessment finished, Edward suddenly spun on his heel to leave; following suit, his entire retinue started trotting in his footsteps like faithful puppies. The king was just on the verge of exiting the room, when, without prior warning, he imperiously held up his hand, skidding the procession to a haphazard halt behind him. Turning back round, the unfathomable monarch gave a friendly glance at Richard and then Simon, whose juvenile eyes had permanently been on stalks gazing covetously at the uneaten food. The hungry stare was not missed by the king, who waved the same jewelled hand at the laden table. "Please eat! We can't have hungry boys in our court now, can we? You never know when you'll need all your strength!" Edward added with a suggestive peer, and then, smiling naughtily, he winked a giant obvious wink at Simon, who, understanding the inference, blushed crimson with embarrassment as the king, with a touch of pathos in his voice added just one more thing before he left. "There now, I can't be such an awful devil as they say I am, now can I?" Without waiting for the response, Edward disappeared along with the others, who went off tripping in his wake, brim-full of the lunch, leaving Richard and Simon filling their empty bellies with the finest food and drink in the land.

However delicious it was, Simon reckoned he could have done better, criticising first the crust and then the filling of a succulent pie, turning his attentions to a joint of beef which he insisted was overcooked, nevertheless stuffing his face to capacity with each. Richard and his company enjoyed the night in the castle, for once eating well, sleeping comfortably in dry warm beds and having a good wholesome breakfast of ham and cheese, before loading up with the plentiful supplies to tide them over for the journey home.

Leaving his fellows alone to tack the horses up, a thoroughly washed Richard, wearing his freshly re-polished armour, followed a tall liveried steward to attend his appointment with Edward and collect the letter for Sir Alain. Obeying the king's instructions at precisely ten o'clock on the morning of 16 August and looking every inch a professional warrior, he arrived at the same room where he'd been interviewed the previous afternoon. As promised, Edward was there and waiting with the same six nobles and two guards, but instead of the friendly humorous king of before, he was strutting up and down screaming, crying and throwing things about in one of his famed stormy tantrums. Shrieking an expletive, the king wagged an opened note, with its red wax seal still dangling off its purple ribbon, at five of the cowering lords, who were doing their best to appease the raging royal.

Wide-eyed, Richard watched as the inconsolable monarch accused his royal cousin, Thomas the rebellious Earl of Lancaster, of treason for refusing to commandeer food off his hard-pressed starving tenants and send it to Arundel to feed the king's private household. All during the rancorous outburst, rather than calming Edward, Hugh Despenser, who was already at loggerheads with the earl over some disputed land on the Welsh marches, egged on the moody ruler in an attempt to alienate his opponent and was unable to help himself from giving a sly smile at his unexpected success.

The king's raging mood miraculously disappearing in the blink of an eye when he saw Richard politely standing armed from head to foot in spotlessly clean mail with his gleaming bascinet neatly tucked under his arm, waiting in stunned silence to receive the all-important letter for Alain. Edward's railing shrieks instantly turning to words of welcome at the sight of the young paladin. "Well, if it isn't the friendly face of half-hung Richard de Mauville, dressed like a veritable Galahad and here to see me and cheer me up when I most need it! I believe my Lord Dussingdale has your letter and the archers I promised should be assembled in the courtyard by now," he added, looking benevolently at the bashful youngster.

Richard looked perplexed. "What archers, sire?" he asked sounding confused.

"The forty mounted archers that I'm sending with you to Carlisle; remember the little men with bows who fire arrows at their enemies! They need something to occupy them, so I'm getting them off their fat lazy arses and sending them with you all the way to Cumbria!" Edward's attempt to be sarcastic was lost on Richard's amazed ears, still disbelieving that he was to be put in charge of forty professional, possibly drunken and probably rowdy bowmen, to hopefully escort them without incident all the way back through the heart of England to the Scottish borders.

Changing tack, the unpredictable monarch once again addressed Richard, who still looked dumbfounded with his mouth gaping open and a little bemused at the impulsive king. Smiling a curious smile, he asked a peculiarly strange question with a mischievous twinkle in his royal eye. "Are you a true and loyal man to your anointed king, young Richard de Mauville?"

"Of course I am, my lord!" Richard replied, sounding a little indignant at the query.

The spontaneous reply apparently pleasing the king, who nodded silently with a playful smirk on his lips as if saying yes to himself. "I know you're of noble birth and I hear you've been well taught by Sir Henry in the laws of chivalry, so today, master de Mauville, I think I shall make you a knight, to ride at the head of this gallant war band, so come here and kneel before your king."

Somewhat hesitantly, Richard stepped forward and knelt at the feet of Edward, suspecting he might be the butt of some form of wicked jest for the amusement of the gathering. Although, when Edward hit him smartly with the flat of his hand on his cheek he realised it was no joke. "There, Sir Richard de Mauville, now get to your feet and buss your king, then go and win me this war in Scotland!" Edward warbled, smiling kindly at his newest belted knight.

Rising unsteadily to his feet, Richard's wobbly knees momentarily disobeyed him, making him almost collapse as he followed tradition and, scarcely being able to believe he was now a knight, embraced the pungently sweet-perfumed Edward. With his young mind in utter turmoil, unprepared for the surprise accolade and not knowing what to say, Richard, whose only testimony to his raised status was his scarlet cheek which still stung from the only blow he was now allowed to receive without returning, mumbled a nervous thanks to the king, who in response immediately commanded the steward to rush off and get an indenture drawn up as proof of Richard's newfound raised status. Then, with the business at hand in mind, Edward dismissively waved Richard away so he could return to his previous dilemma and in a fleeting moment was again loudly making wild threats against the Earl of Lancaster for his reluctance to obey his orders.

Disbelieving his luck at catching the king on a good day, Richard patiently watched as a very exacting, pitifully slow cleric drew up the appropriate document. Getting increasingly frustrated, Richard scoured his brain to remember minute details and tell him everything he knew about his sketchy ancestry, each relevant detail being laboriously scratched down with a goose quill pen clutched delicately in the scribe's ink-stained fingers. Stopping several times to carefully sharpen the stylus, the fastidious clerk wasted more time embellishing the manuscript by adding an intricate and colourful drawing of Richard's inherited coat of arms, 'Or, a boar's head proper, tusked gules', and then to finish off the all-important deed, he frittered away extra precious minutes by proudly adding even more unnecessarily ostentatious flourishes to his handiwork.

After another wasted two hours, the scribe eventually finished the indenture, allowing a late, rather shocked Sir Richard de Mauville to take his place where the men were ready and waiting in the courtyard. Finally arriving, Richard joined his troop carrying not only a bag of gold which jingled with his every step, but a sheath of papers in his bascinet, the written orders giving him command of the forty king's own archers, the letter from Edward for Sir Alain Jeffrys and finally his own manuscript bearing the royal seal and confirming his elevation to knight.

The happy news of Richard's surprise advancement travelled through the castle like wildfire, his long-awaited presence being greeted with a hearty chorus of cheering, led by an ecstatic Simon and joined in enthusiastically by all the assembled men as he walked amongst them towards the impatient Solomon, who showed his aggravation at being made to wait with a stamp of his impatient hoof and a noisy champing at the foaming bit, as were the rest of the horses who'd been forced to stand idle and hang around for most of the morning while the heady laws of chivalry were adhered to.

Following a series of well-meaning handshakes, the occasional hug from the soldiers who knew Richard best, and backslaps from most of the rest, Richard walked through the troops to the horse. Accepting a leg up from Simon, he mounted Solomon, who with no respect for his rider's new elevated position, started hopping up and down on the spot in anticipation of at last moving off, which wasn't far away.

In one movement and a whispered rustle of cloth and metal on oiled leather, the entire company followed Richard's example and were on their steeds waiting for their new master to ask his horse forwards and out along the road between the two sets of curtain walls through the gate to start the mighty three-hundred-mile trek all the way to bleak Carlisle.

Contrary to Richard's initial fears, the archers weren't just a disorderly bunch of peasants who happened to be good with the longbow, but a highly disciplined, well led, highly organised group of expert bowmen, mounted on good steeds, equally adept at horsemanship and practised with arms other than their main weapon. So, with his helmeted head held high and a colossal sense of pride, an incredulous Sir Richard de Mauville led the long column of fifty-one good troops out of the castle, regularly stealing a disbelieving gaze over his shoulder to make sure he wasn't simply dreaming.

CHAPTER 17

Thankfully, the clement spell of weather established itself over the entire British Isles and with it, a real belief that better times were ahead. Where a short few weeks before the population skulked in the shelter of their homes, whether it be a castle, hall, house or hovel, now they were out and about, starting to do the necessary labours to return the land to something resembling what it was like prior to when God hid the sun from their world three years before. It was just the same north of the Scottish border, where now the deprived, starved people came out of their crofts to cast their avaricious eyes south, to what they believed was the land of plenty, jealously coveting the riches they thought the English had, vowing to relieve them of whatever they could as soon as their armies could be re-assembled.

Still incredulous that he had achieved his life's ambition of becoming a knight so early in his young life, Richard rode at the front of his column of men making his best effort not to look too smug as he chatted, riding three abreast, with Simon, who'd nominated himself as squire to the new knight, and the wise grey-haired Dudley Chapman, the bastard son of a high noble and the grizzled war-wise captain of the archers. A veteran of the Scottish wars during the reign of Edward I and well versed in the cunning ways of the enemy, Dudley's high-ranked father successfully made great efforts to ensure that his illegitimate son gained the benefit of a decent upbringing with a military family. A quick learner, he proved to be extremely adept at his chosen trade of war and subsequently was seconded to the king's personal bodyguard as captain some years before Bannockburn. With that great deal of knowledge behind him, he quickly made friends with Richard and Simon as he spent the long boring days of riding whilst relating his many tales of war to both pairs of ears, which listened eagerly to his every word, learning much during the protracted conversations, making the eventless arduous hours flit by, until after a full fourteen gruelling days in the saddle, they at last arrived in Cumbria after a full fourteen gruelling days in the saddle.

The closer the band got to their final destination the more uneasy Richard felt and for the second time in his life his mysterious sixth sense caused the inexplicable foreboding accompanied by a tense feeling in the pit of his stomach. There was absolutely no tangible reason for his discomfort, but there was no mistaking its existence, his suspicions being raised further when the party reached the crest of a hill just outside the ruined village of High Hesket, which should have looked over the mottled green slopes towards the castle and the distant Irish Sea, but instead of the usual breathtaking vista, the expected sight was obscured by a thick, smoky, brown hazy smog, which lay unmoving in the windless valley and seemed to be emanating from very close to Carlisle itself.

At the sight of smoke, the party quickened their pace to a fast trot as they made their way along the grassy banks of the River Eden, where all the dwellings and steads were freshly looted and still smouldering. Nevertheless, the nearer they got to their destination the clearer it became that the source of the fumes was actually coming from the immediate vicinity of the castle.

Trying not to panic, Richard hallooed the contingent to an urgent canter, through the thick woods at Wetheral, past the securely locked and barred fortified priory, arriving at the outskirts of the town with their horses sweating and blowing from the strenuous exercise. Their eyes meeting with utter disorder at the very recently razed, smoking ruins of the now-desolate town of Carlisle, where castle and gateway still stood defiantly, completely unharmed and intact, amid a litter of squashed and badly mutilated corpses of the failed Scottish attackers, who lay in swathes among heaps of rubble at the base of the castle walls, where the taunting black and white banner of Sir Alain Jeffrys still remained defiantly raised above the keep.

Warily, the battered, bruised but still undefeated small garrison opened the gate on the command of Alain, who, unlike the men, didn't think it was the belligerents that had returned to finish the job they had started. Instantly he recognised it was Richard on Solomon at the head of the two lines of very professional-looking horsemen, sadly arriving a little bit too late to rout the besiegers by outflanking them. However, their presence was still highly welcomed by the hard-pressed soldiers, who for two days had repelled a determined band of Scottish raiders attempting to take the castle, their sturdy efforts only being thwarted by the tireless resistance of the better-disciplined defenders and solid repairs which were now almost completely finished.

Once through the gates, an amazing sight met Richard and the fifty mounted soldiers. To their surprise the whole courtyard was jammed to the gunnels with the entire population of Carlisle town, filling the square and making it all but impossible to move through the crowd. Carefully, Richard picked his way through the throng, trying to find Alain and Mary, firstly to deliver the king's message and money, but also to find out what had happened in his absence. The difficult search was made almost impossible by the clamouring, grateful multitude, all of whom wanted to get near enough to the heroes to shout their hurrahs and prayers of thanks as they passed.

Scanning the appreciative faces from his lofty vantage point on Solomon, Richard hoped to see the man he sought among the crowd of anonymous faces gazing approvingly at him and his men, having to look twice when he caught a fleeting glimpse of a pair of singularly bright, very familiar blue eyes staring hopefully in his direction. Quickly losing track of their owner in the mass, Richard desperately tried to re-establish visual contact with them, thinking he recognised them from somewhere in the past, but, unable to halt with the fifty pressing from behind, he moved on, preventing any chance of finding out to whom they actually belonged.

It didn't take Richard too long to find Alain and Mary. Gazing round, he noticed them standing twelve feet above everyone else, waving frantically, trying to catch his attention from some half-finished new wooden steps up to the battlements he hadn't seen before. Richard immediately indicated over to where the exhausted-looking knight and his equally tired wife beamed a weary welcome, clearly overjoyed at the sight of Richard, the reinforcements and hopefully some good news from the king. Anxious to deliver his letter and tell his story about the four weeks spent at the opposite end of the country, Richard managed to cross the courtyard, miraculously without causing any serious injuries to the press of bystanders. Eventually catching up with Alain and Mary, he vaulted off Solomon and tossed the reins to a tetchy Simon, who was annoyed at having been delegated the duty of showing the contingent of archers where to stable their horses and stow their gear. Somewhat petulantly and in a display of poor grace, Simon went about the task, really wanting to be included in the discussion with Alain and Mary, to be present when Richard told them the whole episode of his meeting with the unfathomable monarch, and his surprise knighthood. Suffering from a tinge of jealousy, Simon watched as the three disappeared to the private quarters, where, over another, suitably expensive, pilfered flagon of wine, Richard first showed them the indenture, then relieved himself of the much needed money and lastly the letter from the king, hurrying his story up, eager to hear Alain's account of the surprise attack.

Using his extra special, explanatory deep voice, Alain went into every detail, describing the complicated series of events which led to his urgent evacuation of the town. His basso profondo rumblings caused much mirth to the apparently parched Mary, who was very quickly on her third goblet of the delicious liquor, as she laughingly mimicked him to draw attention to the change in his vocal tone. Aggravated by his tipsy wife's interjection, Alain continued, trying to keep his voice normal whilst telling Richard how the foolish Scottish captain gave away his intent of attacking the castle by setting fire to everything remotely English as he approached, giving what for all intents and purposes were warning beacons signifying his rate of approach, giving adequate time to get the civilians to safety. Alain went on to say how he watched helplessly as the Scottish leader oversaw the sacking and looting of the town and personally supervised the loading of the booty on to ox-carts before commencing his hopeless attempt to attack the greatly improved defences of Carlisle Castle.

To repel the besiegers, Sir Alain lined the battlements with anyone strong enough to hurl down the hundreds of the already stacked building blocks of masonry on the heads of the Scots, who, in another clueless inept folly, hadn't brought any archers with them, expecting the castle walls to be in the same un-defendable ruined state they were in just a few years prior.

As soon as Simon was satisfied that the newcomers to the castle were familiarised enough in their strange surroundings to make themselves at home, with rather too much haste to be decent, he handed over their induction to one of the soldiers he befriended on the journey to Arundel, and racing off like a bat out of hell, made a bee-line to where he knew Richard and Alain would be performing a post-mortem on the attack on the castle and chewing over how well the restored defences had performed when under attack.

Simon was scurrying as fast as his young legs would carry him, and was almost all the way across the yard and about to enter the door to the living area for the nobles, when out of nowhere a young and lovely blue-eyed blonde girl in her late teens jumped in his path, partially blocking his way, clearly wanting, but hardly daring to ask him a question. Stopping him when he tried to push past, the lass mustered all her bravery to politely beg a moment of his time in a language which to his Midlander's ears, was barely any known form of understandable English.

No matter how hard Simon listened to her appeals, her softly mumbled tones were absolute nonsense to him, until at his signalled suggestion she started speaking very slowly, with long gaps between each word, making exaggerated mouth movements and using hand signs to give him a clue. Having arrived at a mutual form of communication, the young woman pointed first at her breast bone and then to the chamber where Simon was heading. "I have seen you with Richard de Mauville. Please tell him Rolfe's daughter Alice is here and urgently needs to see him," she explained a little incoherently, but after some more difficulty and asking the lass to repeat herself twice, Simon at last grasped the gist of what she desired. Having heard Richard speak fondly of the peasant family, he immediately agreed to her request, and grabbing the girl's hand, hurtled up the stairs to the quarters with her in tow. Pointing at the floor to signify that she was to wait outside the door, Simon knocked politely and entered the room, where a tipsy Richard was sitting imbibing a celebratory drink with Alain and an even merrier Mary. As soon as the boozy trio saw it was Simon who'd just entered the room, they motioned him to sit and enjoy some of the alcohol with them. Ignoring the kind offer and with a cheeky grin on his freckled face, Simon told Richard of his rather young and lovely mystery visitor. The welcome yet unexpected news stunned Richard a little bit, as he believed Alice had been killed when their homestead was flattened. So, rising a little unsteadily to his feet, a slightly doubtful Richard instantly asked Simon to let her in so he could see for himself.

Feeling overawed to be summoned into the presence of a knight and his lady and worried she might have been a bit too pushy, Alice was slightly reluctant to enter the room, almost having to be dragged by Simon. Nonetheless, she was more than pleasantly surprised when her hosts greeted her as an equal, inviting her to take a seat and offering her some liquid refreshment as soon as she appeared.

Immediately recognising the blonde beauty as the same little Alice he'd met over three years before, Richard grabbed her and gave her a prolonged hug of welcome, before releasing her breathless body so that she could take her seat and tell her woeful tale.

Scarcely crediting what she was telling him, Richard listened to Alice's rather too familiar, torrid story of capture, torture and abuse at the hands of a nobleman, her subsequent sale into prostitution and imprisonment in a brothel in Carlisle, right up to her recent escape with her younger sister during the chaos following the threat from the Scottish. The more complicated parts of the tale had to be interpreted by Mary, who fortunately for the others was blessed with a very good ear when it came to Northern dialects, some of the gory details making her weep as she translated the long sad saga.

The gruesome particulars instantly sobered them up, as they heard of how a couple of days after Richard and Yolanda left the homestead on the borders, a band of Scottish raiders attacked their small farm early one morning, killing her father and oldest brother in the ensuing fight. With the resistance dealt with, the Scots stole everything of worth from the smallholding, butchering all the animals for the sheer hell of it, taking some of the meat but leaving most of the carcasses where they lay. Bravely, Alice told of how she was forced to watch with her younger sister Joan, as the marauders mercilessly took turns in raping her poor mother to death, before slaughtering the rest of her family, burning the bodies in the pathetic hovel and the other buildings they once called their home.

Sympathetically, Mary halted Alice at that point, noticing her blue eyes getting even bluer as they welled up with the tears she had so valiantly been trying to fight back. Losing the battle against the inevitable, Alice broke down into a bout of inconsolable sobs; her continuous sniffing as the torrents of salty droplets pattered on the wooden boarded floor made her utterly impossible to comprehend. With this in mind, Mary urged Alice to take a few deep breaths, then rest for a while to allow her the time to recover her poise and finally take a couple of gulps of wine to aid her recovery before bracing herself to resume her tale.

Visibly pulling herself together, Alice carried on stoically, telling how both she and her sister were both amazed at being spared from the rape and subsequent murder they expected. They were bound, blindfolded and gagged before being thrown on the back of a wagon and taken northwards. To the best of her knowledge, other than to rest for the night, they made only one noticeable stop, when her keen ears gleaned some possibly relevant information from whispered conversations which led her to believe that the raiders picked up a lost and wounded English knight they found abandoned in the middle of the Trossachs. Having thrown him on the back of the cart with them, they shared the uncomfortable silent ride all the way to the desolate Dunstaffnage Castle. Once there, they were handed to its vile master Sir Thomas Dewar and subsequently given as sex slaves to the same wounded man she knew was the English prisoner, and now recognised as the knight in charge of the same recent attack on Carlisle Castle which allowed them to escape from her present-day captors, who sold her and her sister's services to anyone who was prepared to pay for them.

The description and the timing of the events rang a very recognisable bell with Richard, who, with the help of Mary, questioned the heartbroken girl further, Soon learning between the series of shuddering sobs more details about the English knight, Richard soon came to the thoughtfully considered conclusion that it was more than possible she was talking about the wanted renegade Lawrence Buckenham. His suspicions becoming confirmed when Alice, on being asked, described the tall black horse with a strange hook-shaped mark along its nose he rode while halooing on his men during the aborted attempt to take the stronghold. Richard's interest became even more raised when it dawned on him that the object of his three years of pent-up hatred was less than a full day away, probably heading back north, encumbered by the heavyweight spoils from the latest raid, loaded on the already notoriously slow ox-drawn carts.

Befuddled by the combination of a hefty intake of alcohol, mixed with his desire for revenge, Richard's normally tactical-aware mind became confused. Casting his usual caution aside and ably goaded by a rather over-enthusiastic Simon, who also thought it was a great idea to waste no time and immediately go in hot pursuit of the man Richard believed was Lawrence Buckenham.

Their ill-conceived idea was to simply gallop headlong after the absconded traitor, find him and bring him to instant summary justice. Fortunately for them, though, they were quickly brought back to earth with a bump by Alain, who, although a bit more tipsy than Richard, still had many superior years of accumulated wisdom behind him. Calling on his amassed experience, he wisely counselled the fanatical men-at-arms to stop, wait, conceive a viable plan and carry it out in the morning when they were sober with a good night's rest behind them, rather than hurtling blindly into strange enemy territory in pursuit of an unknown number of armed men.

Carrying on with the reprimand, Alain slurred a little as he taught Richard an unforgettable lesson, pointing out that it was stupidity like his which caused many a fatal calamity in the past similar to the debacle at Bannockburn. Remembering the similarly wise words of the dead Henry, Richard took the point with a petulant nod, apologising instantly for his rudeness, knowing that the wily knight was in fact talking absolute sense.

With a friendly wink, Alain accepted the contrition, adding a footnote to his own good advice by reminding Richard that there was plenty of time, because as well as being slowed down by the laden carts, their intended quarry had no idea that reinforcements had arrived at the Carlisle and wouldn't expect to be chased, as they probably thought the castle's inhabitants would be staying safely at home, licking their wounds and picking up what was left of their ruined lives.

Their differences healed and the bickering over and done with, the company enjoyed the rest of what were now somewhat muted celebrations. Sensibly, Richard avoided the intake of more alcohol, determined to make sure he was clear-eyed and sober in the morning. Meanwhile, Alice had gone off to extract her emotionally wrecked younger sister Joan from a safe cubbyhole she had found to hide away from the outside world. Having to resort to force, Alice eventually managed to winkle her reticent sibling out of the sanctuary, to reacquaint herself with a happy and relieved Richard, who thought both girls were long dead.

Poor timid Joan was nothing like what she was like when Richard first met her; instead of the precocious, cheeky, short and rather chubby young lass he was expecting to see, she was a gorgeous dark-haired, willowy young lady, who looked frightened of her own shadow. Summoning every ounce of her strength, Alice tugged at Joan's trembling hand to haul her into the room, eventually succeeding, the petrified girl entered like a terrified rabbit, flitting her horrified blue eyes repeatedly over her shoulder as if she was expecting to be jumped on at any moment.

After a lot of encouragement and reassurance, Joan eventually gained enough confidence to meekly tell her story. Using a very faint, nervy little voice, Joan stared forlornly into space and spoke as if she was reading a book. Surprising everyone with her accurate and lurid description, she went into some of the more gruesome details her older sibling preferred not to tell. A series of prods from Alice prompted her to speak clearer as the shadow of a girl described every miniscule particular of her brutal rape at the hands of Lawrence Buckenham. The candid account shocked the company when she told of the excruciating pain, how much she bled and how long it took her to recover from the savage sexual assault. Even in her shattered state there was no mistaking the bitterness in her quiet tones as she related the gruesome tale, yet only on one occasion did Joan raise her voice when spitting out some of words as she spoke of the unnamed Englishman who actually committed the wicked atrocity.

The horrendous details of how the two innocents were first abused at Dunstaffnage and then subsequently sold into prostitution moved everyone, especially Richard, who had first-hand knowledge of how such bestial treatment can affect the minds of the juvenile victims. Vowing awful revenge on the perpetrators, Richard inwardly thanked God for his intervention by sending the raiders, which in effect caused both girls to escape from their captivity, releasing them into the friendly hands of Alain and Mary, who promised to put them under their protection.

Having heard all they needed to about the chapter of events which led the two girls up to the present time, Mary suggested it was time to speak of a less-depressing subject and started chatting about more mundane things to take the company's mind off the pitifully sad narrative. Making a good attempt to defuse the tension, she told the girls some humorous yarns about her almost-nomadic life with Alain and then of her own childhood. Mary's unusual view of life made the gathering laugh, except for Joan, who still had a remote faraway look and, as Richard expected, was again re-living her ordeal at the hands of the man she desperately wanted to see suffer as she had suffered at his brutal, child-abusing, despicable hands.

Even before first light, Richard was armed and ready to leave with Simon and only a paltry fifteen volunteers: the maximum number of men Alain dared spare from the contingent at the castle to go on such a perilous journey. Ignoring that in the main it was for personal reasons why Richard wanted to pursue Lawrence Buckenham into Scottish territory, Alain justified it as an attempt to eradicate a known English traitor with his dangerous war band which could otherwise cost the lives of many border farmers. In total, Richard's posse consisted of Simon, six of the king's archers, and his now staunchest ally and old adversary Edgar, who he'd put in charge of the eight reliable men-at-arms he had chosen from the ones which accompanied Richard to Arundel.

The trail left by Lawrence and his men wasn't difficult to follow. The heavily weighed down carts left deep ruts and muddy hoof prints in the still-waterlogged turf down in the dips and valleys, as well as other signs on the English side of the border, such as a couple of burnt-out, looted buildings and the raped or mutilated corpses of the inhabitants. As a one-time poacher-cum-stalker, the country-bred Edgar concluded they were following one heavily armed knight on a destrier, approximately a dozen lighter-armed mounted men on ponies and about twenty infantry, with at least two or possibly three ox-carts to carry their loot. Armed with the knowledge they carried on the pursuit a little more cautiously and using a great deal of stealth they sneaked across the border into the lowlands of Scotland. Making as much speed as possible, Richard's small but well-mounted force rode forward with purpose, quickly enough to catch up with their quarry, yet not so fast as to overtire or lame the horses, as now, being in unfriendly territory, any assistance with injured animals from the locals could be readily ruled out.

Richard nominated the experienced Edgar as chief tracker and every few miles he hopped off his tough little pony to inspect the trail and give an update on the progress, surmising that after only a day and a half's travelling the prey was only three or four hours ahead and getting closer and closer with every mile travelled. The faster they closed the gap between pursuers and pursued the more desperately Richard needed a plan. Knowing they were almost certainly outnumbered, It was decided to leave the track, take a wide berth to circumnavigate the raiders, set an ambush further along their expected path and rely on the archers to thin the enemy's ranks before entering into hand-to-hand combat with the remainder.

Thus as soon as Edgar thought the still-steaming dung from the Scottish raiders' animals was less than twenty minutes old, Richard and his men made a wide detour at speed and used the undulating terrain to remain unseen as they overtook the Scots. Taking a moment to spy on them as they passed, they assessed their numbers to be roughly as they thought, seeing around fourteen men on horses, twenty on foot and a couple of what they suspected were captured young females, trussed and sitting on the back-board of the two laboriously slow covered ox-carts which hampered their forward progress to no more than a pathetic crawl. The overloaded wagons acted against the Scots in two ways: on one hand the soldiers exhausted themselves by having to act as extra power to assist the beasts going up the steep soggy inclines, and on the other, acting as brakes going down, trying not to let the heavy vehicles roll over the oxen on the descent. But regardless of how hard Richard's men strained their eyes, they could see utterly no sign whatsoever of the primary objective, the renegade knight and wanted man, the insidiously evil criminal, Sir Lawrence Buckenham.

Applying his tactical skills to the best advantage, Richard led the men an appropriate distance ahead, keeping well off the road so as not to leave tracks and give a clue to their prey and possibly warning them of an ambush. Then he Selected what he thought was a very good spot to set his trap on a steep upward incline heading due west, straight towards the sinking sun and in consideration of the opposition's slowness, at the point where he expected the target to be just as dusk was starting to gather, but desperately hoping they weren't planning to prematurely stop to rest for the night and thus thwart his well-thought-up plan.

The wait seemed interminable as Simon and the six archers lay in hiding, with four of them concealed behind some dense gorse on the right bank of the trail, while on the left Simon and the other two stayed low, hidden among a pile of large boulders. Meanwhile, Richard and the mounted contingent stayed on their horses, standing back out of sight some fifty paces off the road and doing their best to keep their own and the other steeds quiet by letting them graze in some excellent-looking wayside herbage. For a full hour Richard sat on Solomon, craning his scarred neck, hoping and expecting the foe to come into sight at any moment. Starting to feel disappointed when the sun started to set, he considered giving up, thinking his carefully contrived scheme had gone awry, but unlike his calculations, the planning was sound and more than half an hour later than expected the carts, the oxen and their foot-weary personnel at last crawled into view.

The plan had worked a treat and although badly late they were there and walking straight into the sprung trap with their tired eyes firmly shut. The consummate skill of the expert bowmen was amazing. The slow-moving targets played directly into their eager hands as the train struggled up the gradient. Most of the Scots had to put aside their weapons and shields to use both hands to push the vehicles up the slope, making easy targets for English archers as they fired their bodkin-tipped arrows as quickly as they could. Often with eight or ten shafts in the air at once, they first targeted the riders, nearly all their arrows finding its mark with a satisfying plop as the needle points sunk into the flesh of the disarmed, bewildered troops. The dimming light behind and the glare of the setting sun in front prevented them from seeing where the attack was coming from, causing widespread panic as they witnessed their colleagues so easily killed by the invisible archers.

The Scottish ranks plunged into even more chaos when silhouetted starkly against the brilliant orange sky, they saw Richard leading a body of ten armoured horsemen, weapons raised at the ready, screaming their war-cries and thundering down on them from the crest of the rise. Like a hot knife through butter, they scythed through the confused remnants of the Scots, beating down on their confused heads with their swords, axes, mallets and clubbing maces, splattering their blood and brains over the sweating flanks of the trampling, terrified horses, whose own desperate urge to escape the carnage was suppressed by the busy spurs and the controlling reins to keep them facing the shrinking number of the opposition.

Taking a leaf out of the book of warfare written at Bannockburn by the Scots, the attackers mercilessly pushed their advantage home, even slaying the fighters who yielded, callously refusing to accept their offered glaives, seeking revenge for that humiliating defeat which was still fresh in the minds of the rampaging, vengeful English.

The skirmish was over in a very short while. Richard's triple-pronged scheme had worked perfectly and nearly all the Scots were butchered hardly having even drawn their weapons and not really knowing who it was that so easily routed them. Never before had they seen such skilled, ferocious soldiery. In all twenty-seven of their number were killed outright, pierced by the shafts or with their skulls crushed, another six were mortally wounded, and only one slightly injured survivor had been lucky enough to find shelter from the falling arrows under a cart.

The English victory was completed without having lost a single man in the swift and spectacularly successful attack. It soon became all too clear that, in success, Richard had failed to achieve his goal to locate the renegade

Lawrence. Personally inspecting each individual dead enemy carefully, Richard hoped upon hope to find his vile corpse; quickly realising that his arch-enemy was definitely not among the slain, he unusually resorted to a bout of cursing and swearing in his abject frustration at the lack of finding Lawrence's dead face staring back at him. Dejected and angered by the lack of the evidence of Lawrence's whereabouts, with his own personal reasons in mind, Richard set about questioning the only Scottish prisoner he thought was well enough to withstand interrogation. Along with the many strategically important questions which needed answers, for his own peace of mind, Richard urgently wanted to find out exactly why Lawrence wasn't with his men. The selected man proved to be very stubborn, refusing categorically to utter a single word, let alone give away any sensitive information which might be useful to his sworn enemy, and even after repeated threats of violence the obdurate Scot still remained resolutely silent.

The ineffective grilling technique was being watched by an amazed Edgar, who failed to understand why Richard was being so gentle with the dogged prisoner. "Let me do it and I'll have your answers in no time," he suggested, having had some experience of extracting information for the ecclesiastical courts on behalf of Bishop John de Halghton, the absent governor of Carlisle Castle.

Needing quick responses, Richard accepted Edgar's offer of his services to act as inquisitor. "Do whatever you have to," Richard agreed sadly, giving Edgar a silent nod of approval, and not being blessed with the stomach for torture but knowing that needs must, walked forlornly away from the scene knowing he would have all the desired answers in a very little time.

His departure left the unfortunate fellow to whatever quantity of inflicted pain Edgar decided was sufficient to loosen his mulish tongue. "Tell me everything we need to fucking know! You will eventually, so you might as well fucking do it now before I fucking get to work on you!" Edgar demanded, slapping the victim hard across the face twice, inwardly hoping he wouldn't have to resort to a more vicious technique.

His relatively civilised attempt to loosen the man's tongue met with no response except a shower of bloody spittle, complete with a few teeth, spat directly in his face. "I'll give you just one more fucking chance to tell me and I swear I won't hurt you any more," Edgar promised, almost pleading with his victim whilst wiping the liquid insult off his face, only to receive a repeat dose. "Well you've only got yourself to fucking blame!" Edgar explained, dragging the defiant Scot to one of the cartwheels and tying him to it with his legs stuck out in front. "One final chance to save yourself before I start. I promise you, it ain't going to be very nice for me or for you!" he warned, keeping his head a safe distance away from the stubborn man's mouth, but again receiving no reply. That was it, realising that being reasonable wasn't going to work, Edgar decided to take a more determined approach to the job at hand.

The methods used by Edgar were as crude as they were effective. The practised inquisitor started the gruesome task by staring coldly into the victim's terrified eyes and simply taking hold of the man's own short-handled steel-flanged mace, promptly smashed the man in both knees with it, repeating the strikes twice to make sure the bones were thoroughly broken.

Ignoring the now-talkative man's agonised pleas for mercy and without showing any pity whatsoever, Edgar reminded the blubbering wreck that he should have spoken earlier. "I told you it was going to fucking hurt!" he said, grabbing the howling victim's left foot, then, glaring fiercely into his screwed-up face, started twisting it very slowly, bone-crunchingly clockwise, then anti-clockwise and then clockwise again, causing the man to faint with the excruciating pain. Bringing him back to consciousness with a few beakers of cold water, Edgar once again got hold of the victim's right foot as if to repeat the process. However, the threat of further brutality instantly achieved the desired effect and without too much more of the less-than-subtle encouragement, the poor soul blurted out all the required information without taking breath. Between his long groans of agony, the man gasped out his name and the rest of the answers, suffering another ten minutes of the torment before Edgar was satisfied enough to relay his savagely extracted information to Richard.

Pleased with his results, Edgar excitedly told Richard of all he had learned, including how Lawrence had become increasingly frustrated by the slow progress of the carts and left to go back to Dunstaffnage with a very pretty eleven-year-old, bright, red –headed English girl he'd captured at one of the razed homesteads. Having taken a special liking to the lass he referred to as "his little bit of fresh meat!" Lawrence deserted his men to charge off with her as soon as they crossed the border. The poor soul also confessed when asked how badly undermanned the castle was, as in thinking that for the time being Scotland was safe from English attack, Robert the Bruce had commandeered the best part of the garrison to re-open the border war with King Edward, at the same time ordering Thomas to do his bit and harry the English with the remainder.

The sublime accuracy of the bowmen's well-targeted arrows had spared most of the animals, with all four of the oxen completely unhurt and eight of the fourteen horses surviving with little more than scratches. Sadly, six were mortally injured and needed to be despatched to save them from any unnecessary pain, a volunteer sympathetic trooper doing the job very expertly, ending the suffering of each by a single sharp blow in the forehead with the pointed end of a war hammer.

In the search for any potential enemies possibly hiding in the stolen gear on the carts, Edgar found the two extremely scared, very young captive English girls concealed among the booty. Thinking they might know something relevant, he immediately took them to Richard so they could tell him what they knew about the Scottish raiding party. Using the same hybrid patois he found worked in his chats with Alice and Joan, he soon discovered all about them and their missing friend.

Daylight was fading fast, so with as much haste as the party could muster, they moved everything away from the site of the massacre, leaving the wounded, including the tortured man, to their brutal destiny with the wild animals which still roamed the wilderness in Scotland. Then, after a quick scout round, they found a convenient nearby sheltered spot to rest for the night on a sloped clearing just off the track, below a very imposing massive rock which looked as if it was about to tumble down the hillside at any moment and squash those below. Knowing the boulders had stood unmoving for thousands of years, and presented no imminent danger, they unhitched the exhausted kine and tethered them along with the hungry horses to find whatever they could to eat among the meagre coarse grass.

The evening was a little chilly on the hills, so Richard allowed Simon to light a dry wood fire at the base of the huge rock to warm the company and cook some very appetising, roasted fresh horse meat for them to eat. Using some ingredients gleaned from the stolen goods in the carts, he made what was a delicious meal, accompanied by some scavenged looted ale to wash it all down with.

During the meal, a faraway Richard merely poked at his food while he considered his position. "Do you think I'm being selfish if I suggest we go on and see if we can get Buckenham before he ruins any more poor little mites like those two?" he queried, addressing all the men as one and nodding towards the two little waifs who were too upset and frightened to be hungry. "Or do you think it would be more sensible to cut and run home with that retrieved booty, which, as you know, would be more than a godsend to the people at Carlisle?" Richard asked, somewhat in a quandary as to whether his lust for revenge was dictating the approach or if it was just plain common sense to see the mission through to its natural conclusion.

With that in mind, he gave them all the option to return to the safe haven in Carlisle without any slur being attached to their name, or to follow him and carry on with the mission, yet to a man they all expressed their desire to assist him in his quest. Nevertheless, after giving it a lot of thought, Richard came up with a painstakingly considered, workable plan to achieve both goals, suggesting they should remove all the heavyweight loot from the carts, sift through it and load anything either edible or useable onto one of the wagons and send it off using the fittest and fastest of the oxen with only one driver, the two girls, and a couple of the soldiers to guard it, back to Alain Jeffrys at Carlisle Castle. Meanwhile, Richard proposed to take the other emptied wagon, fill it with troops and to go the short day's travel to Dunstaffnage, where he planned to arrive in that awkward-to-see half-light just before dusk, pretending to be the returning raiding party. To add plausibility to the scheme, Edgar suggested that maybe it would be wise if they propped two of the less-mangled corpses in the driving seat of the cart and dress themselves in the deceased's enemy uniforms.

Thinking that perhaps the ruse might work, Richard agreed, asking the men to audition for the best-sounding Scottish impersonator among them. The job falling to a bowman called Walter Brunt, whose grandmother actually was a Scot and as a small child he had learned to mimic her highland accent with more than a great deal of expertise.

The Scottish night was colder than of late and showing early signs of the autumn which wasn't far around the corner, but still warm enough to sleep out in the open. The afterglow of victory had removed the tiredness away from the soldiers, who chatted excitedly around the last glowing embers of the fading fire deep into the hours of darkness, eventually talking themselves to sleep three hours before dawn. Grumbling and grouching, the sleepy men were woken up at first-light by a buoyant Simon, who wanted them to eat a scant breakfast he'd prepared for them before they undertook the tiresome task of sifting through the piles of stolen goods, most of which were just gewgaws and other useless trinkets taken by the human magpies merely because they were there. Nominating Simon to oversee the task of sorting the wheat from the chaff, Richard gave him strict instructions to pack only the food and any other items he thought would be helpful to the oppressed population of Carlisle, commanding him to discard the rest.

Obeying the instruction almost to the letter, Simon made two separate heaps of essentials and non-essentials, but in a deed of mercy, he sneakily allowed the two sad girls each an item of their choice to cheer them up. One lass chose a bone comb and the other weepily selected a cheap copper brooch she recognised as having belonged to her mother, the kind act of compassion not being missed by the ever-vigilant Richard who could see that the fledgling boy was fast growing into a kind, decent man with a long and fulfilling future ahead of him.

CHAPTER 18

By mid-morning on 5 September 1318, everything was in place and ready to go in Richard's optimistic plan to capture his sworn enemy, the known liar and wanted traitor Lawrence Buckenham. All the edible goods were sorted, packed and already safely dispatched on one of the wagons, allowing just enough room for the two young girls to travel back to England crammed in among the priceless cargo. Richard nominated Edgar to act as mounted guard and one of the most senior soldiers to drive the cart as a replacement for his first choice Simon, who, fearing for his safety, Richard begged to go with the commodities. Nevertheless, stating that he also had an axe to grind with Lawrence, Simon stubbornly insisted on staying, citing as a reason his ability as the only other present able to recognise the wanted man. Reluctantly agreeing to his supplications, Richard gave his go-ahead for the lad to stay.

The heavily laden cart was well on its way back to Carlisle by the time the fifteen remaining troops at last were prepared and in position to accompany the other wagon, which had two of the least-mangled dead Scots securely propped in the driving seat, Simon and five English bowmen hiding under the canvas cover, with Richard and the other seven dressed in Thomas's own bloodstained livery riding openly alongside, all raring to go on the short vengeful trip to Dunstaffnage and hopefully find Lawrence.

Edgar had done his job very well when he extracted the information from the unfortunate Scot he so effectively tortured, learning a lot of relevant details to aid the raiders in gaining entry to the otherwise impregnable fortress. In his agony, the victim revealed exactly how many he could expect to be on guard, the simple password, which Richard would have probably guessed anyway, and even the names of some of the twenty garrison, who had remained to defend the stronghold from the unlikely event of an enemy attack.

The combination of freshly rested oxen, with the considerably lightened cart, made much better speed than expected as it made its way north. The little war- band having to make three unscheduled stops to get the timing just right. And precisely as planned they approached the stark outline of the grim castle, to enter into the vast shadow of the mighty keep, cast by the lowness of the reddening sun as it set in the western sky. The armed party managing to get within about eighty feet of the main gate before they were eventually spotted and challenged, when a very thick Scottish voice called from the high battlements above the arched entrance to ask exactly whom it was that approached so near to curfew. Richard's war band arrived only just in time, as the heavy beamed portcullis was already grinding noisily into place for the night, and was three-quarters in position when the guard peered into the gloom to satisfy himself it was whom he thought approaching at such a late hour.

Struggling to see in the dimly lit shadow, the sentry recognised the uniforms of the riders and the familiar pale faces of the travel-weary-looking cart drivers who both sat so oddly stiff and upright in their seats. Raising his voice to combat the noisy clatter of the winch, the sentry bellowed down to the men on the crank to halt the defensive grating from being fully put in the closed position. Satisfied with the resulting moments of silence, he called down to the late arrivals. Using his hands to direct his voice and make himself heard, he asked for the password: "Who's the king of the English?" he cried loudly and received a derisive jeer from the few others who bothered to man the famously unassailable walls.

Cued by a sharp prod in the ribs from Richard, Walter Brunt immediately answered the question. Already knowing the correct response and hoping it was the same man calling down as he was told it would be, Walter used his best Scottish accent to reply. "Spawn of the fucking devil! Now come on, open up and let us in, Dickon! It's me, Alex!" he yelled back, pretending to cough during the response in an attempt to disguise his voice.

The man, who obviously was the Dickon Walter thought it would be, shouted back, believing he recognised the voice down below. "Where's the other cart, Alex?"

Having an already prepared plausible reply on the tip of his tongue, Walter replied suitably tetchily to impress Dickon that he was annoyed at its absence. "The fucking axle's broke about ten miles up the road, so Ewan and the rest are guarding it, and we've come ahead to get help."

The reply very clearly satisfying Dickon that it was indeed the returning Scottish raiders, so after bellowing down some more instructions to the men on the windlass, the portcullis started to painstakingly and very slowly graunch its gradual way back up into its stone housing, opening the entrance and giving the chance for the English to put their cautiously conceived scheme into action. For a full two tense minutes the giant steel-reinforced, heavy oak grating grumbled its laborious way back up in its slot, the sweating operators fuming at having to undo the strenuous task they'd already half-done. Their audible curses reached above the din to the ears of the bowmen as they blindly lay hidden in the back of the wagon, tensely keeping perfectly still, worried the slightest sound might alert the Scots, as they patiently waited for it to get high enough to permit the mounted riders and cart to enter.

Feeling a sense of apprehensive relief, the eager passengers at last felt the wagon moving forwards. The sound of the horses' hooves and the wheels of the vehicle changing tone as they echoed under the vaulted roof of the stark stone-floored gatehouse, returning to normal as it rumbled into the cobbled yard, indicated the ploy had worked and they were in. Barely daring to breathe, they lay waiting for Richard's signal to grab their bows and use the last remaining light to target any opposition and dispatch them as quietly and efficiently as possible.

The ruse had worked a treat. Even the half dozen ragamuffin stable urchins, who darted out of the outbuildings to help the riders dismount, believed in the half-light that the troops were friendly, until, that is, when one of the more diligent lads realised the cart drivers were in fact corpses and shouted an alarm to the few members of the garrison present. Completely taken off guard and with nobody in absolute charge over them, their ill-disciplined attempt to fight the interlopers was already doomed to failure, as the insufficiently armed Scots scrambled about for the discarded weapons they had foolhardily laid aside, deeming them an unnecessary encumbrance to lug around inside the safety of the unconquerable walls of the never-defeated, mighty citadel of Dunstaffnage Castle.

In total contrast to the leaderless Scottish rabble, the professional, disciplined and better-armed band of English gainfully used the shade in the yard for cover. Leaping out of the cart, they automatically formed up their company as one, then, keeping their exposed backs protected by the high-sided wagon, lined up with the archers standing behind the dismounted, crouching and ready men-at-arms, spaced so that the bowmen could select their targets unhampered.

Most of the Scots were still on the battlements, the fading sun's pink rays highlighting their outlines against the black walls as they scampered for safety, making them easy victims for the carefully aimed shafts. Without a word, the skilled archers plied their trade: accompanied by a mocking musical twang and a zipping swish, the deadly missiles felled the enemy as they desperately looked for shelter from the lethal storm. A scant few of the garrison managed to regroup and fire back several bolts from the cumbersome arbalests, considered by the Scots to be a good defensive weapon, but a bit too slow and clumsy for attack. Two of their short, thick quarrels found marks, one killing Walter Brunt instantly, when, sounding like an angry hornet, a close-range missile passed through his surcoat, mail, gambeson, ribs and lungs before coming out his other side and he tumbled to a halt at Richard's feet. A second projectile, fizzing off the sloped visor of a kneeling soldier's bascinet in a shower of glowing sparks, found its mark in the eye socket of one of the archers, piercing the man's brain, without him ever seeing it come from the darkness of the gateway, where some resistance was being organised by Dickon and the same six men who had erroneously made the demanding effort of raising the portcullis to let them in.

Deciding to fight back and redress their foolish mistake, the seven made a sally from the murkiness of the portal, to attack the difficult-to-see, but vulnerable bowmen, only to have the unseen, supporting fully armoured warriors stand up and slay them in an orgy of bloodletting. In the confusion of the melee, the blades of the busy English swords found easy targets for their honed edges, which cut effortlessly through the poor protection on the Scots, slicing through skin, flesh and bone as if it wasn't there, the spraying blood flying into the eyes of defenders and attackers alike, soaking and blinding them as they used their expertise to overwhelm the resistance with almost no fuss.

The battle was nearly over and finished almost before it started. The whole brief episode totally missed by a bleeding, scratched and bitten Lawrence and an excited Thomas, who, oblivious to any danger, sat drooling, as he listened, mesmerised by yet another depraved tale from his henchman whilst sitting in his usual spot near the hearth with the last remaining two of his favourite dogs laying and warming themselves at his stinking feet.

As usual, the elderly, grumpy and broken Duncan was there, lurking out of sight in his customary position, lost in the shadowy background and giving himself a well-needed manicure with the point of a stiletto dagger, waiting for any summons to fulfil the every need of his master and the conscript captain, who lolled in front of a warming fire, brim-full of some stolen vintage, completely unaware of the lurking danger.

Complacently, they ignored the alarmed pair of hounds when, stirred from their snooze by a distant crashing and banging, they jumped up from their sleep and barked a warning woof. Annoyed by the interruption, Thomas commanded the dogs in no uncertain terms to shut up and resume their places, without bothering to investigate the rumpus. In their sheer contented arrogance, they idiotically put the racket down to one of the many squabbles which often broke out among the ill-disciplined and unhappy contingent of argumentative soldiers, stuck within the miserable confines of the cheerless bastion.

With more than a lustful twinkle in his evil eye, Thomas was totally engrossed by Lawrence's sordid recounting of the defiling of the feisty little red-headed English lass, who'd so recently been heartlessly ripped away from her home, her peasant parents probably murdered, their small amount of belongings taken and she so urgently transported to the castle to satiate the depraved carnal desires of the contemptibly immoral English knight. Slurring a little, Lawrence told of the savage fight she put up in defence of her virginity, showing the scars and scratches acquired during the encounter as proof. His account was listened to by the equally despicable impotent governor of the castle, whose sexual penchant for pre-pubescent females could only be satisfied by each lurid detail of the rapes being minutely gone into several times by his extremely apt and very willing lodger.

Outside, the last of the resistance had totally dissipated. Any survivors of the English onslaught had either gone into hiding or fled out through the gaping portcullis to safer areas out in the hills. The defenders' absence giving Richard's men free-licence to wander uninhibited through the empty castle in their search for Lawrence. Never for one moment did they suspect that he was in fact still at his ease in the main hall, drinking wine, telling degenerate stories and contemplating his second night with his feisty adolescent female captive. The same young girl, who for modesty's sake sat alone, clutching her torn clothes together, sore, abused, but resolved to put up another good fight when her abuser returned, tearfully dreading what was to come in the same lofty room, which had witnessed so many similar ordeals, where the purity of youth had been savagely plucked from the numerous innocents whose lives were never quite the same afterwards.

The search of the stronghold was not simple; a pitch black, moonless Scottish night had descended over the bleak Dunstaffnage Castle, making navigation around the foul, gloomy corridors of the fortalice all but impossible. Fortunately, with his usual forethought and using his practical skills to everyone's advantage, Simon had snatched a cresset light from a sconce on the wall of one of the warren of connecting passageways. Stopping the company, he attempted to ignite the flambeau, finding the low-quality fuel it contained especially difficult to light, eventually managing it with a whispered cheer when the iron torch at last burst into life. The pathetic spitting and spluttering flame successfully burning away the all-pervading damp which was everywhere in the musty dank castle. Slowly drying the pitch out, the torch's flame gained strength, belching its resinous perfumed black fumes which easily cut through the mildewed stench and rancid aroma of an over-cooked supper.

In order to defuse the tense situation and emphasise his distaste for Scottish food, holding his nose with his free hand, Simon blurted out a joke, making everyone laugh. "It smells like boiled rat," he jested, adding after a pause for thought, "mangy with scabs on, as well!"

The scented smoke made the foetid air almost pleasant as Richard, Simon and two others carried on laughing like boys at the impromptu humour. Galloping from room to room, the four went on the deadly serious business of hunting for their quarry, fortuitously stumbling through a heavy oak door into the main hall. The sight which met them stopping the hunters dead in their tracks when they happened upon the two men lounging back at their leisure, laughing and giggling at Lawrence's recounting of his exploits with the ginger wildcat. The colossal fire illuminated a palpable look of utter dread on the shocked faces of Lawrence and Thomas when they turned to see who it was who had so rudely disturbed their comfort.

Lawrence's jaw dropped to the floor when, in the feeble light of the torch, he saw that it was the grim features of a very determined Richard, his young friend Simon and a couple of single-minded men-at-arms who were the culprits. In a moment of blind panic, Lawrence quickly decided his best course of action was to cringe in his seat and pretend it wasn't him who was drinking wine and sitting enjoying himself by the warm blaze. On the other hand, the old Templar's reaction was totally different; jumping up out of his chair Thomas set the pair of dogs on the assailants, simply whispering, "Get them!" to the willing hounds, whose attempt to oust the intruders met with no success.

The fastest clamped its jaws on one of the soldier's padded mailed thigh, only to have its head staved in with the man's weighty mace. Seeing the failure, the second changed its mind and, helped on its way by a brutal kick from an armoured foot, scurried shrieking for safety at the feet of his standing master. Shocked by the ineffectiveness of the dogs, emboldened by the wine, and used to having his every word obeyed, Thomas manfully strode towards Richard, shouting and swearing at him in English and Gaelic, "Who the fecking hell is it that dares ta burst in on me in me own fecking home at this time o' day?" he screamed, incorrectly assuming his tirade would have its normal effect of intimidating Richard and thus drive him and his men from Thomas's presence. The hasty actions had the opposite effect from the desired one, when, casting aside the light, Simon ran forwards, drawing his sword in defence of Richard and halting Thomas's advance when the point of his weapon was held pricking his doublet over his heart.

The sudden fracas frightening poor old faithful Duncan, who, as normal, kept back to remain invisible in the shadows, but when he saw his hateful, abusive, but oddly beloved lord endangered, his old sense of loyalty leapt to the fore. Flying at Simon from behind, the ancient retainer raised the slender blade of his poniard to bring the stiletto down with all his might on the mail coif at the side of Simon's neck. Its needle tip pierced through armour and padding, before driving some metal links deep into the yielding flesh, severing the sinews, veins and arteries on its way into and out the other side of his windpipe. With a look of incredulous dismay on his blood-spattered young face, the unsuspecting Simon slowly crumpled to the floor, his life blood pumping in rhythmical spurts from the small hole in his throat, soaking Richard in the torrent of frothing pink foam.

The sad demise of his beloved friend prompted a spontaneous response from Richard, who, gripping his sword with his right hand on the handle and the other on the pommel, used every scrap of his power to sweep it obliquely down on the collarbone of unarmoured Duncan. Its razor edge passed through the old shrivelled body unhindered, lopping the skull three-quarters off his shoulders as the blade did its work with ease, flopping the old head to one side as Duncan's corpse fell on the already very clearly deceased Simon, who lay twitching spasmodically in the fast-spreading dark pool as it spread though the festering rushes. The stroke which felled the servant also killed the master, as, with hardly any of the impetus wasted on its path through scrawny Duncan, Richard aimed the blade high on Thomas's head, slicing the top off like a boiled egg, sending the pate, scalp still attached, spinning through the air, blasting out the pulpy brain all over the filthy floor, to be cleaned up by the last remaining hound later on.

Badly traumatised at the death of his friend, with a vengeful lust for blood raging through his veins and bent on instant reprisal, Richard rushed at the object of his accumulated hatred and the man he knew was guilty of the series of events which led to the tragedy. Sword raised high with both hands gripping the hilt, in his heart Richard wanted to strike the cowering, blubbering Lawrence instantly stone-dead, bringing the polished steel blade down with the full-force of every sinew and muscle fibre that his tempered body could muster, only to halt it within an inch of Lawrence's horrified face. Making the instant decision that a quick death was far too good for the child-abusing traitor, Richard preferred to see him publicly tried, humiliated and then hanged for his crimes, ideally in front of a baying crowd eating roast chestnuts and buns whilst enjoying the spectacle of his torment.

Although Richard amazingly had managed to control his rage, he still found it irresistible to cause some physical harm to the spineless Lawrence who crouched, sobbing like a beaten child in his utter dread at being slain.

With a mind to just damage him the merest bit without endangering his life, Richard allowed the business end of his sword to slice off most of his left ear, which fell in Lawrence's lap, causing a prolonged squeal of pain and disbelief to issue from his lips as he picked up the lost appendage to clutch it with one hand in its old position on the side of his head whilst curling up in the foetal position to use the sleeve of his doublet to staunch the readily flowing blood.

Acting on a nod of assent from Richard, the two men-at-arms manhandled the gutless coward, still coiled up like a new-born, towards the gaping door, on the way through, carelessly tossing the confiscated ear to the frightened dog as a conciliatory titbit, to take the traitor outside to be bound, trussed and tied to the wheel of a cart, making any hope of escape impossible.

Feeling sick to his stomach at losing his long-time dearest friend and most reliable ally, Richard didn't want to stay in the castle a moment longer than he had to; so, with as much haste as was practicable, he organised a thorough search of the premises. Led by a deeply depressed Richard, the entire group spent the rest of the night, with nothing more than the feeble gleam of some other pathetic torches for light, sifting through as much as they could before dawn

The whole time Richard's thoughts were of Simon, seeing him as he was just a short while earlier, enjoying life to the full, adamantly persisting on staying by his side during the incursion into the castle and bestowing a little kindness to two sad lost souls, to ease their suffering and give them a little reassuring hope. Richard afforded himself a little smile when he remembered Simon's less than complimentary last words about Scottish food, uttered the second before bursting into the chamber where he sadly lost his life.

Wondering what on earth he was going to tell Simon's mother when he got back to Market Deeping, Richard struggled with the thought of how he was even going to look her in the eye, let alone inform her that her one and only precious son was killed under his charge, slain on a foolhardy plan to go deep into enemy territory to selfishly bring Richard's arch-enemy to summary justice without a thought of the potential consequences.

The rummage through the castle bore fruit, when one of the teams of investigators rescued the little red-headed girl from a lofty bleak room overlooking the ocean. Although heartbroken and dreadfully sore with bites on each breast and bruises from kicks in her stomach and groin, she was for the most part intact, lucky to have survived Lawrence's savage attack and subsequent rape of the juvenile.

Elsewhere in the castle, another group of searchers found one of Thomas's personal servants hiding in his master's particularly filthy garderobe. His insignificant life only being spared when he knelt on the stinking, slurry-covered floor and implored them to let him live, telling them he knew something which would be a great benefit to the English. Moaning pathetically about his bad back, sore feet and the long trek through the dismal tunnels, the man was jostled forcibly to Richard's presence in the main hall, to part with his secret information to him alone.

After listening very carefully to what the grim lackey had to say, Richard immediately commanded the man to lead him to what was promised to be something of great value, reluctantly leaving the side of his dead friend to do his duty and hopefully advance his country's cause. Amid another salvo of complaints about his poor health and aching bones, the grumpy old retainer shuffled off, leading the retinue of followers all the way back to the same closet where he was found. Going to a place even the strongest-stomached persons were unlikely to look, he pulled the disproportionately long, badly stained, green and greasy half-rotten wooden cover off the sewage chute. Its removal revealed, either side of the hole where the effluent tumbled over a hundred and fifty feet to the rocks below, a specifically built hiding place, where three locked mildewed coffers of varying dimensions sat in a two-inch-deep, disgusting puddle of human excrement, accumulated over years of regular use by less-than-accurate Thomas, who used the stinking cupboard for its given purpose as well as a place of safety for his ill-gotten gains.

The largest strongbox was roughly three feet by two feet in size, with one about two-thirds as big, down to the smallest of about half the dimension of the first, sitting next to the deep footprint of a missing fourth and much smaller one. On Richard's orders, two of the strongest soldiers manfully struggled to release the largest box from the sucking slime, and after a lot of heaving with no result, they resorted to using a stolen sword to lever the crate out, eventually liberating it with a satisfying juicy squelch, announcing it was at last free to be lifted out of its noisome hiding place on to the floor. Its removal was quickly followed by the other two, which soon succumbed more easily.

The fact that they were locked evidently wasn't a problem, as the wood of the ancient chests outwardly showed all the signs of being almost completely decayed in the wet atmosphere of the festering cubbyhole. With just one carefully aimed axe-strike adjacent to the rusty iron hasp, the smallest of the three flew to pieces, exploding its glittering contents all over the fouled slippery floor. Even in the bad light the filling was easily recognisable as coins of silver and gold from all over the known world and beyond, such as bezants from the east, marks, nobles, guilders and schillings from Europe, and others originating from strange far-off lands with peculiar writing on, or holes in the middle to take a holding string, yet every single one was unmistakably made of a shiny precious metal. Likewise in the second when its contents were easily revealed. However, the third, a coffer very much like the one Richard had seen before in Yolanda's father's house at Market Deeping and made out of an almost jet-black wood, heavily carved with a set of compasses, setsquares, suns, moons and other unknown outlandish symbols, put up any worthwhile resistance, having to be hit five times before succumbing to the increasingly hefty strikes to spill its valuable sparkling insides out with the rest of the very mysterious stolen loot.

Urging his men to make as much haste as possible, Richard oversaw the treasure loaded into some sturdier crates, ready to be stacked on the ox-cart and transported back to Carlisle, taking it upon himself to reward each of the men one of the odder foreign gold coins as a keepsake, knowing how the sight of so much wealth could so easily affect the men, who for all their lives had probably never owned any gold before.

The time to depart came very quickly, Richard himself helping to load the fantastic hoard on board the wagon; along with the corpses of Simon, Walter Brunt and the other dead soldier. Placing all three very reverently behind the driver's seat, Richard covered their dead staring faces with Simon's cloak and to stop them from being thrown around on the bumpy ride he used the weighty crates of money as chocks. Because of the total lack of willing volunteers, Richard's next job was to instruct the men to draw straws, the loser getting the unenviable task of acting as head guard over Lawrence on the long journey home. Knowing what an insidious job it would be to keep a twenty-four hour watch over the evil Lawrence, Richard couldn't help but feel sorry for the unlucky gnarled old campaigner called Roger Wellham, who'd drawn the shortest straw.

Most of the company of troops were for setting fire to the easily defendable stronghold in order to prevent it from being used against them when the war proper resumed and, foolishly, some of them even wanted to hold and secure it for the king. Both ideas were instantly scotched without consideration by Richard, on the grounds that in the first case he was reluctant to burn it as that might alert all the surrounding Scots there had been a raid in the area, and the second idea as impractical, bearing in mind how deep they were in enemy territory, pointing out that to support any English garrison so far from the closest allies would be nigh on impossible.

Without any dissent, they all accepted Richard's logic to a man, leaving their hard-won conquest in the hands of the not-so-bitter old retainer, last seen lounging back in Thomas's favourite chair warming himself by an extra-fierce fire, drinking some of his dead master's best vintage, stroking the last remaining hound, enjoying the fact that his poor aching body had been miraculously cured by the thought of the small chest of precious coins he'd found time to secretly secure and save for his own use before the troops had managed to find him and the rest of the hoard.

As foretold by the red sky the previous evening, it was going to be another fine Scottish autumn day. The risen sun had just started winning its battle against the shredding morning mist by the time Richard arrived at the idyllic craggy spot near to where they camped the night before. Thinking that beneath the dewy turf at the foot of the giant precarious-looking rock would be such a place where he would like to be buried, he got four of the burliest of his group to scrape a hole in the stony upland ground deep enough for the three bodies. Very reverently, Richard personally laid the stiff corpse of Simon, holding his father's bow, slightly apart from the other two in the grave, getting the men to cover all three with some loose scree before asking them to place some heavier rocks on top to stop the local carnivorous animals from digging them up to fatten themselves on the flesh. Gathering all the troops together at the graveside, Richard said a short prayer over Simon, Walter Brunt and the third man, who was only known by the nickname of Moke, which he was named either as a testament to his stubbornly immovable nature or more probably his famously enormous genitalia which he was always prepared to put on display to shock the inquisitive who begged a look.

Richard mentally marked the unique site well, in case at any future date he was in a position to visit the lad, whose enthusiasm had lit his way through some very dark hours. And with a sense of desolate loss, he left the unmarked grave freshly watered by his free-flowing tears to face what was going to be a lonely journey back to Carlisle Castle.

While he was still at the encampment, Richard took a leaf from the final page of Simon's book and let the fiery little lass select a trinket from the nearby discarded heap of heavyweight bric-a-brac, thinking a toy, possibly a doll or maybe a shiny bauble would be something to keep her amused and help her forget her ordeal. Her selection surprised him, when, ignoring the pieces he thought would probably be more attractive to a girl of her age, she chose a cheap, short-bladed and rather blunt lady's dress-dagger with a gold-painted hilt, which in the risen sun, gleamed with fake jewels. Assuming her choice was made in the belief that the gems were real, Richard gullibly let her keep it to play with.

Before doing anything else, Richard made sure the lass was safely placed out of harm's way on the back of the wagon with her new toy. Having done that, he then checked on Lawrence to satisfy himself that the prisoner's hands were tied and bound securely in front on the pommel of the saddle before moving off. The bloodstained captive refused even to look at Richard as he grimly sat bareheaded and unarmoured and on his own unruly high black steed, held firmly by the reluctant, sour-faced, muttering Roger, who clearly hated the chore. Taking the opportunity, Richard reminded the unlucky loser of the draw to keep vigilant while he led the devious captive to Carlisle, repeating that he wanted Lawrence kept alive, no matter what, to face trial, even though the renegade constantly threatened awful retribution on Roger and the men for their part in his capture. Lawrence's ignored warnings turned to offers of wealth beyond their wildest dreams provided by his rich family, if only the guards would change sides and help secure his freedom. The loyal men treated his propositions with the contempt they deserved, knowing that the last thing Lawrence's kin would be interested in was saving the licentious, cowardly turncoat who unfortunately for them, brought eternal disgrace on their good names by happening to be related to them.

The first part of the trip remained uneventful as the short procession resumed its way south to take almost exactly the same route as it had traversed in pursuit of the wanted man. Things changed suddenly after a bungled changeover of the guards leading the prisoner, when Roger grew tired of Lawrence's whingeing and whining and begged a comrade who owed him a favour to take a turn. Having to haggle for a while, he ended up offering a small financial incentive before, with no good grace, the reluctant companion agreed to undertake the unpleasant duty. Irritably reaching across to grab the reins on the black horse's bridle, the man lost his balance as he leant out of his saddle, jabbing the beast savagely in the mouth, making the ill-disciplined animal rear vertically in pain, unseating Lawrence, whose tight bonds made him powerless to steady himself. Somersaulting backwards out of the saddle, Lawrence was unable to break his fall, landing with a sickening crunch behind the animal's back legs, and receiving a hefty kick in his ribcage for his impertinence of being where he shouldn't. The accident roused a hearty cheer from all the spectators, none of whom had any compassion for one-eared Lawrence who lay on the ground bleating like a lost lamb, holding his battered chest while gazing unbelievingly at the very evidently extremely badly broken and displaced shin bones of his left leg.

Following the mishap, there was no way Lawrence could possibly ride any more; so, obeying a command from an annoyed Richard, the instigators of the accident stripped their damaged prisoner down to his underwear to inspect his multiple injuries. Ignoring the purpling bruise on Lawrence's side, they made a crude splint of sticks and unsympathetically bound his inadequately straightened injured limb. Lifting his almost naked, battered, bruised and clearly broken body onto the cart, they tossed it among the pile of the rescued commodities near to where the girl sat quietly playing with her new acquisition. Her repugnance of Lawrence was made audibly apparent to all by a long shriek of hateful vehemence at the first sight of him, spitting out a foul tirade of vile curses they'd rarely heard even from the basest of the soldiers, as she scampered away from the object of her loathing.

Putting as much distance between her and Lawrence as the confines of the wagon would allow, she found herself a place tucked out of sight of the monster, but where she could still see his every move, her tiny blade giving the girl some peace of mind as she gripped it, just in case she might need it. The brief tumult brought back the reality of her heart-rending plight fresh into Richard's grieving mind, which was lost elsewhere, dwelling on happier times back at Market Deeping with a smiling Simon helping his mother and Yolanda. With tears in his eyes, he pictured them in their usual places in the kitchen, gossiping, with their arms white to the elbow with flour, kneading and thumping at the dough in readiness for the next day's baking.

Lawrence was in an awful state; apart from his fractured leg, lost ear and dislocated shoulder from the fall, he'd also gained a couple of cracked ribs from the kick, and a badly bruised mouth and lips where he punched himself with his tied fists as he tumbled over the rear end of the horse. The excruciating pain from his multiple injuries causing him to squeal and wail with every single bump or jolt of the solid wheeled, un-sprung cart, which were plentiful on the long, rock-strewn, rough track. Thanking God for his mercy, when at last relief came as the wagon finally halted for the night.

Feeling too tired and ill to eat, Lawrence refused the offer of a crude supper of some hard dried meat he felt was too much for his pained mouth to eat. Still only wearing his underwear, all he wanted to do was sleep; so, struggling to get as snug and comfortable as he could, Lawrence propped himself up against the rough side of the buck, eventually managing to doze off. However, at each toss or turn in his sleep, he groaned or whimpered, occasionally producing a long howl of agony to issue from his swollen lips. Every little twitch, blink or painful move of his mutilated body was unerringly watched by the unfaltering eyes that never left him, waiting for the slightest chance to exact her savage revenge.

It was another moonless Scottish night as the sentinels kept their vigil over the sleeping camp. Staring away from the encampment, they tried to focus their fatigued eyes into the impenetrable pitch-black void, looking for any tell-tale signs of approaching danger, heeding nothing of note, except for the distant sounds of a wandering fox, hunting for a midnight feast, a far-off stag belling to his hinds and some squabbling dogs, their snarling barks echoing miles through the bleak and empty wilderness. Nearer to the camp, the occasional snort and shuffle from the picketed line of horses could be heard as they satisfyingly munched noisily at their night-time forage and closer to home the sleepy sentries marvelled at the rumbling long drawn out snores of an anonymous member of the company, wondering how his wife could ever put up with such a noise, coming to the conclusion she would be happy he was away at the wars rather than being safely tucked up with her.

Nevertheless, the loudest of all the incursions into the still night were the sickening sounds of a man in inescapable agony. Lawrence's piteous wails reverberated through the gloom, increasing in intensity, until with six close together hideous screams they stopped altogether, returning the camp back into an uneasy hush just as a very thin crescent new moon appeared from behind a silver-edged cloud low on the horizon. Its pallid luminescence gave a little pale radiance to the scene, illuminating the guards who were just visible, wearily leaning on their spears, still staring out into the fathomless void trying to stop their heavy eyelids from closing, waiting for the next series of groans to break their monotonous concentration on the job in hand of protecting the site from any impending potential harm.

As soon as the dawn broke, the camp woke with the practised ease which was expected from a professional body of soldiers. With no fuss, they went about their allotted tasks of preparing for the day. The men went to and fro, checking the animals and feeding them, attending in shifts to their morning ablutions, another organising a cold breakfast of some hard biscuits, smoked herring and small beer for the crew. However, one of the most pressing jobs in the morning was to check on the injured prisoner's welfare.

Undertaking the task himself, Richard hoped to find Lawrence in an improved state to face the forthcoming justice. Unlacing the thick canvas flaps at the back of the cover on the wagon, he peered in, at first noticing how quiet it was within, the reason soon becoming clear, when his eyes became accustomed to the muted light in the back of the gloomy buck.

Inside, a hideous tableau of the girl's revenge was clear to see and the reason for the torrent of overnight screams instantly became self-evident. Half-naked, with his hands trussed in front of him, Lawrence sat in exactly the same spot where he eventually got to sleep and was much as when Richard last saw him the previous evening, except that is, now frozen with horror in front of him, scarlet from head to foot and kneeling in the entire contents of his veins, arteries, bladder and, bowels, the feisty little red-headed girl still clutched the bright-handled little blunt dagger she put to good use on her victim in getting her violent revenge on the sleeping fiend. She'd stabbed Lawrence in both eyes and each side of his chest, slashed his stomach. Yet the main source of all the blood was very obviously from where his penis used to be attached, the offending appendage lying some two feet from where it once lived, the signs of where the blunt edge did its gruesome work, making the morsel of meat look half-chewed where the repeated cuts with the dull blade made their marks in the successful effort to saw it off.

On one hand Richard was thankful to see Lawrence so brutally murdered, thinking how apt it was that one of his young victims had done the deed. On the other he felt cheated that he would never see Lawrence suffer as he had suffered torment at the hands of a hangman and experience the ignominy of being booed and hissed by a hate-filled mob, which pointed grinning and cheering as he was launched into the air, to see his death throes while eating roast nuts, cakes and pies. But it was what it was and all there was left to do was to put his personal bitterness to one side and do his best to snatch the girl out of what was nothing short of a catatonic state, stooping motionlessly like a statue in the thick clotted detritus of a painful bloody death, deeply traumatised by the level of her own bestial savagery.

Summoning all his strength, Richard forcibly dragged the mite away from the corpse out into the fresh air, dousing her with cold water to break the spell, in time snapping out of her trance only for the stark realisation of what she'd done to set in. Her first reaction was to collapse into an inconsolable fit of sobbing, followed by a bout of uncontrollable hysterical laughter, before coming back to reality when she stoically admitted her crime, expecting to be punished there and then for the vengeful deed. The girl's worst fears were quickly allayed by Richard, who felt complete sympathy for the lass. First putting her at ease by finding out her name was Maud, he gently asked her what had happened. Leaning very close to get the full gist of what she had to say in her almost unintelligible accent, she told him how she waited and waited, watching for Lawrence to close his eyes, which in his pain he clearly found to be very difficult. At last succumbing to sheer exhaustion, he went into a fitful sleep. It was then she took her chance, first stabbing him in the crotch as punishment for the rape, and then in her rage she gouged the blade into both his breasts and stomach in direct revenge for what he did to hers when she tried to fight him off. After that she stabbed him in each eye for looking on her nakedness during the assault, before sawing off his penis while he still had enough life in his body to feel the pain she had to endure when he pumped it inside her. Summary justice served and the deed irrevocably done, she merely sat back and watched as his worthless life seeped from him. Then ending her admission of savage murder, Maud ironically crossed herself, adding that she believed he was in hell where he belonged.

The re-living of the events overwhelmed sad abused tiny Maud; finding it too much to bear, she crumpled into a heap and cried herself to sleep in Richard's comforting arms, which gently rocked the poor little thing whilst patting her distraught back in the rhythm of his own broken heart.

Meanwhile, the rest of the contingent carried on as normal, leaving him be as they went about their given tasks, clearing up the mess in the cart and preparing everything necessary in readiness for the last leg of the journey back to Carlisle. Without so much as a brief prayer for the dead, they cast the ignoble Lawrence's mutilated corpse into a wayside ditch to be consumed by the foxes, wolves, and crows which Richard suspected had already gathered at the smell of blood, anticipating that a tasty meal of fresh meat was in the offing to fill their hungry bellies.

With all prepared for the journey, Richard reluctantly stirred little Maud from her nap, the girl refusing point blank to go back into the back of the cart to finish the trip. With that in mind, her new friend Richard allowed her to mount up behind him on Solomon, taking his mind back to four years prior when he did the self-same thing for another of the deceased Lawrence's innocent victims. Feeling her pathetically thin arms clutching tightly around his waist, Richard wondered how many more guiltless young girls there could be whose unhappy lives would be uplifted to be able to celebrate that at last the revolting predator on helpless young females was finally dead and no longer a threat to innocents like sad Maud, brave Joan, timid Alice and most importantly of all, his beloved wife and mother to his child, the beautiful, caring Yolanda.

CHAPTER 19

At last, with a huge feeling of frustrated relief, the welcoming sight of Richard's long-time home, Carlisle Castle, came into view. Relief because it was still standing, with Alain's banner flapping proudly from the keep and from the tiresome travelling, which in Richard's depressed state had become a mighty burden to his disturbed mind. Frustrated because an inner feeling of abject failure was foremost in his thoughts. However, he was thankful to finally have the solace of Alain and Mary's wise words to give perspective to the ordeal, his downcast face lighting up as he rode through the sturdy gateway, where they both stood, hand in hand, ready to greet him back from his arduous trek.

The day was growing late, so Richard's first duty was to show the riches to Alain and Mary, whose eyes popped out on stalks when they saw the colossal amount of captured gold and silver. As a clue to its origin, Richard showed them part of the original dark wooden chest which contained the treasure and which he'd kept for when he finally got to his real home to show Yolanda and compare with the fragments of the one they found in her father's house. Mary instantly recognised the style of the shard as being Middle Eastern in origin, but according to the symbols was made specifically for the Templars and possibly part of the ransom extorted by King John's men, falsely extracted from the people of England, in the guise of it being for his brother, King Richard I's release from imprisonment at Duke Leopold V of Austria's Durnstein Castle. The same treasure which became mysteriously lost in the Wash some hundred plus years before, conveniently just prior to King John's untimely death at only forty-nine years old and rumoured to have been stolen and divided up amongst the guard of Templars charged with protecting it on the foolhardy shortcut across the huge inlet.

All the information rung true to Richard, remembering he had heard that Thomas Dewar's family came from a long line of the less than holy knights, as did Yolanda's father, who he knew was both the son and grandson of members of the notorious dissolute group of religious men who generally made and broke solemn vows as if they were nothing more than idle promises to keep a child quiet when they were being extra annoying.

The next most important task at hand was the placement of poor frightened little Maud. Mary deciding wisely to billet her in her own private apartments to share a room with Alice and Joan, knowing all three girls had probably far too much in common for their tender years. Yet having seen the deeply sympathetic nature of Joan, she felt quite happy they would very soon be chatting together, possibly helping all three to forget the abuse and look to the future, which Mary was determined to make a lot better than their heart-rending immediate past.

As was usual in the lodgings of Alain and Mary, a complete and detailed description of what occurred since Richard left on his trip to arrest Lawrence were to be discussed over supper and a prepared meal was already on the table, along with two of the last remaining flagons of the expensive vintages which once graced the bishop's famed but now almost empty cellar. By the time Richard had bathed and changed, he started to feel a little more relaxed and ready to sit and eat. Although, the sight of some newly baked bread brought back the picture of Simon in his element fresh into Richard's troubled brain, ruining his appetite, a few slurps of numbing wine helping him to cast the demons to one side, clearing his mind so he could tell the story.

Sitting picking at the food, Richard told the tale, repeating why he made the tactical decisions and why he left Dunstaffnage undamaged, sadly reliving the moment when Simon was so unluckily killed. Finishing his unhappy saga, he told of how the despicable Lawrence painfully lost his unworthy life fittingly at the hands of the vengeful tiny Maud.

Alain and a distraught Mary listened to every detail, Mary picking up her hem to mop her weepy eyes on several occasions, especially when she heard of how her culinary-adept helper's met his demise. Shaking her head in disbelief, she commiserated with Richard, whose tears had already been cried in private, knowing how much she would miss the lad who so often tickled her funny bone. On the other hand, Alain, who fully understood the perils of war, pragmatically accepted the loss, saddened but satisfied with the end result, needing urgently to discuss what to do with the treasure with Richard.

Using his extra-deep explanatory voice, he broached the subject with as much tact as he could muster. "I know you're hurting at the moment, but we have urgent matters to discuss, which need to be done sooner than later."

Surmising from Alan's insistent tone that he wasn't going to let the matter drop, Richard looked up from an innocent crust he had been pulling into tiny pieces and torturing in a small pool of spilled wine, asking almost disinterestedly, "Do you mean the treasure?"

Nodding a meek yes, Alain continued "I've had news from Sir Humphrey. Just sit there and listen, and I'll tell you everything I know. It looks as if we need to return to Hereford, as things are going badly tits-up down in Wales, and it seems that civil war might break out at any second."

Hearing what Alain had to say, Richard stopped tormenting the bread and perked up, wanting to hear more. "What do you mean, civil war in Wales?"

"Not in Wales exactly, more like the whole bloody country. It's those bastard Despensers, they've been stirring the shit and now they've wheedled their way into Edward's good books. And now they've got him on their side, they've been arguing over who owns what with Roger Mortimer. Now young Hugh has gone and overstepped the mark by grabbing a load of Mortimer's land near Caerphilly! It's a fucking political nightmare." Alain groomed, stopping to take an enormous gulp of wine whilst casting a quick apologetic sideways glance at Mary, who'd been kept completely in the dark about the political manoeuvrings. "All the barons are taking sides; most of them are pissed off with the king, and the king's thoroughly pissed off with most of them, especially his own cousin, Thomas Earl of Lancaster, whom he never forgave since his men failed to turn up at Bannockburn. Lancaster now has sided with Mortimer against Edward and the Despensers and now they're rattling their fucking swords at each other, and that's it! That's about all I know!" he explained, to appease Mary's curiosity. Once again Alain looked at Mary, whose difficulty in grasping exactly what was going on in the complicated situation was plain to see by her puzzled expression. Shrugging his shoulders at Richard, Alain leaned forwards in his seat and, using an extra deep voice, started to re-explain to his spouse in simpler terms. "In essence, Edward, backed by the Despensers is probably going to start a war he can't afford with Lancaster and Mortimer, which will drag all the other barons into what will be a God almighty mess, especially when the Scots see what's happening and re-start the border war with us!" Alain elucidated. Turning his attention back to Richard and taking another mouthful of drink, he returned to speaking relatively normally. "So I suggest, at least for the time being, we keep our mouths clammed firmly shut about that heap of money, which is likely to be frittered away on a useless war between idiots who'll never agree on anything."

In something of a quandary, Richard returned to idly squashing the morsels of soaked bread while he absorbed Alain's wise words, taking a few quiet minutes of deep thought before stating his intentions, needing only one more thing to be clarified prior to answering. "What about our oaths to Edward?

Shouldn't we give him the money to help his and the country's cause?" he asked, feeling reluctant to break his promise to the king.

Richard's naive standpoint prompted Mary to put her two-penneth in, speaking directly back to Richard with her take on the situation. "I understand what you're saying, Richard, but as you are fully aware, Edward isn't the most reliable of kings. It isn't for nothing they call him the devil king. You've seen him; you know what he's like! In your heart you must have wondered why someone like him can do exactly what he wants to get his own way, no matter whom or how many he hurts in the process! And from where I'm standing it seems most likely that if he gets his hands on that great pot of treasure, it would most probably be wasted on either his new lover young Hugh Despenser or his own personal vanities, with the country seeing nothing of it! So I for one wholeheartedly agree with Alain and he has my support."

Having degusted what Mary had to say, Richard thanked her honest assessment of the situation. Knowing that in fact she was correct, he found it impossible to disagree with her, with resignation in his unhappy voice he agreed that in the best interests of England it would be wisest to hide the treasure somewhere safe, until the discord amongst the senior nobles, arrived at what was likely to be a very bloody conclusion.

Another piece of news Alain had received concerned the imminent return of Bishop John de Halghton, so with a little more urgency than was decent, Alain, Mary, and Richard had their belongings, including the crates of money, packed into the cart, ready to leave, taking with them Alice, Joan, Maud, and only six of the garrison, handpicked by Richard, as escorts to go back down south.

Having got everything prepared, the small party departed with some alacrity, as the last thing Alain wanted was to come face to face with the bishop and have to explain the emptied cellar, where in the place of the missing wine, he left a small bag of gold coins, rightfully liberated from the hoard as a long-overdue part-payment for his services and an explanatory note apologising for his absence, also cheekily saying he hoped the bishop was pleased with the improvements.

The laborious, fortunately incident-free crawl back down south took a little too long for Mary's liking, as it meandered through Yorkshire and then to the Midlands. None of the party being in the least tempted to stop at the unrepaired, dilapidated, weather-ravaged inns, where with utmost certainty, poor shelter, inedible food and the bad hospitality they offered was going to be overly expensive and also in consideration of the nosey hard-up landlords, who were likely to pry into their belongings and find the treasure as soon as their backs were turned.

The long, rough, laborious trek took its toll on the travellers in the dewy autumn weather, and one damp cool evening, as the party ate their scanty rations around a feeble campfire, a thoroughly fed-up Richard suggested that maybe a detour to his home in Market Deeping might be in order. Alain's agreement became assured by a hard stare, reinforced by a bony elbow poked meaningfully into his ribs from Mary, whose chafed-sore backside and legs were completely numb from riding Simon's horse Uther.

The last day of September had just gone and with the arrival of October there were many chores to perform before the cold weather closed in. It was the same in the old merchant's house where Yolanda, accompanied by the ever-present Matilda, had started on the seasonal stocking of the store cupboard ready for the winter. She was meticulously checking the small crop of edible summer produce for spots and bruises which might turn the whole lot bad, before packing them in carefully cleaned barrels and crates, where they hoped the crop would survive until the next harvest without rotting.

Supposedly helping with the job at hand, two of Yolanda's youngest siblings watched, hoping to lend a hand with the disposal of any rejected fruit. The youngsters were bickering over a juicy-looking apple with nothing other than the smallest of blemishes on its cherry-red ripe skin, when all four were distracted from the task at hand as the unusual sound of a small body of horses met their ears. Gazing at each other with expectation, all four wondered if their ears were merely playing mean tricks on them, when, overtaken by hope, first Yolanda, closely followed by Matilda and then the reunited teenagers, galloped to the front door to see who it was that rode so purposely towards the house.

There was no hiding their surprise when they saw a covered wagon with eight riders sadly ambling their way directly to the building. Both women squealed with delight when they instantly recognised Richard on Solomon at their head and then, scanning their eyes across the band, they expected to see Simon's grinning freckled face beaming at them and waving a frantic hello from Uther's back. Thinking their eyes were playing tricks, they looked again and, seeing there was no sign of Simon, Matilda's maternal heart pounded a single giant beat and broke instantly.

Without needing to see more she knew the truth, her inexplicable, motherly sixth-sense telling her that her absent and much-beloved son Simon was indeed dead. That evening the usual homecoming celebrations were ignored, and minus the normal repartee, the travel-weary company gladly ate the fresh food put in front of them, all except Richard and Yolanda, neither of them having an appetite after the sight of a distraught Matilda, who had simply disappeared when her worst fears were confirmed by the pathetic tale.

Not waiting to hear the whole tale as the red-faced, sad Richard stumbled through the pitiful saga concerning her young sons demise, she ran off as fast as she could, to lose herself somewhere secret and be alone with her grief. The search party sent out to find her arrived back at dusk cold and empty-handed, not having a clue where she was, coming to the conclusion she had cried herself to sleep somewhere secret out of harm's way.

For the whole of the next three days the sombre atmosphere in the old merchant's house stayed as it was, without any joy, laughter or the telling of stories, normally so eagerly listened to by the relieved family and friends of those returned from war. In the depressing atmosphere Richard didn't even bother to mention his unexpected knighthood, preferring to save the good news for the more joyous days which at that time were hard to believe would return to the saddened de Mauville household. The only animated member of the distraught family was Sam the lurcher, who'd become puzzled by the morose atmosphere and enthusiastically fussed each person in turn with licks and wags of his busy tail. Sam's wholehearted attempts to be friendly met with what seemed to him as rejection as he was sent away to his bed, the resulting confused whines and whimpers starting to even get on the patient Yolanda's nerves in her frustration of having no news of Matilda's whereabouts. Ignoring the melancholy, Alain and Mary carried on normally as if nothing had happened, having suffered similarly themselves and seen it several times before when the families of the fallen struggled to come to terms with the loss of a loved one.

Nearly a complete week had passed when they finally gained some information concerning their absent companion and it wasn't what they hoped to hear. Yolanda's youngest brother Peter had returned following a hunting trip with Sam, bearing tidings he heard from a begging friar whilst out and about in search of game. Cutting short his trip, he rushed home to tell the sad news of a woman fitting Matilda's description, who was found drowned, face down, in an adjacent village's pond with her clothes stuffed full of rocks. Yolanda completely broke down on hearing the woeful tale in realisation that her only real fellow female friend had tragically committed suicide in her mentally distorted grief-stricken state.

Taking all of the next week to come to terms with the catastrophe, Yolanda only started to feel a little better after the following Sunday's Mass, where against the written laws of God and the Church, candles were lit for the departed soul of simon's mother, and prayers said by the same greedy priest who had needed a financial inducement to circumnavigate the normal channels and perform the marriage ceremony for Richard and Yolanda. Again accepting another very large donation, he prayed for Matilda's eternally damned soul to ease her time in purgatory, for a woman whose only sin was to take her own life in a moment of inconsolable blind anguish. The delighted greedy priest, counted the purse of strange gold coins twice, testing each one in turn, pouching them securely out of sight and then in a show of his virtuous generosity, offered to pray for Simon completely free of charge.

The day after the church service, Alain and Mary departed from Market Deeping, taking with them the three girls, six mounted escorts, along with the wagon and all their gear, including the packed treasure. Refusing to take the responsibility for it himself, Richard knew the wise head of his respected advisor was more suited to deal with such wealth. And with a tear in his eye, Alain promised to return when duty called Richard from Yolanda's side, telling him to make up for lost time with his lovely young wife and family and enjoy the calm while it lasted, which, in his considered opinion, wouldn't be for very long, as there were already rumours of a new wave of Scottish raids into English territory to the north, a growing crisis on the Welsh marches on the western side and the permanently grumbling French to the east, who in all likelihood would most assuredly take the weakened status of the English ranks to push home their claims on the disputed territories of Aquitaine, Guyenne and Gascony.

It was true, Robert the Bruce was planning on using the strife in England to expand the border war and orchestrate incursions even further south than before. Trying to make up for the unprofitable time wasted during the prolonged spell of dreadful weather, the Scots urgently needed to replenish the stocks in their impoverished land, where prices for even the most basic commodities remained sky high.

Invited to assist the Bruce at his headquarters in Stirling Castle were the wisest and most trusted of his loyal followers and their attendant squires, including Robert's bodyguard Walter Grint and a sixteen-year-old boy called Robbie, who stood behind his foster father watching with his bright blue eyes like saucers, as the Scottish king plotted his latest campaign to raid the great city of York. Justifying the proposed daring incursion with a lot of satisfaction, Robert told the war council that it was part of a pact he made with the French, who promised mutual assistance if either of them were threatened by King Edward, in his well-publicised, ambitiously bizarre plans to subjugate all his enemies and thus ingratiate himself with his unhappy subjects, that still referred to him as "the devil king who beggared the nation".

Taking Alain's good advice, Richard went about being a good husband and father, living in the same house, which seemed so empty since the loss of Simon and Matilda, where Yolanda's siblings were growing up fast and the old man stayed seated upstairs incapable of doing anything except gaze vacantly into the street, listening to the family living their happy lives, wishing he could be there enjoying his old age, instead of being locked away in his shell, rueing the day he was bewitched by a woman wanting nothing but his wealth.

And so it remained for over a full year, until one day in late February 1320, the long-expected knock on the front door beckoned Richard back to Alain's side, where his knightly services were once again required, to play his part in saving the beleaguered nation from the addle-minded king and his outlandish ideas to make himself popular with his unhappy subjects, who hated the very ground he walked on.